SPLIT

Also by Libby Creelman

The Darren Effect
Walking in Paradise

SPLIT

Libby Creelman

a novel

Edited by Bethany Gibson.
Cover and page design by Chris Tompkins.
Printed in Canada.
10 9 8 7 6 5 4 3 2 1

Library and Archives Canada Cataloguing in Publication

Creelman, Elizabeth, 1957-, author
Split / Libby Creelman.

Issued in print and electronic formats.
ISBN 978-0-86492-861-0 (pbk.).--ISBN 978-0-86492-725-5 (epub).--
ISBN 978-0-86492-841-2 (mobi)

I. Title.

PS8555.R434S65 2015   C813'.6   C2015-901810-2
                        C2015-901811-0

We acknowledge the generous support of the Government of Canada,
the Canada Council for the Arts, and the Government of New Brunswick.

Nous reconnaissons l'appui généreux du gouvernement du Canada,
du Conseil des arts du Canada, et du gouvernement du Nouveau-Brunswick.

Goose Lane Editions
500 Beaverbrook Court, Suite 330
Fredericton, New Brunswick
CANADA E3B 5X4
www.gooselane.com

Oh, give us pleasure in the flowers to-day;
And give us not to think so far away
As the uncertain harvest; keep us here
All simply in the springing of the year.
—*Robert Frost, "A Prayer in Spring"*

PROLOGUE

The last time I saw my sister we were standing in a clearing beyond a string of cranberry bogs connected by various flumes and channels, linked one to the next by the flow of water. There was a stagnant, buggy swamp on one side of the clearing and a hayfield on the other. April was waving our father's .32 pistol in her bandaged hand like it was a sparkler on the fourth of July. We had been sixteen for nearly four months and, as I learned later, had certain legal rights, but discharging a firearm was not one of them.

Everybody who mattered was there: Mom and Dad, Dr. Jean Moss, our dog Petunia. The station wagon—a green AMC Ambassador with wood-grained side panels—was parked at the edge of the clearing, beside Jean's Datsun.

April and I hadn't driven the Ambassador a whole lot that summer, which was a shame, because driving relaxed us. We enjoyed the springy, embryonic feel of the pedals under our bare feet, our soles gripping them like hands, our bums wiggled to the edge of the hot vinyl seat.

The first car April and I drove was a beat-up Ford Falcon, three years earlier, the summer we were thirteen. It was a 1966 model and already six years old when my father came down our long dirt driveway with it, avoiding the potholes with a care that never lasted.

It was cause for excitement when my father went poking around for a new car, usually in Dover but sometimes as far away as Plymouth, and although we awaited his return with anticipation, these new cars were only new to us. It never occurred to April and me that people somewhere were purchasing brand-spanking-new cars that would become good buys, later, for families like ours.

We were permitted to drive the Falcon around the property and down our driveway to where it met Assabet Road, just to see if Mom needed anything at the vegetable stand. Exploring beyond the stand was not permitted, a rule imposed by our parents after we struck a pin cherry tree on our way back from the post office.

As always, we had been sharing the steering wheel, perched side by side on the bench seat, navigating smoothly without a word between us. But when the wheel started vibrating violently, we were powerless to stop the car from running off the road. Although we'd been moving at a crawl and the cherry tree bent gracefully without snapping, the Falcon's licence plate fell off, and April banged her head on the dash and got a bloody nose.

"Goddamn," she said tearfully, putting her hands to her face.

When she felt the blood in her hands she turned to me with astonishment.

"Don't cry," I said. "Please don't cry, April."

There'd been a leak in the power steering rack. Even so, we weren't allowed to drive side by side like that again.

The Falcon was followed by a Volkswagen Beetle, which my father associated with all things anti-establishment, anti-war, anti-racism. But we didn't have the Beetle long. Impractical, my mother pointed out, with a back seat that could barely accommodate a couple of dogs, never mind a couple of daughters.

April had never held a gun before and it was heavier than she expected.

Mom and Dad were standing beside each other as though they were together in this, which they decidedly were not. Dad looked like someone who'd never had a tenth of a second's patience in his life, which was nearly true, and Mom looked terrified. Ticking sounds came off the Ambassador as its hot motor settled, but like many things in that clearing, the car had a shimmering, wavering quality and I couldn't focus on it properly. I thought how my mother liked the station wagon for its roominess. I stood next to her, while April, now in possession of that gun, was keeping her distance from everyone. Beyond April stood Jean. I couldn't bear to look at him.

Twenty minutes earlier, April and I had been riding in the back seat of that same station wagon that was now turned into a mirage, Petunia between us and Dad gassing it down an unfamiliar dirt road that dove in and out of woods and alongside a string of cranberry bogs. Despite my father's apparent hurry, we never got so far ahead that we lost the white Datsun that was trailing us.

Halfway to the clearing—though we didn't yet know about any clearing—April announced she was carsick.

At first, my father ignored her. When he finally stopped the car, April jumped out and walked ahead so that Jean, sitting in his idling car behind us, would not see her puke all over the ground. She bent forward with her hands on her knees, and I saw how the bandage on her wrist was already frayed and loose. Her body convulsed, but without result. She lifted her face and stared at me.

Puzzled, she thought my name: *Pilgrim*.

Beside me, Petunia sneezed and tossed her head. She was on her hind legs in order to study April's every movement.

Perspiration broke out on my forehead. I swung open my door, leaned out, and vomited onto the road. I sat back and let the chill finish running through me. Petunia moved onto my lap and politely sniffed my mouth. I nudged her away.

My father shouted at April, "Get back in the friggin' car, young lady."

She sailed back towards us. She had not seen me be sick. She gave Jean a tiny, covert wave, got in, and whispered to me in wonderment, "I feel fine all of a sudden," which annoyed me.

We left the woods and skirted another cranberry bog, and I realized harvest had begun. The bog was bathed in water and a picking machine was making its way across, creating a crimson wake as the berries loosened and popped to the surface in the millions. It seemed early for harvesting and I nearly remarked on this to my father, then thought better of it.

My mother asked, "How much longer, Russell?"

He didn't answer. After another few minutes the road ended beside the swamp. Opposite the swamp was the field dotted with bales of hay. I wasn't sure whose land this was. In fact, I wasn't sure where we were. But the bales of hay gave me a feeling of comfort. Someone would be coming back to collect them.

"Everybody," Dad said. "Out."

These were the words Petunia was longing to hear. The moment I opened my door she scrambled over me, gouging my bare thighs with her toenails. April was next out, eager to be close to Jean again, then lost her nerve. Our family formed a semi-circle against which Jean seemed to brace himself.

Petunia was officiously trotting about, sniffing at things before squatting over them and urinating.

"What the heck is going on, Russell?" Jean asked.

A catbird called down from the willows bordering the swamp, impersonating a red-winged blackbird. My father slapped his arm. Suddenly the mosquitoes were on us. The air felt muggy and close.

My mother was tense. I tried to convince myself this was about her, something she had done and about which we knew nothing, but my father stepped close to her and put an arm around her shoulders. I felt a sudden lashing anger towards her—for her lack of make-up and style, her wild hair, petite frame, those bony hips through which April and I had entered this universe minutes apart.

"April," my father said. "Could you put a collar on that dog?"

"Dad?"

"It's in the front seat."

April went obediently to the car and fetched the collar. While she was slipping it over Petunia's head, Dad got a rope out of the back of the car. He tied one end to the trailer hitch, then

11

approached Petunia, who, delighted by his attention, wagged her tail with frenzy. He passed the rope through her collar, attaching her halfway along its length.

Everyone watched as he walked the other end of the rope to the edge of the dirt clearing and tied it to the trunk of an alder.

My father turned around and shouted at Jean, "What were you thinking?"

Jean stepped back, and when he did, I saw how young he was, though he was ten years older than April and me. It was time for him to go home, to his own land. It was not just his clothes and radiant dark skin and melodious voice. He was an outsider, and it was hard to keep feeling sorry for him, especially since he didn't love me.

"Moss, you're fired. Your medical practice in Cranfield is terminated. If I ever see you again, I'll shoot you."

Jean laughed in a weird way.

My father lurched back to the car, opened the passenger door, and reached into the glove compartment. I had never before seen him so enraged. He would come back from that lost place, but I couldn't know that then. None of us could. When he stood back up and faced us, he had a small pistol pressed against his thigh. I didn't even know we owned a handgun.

He passed it to April, and she took it in her bandaged hand. It was heavier than I expected.

Part One

ONE

To my astonishment, I fall asleep on the flight from Halifax to Boston. I can't remember when I last felt so relaxed. My decision—which Ethan called rash—to make this trip seems to have done me a world of good. Other than a couple behind me, I'm alone in executive class. I drift in and out while they argue cordially, if not very quietly. She has a British accent and is of the opinion the banks should not be rescued. The man is more sympathetic. "The global economy is falling off a cliff, Fiona." He's either Canadian or American. I open and close my eyes while she laughs at him. "Falling off a cliff? Is that the official word, then?" But after we land at Logan, I can't remember what they were saying earlier. When I turn to look at them, they smile tensely and I wonder if I was snoring. My face has the soft, collapsed feeling that follows unexpected rest.

We wait on the tarmac an hour and a half for a gate to open. "Sorry, folks, shouldn't be much longer," the pilot tells us every fifteen minutes without a trace of apology.

When I get to Customs and Immigration, the official seems affronted I've not been back to the US in thirty years.

"Not even a stopover on your way south?" he asks suspiciously. He is a small man with incongruously wide shoulders. Maybe the hiring committee thought he looked intimidating. That people would hesitate before lying to him.

But I am not easy to bully and I stare blankly as he flips back and forth through my passport with mounting disapproval, as though he would like to deny me entrance for having been gone so long, but we both know that in the end he will have no choice but to wave me through.

I rent a Honda Civic. The freckled girl at the rent-a-car asks how long I'll be needing it and my eyes wander to the calendar propped on the counter. It's early October. A week? Several weeks?

"A month, to be safe," I tell her.

As I insert the credit card, I joke, "I hope my husband hasn't cancelled this card."

The girl doesn't respond. She avoids eye contact as we await the machine's decision.

But Ethan is not a spiteful man, as it turns out.

"I'll need to see another piece of ID," the girl says, as though she is just remembering this.

I locate the Honda in the rental lot. A hubcap is missing and the power windows are sluggish. I consider returning to that freckled girl and demanding a worthier car, but I'm anxious to get on the road. I make my way to the Southeast Expressway and out of Boston.

———

It was several weeks ago that Mrs. McNadden first began calling and urging me to make a visit to Cranfield. It felt as though she were calling me every day.

"I'm trying to locate a Pilgrim Wheeler," she said the first time.

I recognized her voice immediately. "Speaking."

"This is Lois McNadden. Do you remember me, Pilgrim?"

"Who?" I asked, stalling. I was alone in the house, upstairs. I can't remember now what I'd been doing.

"Is that you, Pilgrim?"

"Mrs. McNadden?"

I slipped into my daughter's bedroom and closed the door, stunned by the familiarity of this woman's unique jumpiness, as though I was only ten years old and had just come down the stairs and caught her snooping around our kitchen.

Mrs. McNadden was our nearest neighbour, half a mile up the road. She liked being in our house, roaming our property and inquiring after my father's projects, despite the terror he playfully set out to arouse in her. My father teased and drove her off, but like the dogs, as soon as she was out of the house she wanted back in.

"I found your number through directory assistance," she said. "I had to search your father's things to get your last name."

Katie's bed was unmade. The sheets were stained. Candy, drool, juice, jam?

"I'd been looking for a Pilgrim Bell. Silly me. Of course you've married."

"What's happened?" I asked.

17

"Your father has passed on, dear. That's the reason for my call, in a nutshell."

"Was it sudden?" The stains would come out with the Spray 'n Wash. I prayed it was sudden.

"Yes. Sudden. He was in the barn, fiddling with one of the scoops. There was something broke on it. That's all I know. Those things are ancient. Rodney was there."

I didn't know any Rodney, but why would I? There were always a couple of boys hired by my father and paid peanuts to sweep the barn, clean the tools, follow at his heels just in case he came across some wood that needed to be stacked, fence mended, brush cleared.

"Scoops?" I asked. "You don't mean to say he was still trying to harvest cranberries?"

Mrs. McNadden laughed. A laugh of fondness. For my father?

"How is my mother taking it?"

"Marsha is not much changed, I dare say."

I thought about that for a minute. "I'm not sure I know what you mean. Have you spoken with my sister?"

"April?" she said lightly. "April disappeared off the face of the earth, dear. You were there."

I had a crushing desire to hang up.

"It hasn't been easy for us keeping track of you two," she went on. "At least you sent a few Christmas cards."

What was this *us*?

"You moved to Canada. My recollection is that Montreal—"

I interrupted. "I'm in Newfoundland now. A city called St. John's. What about you? Still living in Cranfield, Mrs. McNadden?"

"Good heavens, what a question. But I had to get rid of my hens, Pilgrim. The air has gone queer and the pastures are being invaded by trees. Your father was always so helpful. I thought we might have the service on Sunday."

We?

I could hear Fred sniffling and snuffling on the other side of Katie's bedroom door. In a minute he was going to start scratching and leaving marks in the paint.

"This Sunday?" I asked. "In four days?"

"That doesn't suit you, dear?"

"No. I can't make it as soon as that, Mrs. McNadden."

"Your husband will understand."

I wasn't so sure about that.

"Your mother won't know the difference, dear, but it would still be nice for her to see you, after all this time."

I didn't think to bring sunglasses, and the day is crazy-brilliant under a sky of uninhibited blue. Now that I'm here, I'm nearly jubilant, exultant. I know I should be cautious, that soaring spirits can have a sudden, painful plummet, but it's been so long since I've felt this way, I embrace the mood with an ache that reminds me how I once craved cigarettes.

The expressway is pock-marked, narrow, and closely banked by trees monstrous after the midget spruce of Newfoundland. They are turning orange and gold and scarlet as though bursting into bloom. My pupils are so shuttered by the intensity of the light that when an animal charges out from the shadows and darts across the expressway, I think at first it's a small dog.

But no, it's only a squirrel, and then it's gone.

I wouldn't mind a cigarette.

"What do you mean," I asked Mrs. McNadden in a friendly way, "my mother won't know the difference?"

"Dear, your mother lives over at Sunset Hills. She has a terrible disease. I've never seen anyone so addled."

"Alzheimer's?"

"Your father had such a time with her until he booked her in there. She never came in out of the cornfield. She was out there all night. Or at the stand, trying to sell vegetables in winter. It was the saddest darn thing."

It appeared Mrs. McNadden may have gotten over her fear of my father.

"Was he able to visit my mother there, at this Sunset place, very often?"

"Your father was getting on, dear."

"I know that."

"He wasn't keen on driving. She barely recognizes anyone. And my, can she get worked up. Well, you remember your mother. Your father was the only one could handle her. He could fix anything."

Mrs. McNadden and my mother could not have been more unlike. Mrs. McNadden was groomed, even in her work clothes — clean coveralls, a ribbon in her hair, a flick of pearls at her throat; her day good or bad depending on the tone with which someone, say my father, spoke to her.

Whereas Mom was untidy, her hygiene wanting. She might wear the same jeans and sweatshirt right through August. There was usually soil under her nails and a bobby pin creeping out of her hair. Sometimes, bringing lunch to her at the stand during the corn-frenzy days of summer, I would see grains of sleep in the corners of her eyes. As though she had risen from her bed, stepped into her work clothes, and gone out the door. Before the sun was even in the sky.

She could appear so distant and lacking in personality that occasionally people wondered if she was slow-witted. But she sold sweet corn that was never more than a few hours off the stalk, lemon-yellow summer squash, string beans that were crisp and unblemished.

Throughout the growing season, a dozen cars were parked helter-skelter at our stand, which was cavernous and dim with a low roof. From outside, you could just discern the sloping wooden shelves and hanging scales, and Mom—pencil behind her ear, paper bags tucked under her arm—moving like a shadow from customer to customer, filling orders. Some received a baker's dozen, some did not; some a generous half pound, some not. No one—not her daughters, not her customers, not her husband—knew her thinking on this matter. When my mother bothered to make a decision about someone, it was swift and unspoken.

The air inside the stand was sweet-smelling and humid, warmed in part by the vegetables themselves, picked shortly after dawn. Most never lasted longer than a day in the stand, but April and I took those that didn't sell down to the house by wheelbarrow for freezing or canning. Or they were given away to Mrs. McNadden, who was crazy for snap peas.

———

When I am fifteen minutes outside Cranfield, I call Mrs. McNadden on my cell. She sputters, surprised, suddenly sounding elderly. She tells me she'll meet me at the house. I imagine her grey-haired. Hollow-boned like a sparrow. I think what a magnanimous person I am after all. I have made the decent decision. I am coming to the rescue of a woman I probably never liked.

I turn off the expressway onto Route 17 and follow it to Cranfield's centre, where it intersects with Assabet Road. The post office is gone and an establishment we simply referred to as Otto's is there, but boarded up. At one time, Otto's offered gas, a few dried goods, penny candy, but I see now it was no more than a shed.

Otto was a short, messy, scary man. Whenever he was outside pumping gas, you knew he was waiting to rush back in to shout at any Negro kid he suspected of stealing cigarettes or candy in his brief absence. My father said he was a primate.

Beside Otto's shed stands a new — to me — Shell service station, housing a Papa Gino's Pizzeria. I don't see a car or person anywhere and am wondering if the service station is open, but then a face appears in the window of the pizzeria.

Beyond the service station is the blocky congregational church where my parents were married.

I turn onto Assabet Road and proceed slowly, keeping my eye out for our driveway. But it's impossible to miss with my mother's vegetable stand still there, barely upright, just before the turnoff.

The driveway is badly rutted and I take my time, not wanting to damage the rental's muffler, and pass fields now overrun by grasses and raggedy wildflowers gone to seed, though in places I can make out the old furrows. I've gone no distance at all when I notice a sign, partly hidden by Queen Anne's lace and purple vetch, advertising pumpkins and squash.

It takes a while for everything to come into view: first the house, then the sheds, then the barn and greenhouses. Beyond them all is the bog, which even at this distance looks dryer than I remember. Almost like a meadow now. Did my father manage to drain it after all?

Sugar maples with their blazing fall foliage surround the house. The roof has an unhealthy look, brittle and crumbly. In front, the grass is still bright green but unmown. Here pumpkins and squash are heaped, ready for purchase.

I am there, testing a large pumpkin with my toe for rot — but there is none, indicating no real frost yet — when Mrs. McNadden arrives. She's driving a beige Taurus that sounds like a motorboat. She sits low in the car, the way small — or elderly — people do, her chin up to help locate the road over the steering wheel. When Mrs. McNadden emerges, she's in an ankle-length fur coat and white heels. A checkered silk scarf is wrapped in a complicated fashion at her neck. She grazes my arm in greeting and I recall the undemonstrative nature of the New Englander. She asks me how my flight was. I hardly recognize her, and though she looks aged and tired, it dawns on me she was once a striking woman. I get a whiff of sour clothing.

"You must be exhausted," she remarks, taking a set of keys from her purse and walking ahead of me towards the house. She moves so slowly I nearly step on her heels. "Do you have the time, dear?" she asks.

I hadn't expected to be tested by her so soon. "Going on three," I tell her. "Ten to."

She stops to peer at her wristwatch. "Ah, the Bell internal clock," she says wistfully.

My family never locked the house and I would not have known a key existed, but at the kitchen entrance she unlocks the door, then grabs the door frame and hauls herself up into the house. This is a steep step, at least a foot and a half from the ground to the threshold. It was always like this, the first challenge to anyone thinking of entering the house.

Mrs. McNadden crosses the room to the refrigerator. I pause just inside the door and scan the kitchen from left to right: the window and curtains with the pom-pom fringe, a dog's bed in the corner, the cupboard where the eggs were stored, an unfamiliar—new, efficient-looking—woodstove, the sink and gas range and peach Formica counter, and Mrs. McNadden in front of the olive-green refrigerator. To my right, the doorway to the rest of the house.

Burpee seed catalogues are stacked on the windowsill. A glass and toothbrush rest on the drainboard by the sink. My father brushed his teeth, put his coat on, and went down to the barn to fix a cranberry scoop.

"Not much here," Mrs. McNadden mumbles, inspecting the contents of the refrigerator. She wobbles on her high heels. She opens the freezer and takes out a box.

"I thought so. Éclairs. I don't mind them frozen, do you?"

"There isn't a dog here, is there?" I ask.

"Heavens no." As she is pulling out a chair, she glances at the dog's bed. Clumps of wiry hair cover it. "Your father was terribly fond of that dog, a houndy kind of creature. Died last year. Used to sleep there, rolled up in a ball, and moan. Your father said she had bad teeth, but he wouldn't put her down. Now, your father had great teeth. Mine have seen better days. Have a seat, dear, and help yourself to an éclair. But keep your coat on. You're going to want to think about how to heat this house."

"I wonder if there's oil in the tank."

"No, dear. Last year your father stopped paying and they cut him off."

"What about propane for the stove?"

"Hardly."

I walk over to the stove and turn a couple of the control knobs.

"So?" she says.

"You're right. Nothing."

When I sit down across from her, she says, "Go on, help yourself," and she pushes a single éclair to me across the grimy tabletop. "Thank God you're here," she adds. There is a glob of whipped cream at the corner of her mouth.

"I guess you heard we might be having a black president?" She takes another éclair from the box and bites into it. It seems Mrs. McNadden is ravenous.

"I find that doubtful."

"You're not alone in your opinion," she mumbles. The inside of her mouth is awash in cream. "Yet he's gaining in the polls."

"Is he."

"I don't know what your father would make of it."

"Really? He'd be over the moon." Wouldn't he?

"I see you still chew your lip. April probably does, too."

"What kind of fur is that you're wearing?"

"Muskrat."

"Nice," I say, deciding the dog bed is not solely responsible for the fusty odour in this room.

While Mrs. McNadden sits there, recharging herself, I feel myself deflating. Everything is going right out of me. I don't even crave a cigarette anymore.

"There was nothing else in the refrigerator?" I ask.

"What did you have in mind, dear?"

"Something to make a proper meal with?"

Mrs. McNadden looks at me with a deceptive blankness.

The house is cold and filthy. Dried mud is tracked across the floor and there are unhygienic smells that don't fit with my memories. In the light of the late afternoon sun float dog hairs and other detritus we have disturbed. I wouldn't eat off this tabletop if you paid me.

I glance across at Mrs. McNadden. Was my father also this hungry? I wonder how much cash you can make selling pumpkins and squash.

"Still small," she observes of me. "That was always a worry for your poor mother, that you girls were so small."

"What about Mr. McNadden?" I ask.

Her head jerks up.

"Is he still alive?" I say.

"Goodness, no. He died in '85. Cancer."

"I'm sorry to hear that."

"What about you? You're married, of course. Any children?"

"A daughter. Katie. She's thirteen."

"Now that's a sensible name. I've never met a Kate I didn't like."

"Where exactly is my mother? Where is this Sunset Hills?"

"Sunset Villa. It's a dandy spot. I don't know how Russell got her in there."

"Would you like to come with me, Mrs. McNadden, to see my mother?"

"No, I can't. I've got too much to do."

"Really."

Mrs. McNadden heaves a sigh, as though I have pushed her too far. I realize she doesn't like me — has never liked me.

And I am beginning to get a clearer memory of what I thought of her: that she was a silly, shallow woman. Of average intelligence, my father would have said. I imagine my mother tolerated her because she didn't know any other way, and my father simply enjoyed alarming her. That she kept coming back where she may not have been respected caused me to think little of her.

"Can you give me directions to it?" I ask. "I assume it's not in Cranfield."

"There's nothing in Cranfield. It's in Dover."

"Dover. That's west on 17, right?"

Mrs. McNadden nods, then decides to get to her feet, moving none too swiftly yet still managing to convey a little huffiness.

"Do you want to take the éclairs with you?" I ask.

She turns back but avoids eye contact. "You don't want them?"

"No."

"Are you certain, dear?"

"Absolutely. They're yours."

"Her name was Hazel."

"Who?"

Mrs. McNadden's eyes slide towards the dog's bed. "Hazel. It just came to me."

My family mostly inhabited the kitchen, so perhaps it's not surprising it seems so worn, so stripped down. It was the warmest part of the house in winter due to the woodstove, and the coolest in summer because of an old, towering maple. The rest of the house has a more preserved appearance and, compared to the kitchen, is stark and tidy though still grimy. I pass through the dining room — never more than a passageway after a section of it was carved off for the bathroom — to peer into the living room, then wander over to the foot of the narrow stairs. But instead of ascending, I pause outside a room that was at times office, storage space, guest bedroom. Though the only guest we ever had was Dr. Panama.

I am like a toddler circling a hot stove, over and over, too smart to approach, too self-destructive to stay away.

I place my palm on the wooden door to this room. Although I had planned on leaving this for later, I pop the latch and peek in. I catch my breath. I expected the room to be either empty or used for storage, but from the rumpled bed and a certain weak smell I realize my father was sleeping here. A pair of his work pants hangs from a nail, the hem let down — or fallen down — exposing a line of dirt along the fabric. Ratty towels are attached by plastic clothes pegs to a rope strung from one corner to another. A cup and saucer rest on the bureau top.

Of course: in his last years my father must have stopped climbing stairs. Even so, I'd have thought he'd sleep in any room but this one.

TWO

Everything was straightforward at first. Our father's sperm located and pierced our mother's egg. Within days we were a throbbing cluster of cells. And then, we split. A tiny rupture, but it produced a deep rumbling sound that was still there in our first awareness in the dark. What was meant to become one girl, became two. It was risky. So much could have gone wrong.

Eight months later, in April of 1959, Mom gave birth to us at Jordan Hospital in Plymouth, Massachusetts—just over a mile from the Mayflower's landing site where 102 weakened passengers once stepped ashore to begin a life of religious freedom in a hostile environment.

I was born first. April emerged six minutes later. We were slippery and confused.

The day was overcast but spring-like. You could smell the earth, and everything was softening up out in the fields. Parents were being warned of the risk of suffocation posed by the new polyethylene dry-cleaning bags, and Mack Charles Parker, a twenty-three-year-old Negro arrested in Mississippi on weak evidence for raping a white woman, was kidnapped from his jail cell by a mob of masked vigilantes and murdered.

We had hair as pale as our skin, although no photographs exist to substantiate this, since my parents did not own a camera then. Later it turned auburn. Our father called it strawberry-roan, as though he were describing a horse.

Dad could not always tell us apart, even later. He was bad with faces. He threw our names — Pilgrim-and-April — at us the way he might spread grass seed: a sweep in our general direction, hoping the names would take root appropriately.

Until kindergarten, we thought our name was Pilgrim-and-April.

We lay together in our crib. My gaze slid along the distant yellow walls to the maniacal movement of green outside the windows until a blurred figure crossed the room and dropped the shades. My eyes travelled back to the slats of the crib, then came to rest on Pilgrim-and-April. It eased my eyes to be able to focus on something so close. Her thumb was in my mouth and I was aware of the sound of her clicking heartbeat, the smell and taste of her sour, honeyed skin.

Years later, I would still remember the smell of Pilgrim-and-April's baby skin. Like rising bread. Like apple juice.

As my depth perception improved, I strained to focus on what lay between us, but there was nothing there.

Biting, chewing, licking each other — these were central to our long and difficult separation and individuation process.

What is me? What is not me?

Our arms and legs were riddled with teeth marks and small bruises. But as soon as one of us bit the other, we both drew back in tears.

Was that me? Was that not me?

Eventually our parents took shape and became recognizable, but it was our mother's attention we vied for most.

We teased her—one of us running off in one direction, the other in the opposite direction. She'd call out to us in frustration and we'd laugh so hard we'd fall over. Or we threw our food off our highchairs in tandem. Carrots, then apple slices, cheese, macaroni. We waited for our mother's exasperated response: a frown, sigh, or mild scolding—all were hilarious.

But if our father—the large person with the furry face—was present, we were less likely to play these games. He brought a stillness to a room.

"Ju-ju," April said. Despite our father's presence, she had pushed her scrambled eggs, including what she'd sampled and spit out, off her tray and onto the floor.

We didn't like the eggs. They were mushy.

Outside it was cold. The doors and windows were closed and the air was stale—it could have been like this forever, since our sense of time was still developing. Behind us, there was the persistent, engulfing heat from the old Franklin stove. In front of us, our parents were just sitting to the table for their own supper.

"Ju-ju," April said again. Her face was red and shiny. This wasn't just about soggy eggs.

"Dow-dow," I told her.

Ju-ju. She shook her head stubbornly.

Dow-dow.

"They're talking more," my mother said. "I was beginning to worry."

"They talk a mile a minute," my father said, his eye on us as he ate.

"To each other, true, but that's indecipherable."

"Dow-dow," I repeated and banged my cup against my tray.

My father scrutinized me. "Is that April?" he asked my mother.

My mother pointed her fork at me. "No, that's Pilgrim," she said. "I tied green embroidery thread around her wrist. You see?"

"You're sure?"

"Russell, I put red on April, green on Pilgrim. I did it for you. So you can tell them apart."

"Dow-dow," I demanded and shoved my own egg over the edge of my tray.

"What does she want?" my father said, frowning. "They just got up there. And now she wants to get down?"

"Honest to Pete. Are their chairs too close to the stove? Are they too warm there?"

My father rose and made his way around the corner of the table. We watched him coming towards us. He lay his hand against April's cheek and then to the top of her head.

"Yeah, she's warm," he told my mother. He picked up April's chair and set her down again several feet from the stove.

He turned to me. "Juice?" he asked.

Delighted, I kicked out my feet and slathered a fistful of mashed carrot across my face.

"They're asking for juice, Marsha."

I would get used to my father talking to one person while bearing down on another. He was fiddling with my embroidery thread, which had stained my wrist green from April sucking on it. Then he touched a finger to my chest.

"Pilgrim," he said, telling us both.

He glanced at my food and picked up a cranberry between two fingers and pressed it to his lips.

"Mine!" April screeched and he put the cranberry back on my tray.

"Did you hear me, Marsha? They want juice."

"Russell, I heard you loud and clear," said my mother, already up from her supper and opening the refrigerator. "I'm not on Mars."

"Ju-ju," April said to me, laughing, her damp head thrown back.

When we were four, my father separated us to punish us. This happened only once.

It was late winter. April and I were in the habit of spending our mornings in the chicken coop where it was warm and the hens were companionable, always so amusingly curious about our footwear. But one day we left the door to the coop open and the hens traipsed out, passed the house unseen, and were making their way down our driveway to Assabet Road when they were intercepted by a stray dog, who killed several of them. Dad was beside himself. He put April in the truck with him and drove off.

Convinced that she was gone forever and I would never see her again, I plunked myself down in the middle of the kitchen floor,

33

grief-stricken and inconsolable. In the truck, April was staring out the window, hardly able to breathe and certainly unable to hear anything Dad was saying to her about learning a hard lesson.

My father's hunch that this would be the best punishment was inspired. Ten minutes later he turned the truck around and brought April home. I met her at the door. We touched each other's hands and arms, shoulders, face—all over, lightly and quickly.

Mom was saying she had a brainwave. "Who'd like a bowl of ice cream?" she asked, her eyes bright, despite the severe look she was giving Dad and the fact that supper was only an hour away.

For a while after that, whenever we were separated, we panicked, thinking we'd never see each other again.

"Is April gone forever?" I would ask Mom.

"No, sweet pea," Mom would answer, fixing dinner or washing dishes or just staring out the window with her hands on her hips. "She's only gone with Dad to get the new chicks from Mrs. McNadden. You know that."

My father smelled of sweat and animals and sported a beard —not so unusual in the 1960s in that part of the world—that was already salt and pepper by the time we were born. When I was twelve I did a report on the last Czar and Czarina of Russia and found my father was a dead ringer for Rasputin: the austere face, blunt jaw, brick-like nose, a blurry arrogance in the eyes. For several weeks I fretted that Rasputin had never died a dozen deaths, but instead lived on through the remainder of the century, marrying my mother and living with her in Cranfield, Massachusetts, a small town whose industries were rooted in a landscape of hardwood and hemlock forests, family farms, and the bucolic business of cranberry bogs—originally built, sanded, sown, and harvested by the hands of immigrants.

Our land was surrounded by these bogs. My father was raised here, as were his own father and grandfather, and at one time the property had included hundreds of acres. But down the generations much of the land was sold off, parcel by parcel, to Ocean Spray. It was my father's grandmother, Lulu Gladwin Bell, who was responsible for installing the indoor plumbing, electricity, and telephone.

April and I were never embarrassed that our parents failed to support themselves in a conventional manner. It wasn't until I left home I saw we might have been. While the vegetable stand kept my mother and a couple of part-time workers busy for several months, I doubt it brought in enough cash. I realize this now because of the assorted jobs my parents took—though for my father, it was often on a short-term, abruptly ending basis—and because of certain other memories.

Both my parents were, at different times, substitute teachers —certification was not required in those days. One winter my mother worked at Mayflower Paints in Dover; another year my father delivered the *Dover Weekly* throughout the county. I often accompanied him, leaning out the window of our truck to ram the folded newspapers into the plastic mailboxes erected at the ends of driveways.

He was also employed at the Plymouth Seafood Market, but that lasted less than a week.

"Microscopic staircase times two," was how Dad described our matching DNA, which carried the directions, he said, for assembling a human being.

April and I had matching DNA. "This is not typical," my father said. "Not conventional."

Nearly miraculous, it seemed.

April and I had just started kindergarten and everything about it frightened us: our teacher, the children, the school bus. My parents were trying, in their different ways, to give us confidence.

"Dad, are we the only ones?" we asked.

"Possibly," he said.

We were squeezed together in the Beetle's bucket seat beside him, because three piglets stood terrorized and shaking in the back seat. Dad had got an unexpected deal on them in Dover. He put a blanket down in case they shat, which proved to be a smart plan. Not long afterwards, my parents got rid of the Beetle.

"Born the same damn time," my father went on. "One set of Bell babies coming up."

"Pilgrim was first," April corrected.

"Well, yes. Six minutes later, you finally poked your head out."

"What did we look like?" I asked.

"A pair of princesses."

"What did we say?"

"'Hello, Daddy.'"

April and I exchanged a smirk. We did not believe this for one second, though we wondered if he'd had food in his beard, the way he did now, while we were being born.

April always said I came out first because I was braver. She wasn't serious, but it was comforting to imagine that neither one of us had been thrilled about leaving our mother's shadowy interior. Most of our childhood, we never wanted to go anywhere, either. We liked it at home, on our little farm.

"Billions of people in the world and no two identical," my father said. "Except?"

"Except for us."

He nodded and had a quick look behind him at the piglets, which had begun squealing feebly. "Except for the two of you."

We pitied other human beings, even my father, who had probably never been afraid of anything, not even the dark. It must be lonely, we thought, to be unique.

We were passing through the centre of Cranfield, and April and I stared at the congregational church. My father, who had only been inside the one time—to get married—assured us there was nothing in there worth seeing. But we had recently found an old catechism book of Mom's and had some concerns. When we had asked Dad about God, he told us we were crazy as a pair of loons.

Mom had been less certain.

Dad said she was hedging her bets.

"That's God's house," April said now, pointing at the church.

"Girls, never mind about God."

"But Dad, what about hell?"

"Everyone's on fire there, Dad."

"For eternity."

"Listen to me," he said, then hesitated, glancing at the two of us while he drove. "Pilgrim-and-April?"

"What?"

"Heaven? Hell? That's a bunch of bull. You go nowhere but under the ground."

We looked at each other. We had already decided we would die on the same day.

"If God didn't make us, then who did?"

"Your mother and I made you. I've explained that. We provided the gene pool."

"So where did you and Mom come from?" April asked.

"Where did the first human being come from?"

My father exhaled audibly. He may have been growing bored. "Africa."

"Huh?"

"The origin of the species was Africa."

"Huh?"

"Human beings came out of Africa. The continent of Africa." He sounded exasperated now. "Where did you girls pick that up? The school bus?"

We shook our heads. We would never dream of speaking to anyone on the school bus.

"'Huh' isn't a word," my father scolded. "You sound like a couple of hillbillies."

"The Garden of Eden," April whispered to me. "Had to be in Africa."

"What was that?" my father barked.

"One of the pigs is shitting," April said.

But we imagined God anyway, because we needed someone to have put us together to look flawlessly alike. God was a man so shrunken by circumstances he could squeeze inside my mother—where we floated with our fingers in each other's mouths in a cacophony of heartbeats—and work for eight months shuffling back and forth between the two of us, building us detail by detail so that we were replicas of each other. He spent a long time attaching strands of hair in the exact same spots on our scalps. Another day was spent mixing the pigment for our eyes, a blue-grey that would be perfectly matched. Back and forth he went, never stopping. Checking, re-checking. The curve of our necks, the lobes of our ears, the length and width of our legs. But he grew weary, and gave April several moles on the inside of her arms, none for me. He was sloppy with the freckles on our faces, too.

This sloppiness was frightening. What if more than moles and freckles went astray? What if God—that clever little man —decided to unmake us?

We had a recurring nightmare in which, instead of growing bigger, we grew smaller. I would watch with horror as April's face and body disappeared into a block of flesh the size of a loaf of bread, her eyes and mouth and limbs shrinking to pinholes.

We woke screaming. Mom came hurrying down the hall in her bare feet to our room. She guided me out of bed and in with April.

"Hush, April," Mom murmured, reaching out to rest her hand on April's head in the dark. "Hush, Pilgrim," she said, putting her other hand on me.

Mom had always been able to tell us apart, even when she couldn't see us. She could identify us by our voices, our cries, our smell, our footsteps. "Just any little thing," she would say.

Unlike our father, who often remarked that listening to us chattering away in another room was like listening to one girl questioning and answering herself.

Knowing something about raising a daughter myself now, I can see that April and I were obedient, fastidious girls. By the time we were six, we went cheerfully to the bathroom on our own to wash up before bed. We had a good sense of time and rarely needed to be reminded. Dad said we were like two clocks set to the same timetable.

We carried in our pyjamas. One locked the door and the other pulled aside the shower curtain so we could check the bathtub. We had dreamed God grew to be the size of a man, then drowned in the tub. While this was upsetting, and a pity for God, he was no longer in a position to unmake us and we had met the dream with some relief.

We filled the sink with warm, soapy water and submerged our four hands and washed them together. Sometimes, when April took an especially long time with one of my hands, scrubbing beneath the nails with the nail brush as instructed by Mom—pinworm eggs being her worry—I would feel myself drifting into a sleepy trance.

My eyes popped open when there was a knock. Mom asked if we needed help.

"No," we said. "No thanks, Mom."

Or there would be breathing on the other side of the door. We were still a fascination to our father.

We brushed our teeth, combed and braided our hair, beginning and ending each task at the same time. We synchronized by facing each other, as though we were watching ourselves in a mirror.

We removed our clothes and checked the other for signs of change. Sometimes another freckle appeared out of the blue on April's torso and I would feel a tiny pinch of worry.

"What do you love about me?" she asked.

"Your elbows. What do you love about me?"

"Your feet."

When there was a spongy development on our chests, we knew they were mammary glands. They were common to female mammals—not just our mother but the pigs and cows and sheep—and we had been expecting them. We kept an eye on their progress for several months as they enlarged, then told our parents we required brassieres. The Sears and Roebuck catalogue was taken from the top of the refrigerator. My mother suggested a training bra, but we had our eye on the Petal Burst by Wonderbra and were backed by our father.

"Why not, Marsha, what's the harm?" he said.

We ordered pink. My mother said we were out of our minds. We'd never fill the cups.

But when the package arrived a month later and was opened, we discovered Sears and Roebuck had made a mistake. They'd sent one pink bra and one white bra. We were both dying for the pink, which was far lovelier, so Mom had us pull straws. I got the short straw and the white bra.

April hesitated as she considered offering me the pink one. "We'll share," she said at last, and we did.

In the bathroom, after supper, we tried them on. As my mother predicted, we did not fill them, but we would grow — there were so many days and months and years ahead for that. We looked smart and stylish. April said I was like a lady in the *Boston Globe* fashion section. I said it was too bad they were hidden by our T-shirts. The handle on the locked door rotated soundlessly and we turned in unison to observe it.

THREE

After Mrs. McNadden drives off with the éclairs resting on the seat beside her, and I've stood too long in my father's bedroom staring at the rumpled bed and little clothesline and dust everywhere, I wander back into the living room. A card table is set up in a corner and covered with a jumble of papers—letters, flyers, magazines, newspapers. I riffle through them and find information on a homecare facility in Dover called Sunny Gardens Homecare. Although Mrs. McNadden referred to it first as Sunset Hills and then as Sunset Villa, I assume this is where I will find my mother.

I get back in the Honda. At the end of our driveway I stop the car and gaze out at my mother's old vegetable stand. There are holes and gashes in its siding and it has the appearance of being damp, almost wet. Fragile like an eggshell, yet taking a long time to come down on its own. The sign that once hung over the front of the stand, "Marsha's Fresh Fruit and Vegetables," is nowhere to be seen.

Behind the stand, a pile of empty crates and broken boards is sinking into the ground. Here is where the grey Mercedes parked, waiting in the flickering sunlight. Inside, Mrs. Lewis would sit smoking her cigarettes, the windows up and engine running. There were not many air-conditioned cars in those days and we were awed by this.

In the roomy back seat of that cool Mercedes, Mrs. Lewis's two granddaughters played with their Barbie dolls and one of the small dogs they were always kissing and cuddling. Smoke would curl above the girls' heads and over the tops of Mrs. Lewis's crutches, which rested against the empty passenger's seat.

Eventually Mom would come to the car window to take her order, a gesture of kindness for which Mrs. Lewis later demonstrated her eternal gratitude.

On my way to Dover along Route 17, I pass fields reclaimed by small pines alternating with modest plots still being farmed —mostly corn and pumpkin, by the look of them—but this has become a landscape chiefly of cranberry bogs, which look neater and more geometric than I recall. Harvest is well underway and the bogs are flooded. Huge trailer trucks are parked at the shores to receive the red berries, seamless rafts of which are floating brilliant in the sunlight while workers drag booms through the water to corral them.

On the outskirts of Dover the cranberry bogs give way to a series of subdivisions I don't remember. The fronts of houses display American flags and hanging flower baskets, while the backyards look like busy places, with swing sets, swimming pools, raised vegetable beds.

With improved roads, I discover it's now only a twenty-minute drive to Dover, where April and I, along with the other woeful children of Cranfield, were once bused for school, a journey that had seemed endless. In my memory Dover was a somber place, with ragweed growing up through cracked sidewalks and chain-link fences barricading silent red-brick mills.

But Dover has changed. Now I see strip malls and super-markets, gas stations and traffic lights, car dealerships, swimming pool outlets, real estate brokers, fast food.

Sunny Gardens Homecare is off the main drag, towards the river. This must be it, this splayed bungalow, though there is a stillness about the place. The sun is low now and the air beginning to carry a chill.

I park and walk up the wheelchair ramp and across a wide porch. I open the door onto a large common room, low-ceilinged and dim, though several table lamps are on. Sofas and armchairs in floral upholstery are pushed up against the walls. A few sun-starved begonias and geraniums are set among plastic flowers on coffee tables and windowsills, and doilies cover every conceivable surface.

It's not until I've stepped into the room that I notice the man slumped in a wheelchair. He moans, and then I see across from him a small woman perched on one of the sofas. She's smiling.

"I've got a terrible head cold," she tells me.

A woman with a tremendously high platinum-blonde updo appears. Perhaps an alarm went off somewhere, in some office, the moment I opened the door.

"Can I help you?" she asks.

"I think this is my mother," I say, staring at the woman on the sofa. "This *is* my mother. Marsha Bell."

"Really," the woman says. I watch her brain working. "How lovely." She turns to my mother. "Isn't that lovely, Mrs. Bell? A visit from one of your daughters?"

"I've got a terrible head cold," my mother tells her.

"Not again?" the woman says brightly. She turns back to me. "I'm so glad to finally meet you. I'm Nurse Allison. The administrator, Ricky Milton, he's off. Him and his wife are enjoying a little holiday."

"Nice to meet you. I'm Pilgrim Wheeler. I was Pilgrim Bell."

"I know," she says.

"You do?"

"Sure. You're the one whose sister vanished. You went to Dover Regional, right? I'm younger than you, but I remember everything about it. What your twin sister did."

I laugh, because I don't know how else to respond.

"I'm so glad to finally meet you," she says again. "Supper is just around the corner. Normally I have to get prior approval for guests to join us, for the obvious reasons, but I think we can make an exception, seeing as you're already here and all."

"Marsha Bell," my mother says. "I'm Marsha Bell. Over here."

"I have to dart back to the kitchen now, but let me introduce you to Mr. Godfrey," Nurse Allison says, indicating the man in the wheelchair. She lowers her voice. "Stroke."

He's in slippers and pyjamas. A blue cardigan is draped over his shoulders and in his hand he strokes a length of velvet ribbon.

"Mr. Godfrey," I say. "Hello."

"His wife was here for the afternoon, per usual, but had to run home. She'll be back for supper. She doesn't live far off."

"Are there many others here? Other residents, I mean?"

She looks surprised by my question. "Yes, Pilgrim. Nineteen residents in total, to be exact."

I glance around. "Where are they?"

"In their rooms. Or in the dining area, waiting for their supper. They're starved." She winks. "But clean their plates? Not on your life."

She's backing away as she tells me this, and I'm soon left alone with my mother and Mr. Godfrey.

"Hi, Mom. It's me. Pilgrim," I say awkwardly, taking a seat beside her.

But my words appear to go nowhere near her. In fact, she looks a bit cross. Each time she glances at me she seems alarmed by my presence. I wonder how long she's been in this place. When I lean back to rest my head on the sofa, she does the same. The warm air envelops me, and I figure a lot of napping must get done here.

When Mr. Godfrey moans again, my mother jerks forward. "You better keep an eye on him," she tells me. She sounds a little panicky and I shrug off my sleepiness. Might they have coffee somewhere? Even instant would be welcome. There is a sharp, spicy odour—urine, it dawns on me.

"I will. I will certainly keep my eye on him."

"Are you new here?" my mother asks me.

"Yes. I'm visiting. I'm here to see you."

"What's your name?"

"Pilgrim."

I watch her closely for signs of recognition, but there are none. Yet I recognize her, there in her eyes—that simple, hopeful expectancy. My mother depended on me, and on April and my father, for her grounding in the universe. Her life did not have a wide scope.

"Just don't put those thingamajigs in the hello again. *They* know, those nuts and bolts."

The door opens and in comes a bit of fresh air, along with a woman who must be Mrs. Godfrey. She stands there opening and closing the door for a minute, trying to fan the room. She is wearing designer jeans, runners, and a sporty lavender jacket. I sense she is a bit wound up about something. She looks at me and asks, "You don't mind, do you? There's no oxygen in this place. They hate me doing this, all they care about is the cost of things, it's no wonder they're all dying in here. Ha! No one can breathe."

"I don't mind," I say, smiling. "I agree it is a bit stuffy."

"I used to turn down the thermostat. Until they caught on," she says, crossing the room. "Got my hand slapped for that." She pulls a chair up beside Mr. Godfrey and adjusts his cardigan. "Hey, Jimmy. I'm back." He lifts his head a wobbly inch and looks straight across at me. His eyes are crystal blue.

My mother gets to her feet. It takes her some time to manoeuvre around the coffee table until she is hovering over Mrs. Godfrey. She is wearing baggy sweat pants and a pink turtleneck, no bra. My mother never wore pink.

"Now, now, Mrs. Bell, it will ruin your appetite." Mrs. Godfrey leans in my direction and whispers, "I have some gourmet cookies in my purse."

"Oh."

"Nothing gets past her. Are you her daughter?"

I nod.

"I heard about your father's heart attack. That's a shame."

"One of the dogs is choking," my mother offers.

I stare at my mother.

"I only met your father a few times," Mrs. Godfrey continues. "He looked as though he was losing traction. Say, are you okay there?"

"To be honest..." I wave my hand. It would be ridiculous if I cried.

"Take your time," Mrs. Godfrey says.

I hold my breath, tightening my stomach muscles like I'm trying to stop hiccups. Katie used to be a terrible one for hiccups when she was a baby.

"Earlier today," I begin, my composure returned, "I glanced at some of my father's papers. I didn't see a deed to the house. I don't know where, or if, there is a bank account, or how he was financing my mother here."

"He wasn't. Medicaid is," Mrs. Godfrey says abruptly. She seems a little put off by my ignorance. "With all due respect, I doubt he had much in his bank account."

She turns and pats down her husband's hair, and my mother takes a step back.

"Has your husband been here long?" I ask.

"Six years. Long before your mother. Your mother has only been here a year or so. She's really quite functional, you know."

"Have you seen anyone else visiting her? A Mrs. McNadden? A neighbour of ours."

"Diabetes?"

"I doubt that. I watched her devour some pastries earlier today."

"Fur coat?"

I nod.

"She used to visit your mom at first. With your dad. When they stopped coming, I figured they were no longer driving. It's easy for me. I'm just down the road. Right, Jimmy?"

"Mom, where are you going?"

"She always gets a bit of the wanderlust in her right before suppertime," Mrs. Godfrey explains. "You could head her off at the pass if you hurry."

My mother is entering a corridor. Though she is moving unsteadily, she is not slow. I come up behind her, but am reluctant to touch her. When I glance back at Mrs. Godfrey, perhaps for encouragement, I see she has turned her full attention on her husband, whispering and stroking him.

"Mom. Hey, Mom. Wait up."

But it's been decades since anyone has called her that.

"Where are you going? Don't you want supper? Marsha?"

She stops and I take the opportunity to squeeze past her in the narrow corridor. She holds perfectly still and observes me. She is humming quietly.

We are standing just outside a small bedroom. I glance in and see a sagging bed covered with a familiar quilt, a window—that's good, a view of sorts, even though it's of the parking lot—and piles of books and magazines and miscellaneous items on small tables. I think I might recognize these tables. On the wall is a series of colour snapshots of our farmhouse, including one of the vegetable stand from the seventies. It looks like the end of a long day. Inside, my mother and a few customers stand in the shadows. Another photo depicts two girls sitting on our lawn in party dresses.

"Is this your room, Marsha?" I ask stupidly.

She nods. "Come in. There's something I want to show you."

I wonder if suddenly she knows me, but when we go in, she sits on her bed and takes off her slippers and holds them in her hands, examining them. "Damn it," she says. "What the hell?"

I peer closely at the photo of the two girls. I have no memory of the photo itself or the summer day it has captured. The girls are posing for the camera, holding toy mirrors and combs—the early days of colourful plastic toys. I can't believe my parents were able to afford those dresses.

"What was this?" I wonder aloud.

"Birthday party."

"Huh." I stare at the two girls. I haven't the slightest idea which one is me.

The smell of supper hits us both at the same time: heavy cafeteria fare. My mother picks a tennis ball off her night table and tries to put it in her pocket, but it's too big. She places it on the bed, then looks under her pillow for something. She picks up the tennis ball again and returns it to the night table.

I sit beside her.

"Honest to Pete, I'm frustrated," she tells me.

"What do you need?"

She kicks her feet. "Would it kill you to hurry?"

I glance down and see the toes of her slippers poking out from beneath the bed. She must have tucked them there while I was looking at the photos. I bring them out and help her get back into them.

"Have you been here before?" she asks me.

"No, just came today, to visit you."

"You're a good girl. Who are you?"

"April," I tell her.

Suddenly, she looks suspicious. She studies me. I realize that the eyes themselves don't get old. It's everything around them that does.

"A coincidence," she says grudgingly. "I have a daughter by that name. Like you, a good girl."

"Here you are!" Allison says, breathless, in the doorway. "Come on, come on. Guess what, Marsha? We made Jell-O special just for you. No fruit."

"I don't like those nuts and bolts," my mother says, shaking her head and rising from the bed with both of us at her elbows.

I glance at Allison and our eyes meet. I'm thinking she looks like the type who may still smoke in this day and age. Who still believes there are times when a cigarette can do a woman good.

Dining takes place in a large room with a blue-checkered theme: table cloths, lamp shades, curtains. Department store photos of butterflies and tulips have been mounted on the walls. The linoleum flooring is scuffed but probably sensible.

Although Allison said nineteen residents, I count only eleven. They are not a chatty bunch, though to be fair, they are eating. Or trying to, because a few have trouble masticating and another few believe their meal has been served to a neighbour. Allison and another staffer move expertly among them to settle any misunderstanding or confusion.

But before supper is finished, I escape out the back of the facility, relishing the first of the five cigarettes Allison gave me just before we came in for supper. At first she was startled by my request, then couldn't make a gift of the smokes fast enough. She seems to think I'm some kind of celebrity.

Circular flower beds bordered with white stones decorate a deep, sloping lawn. This is the kind of ho-hum landscaping my mother would have scorned. At the bottom of the lawn, I find a path that takes me through a thicket of scraggly brush to the riverbank. The light is fading, but not far up the river I see the cotton mill. So here is the red brick I remember so vividly. The town of Dover has seen decades of new prosperity, but at its core stands the Dickensian monster that started it all.

I sit down. I am being hit by a vigorous nicotine rush and feeling a little nauseous. My first smoke in twenty-five years.

Even so, I am relieved to see that mill: like an American castle, with towering smoke stacks and multi-pane windows designed to let in the light, though never to open and allow in some fresh air. Inside, a hundred years ago, boys and girls with nimble hands and feet ran up and down, over and under, rows of spinning bobbins that seemed to go on for miles. Children flecked head to barefoot toe in white lint.

As I watch, the river turns black and featureless beside the mill. It's odd to see well-spaced weeping willows — fast growers — up there along the water's edge. And just as odd to see the mill parking lot filled with cars. The windows — one here, another there — begin to glow yellow.

The cotton mill has become a goddamn condo.

It occurs to me I should give Ethan a call, at least let him know I've arrived safely. Our conversation about me coming here, alone, had been a tricky one. He felt I should have been willing to wait a few days so he could accompany me. That frankly I should have been touched by his offer.

But instead of taking out my cell phone, I light another cigarette. It's been only twenty-four hours since the fuss that followed my experimentation with Vietnamese cuisine. I didn't think it was as bad as they were making out. Katie pushed her plate away almost immediately, and even Ethan seemed reluctant to finish his dinner. I excused myself and went upstairs.

After a while, of course, Ethan followed me up, and when he saw the suitcase open on our bed, suggested I was being rash. "Come on," he said. "Jellyfish salad? Where did you even find—"

That's when I told him that, actually, I was not being rash at all.

"The thing is," I said. "My father died three weeks ago."

Ethan's expression was a little disturbing, so I added, "That's hardly rash, you know. Anyway, I have to go to Massachusetts."

"He's already dead," Ethan insisted. "Both your parents died when you were sixteen. What's really going on?"

"You're not listening, Ethan. My father never died. Well, I mean, not until recently."

"Are you for effing real?" Katie asked, standing in the doorway. Fred was behind her, thumping his tail and eager to make eye contact with me.

"Language, Katie," Ethan cautioned, then to me, "Hold on now, Pilgrim."

He was standing in the middle of the room, his legs spread, his arms folded over his chest and that crease between his eyebrows. He reminded me of a coach who'd just made a bad decision—put in a weak player or set in motion a moronic play—but would accept the consequences.

"I lied. My father died three weeks ago. Katie, honey, I'd prefer if Fred didn't come in right now. I'm not up to him jumping all over my things while I'm trying to pack."

Ethan watched me choose some sweaters. When he spoke again, his tone was bizarrely hopeful. "What about your mother? She's dead, isn't she?"

"Nursing home. Apparently."

"You lied?" Ethan asked.

"I already admitted I lied. But it doesn't matter. I haven't spoken to them in decades."

"Who doesn't speak to their parents in decades?"

I shrugged.

"Holy crapola," Katie said.

"Is there something I need to know, Pilgrim?"

I shook my head.

"Who lies about their parents being dead?"

I closed the suitcase, then reopened it, took off the shoes I was wearing, threw them in, and closed the suitcase again.

"Who does that?"

I gave him a look reminding him Katie was in the room.

"I'm asking you to wait until the weekend, Pilgrim," he said, trying to sound calm. "We'll all go."

Katie looked alarmed. "What about Fred?"

"No," I said. "I'm going alone."

Ethan lurched for the suitcase, but I was quick to sit on it and he stepped away.

When I left the next morning it was still dark, the cab weaving out of Country Walk Estates. Once a misty forest of scrubby spruce and knee-deep ponds, the land had been stripped prior to development, so that from a distance Country Walk Estates gave the impression of a lunar settlement, not an exclusive residential area. It wasn't until you were closer and saw the luxury cars and jeeps, tennis courts, private playgrounds, and three-stories-high single-family houses, that you knew you were home.

Like anyone was out taking a walk in the country.

We had moved here, to Newfoundland, only a year ago, following Ethan's upward trajectory in the oil and gas industry. Sometimes, I could barely remember our life in Calgary, our smaller house, my busy job, weekends skiing, an excursion to the rodeo, or just doing errands.

"Not a bad day," the cabbie said, catching my eye in the rearview. I looked out. We were crossing a gully. I considered pointing out it wasn't really day. The spruce and fir and ponds were creeping up out of the night and the world seemed too still, as though marking my progress with some profound judgment. I thought I saw a moose in a meadow, but then the view was gone and I would never know for sure.

A memory of Mrs. McNadden came to me then, of a wet evening in September. I knew it was September because April and I were refusing to return to kindergarten. We had stuck it out a week.

Mom said we had to. All children went to kindergarten now. It was common practice. We said we would go on a hunger strike in protest. Mom said, "For goodness sakes I wish your father hadn't told you about that Indian man."

On this evening, we were standing in the living room with the fireplace at our back. The crate of firewood was to one side, and to the other the small table that held the *Webster's Dictionary* and the porcelain figurine of a shepherd boy in blue coat and white britches. The table legs were wobbly and we were always careful not to knock it. Above the table hung my mother's antique wall clock that she wound faithfully each Sunday night. It tick-tocked now, a sound so constant and familiar we sometimes forgot it was there.

Of Mr. McNadden, my memories are less distinct, since he was a conventional husband and generally at his place of work. But I believe he was in the room, sitting beside his wife on the sofa with the green-and-white floral slipcover.

Dad had hollered to us to come into the room. We knew he wanted other people to be as captivated with us as he was, and in the case of Mrs. McNadden, perhaps shocked.

He said, "Tell us a ghost story, girls."

"A ghost story?" one of us repeated.

"Yeah," he said. "Like the one you told me yesterday. With the bathtub."

That wasn't a ghost story.

"Unless you have another one."

April and I turned to each other, so close I felt her eyelash flutter against my face and her breath enter my mouth and nose. We turned back and met Mrs. McNadden's observing eye.

"It was pitch black," one of us, speaking barely above a whisper, told her.

The other nodded emphatically.

"I had to get up in the night—"

"—to go pee-pee."

"It took a long time to find the light in the bathroom."

"Someone had cut the string."

"I had to stand on the toilet to reach it."

"When I turned on the light—"

"—there was a dead man in the bathtub."

Mrs. McNadden had been leaning towards us in order to hear. Now she drew back and glanced at our father, who was tying his shoe and grinning. This worried us.

"So I went and got my sister out of bed. I told her—"

"—there's a dead man in our bathtub."

"She woke me up."

"But I was so sleepy."

"So we went back to the bathroom—"

"—and I showed the dead man to my sister."

"It was true."

"There was a dead man in the bathtub."

We did not reveal the dead man was God, knowing Dad's opinion of him.

"The string was a nice touch," he said. "You didn't mention that yesterday."

We took each other's hand and stared out the window at the rain and pretended we were alone in the room. We could hear the rustling sound of Mom flipping through the pages of the Burpee seed catalogue Mrs. McNadden had brought to the house. She was looking for my mother's advice on the best annuals to grow from seed. "Where do the girls come up with these things?" we heard Mrs. McNadden ask after a moment.

"It was just a dream they had," Mom said. I glanced at the catalogue. The pages had dark, wrinkled spots from the raindrops. "Go on, girls. Go find something to do."

"You don't find it disturbing?" Mrs. McNadden persisted.

"Russell is just trying to get a rise out of you, Lois," Mom said quietly, embarrassed for her.

———

Still nauseous from Allison's cigarettes, I stretch out flat on the riverbank.

I did not see my father grow old, so I have to imagine him old. Whereas I know that my mother has become smaller and that she sports a new hairstyle: short and curly and grey. The last time I saw her, her hair was dark and richly hued, bountiful if untidy. I did not see my father develop a closer, perhaps intimate, relationship with Mrs. McNadden, so I have to imagine that, too. Did their relationship then cool when they reached their eighties? Did my mother know about it? Did it crush her? Did it trigger an Alzheimer gene? Did it really happen?

I lie there, staring at the fading sky above this ordinary New England town, and speculate on what my father and Mrs. McNadden might have gotten up to after I left. I struggle to crack open long-shuttered memory cells to foresee events, but all I have is an aftertaste of things.

It's dark now. A star. The condo/mill is glowing. All around me, mice, moles, nocturnal birds, and snakes get busy transporting themselves. A fish splashes.

FOUR

April and I never returned to kindergarten. This was due in part to our brief hunger strike, and in part because my mother didn't much care for Miss Beattie, the kindergarten teacher.

It was the Saturday after that first week of school, and we were just a day into the hunger strike. Weekends at the stand were still hectic, but Mom had taken us with her that morning. We played on the floor under the shelves or near the cupboard in the back, where Mom kept her cash box, tools, and spare clothing.

Miss Beattie lived in Dover but happened to be in the area that day. She was a big woman and looked even bigger wearing the red poncho she had crocheted herself—we knew this because she had bragged about it the first day of school.

"I'd like to discuss the twins attending kindergarten separately," Miss Beattie said to our mother. "There's an afternoon session," she went on, uncovering her purse from beneath the poncho. "One twin can go in the morning session, the other in the afternoon. Principal Gaines has given his approval. Those carrots look nice."

April sneezed and Miss Beattie, startled, glanced down. She did not seem pleased to find us sitting so close to her feet, holding hands and staring up at her.

"Gesundheit," she said anyway, and my nose tickled.

My mother counted out Miss Beattie's change.

"They can't attend separately," my mother said, turning to another customer. Perhaps my mother's simple unequivocal response aroused some stubbornness in Miss Beattie, because she hung around, holding her bag of carrots, leaning against a shelf of turnips.

"I'm concerned about the twins," she said, approaching my mother again when she was free. "It's my feeling they lack a healthy sense of individuality."

My mother didn't understand this kind of talk. She stared at the teacher, weighing the value in explaining the hunger strike to this pushy woman. She was already worried about us not eating. And that was in protest to attending kindergarten *together*. What might we devise, my mother wondered, if told we would be separated all day?

"Individuality?"

"Yes," Miss Beattie said with a smile, encouraged by this one word from my mother to further her point. "You see, they only speak to each other, in gibberish. They never even look at the other children."

April sneezed again, but this time Miss Beattie ignored her.

"Do they speak to you?" my mother asked.

"Well, yes, but they whisper, so I must stop what I'm doing —this is very disruptive—to get close enough to hear them. Then all the other children become intrigued and immediately want to know what they've said." She heaved a sigh beneath her poncho. "And so it goes."

We watched my mother. She looked cross.

"Separate sessions," Miss Beattie said, "will allow them to acquire some individual identity. And I'm certain it would have a positive effect on their language development, Mrs. Bell. I learned all about this in teachers college."

"When they speak to you, do you understand them?"

"Yes. But as I said, it's just whisperings."

"What do they say?"

"They ask to go outside, or go home, that kind of thing."

At the end of the day, Dad arrived with the tractor and wagon and helped Mom close up. April and I were starving. Even the smell of raw vegetables was agonizing. We listened to my mother tell my father about Miss Beattie's visit. She looked cross again. My father lifted us, one then the other, onto the wagon beside a basket of beets.

Dad drove the tractor and Mom stood alongside him, one of her hands gripping his shoulder. Mostly he was talking and she was listening, but we couldn't hear them above the sound of the tractor engine. The air was crisp and the sun had already dropped to the tops of the trees. A flock of sparrows was darting around the garden edges.

My teeth hurt.

Me, too.

Really hurt.

April and I looked at each other.

"Because we're hungry," I said. We thought of Miss Beattie and the classroom of children gaping at us. April patted my arm and then left her fingers resting on my wrist.

When we arrived at the house, Dad came over and lifted us out. "So, girls, what are your thoughts on supper?" he asked.

We were rubbing our jaws. Even so, we shook our heads.

"You're not still on about that hunger strike, are you?"

We nodded.

Mom was more direct. She passed behind my father, hefting the basket of beets, and said, "Next year. First grade. That really is the law. Make that clear to them, Russell. And they have to eat supper tonight. Every last bite."

The eating would be no issue, despite our tender teeth. We looked at Dad, who put his hands on our shoulders and steered us towards the house. "Your mother's had one of her brainwaves," he explained. "No kindergarten. You can already tell time, anyway. You'll go straight through to first grade next year. You won't be able to get out of that one."

"It's the law," my mother said again. We were in the kitchen now and she was already making supper. "Sit down at the table, girls, this instant. What's the matter with your mouths? Are your teeth bothering you?"

"A little bit."

"You know that's because you're starving, right?"

Several times during the following year, our father—prompted by our mother, who was of the mistaken belief we were more attentive to him—made an effort to talk to us about the whispering. "Your mother worries about you," he would say. "Your mother's had a sleepless night. You need to help her, be good girls." And once: "Your mother is driving me up the friggin' wall."

He spoke and we listened. He looked at our faces—perhaps wondering who was who—and pulled on his beard.

"The whispering is problematic," he said unconvincingly one day when we were alone in the house with him.

At home we spoke normally, but we whispered everywhere else: the supermarket, the post office, the feed store, and, of course, during our few days in kindergarten.

"People have trouble understanding you," he tried to explain, not looking at us and perhaps distracted by some other unrelated thought. It went against my father's grain to suggest conformity. "Your mother just wants you to fit in. You don't do yourself any favours with that funny talk."

We started to interrupt but he put a hand up. "I *know*. But no one else understands what you're saying. That woman...that teacher...Miss Beattie," he said with a sour expression. "What did she call it? Elective mutism?"

April scowled. "Miss Beattie..."

"...is a meanie."

He didn't make much of an effort to hide his smile.

The following September, April and I went obediently, though fearfully, to first grade. Over the years we got used to the other children and learned their names and eventually did not whisper our answers to the teachers. But it was always important to us, even as we got older, that people knew we were twins. Whenever I met someone on my own, I let them know right away that I didn't just have a sister, I had a twin sister. I wasn't comfortable talking to anyone unless they knew this.

April and I were slow to make friends, but we did become less vigilant and shy. This may have been due in part to Lottie Barboza, who moved to Cranfield in the second grade and surprised and baffled and befriended us, although it would prove short-lived.

Lottie had been living in Plymouth until she and her brother, Amado, arrived in Cranfield to live with their aunt. Most of the Negroes we went to school with were descendants of Cape Verdean immigrants who'd come to the Cape Cod Peninsula for employment in the whaling and shipping industries, then later to work the cranberry bogs, and they had Portuguese names, like Rosa and DaSilva and Lima. Some, like us, lived in the old farmhouses, others in the newer ranch-style houses, while there was the rare old-timer who still lived out in one of the pickers' tarpaper shacks, now nearly swallowed up by woods.

April and I were approached by Lottie on the school bus. We'd been sitting for a year at the front, avoiding the nightmarish racket at the back. Her stop was after ours, and for several weeks she boarded the bus on the heels of Amado, fixing on us a look of casual curiosity, to which we were accustomed. Sometimes she brushed by in a hurry, while other times she trailed by groggily, as though she had just tossed aside her bedcovers, but always she gave us a good once-over.

Then one day she stopped. She was wearing her favourite outfit: a red faux leather jumper and blue knee socks. "You identical twins?" she asked.

We glanced at each other, then back to her, and nodded.

"I knew it." Suddenly, she was trying to sit between us. "Move it or lose it," she said, but in a good-natured way.

I was sitting on the outside and April was by the window. We exchanged a nervous look, but made space for her. She wedged herself in, wiggling her bottom, then glanced back and forth between us, as though checking us trait by trait, before letting out a soft whistle.

Lottie was the first person to enter our universe other than our parents. She took to us with zeal and was especially encouraging about our whispering, which she adopted herself. For a month, the three of us shared a seat as the school bus jolted over the country roads, our bodies loose and rubbery. Lottie sat squeezed in the middle and talked away in a rattling, fast-paced whisper, but always stopped to listen attentively when one of us wanted to place a comment or question to her ear.

But as fascinated as she was by us, we were by her: the way the dark skin on the back of her hand rotated into a tender paleness on her palm; the softness of her hair, which did not look like it should be soft. The way a bug bite or scratch left a permanent pale scar on the skin of her face or arms, as though everything left a more lasting impression on her.

"How did you get that?" I whispered, cupping my question to her ear with one hand and pointing with my other to an indentation on the back of her hand.

"Amado poked me with a pencil."

The three of us put our hands on the seatback in front to brace ourselves as the bus driver, Mr. Philpott, accelerated into a turn.

Amado had an afro that rose like a halo around his head and he wore a smart-looking plaid vest over wide-collared shirts. It seemed he frequently stabbed Lottie with sharp objects.

"He's not very nice to you, is he?" April said.

"I hate him," Lottie said. "I hate that evil Amado."

We nodded. It was incomprehensible to April and me to hate a sibling, but on the other hand, having one who stabbed you with a pencil or stick or nail on a weekly basis without any apparent consequence seemed inexplicable and foreign.

Days later, she let slip he was punishing her for sitting with us. There was a bandage on her arm, just above her elbow.

At Lottie's suggestion, we scheduled an after-school visit to our house. She said Burry's Scooter Pie was her favourite snack.

But Amado must have got wind of our plan and decided it was the last straw, because Lottie boarded the bus one morning and just sailed past us. We were making room for her on the seat and were bursting to tell her that our mother had immediately agreed to buy a box of Scooter Pies when we explained for what purpose. But Lottie gazed straight ahead, her face blank, and made her way to the back of the bus with her brother. We turned a few times, hoping to catch her eye, but her chin was aloof and set, her look elsewhere.

Amado leapt out of his seat and shouted, "What you two-headed freak lookin' at?"

Kids snickered or stared nervously at their laps. Everyone knew Amado was as mean as mean could be, and April and I spun around and moved closer together, extinguishing forever Lottie's place between us. When I glanced up, my eyes met Mr. Philpott's in his massive rearview mirror. He had been watching us for weeks. It was no secret to anyone he was in support of Lottie returning to the back of the bus with her brother.

FIVE

Barack Obama and John McCain clash over the war in Iraq, tax policy, the environment, Guantanamo Bay, the financial crisis. Meanwhile, my father's new woodstove burns well enough to eventually heat the kitchen if I keep the door shut to the rest of the house. I scrounge around and find scraps of dry wood — in a corner of a shed, the back porch, piled beneath a tarp in the kitchen garden.

But after a few days the wood is nearly gone and I start wondering how I will keep the kitchen warm. Then, one morning, a man backs his truck up close to the kitchen door and dumps a load of firewood on the lawn. He tells me he's Rodney. His skin is brown, with features that make me think Black Portuguese, yet he has blue eyes and light-coloured hair. He limps, his hips moving as though independently of each other. He tells me he was with my father when he fell down in the barn and died. I had imagined Rodney was a youngster, one of those boys who used to roam the neighbourhood, looking for the odd job. Then I realize there was a time when he probably had been one of those boys.

"Would you like some breakfast?"

"No, ma'am."

"Coffee?"

He shakes his head, glancing over my shoulder at the house. I realize he's never been inside.

When he's in his truck again and driving off, he looks at me out the driver's window. I suspect his was the face watching me the day I arrived, through the pizzeria window. He'd been waiting for me. There is a tightening in my chest—a feeling of responsibility that saddens me.

Within a week a routine sets in. Each morning I wake up on the living room sofa, where I'm spending my nights, go out to the kitchen to light the woodstove, then return to the living room and crawl back under the blankets.

The sofa still has its slipcover of green-and-white floral, which is not as grimy as I would have expected, but musty. The shepherd boy figurine sits on the end table, but the *Webster's Dictionary* is gone. Jam jars of dried flowers are displayed on the fireplace mantle like a shrine to summertime: purple aster, feverfew, lamb's ear, larkspur, yarrow. They look so dry and papery I dare not even breathe on them. My mother's wall clock has stopped at 5:05.

Once the chill is off the kitchen, I get up, make coffee and toast, and have a cigarette while I wait for the nursing home to open. I am surprised by how tiny the kitchen seems, how low and narrow the counter with its Formica top and chrome trim. Without gas, I can't cook, but there is an electric kettle for hot drinks and instant soups, and I usually get take-out in Dover on my way home at the end of each day. There is little food, anyway—perhaps Mrs. McNadden had already taken for herself what might have spoiled.

One day I find a mood ring in the refrigerator, buried under the gummy vegetable debris at the back of one of the crispers. The stone is black. I slip it on and wear it for a couple of hours, but it never changes colour. Later, I find a compact of eye shadow in the egg cupboard, so brittle with age it makes a tiny cracking sound in my hands. With it is a carton of eggs that I toss out.

When there is sun, I go outside because it is warmer and dryer, but I don't wander far.

Then there comes a particularly mild morning when the air feels so supple and inviting, I finally venture out across the property behind the house, keeping my eye out for snakes though it's late in the year. Mist is coming off the bog beyond the barn and the air is thick and sweet. Tiny flies hang in whirling groups, mating in the brief rising temperature of this fall day. The ground is spongy, as though aching to flourish and reproduce, not be locked down and subjected to months of hard cold.

I pass the sheds, where many of the windows are broken, though I don't know if this is the work of trespassers or storms. The greenhouse next to the barn appears small and boxy by today's standards. A cold frame lies at its entrance, as though left by someone whose intention was to return after lunch to remove it. Bedstraw and butter-and-eggs are growing up over it. The far end of the greenhouse has started to sag.

I avoid the barn and meander in the direction of the old cornfield, shadowed by a group of blue jays whose call is bell-like, robust and intimate. But no evidence remains of the sweet corn that grew in long straight rows, where my mother toiled alongside those boys corralled by my father. I try to picture Rodney among

71

them, coming down the driveway on hushed summer mornings, eager to pick corn, then strolling off an hour or two later with a bit of cash in his back pocket.

I gaze out across the land, the air holding so much humidity it has a tangible luminosity. The cornfield has surrendered to weeds and small trees and shrubs. It is easy to imagine nothing but woods here in a few decades.

On my way back I stop at the barn. The sliding doors move on their runners with a rattling, metallic whine. Inside, it's gloomy and smells of old hay and rotting animal feed. Cranberry rakes and scoops are propped against the outside of a stall, while one scoop lies on the barn floor, looking busted and archaeological. I'm guessing this is the contraption my father was examining in the last minutes of his life, and this is where he lay in the first minutes of his death. I nudge the scoop with my toe. The handle is broken and separates from the basket. Scraps of vines and leaves are caught in its teeth.

There is no sign of blood on the wood floor. Faded or washed away after all these years. I hear mice scurrying around in the loft among the few ancient bales of hay.

I leave the barn, pass the house, and wander down our driveway towards the stand, passing what was once well-tilled land, where my mother grew, at one time or another, tomatoes, lettuce, beans, and peas; cucumbers, zucchini, squash, and pumpkin; root vegetables. A flower or two for drying. It seems nothing has been sown here in years, but then I spot what looks like chicken wire fencing, and I wade out across the old furrows to a tiny garden patch in the middle of this field of weeds.

"Ah, here they are," I say aloud, relieved, for some reason, to find where my father was growing those squash and pumpkins he'd been trying to sell, though I wonder about the location. Was he hoping to avoid vandals?

The blue jays follow me back to the house. In the kitchen I scrape together some leftover take-out and throw it into the yard.

I stand behind the screen door and search the yard for movement. A cold shiver runs down my back, as though I am being watched. Minutes pass. When the jays swoop down onto the food scraps, my pulse quickens. But there is just the rustle of their collapsing blue wings in this otherwise hushed world, and I wonder if it's the silence, rather than the untamed plant growth or dire state of the buildings, that troubles me. The farm animals are as gone as my father, every last one. I imagine them dying and disappearing, one by one, species by species, over the years. Of sickness, old age—my God, I hope not of starvation.

We didn't raise a lot of livestock, and those we did were usually for our own consumption—a few lambs, pigs, chickens, turkeys. But not all earned their keep. Some my father found and brought home just because he could. Like the geese and ducks—we ate neither their eggs nor their meat. And there was Happy, a mare saved from the glue factory by my father, who thought we might like to ride her. Her name a misnomer if there ever was one. She was old, produced vast quantities of rank urine, and made every effort to bite you, the moment you turned away, with her brown teeth. So sway-backed that riding her was painful.

Who were the hangers-on? The hens, perhaps. Or that dog, Hazel, who slept in the kitchen and died last year—a houndy kind of creature, was how Mrs. McNadden described her.

My father outlived them all, as though it were good manners to let them go first. And not just the animals. April, me, my mother. We all left before he did.

―――――

One morning, I arrive at Sunny Gardens Homecare and although it's past nine, the door is locked. I knock loudly and see movement inside. Clearly I am being ignored.

To keep warm, I begin pacing up and down the veranda that wraps around the building. I turn a corner and there is Mrs. Godfrey hunched up against the house, hurriedly wiping her cheeks with the back of her hand.

"Still locked?" she asks.

"I'm afraid so."

"Bastards."

"Can they lock us out like this?"

"They can do anything they like. You've got to play along, they've got all the power."

"I thought it opened at nine?"

"A crisis must have arisen." She looks at me and smiles grimly. "Don't be alarmed. Not a genuine crisis."

"I'm going to give it another try." But the door is still locked. Suddenly I want more than anything to get inside that building. I thump on the door with my fist until it is opened by an unfamiliar man with a stony expression. This must be Mr. Milton, the Homecare Administrator, who has been away. He is heavyset in the manner of someone who was once beefy and enjoyed intimidating other men. Now he carries a galactic belly and has a steel-grey flat-top. He stares at me without offering any greeting, and I feel my confidence scatter. Age, I suspect, has reduced him to bullying women.

He eyes Mrs. Godfrey as she slinks past him.

"Good morning, Mr. Milton."

"Mrs. Godfrey," he says.

He turns back to me. I tell myself to make an effort to get along with him.

I introduce myself, annoyed by how timid I sound, and his response is silence. Impulsively, regretting it instantly when I realize it means I'll have to touch him, I thrust my hand out, forcing him to engage with me. He receives my hand with lethargy, but then surprises me with a wide smile.

"Welcome to Sunny Gardens Homecare," he says.

I step in and see that a few residents, including Mr. Godfrey, are in the common room, but not my mother. Shaken and not sure why, I wander down the hallway to her room, fairly certain Mr. Milton's eyes are on my body, checking me out. I find my mother sitting on the edge of her bed in the same clothes she's worn every day since I arrived: the pink turtleneck and baggy sweat pants. As soon as she sees me she starts crying.

I sit beside her and take her hand. "What is it, Mom?"

"I think they poisoned one of the dogs."

"Who did?"

"She's like a flower."

"Don't think about that, Mom."

She shakes her head as though she can't help what she thinks. "I'm just a little blue today—Russell can't keep his mouth shut."

This is the first time she's mentioned my father. Did anyone try to explain he'd died?

Her hair is a mess. I glance around the room for a brush or comb but don't see either.

"What did you have for breakfast?" I ask her.

A stupid question, but I don't know how to talk to her.

"Why do you ask?"

And then occasionally she seems so lucid.

"Because I think some of it dripped on your beautiful pink turtleneck."

She has likely missed the sarcasm, but my grinning is contagious. She laughs, leans in and says, "You were always my favourite."

"I wonder if you would like to change your clothes?" I ask, to steady myself. "Then maybe we'll find some lip balm for those lips of yours."

"Is Russell here? I want to go home."

"That shirt smells a little sour, Mom. Like it needs to go in the laundry."

I'm not sure she understands, but she is listening. I close her bedroom door, ignoring the note taped to it: "NOT TO BE CLOSED UNDER ANY CIRCUMSTANCE," and open her chest of drawers. It's full of clothes, all neatly folded and clean.

But she seems confused and alarmed by my efforts to undress her, which must explain why the staff avoid undertaking this task on a daily basis. She is stiff and unyielding. Success is only possible when I guide her limbs slowly and gently. It takes ten minutes to get the turtleneck off, revealing a torso speckled with age spots and small bruises.

Even so, my mother has a right to be clean. To wear clothes she would choose herself if she were able to remember what they might be.

When we emerge she's in a floral button-down blouse and green corduroys. We are both proud of ourselves, but when Allison sees us she looks like her heart might stop.

"We'll never get that off her. All those buttons. You know she can't stay still. You should have asked first."

"Marsha," Mrs. Godfrey sings out from across the room. She's at her post beside Mr. Godfrey, who is stroking his velvet ribbon. "You look splendid. The bee's knees."

"Allison, she's my mother. I can help her."

"No, you cannot."

"That's just it," Mrs. Godfrey says. "You cannot."

"Only staff are permitted to dress residents," Allison explains to me, giving Mrs. Godfrey a stern look.

"Is that official?" I ask.

"I'll tell you what it is. It's a liability. What if something happened to your mother while you were dressing her? What if she fell on you and neither of you could get up? These are real safety concerns."

"I doubt she weighs a hundred pounds, Allison." But I think of her bruises and wonder if she has already had a few stumbles.

"Staff here have all the requisite training," Allison says.

"Can I brush her hair?" I ask. "Or is there something I need to sign first?"

Allison hesitates.

"It's like a rat's nest in the back," I point out.

"Of course she can," Mrs. Godfrey says. "Don't be ridiculous, Allison. How can that be a risk?"

"It's not up to me," Allison says, watching the movements of my mother, who has become particularly restless. She has already sat in three different places since entering the room. Each time, she leaps up as though someone has called her name. "I'll have to check with Mr. Milton," Allison says finally, then adds, "But I think 'rat's nest' is a bit of an exaggeration."

After she leaves, Mrs. Godfrey is silent. I sense she would

rather be alone with her husband. I wonder if the staff has decided she can't be trusted and the two of them are not permitted in his bedroom alone. Soon that could be me, I realize.

My mother, who is now hovering around Mrs. Godfrey, says, "She's a little blue today."

"Why don't you come sit beside me, Mom?"

Mrs. Godfrey takes a hankie from her sleeve and blows her nose.

"Yes, I am," Mrs. Godfrey says. "Well put, Marsha." She glances at me apologetically. "I just want to be with him. These damn people and their rules. We just want to touch the people we love, don't we?"

Allison returns with Mr. Milton. Behind them, a woman with a walker follows.

Mr. Milton scans my mother's blouse as though counting each button, then looks at me and says, "You had a question about brushing your mother's hair?"

"Yes."

"That will be fine. I can allow that."

"Thank you. Another thing. My mother seems particularly agitated today."

"That's typical," Allison is quick to say. She is helping the woman with the walker get settled in a chair.

"Really?"

"The only predictable element of dementia," Mr. Milton says authoritatively, "is its unpredictability."

"But how do we know if she's in pain?" I ask. "She might not find the words to tell us."

"She'd moan, or cry," Allison explains. "Or rub the part of her body that hurts."

I nod. It sounds both reasonable and heartless.

"She mentioned someone had been poisoned," I say. "Maybe that's her way of saying she doesn't feel well."

"What?" Mr. Milton says. "She's claiming someone poisoned her?"

"No, not her. She said a dog had been."

"A dog? That's different. There are no dogs here."

Everyone is watching me.

"Well, it's what she said," I say stubbornly.

"No pets here," the woman with the walker croaks. "Not allowed." Then, as though she has surprised herself by having spoken, she begins fussing with a knitting bag hanging from her walker.

Allison approaches me and puts a hand on my shoulder. "You know what they say. What doesn't kill you makes you stronger."

Mrs. Godfrey scoffs. "Nonsense. What doesn't kill you exhausts and weakens you. It's been scientifically proven. The DNA becomes truncated and the cells die."

"If you'll excuse me, ladies."

"I try to stay optimistic, Mrs. Godfrey."

"Suit yourself, Allison."

Later, Mrs. Godfrey, who has lived all her life in Dover, tells me Mr. Milton used to work for his brother, who owns a Mazda dealership on Main Street.

"They were pulling in the money and making enemies all over the place," she said. "Then poof!"

"What?"

"Some indiscretion involving warrantees. That's the most I know. Not long after, the home here was hiring, and on he came as Homecare Administrator. I was floored. And made my opinion known. Well, you know that was a mistake."

"He must have certain qualifications and training?" I ask.

She looks at me. "Apparently he must." She crosses her fingers and says, "He and Allison are like this."

"I rather like Allison."

Mrs. Godfrey nods. "I'm just letting you know."

She leans down and slides one of her husband's slippered feet back onto the footrest of the wheelchair. His legs are stiff and immobile. A grimace crosses his face and the velvet ribbon slips from his hands. Mrs. Godfrey immediately pries open his fingers and slips the ribbon back between his thumb and forefinger. She looks at me.

"They're understaffed here," she says. "The Director of Nursing quit over a month ago."

"Why?"

"A difference of opinion on some practices. The use of anti-psychotic drugs, for example. I watch them like a hawk with Jimmy, but I worry they slip him something at night."

We both look at him. He does seem brighter in the afternoons, but I keep that observation to myself.

"If your mother is agitated, Pilgrim, I wouldn't bring it to their attention."

"I see."

Meanwhile, my mother is moving the potted plants around the room. I'm dismayed that she can't seem to distinguish the real ones from the plastic.

"They have this little trick they do," Mrs. Godfrey whispers. "I caught them doing it with Jimmy in the early days, when he was a bit more footloose. Before his second stroke. Boys oh boys, did I ever give it to them."

"What trick?"

"They roll the wheelchair up to the wall and lock it. The resident doesn't have the strength to get out. Staff don't have to worry about them wandering down the road while they're out back for a smoke. Jimmy and your mother are lucky—they have someone to look out for them. Of course, your mother's quite functional. You can see that for yourself."

My mother is sitting beside me now, tapping my knee with her finger.

"What is it, Mom? Is there something I can get you?"

"Did you see where Russell went?"

•••

Mom was washing the dishes while Dad stood beside her, his rear end slouched against the kitchen counter. April and I sat by the woodstove, reading from the same copy of *Bleak House*, assigned to us in our grade ten AP English class. I held the book while she turned the pages. Sometimes I was a sentence or two behind her and she waited for me to catch up.

Their conversation did not penetrate us until my father said, "Marsha, the guy didn't know the difference between a bay scallop and a sea scallop—or pretended he didn't."

"Couldn't you have said nothing?"

"He was a cheap bastard."

"But, Russell—"

"Marsha, you're making a federal case out of it."

He left the kitchen as though he were embarrassed to have spoken harshly, or thought of something he had to do elsewhere.

After a moment, my mother came across the room and sat in the chair by the window. She was cradling her soapy hands in her lap and the winter light silhouetted her so we couldn't see her face clearly until we came closer. April took the book from my hands, bent a top corner, and slid it onto the kitchen table.

My mother didn't look pitiful when she cried. Not like the rest of us.

April and I put our hands on hers.

"What did Dad do?"

"It's not Dad. I'm worrying about silly stuff."

April stroked the back of her hand. "Like what?"

"Silly stuff."

But we knew, or knew in part. Dad had got a job at the Plymouth Seafood Market, but it had only lasted four days.

"I'm just a little blue today," Mom told us. "That's all."

That's when I saw Mrs. Lewis. "What's she doing here?" I said, standing up.

My mother twisted around to peer out the window. Presto, my father was back in the room. We stared out at that grey Mercedes, puzzled by its appearance in our driveway. It was not the right time of year. The stand was closed.

Yet there sat Mrs. Lewis in her car, finishing her cigarette and somehow conveying to anyone watching that she expected to be greeted.

"Maybe she's looking for a dozen eggs," my mother suggested. She wiped her face with her sleeve and stood.

"She never has before," my father said. "Let her come to the door."

"You know she can't, Russell," Mom said, going out.

"Stay inside, girls," my father ordered, but we ignored him.

Mrs. Lewis smiled at us coming across the yard. Her automatic window was descending with that pleasant whirring sound that made me think of summer. When she reached for the car's cigarette lighter, I saw her hands were shaking. She turned her head towards us awkwardly.

"We're having a nice respite from winter today aren't we, Marsha?" As she spoke, she exhaled smoke through her nose, which was red and finely veined.

"Yes, that's true."

"And to top things off nicely, Daisy's had her puppies," Mrs. Lewis said.

It irritated me that Mrs. Lewis would speak of something that was important to her as though it should be important to my mother, too.

"Open my back door there and take a peek."

My mother opened the door. On the seat directly behind Mrs. Lewis was a box. I had a hunch that whatever was inside was alive, pulsing with DNA.

"Do you see the box?" Mrs. Lewis asked, like suddenly she was in hurry. She was staring straight ahead. "One of you girls, open that box for your poor mother."

April leaned in. When she noticed Mrs. Lewis's crutches on the floor of the back seat, she hesitated and nearly backed out. I moved in, pressing on her, and she opened the lid of the box and a small head sprung up. It was a puppy, the size of a squirrel, with a black nose and ears, and with fur the colour of rich butterscotch. It licked April's fingers ravenously.

"Her name is Petunia," Mrs. Lewis said. "I name all my pups after flowers. But I won't hold it against you if you change her name. If it doesn't suit you."

April held her breath and I asked Mrs. Lewis, "Is she ours?"

Mrs. Lewis laughed. "Yes, young lady, that's exactly why I'm here, sitting in your driveway."

We waited a moment for our mother to speak, but she didn't, so April leaned back in and lifted out Petunia, who went nuts, wagging her tail and licking April's face.

We already had two dogs. Tansy and Bandit were mongrels with skinny, alert bodies and an appetite for trailing us anywhere and sleeping out of doors. They were watchdogs and happiest in each other's company. We had never had anything like this before. A genuine pet.

"Bring Petunia to my window so I can say goodbye to her," Mrs. Lewis said. "There, there, my itty-bitty girl. She's an affectionate dog, Marsha. We call that an apricot coat. She's of good pedigree. Wait, don't move, let me give you her papers."

When I touched Petunia she grew even more delirious. She tried to crawl out of April's arms and onto my shoulder. She nuzzled my ear frantically. She wanted to come live with us and had forgotten all about Mrs. Lewis, who was waving an envelope at my mother.

"Has no one ever given you a gift before?" Mrs. Lewis scolded.

"Of course," my mother said. "Of course they have."

"You've always been so kind to me, Marsha, even when you're inundated with customers. I'm eternally grateful to you for that."

My mother smiled. April and I were thinking about our father, who was likely watching from the house, wondering what in damnation was in the envelope. He wasn't going to be happy about the puppy.

"Petunia looks like a sweet dog," my mother said, taking

the envelope. Her face was still blotchy from the crying and I wondered if Mrs. Lewis had noticed.

Petunia was like our doll or baby. The first few weeks, she had such little stamina she had to be carried. With the exception of my father, it was everyone's pleasure to accommodate her. She'd get halfway across the kitchen floor, tire, and fall asleep on the spot. She liked to curl up inside my father's shoes, and when she got bigger and could no longer fit inside them, she still preferred his over anyone else's. We often found her asleep in the shoe pile behind the door, her head resting on the toe of his boot.

As Mrs. Lewis promised, she was affectionate. If I pressed my face against hers, she'd press back, and we'd doze in bed or on the sofa, side by side, cheek to cheek, until she stirred and lifted her head to lick my face. But as she grew, she became a dog of industry. She took pleasure in swimming, digging, hunting, herding the ducks and geese, for which my father grudgingly began to admire her. He even expressed annoyance with Tansy and Bandit, who seemed only concerned with self-preservation: lazing around in the summer, panting and snapping at flies, or huddled under the kitchen table in winter, trying to stay warm between meals.

Even so, my father said her name was absurd. He referred to her as "that pillow dog" and promised to give her a swift kick if she got too close to him.

"If someone doesn't get that pillow dog out of my way in the next three seconds..."

It made April and me jealous, since Petunia seemed far more loyal to him than to us, and yet we were the ones who showered her with love.

•••

By the time I return to the farmhouse, my irritation at being scolded for dressing my mother has evolved into anger. But I'm happy to see that Rodney has reappeared and is stacking the wood he dropped off over a week ago. Despite his limp he is strong, his body muscular and efficient like a gymnast's. It is probable I knew this man when he was a boy, but I can't for the life of me remember him. I wonder if I'm supposed to pay him, though I doubt my father did. I have discovered my parents had a checking account in the Dover First National Bank with a balance of $152.13 and no transactions for several years. It appears my father was cashing his social security checks at the IGA in Dover, while my mother's benefits are being paid to Sunny Gardens Homecare. Medicaid is picking up the difference.

I discover this information when I look more closely at the piles of papers on the card table in the living room. Most are bills — including one from Tooksbury's Funeral Home and Cremation Services — and requests from charities. I also find my father's death certificate, I assume placed there by Mrs. McNadden, and his will, which I ignore. Perhaps Mrs. Godfrey can recommend a lawyer.

The sound of Rodney's horn reaches me, and I glance out the window to catch sight of his truck leaving the property. I feel both abandoned and relieved.

There is also a shoebox tucked almost out of sight under the card table, which I stare at a moment and decide to open later.

I gather the requests from charities and toss them in the woodstove, then wander back through the house to the base of the stairs. Until now, I have not ventured up to the room April and I shared for sixteen years.

Our room was the second down a short hallway, now banked with black dustballs. The latch has been removed and the door held shut by a rope wrapped around two nails driven into the door and door frame. The nails are high, possibly beyond the reach of someone my mother's height. It takes time to untie the rope, and I grow increasingly annoyed that she may have been barred from this room.

The entire house has a film of abandon, disuse, and dirt, and my childhood bedroom is no different. But there is something not right about this room—as though a stranger has been in, like a hotel maid, tidying things up. I assumed the room would have been emptied out, but on my bed are three stacks of textbooks, sorted by size, which should have been returned to Dover Regional High a long time ago. On my bedside table, a tower of neatly folded days-of-the-week panties—a common birthday present from my mother. Yellow Wednesday on top. On the windowsill, a pair of knitting needles has speared a ball of light blue yarn that I suspect was once navy. I push open the narrow closet and it exhales mothballs and something reminiscent of watermelon candy. Two pairs of Dr. Scholl sandals rest on the closet floor beneath quietly rattling wire hangers. A black Danskin bodysuit droops from a hanger among several patchwork maxi-skirts.

I recall the eye shadow in the egg cupboard and the mood ring in the refrigerator and realize that as my mother's illness progressed, she must have embarked on a number of nonsensical missions that involved transporting objects out of her daughters' bedroom. I imagine how it would have happened: slyly, disobedi-ently. How my father would have scolded her and eventually put an end to it with hammer and nails and rope.

I stand in the middle of the room, turning as though I no longer recognize a door for what it is: an exit. I remember I briefly took up knitting—before the cigarettes—to pass the time during my last year at home, and that at one time April and I shared a crush on Rod Stewart, in the way other siblings might share a candy bar. I tilt my head back to stare into Rod's brown eyes where he poses, showcasing a mullet and beaded choker, on a poster tacked to the ceiling, and recall what had seemed a complicated poignancy in his feelings for poor old Maggie May.

But all that was before Dr. Panama arrived.

Apparently, desire can make a first-class fool out of any of us.

Part Two

SIX

In the winter of 1974 Nixon extended daylight savings in response
to the energy crisis, and April and I went to school in the dark.
We were fourteen. Across the country, people were anxious and
confused, faced as they were with lines at gas stations, a national
speed limit, and rumours of a toilet paper shortage, but April and
I knew only how cold and black it was an hour earlier each day.
Dad found us a flashlight to guide us down our long driveway to
Assabet Road to catch the school bus, though we rarely switched
it on. It seemed warmer, somehow, without that sad spotlight
of yellow on the frozen puddles and hard mud ahead of us. We
held on to each other and said little, breathing wetly through our
scarves. Across the road from the bus stop, our mother's stand
was a dark smudge that gradually, as the weeks passed, emerged
from the night.

It was on one of these mornings that a local eight-year-
old girl died under circumstances that were, in my father's
words, debatable—by which he meant preventable—and as a

consequence he began concocting a plan to install a doctor in our tiny town of Cranfield.

Samantha Ann Molinski had been running a fever three days in a row, but her mother figured it was a run-of-the mill flu. It would have been inconceivable to Mrs. Molinski, as it may have been to most homemakers in that place and time—homemakers whose cash was limited and who did not fly off to the family doctor the way we do now—that an aggressive bacterium was consuming her daughter's body.

By the fourth morning, a rash had inched its way up Samantha Ann's torso, almost before her mother's eyes, and she wasn't talking any sense at all. She was talking about candy corn. Mrs. Molinski telephoned Dr. Bruck in Dover, who listened briefly before interrupting to say, "Bring her to the clinic. Don't waste a second. Don't stop for anything."

I imagined Dr. Bruck on his feet, standing over his mahogany desk in a haze of cigarette smoke, backed by his shelves of wooden decoys—mallards, redheads, pintails—leaning into the phone and doing his damnedest to convey a sense of urgency.

"Wrap her in a blanket. Lay her in the back seat of your car. Come right away."

Dr. Bruck later announced that he'd had a strong intimation, based on Mrs. Molinski's description, that Samantha Ann was running out of time. The doctor's comments enraged my father. Didn't the sons of bitches make house calls anymore? He talked about nothing else for months.

Eventually my father did some research—or did not do some research, as it turned out—and claimed to have gotten his hands on a joint state and federal program that promised to provide not only capital for a new office and all the requisite medical furnishings, but also a salary befitting a doctor.

Only in retrospect did it seem ludicrous and zany—not to mention fishy.

That winter and spring, we took Art with Miss Fujioka. We sat at large desks designed for four students. Phil Archer sat across from April and me. Cindy Plank had been sitting next to Phil, but she transferred herself to Girls' Health after a week.

We were well into watercolour painting and Miss Fujioka was furious with the class for its lack of progress. We still had acrylics and oil pastels to get through before being let out for summer. April and I were among the few who had not fallen behind, but she was furious with us anyway, because we were painting the same scene—a red barn—and we worked on our paintings in tandem, the way we had once dressed and eaten.

Phil Archer had oily shoulder-length hair and wore his leather jacket to class. He may have been paranoid someone would steal it from his locker, or he may have been, like us, still feeling the cold after the early morning rise for school. He was a year ahead of us. We remembered him from the spring before, when a television set had been set up in the school gym by the French teacher, Madame Petersen, for the edification of any student with a free period and an interest in viewing the Senate Watergate hearings. Madame Petersen wore mini-skirts and had knock knees and a mysterious disease, or so you had to assume, that made her skin purple, grey, and pink by turns. During the coming of warmer, then hotter, weather, students wandered in and scattered themselves in front of the television set. April and I sat cross-legged at the back. While we made little sense of the hearings, we were fascinated by a group of older, long-haired boys who wore peace signs and frayed hip-hugger jeans. They smelled vegetatively peculiar—we suspected this was marijuana.

Phil Archer had been one of those boys.

Madame Petersen, being young and enthusiastic, would join the students and engage them in conversation during the commercial breaks. Our fascination with their seriousness was almost a longing inside us.

"The White House must take responsibility," Madame would say, her dark-rimmed eyes moving from student to student. "You, the youth, you must demand it."

Phil's painting was born of his imagination, which provided another source of fury for Miss Fujioka, since she had instructed the class in no uncertain terms to work from a photograph or assemble a still life. His painting—which would never be completed anyway because half the time he didn't trouble himself to attend class—depicted a tornado-like event orbited by objects April thought might be red apples but I suspected were human heads.

"It's a personal reflection on the Kent State massacre," he told Miss Fujioka one day.

"I suppose you were there, Phil?" Miss Fujioka asked, not waiting for an answer. She was not at all like Madame Petersen.

Phil glanced across the table and caught us listening.

"She really bums me out," he muttered.

We were shocked he had spoken to us and concentrated on our identical barns.

"What are you two painting?" he asked us.

We told him.

"Heard of Kent State?"

April told him we hadn't and I giggled.

"You think that's funny?" Phil asked me. He put his brush down.

I felt my cheeks burning.

Miss Fujioka's head popped up from the other side of the classroom. "Enough talking, Mr. Archer. You're on thin ice as it is."

"Kent State is not funny," Phil said.

Just ignore him.

"The National Guard killed four students."

"We know about Kent State," April said aloofly. "Everyone does." We dipped our brushes in brown paint and applied it to our roofs.

A few years earlier, Dad had argued with Mom for days about taking the family on the Amtrak train out of Boston with the other demonstrators for an anti-war march on Washington. He insisted it could be a real eye-opener for the girls, but Mom said it could be a real mess like Kent State and he would have to go alone, which he didn't.

Phil was profoundly impressed by this. He said our father was far out. His own parents weren't into the scene, but Phil would have gone with our father in a heartbeat.

"Are you going to use that brush?" April asked him.

Phil handed it to her and said, "You can keep that as long as you want."

Then, months later, during summer break, he called the house asking for her.

———

It was August, and April and I were packing a lunch to bring Mom, who was too busy to leave the stand. While it was humid and nasty in Washington—where Nixon had quit and flown off to California and Ford had taken over, though no one had actually voted for him, my father pointed out a hundred times—in Massachusetts the weather was perfect for anyone trying to grow vegetables: full sun, little wind, a good soaking of rain every few nights. Dad, who'd already had his lunch, was standing by the Franklin stove, picking at his teeth and ruminating over Samantha Ann Molinski.

The phone started ringing just as Mrs. McNadden stepped up into the kitchen with a carton of eggs. Dad turned and stared at her as though unable to identify either her or that ringing sound.

I was washing the dishes and April was wrapping up a sandwich.

"Dad."

"The phone."

Startled, he glanced over at us, saw that we were busy, then looked back at Mrs. McNadden, who was at that moment slipping the carton of eggs onto the table as though she hoped not to be seen.

"Grab that, Lois," he said. "You're closer."

The phone was on the wall behind Mrs. McNadden, but there was no doubt this request threw her off. April looked at me and rolled her eyes.

"Me?"

"Grab it! Lois, quick!"

She whipped around and plucked the phone from its receiver. "Bell residence."

The three of us smirked.

"May I ask who's calling?"

"Ready?" April said to me, picking up Mom's lunch.

"April?"

We turned. Mrs. McNadden was holding the phone at her belly, with a hand over the receiver. "It's for you. He's identified himself as a Phil Archer."

We were all silent a moment.

Then April took the receiver from Mrs. McNadden as though this was her fault and went into the next room with it, stretching the cord as far as it would go. She kicked the door but it wouldn't close all the way with the cord there. I heard her say, "That wasn't my mother."

Behind me, Mrs. McNadden began explaining to my father she was dropping off a dozen eggs because that morning Marsha had mentioned we were getting low. I knew Mom would have only been making chit-chat. We had enough eggs to get by. If my mother understood people at all, she would not have offered up information like that to Mrs. McNadden.

"I promised Marsha I'd drop off a dozen on my way to Dover."

I glanced over my shoulder and saw my father was waking up. He stepped around the table towards her. She looked for a minute as though she might sink to her knees.

"Marsha said she was low on eggs," Mrs. McNadden tried again. "So I was—"

"Low on eggs?" My father sounded as though he didn't believe her. Mrs. McNadden slunk back a few inches. Her cheeks had little red circles on them.

He turned to me and caught my eye and held it as he moved closer to her, eliminating the space between them she had just created.

"Since when did the hens stop laying?" he said to me in a false voice of interrogation.

"Beats me," I answered, depositing a handful of cutlery onto the drainboard with undue clatter. "There's eggs in the cupboard."

"I didn't say they *stopped* laying, Russell."

My father flipped open the carton to reveal Mrs. McNadden's shining eggs. She had washed them, something we didn't bother with unless we were selling them at the stand or they were too badly caked with chicken shit and bits of straw — even for us. Mrs. McNadden put her hand on the door latch behind her.

"All righty then," she said, pushing open the door. "I'll be off."

After she was gone April came back into the kitchen and hung up the phone. She looked at Mrs. McNadden's eggs. "You've got to be kidding me. Did she actually wash those?" She was trying to pretend nothing was out of the ordinary, but Dad had already forgotten about the phone call.

"You can frighten the bejesus out of that woman, girls, simply by breathing on her. Am I right?"

We nodded and exchanged a look. I dried my hands and April picked up Mom's lunch, then we slipped outside and set off for the stand.

"What did Phil Archer want?" I asked once we were away from the house.

"He wants to meet me at the movies on Thursday."

We were passing the tomato patch. Dad liked to come out and pick the ripe ones off the vine and eat them as he stood there. Sometimes he even left the house with the salt shaker in his pocket. It was a habit of his Mom tried to discourage.

After a moment I asked, "Did you tell him no?"

April stopped, shoved the packed lunch at me, and covered

her face with her hands. "I told him yes. I'd rather die." I thought she might fall over in the road.

"Call him back and say no."

"We don't know his number."

"Ask the operator."

"I'm afraid to."

I took a deep breath. "I'll go."

"That's not fair to you."

"I don't mind."

"I have to tell you something," April said.

"What?"

"Phil said I'm pretty."

"He said that on the phone?"

She nodded.

"That's pathetic," I said.

"I'm pathetic! I said yes to Phil Archer."

We were at the end of the driveway, across the street from the stand. A handful of cars were pulled off onto the shoulder. Most had kids and dogs crawling around inside. I was still holding Mom's lunch.

"Can't we just get his phone number and call him and say you've changed your mind?"

"That's mean, Pilgrim."

"I'll go," I said again. "He won't know the difference. You're too shy, April."

She nodded. "I am shy."

"Shyer than me."

She nodded again. She wasn't sold on this. I could tell a part of her almost wanted to go, now that I was. But we couldn't both go.

"No, I'll go," I said firmly.

"Thanks, sweet pea," Mom said, when she saw her lunch. Her hair was falling out of her kerchief and I knew she was busy.

April had wandered down the road a bit. She didn't want to hear me ask Mom for a lift to the East Dover Shopping Mall next Thursday. After the supper dishes were done, I explained to Mom.

"Your father won't take you?"

"Nope. It's to see a movie with some friends."

"Of course I'll take you." She was surprised. She wanted us to have friends.

Thursday came and April almost changed her mind and said she wanted to go, then got nervous again and said nothing. Several times we went over how I would act—that I would speak loud enough for Phil to hear me and would try not to drag my feet.

We had a way of walking that my father described as half shuffle, half swagger.

"Pick up your feet, girls," Dad would say to us. "It's a cinch, once you get the hang of it."

Just before I left, April came up to me in the kitchen and slipped her mood ring on my finger.

"He mentioned it one day in art class," she explained.

I was puzzled.

"You must have been over at the sink, washing your brushes." She paused, then whispered, "Do you think he'll kiss you?"

"Gross."

She put her hand on my back and gave me a little push. "Better go. Mom's out waiting in the car."

But when I turned she grabbed the sleeve of my sweater and pulled me back.

What?

She dropped my sweater. *Nothing. Go.*

I got in the car with Mom and closed the door. After a minute I looked over at her and she said, "No April?"

"Nope."

"I see."

Later, she asked me who I was meeting.

"Phil Archer," I told her.

"A boy?"

I nodded.

"What?"

"Yes. He's a boy."

"He's the only friend you're meeting?"

I nodded.

"Pilgrim?"

"*What?*"

"You're on a date?" I could tell by her voice she was pleased with this.

"I figure."

She didn't say anything else until we pulled up at the entrance to the East Dover Shopping Mall.

"That's why you didn't want your father to drive you."

"Mom, please don't tell Dad."

"Oh, for goodness sakes."

"This will never happen again."

"Pilgrim, you're only going to the movies. You'll have a nice time."

"No, I hate him. He's pathetic."

"Are you going to get out of the car, or are you going to leave this poor boy hanging?"

"Promise me you won't tell Dad."

"If you don't want me to, I won't. What does April have to say about it?"

I found Phil standing in front of a poster for a movie, deeply engrossed in the ten words written there. He had his hair pulled back in a ponytail and was wearing his leather jacket. I felt sick as I approached him and then had to stand beside him several seconds, waiting for him to notice me.

"Phil."

He turned. "April. Excellent."

He reached for my hand and I thought we were going to buy our tickets, but instead he led me past the bathrooms and down a corridor I'd never known about and out a back door beside the loading dock to Filene's Department Store and across the parking lot.

"Aren't we going to the movies?"

"What?"

"Aren't we going to the movies?" I asked more loudly.

"All in good time, milady, all in good time." He was speaking with an English accent.

I followed him to a blue Pontiac parked at the far end of the lot.

"Your chariot awaits."

"Whose car?" I asked, stalling.

"Come on, just get in." He'd dropped the accent.

I felt stupid and got in. He sat behind the steering wheel and I watched him remove a slender pipe and matches from a jacket pocket, then a plastic bag, presumably of marijuana, from another pocket. I wondered if Phil was a dope dealer like Amado Barboza, who had conducted business at the back of the bus before dropping out of school.

Phil gently packed the pipe using the tip of his finger, then put the pipe in his mouth and lit a match and drew in noisily. The bowl of the pipe caught and smoldered and let off a swampy odour.

I was hoping he wasn't going to share it because I didn't know what was expected, but he jabbed the air in front of me with it, indicating it was mine for the taking. His lips were pressed together and he was holding his breath.

"I've never done this before," I confessed. The pipe was now in my hand.

He put a finger up as though warning me not to go anywhere. His expression was pained. Then he exhaled explosively and some smoke—I would have expected more—exited his body.

"Really?" He sounded winded. "Hurry before it goes out. That's not my good pipe. I can't find my good pipe."

I didn't know if I should try it. It was hard for me to make a decision without April.

He was coaching me to inhale slowly and not let the smoke escape my lungs for as long as absolutely possible. I nodded and put the pipe to my lips, inhaled slowly and burned my throat. I gave the pipe back and coughed for several minutes, while Phil sat on the other side of the car, growing farther and farther away, and smoked away at the pipe by himself. When I was done sputtering he handed it back to me without comment. I had no idea the effects might be cumulative.

"Your father probably smokes pot," he said.

I shook my head.

I figured Phil would start lecturing me about that liar Nixon now, but he just smiled knowingly.

"It's finished," he said and placed the pipe on the dash. I stared out the window at the mall, where people were being sucked into the entrance. In front of us a flock of astonishingly beautiful pigeons were waddling around eating bits of the pavement.

Meanwhile, Phil had removed the elastic band from his ponytail and was running his hands in and under and through his hair over and over again. It looked silky, not greasy at all, and gave off an herbal shampoo smell. I knew it was rude to watch him but I couldn't look away. He was like someone in a novel. I felt like I knew him through and through, but then I realized that was not possible. Maybe if I touched him I would know him instantly, but I suspected that would not be possible either. Also there was the problem that he did not know my true identity.

"Do you have any brothers or sisters?" I whispered.

"What time is it?" he said. "I don't wanna miss the beginning."

"It's 7:42." I felt tremendously opposed to going anywhere. "It started already."

He dug around for his watch buried beneath the sleeve of his jacket. I sympathized with the struggle he was having trying to get to it. "Shit. It's exactly 7:42. How did you know that?"

I shook my head.

He put his hair back in the ponytail and most of his things back into his pockets, then zipped up his jacket and said, "Let's go. It'll still be the previews."

I giggled and pointed to the pipe he'd left on the dash before getting sidetracked by his hair.

It seemed to take him a while to understand what I was pointing at, but when he did he said, "Right on, April. Thanks."

I giggled again, which was embarrassing, but I couldn't help it.

He leaned over my lap to examine my hand. "That's the kinda ring that turns colour when you're happy or sad, right?"

I took a deep, trembling breath. "It's supposed to."

"It's brown," he said. "What does that mean?"

"Brown means you're nervous."

"You are? You mean of cops?"

"No. But this isn't my ring. I lost mine. I think April is nervous, or worried."

Phil was still bent towards me, peering at me with glassy, perplexed eyes. I realized what I'd just said and felt a stab of panic. Suddenly I needed him to move away. He was not a character in a book or someone I could ever know through and through. He was a stranger. I thought of April and decided she was okay.

Phil leaned back and said, "I hear ya," a comment that carried little meaning but worked for both of us.

I opened the car door and got out.

We saw *Airport 1975*. Because we were late, we missed the beginning and had to sit in the front row. I spent some time trying to get the characters sorted out: nun, star, alcoholic, child, stewardess, captain-hero. My eyes saw cardboard and plastic models when they should have seen drama. At one point Phil disappeared and returned—it seemed hours later, and though I had pretty much forgotten he existed, I was relieved to see him—with popcorn and licorice.

"What did I miss, milady?" he whispered, his breath warm against my ear and giving me goosebumps.

I tried to speak but could only lift a hand and move it in front of my face a few times. He nodded patiently, waiting for words, but I turned back to the screen. I could feel him watching me and figured he thought I was stupid. It didn't occur to me he might think I was stoned.

It was dusk when the movie let out. The Ambassador was waiting at the mall entrance. I said goodbye to Phil, whom I appreciated for having no more interest in chatting now than I did, and who trudged off across the parking lot, possibly to the Pontiac, but I would never know for sure. I got in the back seat because April was in the front, where I expected her to be, with my mother and Petunia, who was beating her tail back and forth with delight to see me.

I was glad to be alone in the back. I was experiencing a heavy sluggishness I'd never felt before and would of course have opportunity to experience later, but all I knew was that I craved isolation.

April turned around and put her chin on the back of the seat and stared at me, patiently and lovingly, trying to get a sense of my thoughts. She knew I would not be inclined to talk about my date with Mom present.

"What's the matter?" she asked after a bit.

I shook my head. I felt cold and couldn't speak. I wanted, merely, to savour the memory of Phil's creaking leather coat, the smell of his clean hair, the mystery of the Pontiac, not to mention Charlton Heston's bravery and everything else that was achingly unrealistic about the movie. I wanted my own thoughts and I didn't want to share them.

"What's that funny smell?" my mother asked.

"Just some licorice," April said, flipping back around to face the front.

My fingers wrapped around the mood ring. It felt warm and smooth. I couldn't begin to guess at its colour now.

SEVEN

Within a year of Samantha Ann's death, my father had nearly brought to fruition his plan to secure a doctor for Cranfield—a plan he laboured over in solitude via the telephone and US Postal Service that summer Nixon quit and I got high with Phil Archer. Then, in September, he was temporarily derailed when the Boston school board implemented a desegregation plan, and black students from Roxbury were bused to school in South Boston's Irish neighbourhood.

"What a sin," my mother said each morning, peering over my father's shoulder at the *Boston Globe* and its grainy photos of frightened students escorted by state troopers to a school where they were unwelcome. "Those poor, poor children."

"The goddamn cradle of liberty," my father would say, throwing the *Globe* down and putting on his coat. "Well, I'm ashamed to be a citizen of this state. Deeply ashamed."

I went to the door and watched him whistle to the dogs. Bandit and Tansy leapt into the back of the truck. I felt rejected, as though the dogs were forgiven for this injustice, but my sister and mother and I, as citizens of Massachusetts, were not. We wouldn't see my father for hours.

The doctor my father eventually located was from a place called Little Dove Cay, which was in the Bahamas, and while it's probable the racial violence in Boston factored in this choice, none of us would ever really know the details.

In the months leading up to his arrival, April and I amused ourselves by referring to him as Dr. Panama. We were fully aware we were making a mistake by over a thousand miles, because Dad had brought out the atlas, but we both liked saying "Dr. Panama." We liked the drawn-out, hilly sound of it in our mouths, and the way it made us feel, unaccountably, like young ladies.

This was in the late spring of 1975. Although we had only just turned sixteen, Dad had begun to talk about college. He urged us to consider a future in Canada, where, he said, post-secondary education was reasonably priced and you could see a doctor free of charge.

My mother would laugh in a weird way when my father recommended Canada for college. "He's kidding, girls, you have years to make up your minds," she would say. "You don't want to go way up there, anyway. You'd have to speak French."

"They wouldn't have to speak French, Marsha. It's not mandatory."

"Yes, they would," she said forcefully. "You don't know everything, Russell."

Although I did not want to consider a future anywhere but where I was, somebody in the house was sending away for course catalogues and university applications, which made their way to our bedroom where they were examined by April. We both knew that if steps in this direction were taken, we would take them together. Neither one of us could have endured, in the spring of that year, the idea of a future not shared.

As the days got longer, the evenings became brilliant and the nights shorter. Outside our bedroom windows gargantuan trees pressed their leaves against the house, and here the birds awoke in the murky early hours to trill and whistle and trumpet, long before there was any sign of the rising sun.

Petunia, who slept with us, didn't mind the birdsong. It was calming just to see her there, sleeping on her back beside me, her paws folded across her chest and her exposed belly tender as a cushion.

"That's how romance is communicated in the avian world," Dad informed us. "You girls get no sympathy from me."

"They wake us up so early," April complained. "It's so annoying."

"Try going to bed earlier, Princess."

We tried. We lay in bed, restless, wide awake in the twilight.

"You need to adjust your internal clocks," my father told us. "If you want to fall asleep earlier."

"*Dad.*"

We had been hearing about our internal clocks forever. If you asked my father what time it was, he was able to tell you, give or take a minute. He also had an internal alarm clock so he knew when to wake up, when to come in for lunch or supper, when to meet the men who delivered the hay or those who took the lambs and squealing pigs away for slaughter.

He'd never worn a wristwatch in his life. And neither had we.

Yet it would be unfair to blame our restlessness entirely on the rhapsodies of birds. We had never had a real visitor before, yet now one was headed our way—one who was male, which was exciting, and a doctor, which was boring, and a Negro, which was unexpected—from the warm seas of the Caribbean, where Christopher Columbus had butchered and enslaved the indigenous people, which was something we learned not at school but from our father.

My father must have faced some challenges in attracting a doctor to Cranfield. I don't know how he found Dr. Panama, who had recently completed medical school in Jamaica. In the end, I was Dr. Panama's first and only patient in our town, not including the livestock he treated.

My guess is that I was his first patient, ever.

He arrived by Greyhound bus in July, smack in the middle of Mom's busiest days. We had been anticipating him for weeks and then there he was, stepping down onto the pavement outside the post office in a swirl of warm exhaust. April and I had not expected to be sent to meet him and had walked the two and a half miles in the summer heat. My father had promised he would be along in the station wagon any minute—which he wasn't—and we ran out of the house, not looking for our sneakers, so that by the time we reached the bus stop the soles of our feet were sore from the hot asphalt.

Tansy and Bandit had followed us, and they lay now at the side of the road beneath the insufficient shade of some jewelweed, panting like madmen. Their tongues were raw and gluey-looking from thirst. It was the kind of heat that could make a green tomato turn red by day's end, a perfect zucchini rot on the vine overnight. There were not enough minutes in the day to accommodate all my mother had to do. The vegetables stubbornly surged onward with their uninhibited flowering and fruiting, and my mother raced to keep up with them.

To hear her complain, you'd think the plants pursued a private vendetta against her. Time was a harsh master, according to my father, who observed my mother's frenetic state with both admiration and disparagement.

April and I had been ruled by a wild, giddy curiosity since hearing about Dr. Panama, but as the Greyhound bus pulled off Route 17 with an explosive downshifting of its gears, we felt simultaneously subdued and fidgety. We expected Dr. Panama to be black as night and, possibly, incomprehensible. He might speak another language. Or pronounce his words garbled and thickly accented. We might agree to something we did not have the authority to agree to. It was also possible he might hate us because we were twins, or because we were white. Other than Lottie Barboza, we had never known any Negroes personally. Though we did not know many people personally, period.

But we weren't supposed to call them Negroes, or colored people, or people of color, anymore. My father said the correct terminology was Black Americans and had been for a good while. He claimed my mother could take some of the blame on this, as she was outmoded.

"Your mother's a hick at heart," he'd said. "It wouldn't hurt her to read the newspaper front to back every once in a while. Just forget you ever heard the word 'Negro.' It's offensive to Blacks."

"Dad—"

"And don't forget, girls, the human species originated in Africa. Put that in your peace pipe and smoke it," he added, which made me think of Phil Archer.

"Dad, is it Blacks for short?" April wanted to know. We were only days away from Dr. Panama's arrival.

My father scowled. "What?" He suspected April of being flippant. But I'd had the same question. It was essential we get this right.

"First you said Black Americans. Then you said Blacks."

My father tugged at his beard and squinted into the distance. April moved a couple of inches closer to me until we touched.

"Mr. Philpott calls them mulattos," I offered.

"Who the hell is he?"

"He's the bus driver, Dad."

"He speeds up at their stops if they aren't out yet."

"Whose stops?"

"The Negro kids."

"You mean Black Americans."

"Black Americans. Mr. Philpott doesn't wait for them like he waits for us, when we're late. The way he honks the horn for us."

"You know what that is, Pilgrim, don't you? That's discrimination. Why hasn't this bus driver been taken to task?"

"Dunno."

"Someone needs to have a talk with Mr. Philpott about the civil rights movement. Someone needs to take this hillbilly outside and—"

"*Dad.*"

"I didn't mean myself, girls."

But I realized, as the Greyhound bus stopped and stood idling like a big, hot animal, that we still didn't know if Dr. Panama should be referred to as Black American or just Black, and come to think of it, he wasn't American. He was Bahamian. Black Bahamian?

But it didn't matter, I thought. We would address him by his name.

I panicked. The door of the bus swished open. "What's his name?" I asked April.

"Dr. Panama."

"No! His real name."

A young man stepped down through the bus's accordion doors and jogged over to us. He was the only passenger to get off and we were the only people waiting there. Here comes the origin of the species, I thought, which was a little wicked of me, but I was nervous. The driver stepped down after him and slid open the outside door to retrieve his luggage. Although Dr. Panama was darker than any of the Negroes we knew, it was his eyes that were the blackest I'd ever seen, yet at the same time bright and flashing. He smiled with his eyes and mouth, even his teeth. His entire face expressed kindness. I'd never seen that before.

He was shorter than my father. He looked way too young to be a doctor.

"The welcome committee," he said cheerfully. His accent was a blend of Bahamian and public school British, though I didn't know that then.

He put his hand out to me first, which would become a memory I coveted. He was wearing a red tie and blue sports jacket, and polyester grey trousers that held his thighs in a mesmerizing manner. The effect of the hot walk rushed at me. I felt drained, unfriendly, and shy. When I didn't budge, he glanced around, perhaps looking for a vehicle.

"What a relief it is to get off that bus," he said in his chirpy, peculiar voice.

April was feeling sorry for him. She was always more empathetic than me. And could have better manners. When he put his hand out to her next, she forced herself to take it.

"Brilliant," he said. "Do either of you speak English?" Then he smiled, and again I was struck by his teeth. April laughed awkwardly. He had made a joke.

But I could see his peppy energy was dissipating.

When the Ambassador finally pulled up beside us and honked —unnecessarily—Tansy and Bandit rose from the dirt and approached the car, their heads low, their tails scarcely wagging. For a moment the only sound was the cooing of a mourning dove.

"So you've met the strawberry-roan girls," my father said, getting out of the car. "The Bell babies. Sorry I wasn't here. Been up to my neck."

I half expected my father to say something derogatory about the tie, but he kept his mouth shut.

Our visitor glanced back at the two of us, with our scratched knees and ratty braids, and appraised us openly. We were a young-looking sixteen, despite our well-worn Petal Burst brassieres.

"I've had that pleasure," he said politely.

In that moment, somewhere inside me, a shift occurred.

It took five minutes to get home. We learned his name was Dr. Jean Moss. In the back seat April and I held hands and tried not to giggle.

He had a funny name.

It was an unusual day.

We also learned we were not yet fully prepared for Cranfield's first doctor. Much of the necessary medical supplies were still en route, or—when Dr. Panama asked specifically about some items—not yet ordered. And the location of his office, along with his private lodgings, had yet to be determined. For the time being, he would be staying with us, in the spare bedroom under the stairs. My father repeated how he'd been up to his neck, and at least two of us in the car knew this not to be true.

I contemplated all the foolish antics we had carried on with that summer, imagining Dr. Panama and how he might act and speak and look, and I was struck by how unpredictable life could prove to be.

My father drove down Assabet Road humming, an indication of mild internal turbulence. The countryside went by. Clouds had formed and a breeze had come up. In the wayback the dogs were restless, their noses lifted as they sniffed the change in air. The sweltering walk to town seemed long past. Beneath this threat of shifting weather, the countryside glowed.

"Looks like rain," my father said, as though we were suddenly incapable of seeing the hands at the ends of our arms.

I watched Dr. Panama inspect the sky. I was curious how he felt about rain. My parents appreciated rain. There never seemed to be enough of it, this time of year. But to Dr. Panama it could mean hurricanes and monsoons, flooding, tidal waves, loss of life. I worried that my father might instill fear in him, though quite by accident.

I wondered if we would stop at the stand so he could meet Mom, and was relieved when we turned off Assabet Road towards our house, not a word from my father. There were cars parked in the dirt apron surrounding the stand and along the sides of the road. It was the height of the corn frenzy. A few customers stood indistinct in the shadowy light inside the stand, but most were gathered outside around my mother where she was selling the sweet corn from the back of the flatbed. The ears had been picked that morning and piled high at the start of the day, but she was getting down to the last now. Corn husks lay trampled at her feet.

On the other side of the stand, the grey Mercedes was parked with its windows up and engine running. Inside, Mrs. Lewis was smoking, waiting for my mother to come to the window.

I thought the world looked magical, so leafy and emerald green, and tried to imagine how it looked to Dr. Panama. In the late fall and winter our house and barn were easily visible from the road, but in the summer the trees around our house shrouded us with leaf, as they did that day.

We gave him a tour of the farm. My father charged from one point to the next, too fast for us to keep up, as though he were trying to shake off Dr. Panama now that he was here. April and I fell behind, and Dr. Panama did an unusual thing: he waited for us to catch up to him. When I got into bed that night I remembered how he'd stood sideways, observing us, and how I'd felt self-conscious, hoping we were both remembering to pick up our feet and not shuffle.

"I think he's waiting for us," I whispered. Petunia was in my arms. Once we caught up with Dr. Panama, Petunia stretched her neck out to sniff his elbow, and he stepped back, checking his arm as though she might have left something unpleasant there.

"Why are you two smiling like that?" he asked us.

April looked alarmed, so I said, "You have a funny last name."

"Pardon me?"

"You have a funny last name," April said.

"Moss," I said. "Like a plant." I handed Petunia to April. She was getting heavy, but did not want to be put down, particularly around this newcomer.

"How do you spell it?" April asked.

"It's hopeless, trying to tell the two of you apart," Dr. Panama marvelled, shaking his head.

"How do you spell it?" I asked.

"M-O-S-S," he told us, in a voice thick with amusement. "And if you repeat each other like that, all will be lost for me, I'm afraid."

"We've never heard that name before," April said defensively. "For a human being."

"We share one hundred percent of our DNA," I explained.

He tilted his head back and laughed. I could see he appreciated what I'd said.

For sixteen years my parents had orbited me like planets around a sun, while I was so close to my sister, whose pale skin and strawberry-roan hair were my own, that there seemed barely air between us. But the more I would come to know this dark-skinned Dr. Panama, the more I would long to claim a distant kinship with him.

We were almost to the barn. My father was behind it, standing in the paddock with a couple of goats, shouting and pointing to the bog.

"What's he telling me?" Dr. Panama asked, examining us in turns.

"He wants to show you the cranberry bog he's restoring," I answered, before April could.

Behind the barn, pasture descended to a marsh my father claimed was once a working cranberry bog. His scheme to return it to cultivation had been eclipsed that year by his search for Dr. Panama.

I knew instinctively that the doctoring project's appeal to my father had been in the challenge of its planning, in the same way burglary and wiretapping might have been for Nixon and his men. But now that Dr. Panama was here, out in the open, halfway to the barn, nodding and smiling and eager, somebody would have to take responsibility for my father's actions.

The rain held off until night. Mrs. McNadden stopped over after supper to meet the new doctor and was shaking the rain from herself when Dr. Panama walked into the kitchen. She was taken aback to see him. My father's face was full of mischief, as though he had been waiting for her reaction. I don't know if he had never told her the doctor was Bahamian, or she had just assumed he would be white. Later, when her pig bit her, she wasted no time in going to Dr. Bruck in Dover. My father wasn't so amused then.

"It's raining buckets out there," she said nervously. "Well!" And she looked Dr. Panama squarely in the face and smiled like a trooper.

Because we had guests, we all went into the living room. My mother offered everyone a glass of water. I was the only one who did not sit but stood in the doorway and watched Dr. Panama.

In response to our questions, he told us about his home, where it never snowed, although, as it turned out, hurricanes were not uncommon. He described how, on the smaller islands, the ocean would wash up onto one shore, splash through the houses, then exit out over the opposite shore. People opened their front and back doors to make it easier for the water and to reduce its destructive force. I wasn't sure if he was kidding or not. He described a coconut grove blanketed with white sand. No, he wasn't big on swimming, but yes, he fished. He enjoyed fishing but had trouble keeping track of time if he was out on the water trying to catch a few groupers.

He was rambling, which embarrassed us, so we laughed nervously and he suddenly looked worried. I watched him stroke one of his ears and sit up straighter.

He had been travelling for days by bus from Miami and smelled strongly and uniquely of perspiration. I was told to take him to the cellar to show him how to turn up the thermostat on the hot water heater before taking a shower. As I left the room I glanced at April, who looked concerned that I would have to do such a thing on my own, but I didn't mind. I wanted to get closer to him. He had one of those good-bad smells.

"Which one are you?" he asked after I had showed him what to do with the thermostat.

"Pilgrim."

"Pilgrim."

"Say it again," I said.

He smiled, because he wouldn't say it again. Instead he asked, "And the other one is April?"

"Yes."

"What are you sniffing at?" he asked, glancing around at the piles of junk on the dirt floor.

"Mice." I noticed his lower lip was pink like mine and April's, but his upper lip was brown like the rest of his face. It should have made him seem different from me, but it made him seem the same.

"They inhabit the basement?" He seemed a little anxious about that.

"Not now, not in summer. They moved back out to the fields."

"Yes, of course."

"And there is the possibility of snakes. Which eat the mice."

Snakes gave me—and April and my mother—the heebie-jeebies, and I shivered a little just to think of them, the way whole families hung from the swamp maples in spring, lazy and motionless in their hammocks of air.

He looked puzzled.

"It's cool down here," I explained. "They like that in the summer."

He nodded. Perhaps he was at a loss for words.

"But we haven't had any in years," I said, assuring him as much as myself. "Dad plugged all the holes where they were getting in."

Neither of us made a move to go back upstairs. I could hear the talking above, a soft rumble. I demonstrated again how you lifted the lever on the thermostat until it made a clicking noise. "I hate cold showers," I said. "Don't you?"

He looked at me and grinned. "Pilgrim?"

"Yes."

"And the other one is April?"

"Yes. I mean, no."

He pretended to look surprised, and I giggled and said, "Okay, yes. I was kidding." I thought how fantastic it would be if he accidentally touched me.

I heard footsteps above. "Mrs. McNadden is leaving," I said. It seemed like such a pointless, yet hilarious, thing to say. I felt the same bubbly way I had in the blue Pontiac with Phil Archer.

He gazed at me with awe.

"Your father was correct," he announced.

"Huh?" I felt myself blush. What had Dad gone and said about me?

"He said Cranfield needed a doctor and not to worry."

"About what?"

"About prejudice. That good medical attention was the thing."

"Oh, right," I said quickly.

"I was doubtful, but we had a frank discussion about it."

I nodded.

"What are you thinking, Pilgrim?" he asked. "You look so serious."

"Just, how old are you?"

"Twenty-six. How old are you?"

"Sixteen."

As he followed me up the stairs I knew he was watching me. The soles of my feet were filthy and I was careful to step in such a way that he couldn't see them.

April wouldn't talk to me as we got ready for bed.

We spent the next several days preparing for the opening of Dr. Panama's practice. Boxes arrived by Greyhound bus and were left with my mother at the vegetable stand. April and I carried them down to the house, and they rattled as the mysterious medical contents shifted from side to side. We stacked the boxes outside Dr. Panama's bedroom door. He was inordinately thankful, which embarrassed us. We couldn't look him in the eye when he showered us with his gratitude. I think even my father found it unsettling.

Mrs. McNadden was the one who located a place to serve as his office. Her brother-in-law owned a duplex on the other side of Cranfield, and he and his family were only occupying half of it. I thought the place looked a bit dodgy for a doctor's office. Run-down, with peeling brown paint, a bunch of tires strewn across the yard. My father reported the inside wasn't much better but a day's painting would remedy that. Mrs. McNadden explained her brother-in-law's children played with the tires. She promised to ask him to get rid of them and conduct a general tidy-up.

He asked April and me to call him Jean, rather than Dr. Moss, but when he was out of earshot we still called him Dr. Panama.

Later, looking back, I would see I'd made a fool of myself trying to be charming and funny. But at the time I couldn't stop myself. My chatter about DNA and gene pools — it was easy to parrot my father — seemed to entertain him. In my gloom weeks later, I would wonder if he'd been exhibiting a trained politeness rather than true amusement.

"You're talking too much," April informed me several times. But she wasn't being funny, like me. She had clammed up since the arrival of Dr. Panama, and I figured she was jealous that I was paying more attention to him than to her.

When Dr. Panama and I kidded around, April stood on the sidelines, wearing a half-listening expression, as though she were always on the verge of finding something better to do.

Occasionally a shy smile flickered around her mouth and I felt less of the guilt I resented feeling.

Since our visit to the cellar together to examine the thermostat, I would tease Dr. Panama by requesting him to repeat things.

"Say that again," I insisted.

"No."

"Yes."

"What?"

"What you just said, 'What is your favourite colour, Pilgrim?' Say that."

"What is your favourite colour, Pilgrim?"

I giggled. "Green."

"Say that again."

"Green."

He looked across the room at April. "And what is your favourite colour, April?"

"Red," she told him reluctantly.

He watched her for several seconds as though listening to something she wasn't saying. "Outstanding," he said. "You two are opposites on the colour wheel."

Then we had a hot spell. Dr. Panama came back from his office one afternoon and didn't look that good. His face had lost its softness. He looked older, like a real doctor. He offered to help my mother, and she reluctantly gave him a bowl of peas to shell, which he took and sat down with at the kitchen table.

April and I were hanging around, sucking on ice cubes.

"Not busy today?" my mother asked him.

"Busy?" he repeated a touch rudely. I might have taken it as a warning. He was putting the shelled peas back in the bowl, which rested on his lap, and making a pile of the empty pods on the

123

table. I went over and playfully tossed a few of the empty pods back in the bowl. He carefully picked them out and returned them to the table without comment.

I did it again.

"Please don't do that." He examined my face, then my body. Perhaps he was determining which one I was.

I did it again. I was beginning to hate myself.

"You're being a pest, Pilgrim," April hissed.

Dr. Panama gave April a quick once-over. People always did this, like we were a science experiment. It made me feel worse.

"Mendel the Monk loved peas, too," I said, my mouth full of ice cube, which was probably vulgar of me.

He barely glanced at me. "What are you trying to say, Pilgrim?"

What I knew about Gregor Mendel, the nineteenth-century German monk, came from biology class, not my father. For that reason I might have begun to falter, but not that reason alone.

"Haven't you ever heard of the father of genetics?" I asked grandly. "It's all very simple. The purple pea is dominant, the white pea is recessive." I tucked the shrinking ice cube into the pocket of one cheek and said more clearly but with a little dread, "Or maybe it's the other way around. Maybe the white pea is—"

"You are terribly mistaken, Pilgrim, if you presume the laws of heredity to be so rigidly straightforward," he interrupted, not looking up from the peas that he was now speedily shelling without my interference. "You might want to consider you're speaking to someone who passed medical school with high marks and complimentary references."

"Say that again?"

"I am more a master of knowledge in these subjects than anyone in this town."

He banged the bowl of shelled peas onto the table. My chest tightened. In those moments I felt a barrier drop between Dr. Panama and me like the weighty curtain at the end of a school play. I was cut off. Out in the cold. I resented him as I would a teacher who assigned too much homework, or someone I'd just met who made an unfriendly remark about twins. This was a hard, unforgiving side to him that I didn't want to believe existed.

I looked at April but her face was blank. My mother began inspecting the inside of a drawer as though she had not been listening to the conversation.

"Big deal," I said, turning to spit my ice cube in the sink. "Big whoop-dee-do." I marched upstairs to sulk, though the heat up there was atrocious.

The hot spell continued. Sleeping was a misery. I hoped that when the sun set it might turn cool, but instead the heat seemed to be released from every object and creature it had settled into during the day. Heat *became* the dense, black air. Everything I heard—Petunia's soft, fretful dreaming, a creak in the walls, a whistle—was amplified and oppressive. It stayed this way until two or three in the morning, when the air lifted and I heard a violent rustling of leaves outside our windows and imagined limbs swaying under this sudden breeze. That's when I reached down for my sheet, long ago kicked off, and finally slept.

When I woke, I was hot again. My sheet was sticky and weighed a ton. Boiling yellow light filled the room. April was already awake.

I rolled over and looked at her. She was facing the wall, her back to me.

"What's the matter?" I asked.

At first, she wouldn't respond. "Dad's angry," she said finally. "It has something to do with Dr. Panama—Jean. I mean Jean."

I told myself I could care less. I was still sore about his disparagement of my knowledge of genetics a few days earlier, but the truth was, I was more embarrassed than insulted. I would not be surprised if he never spoke to me again, which would be awful.

"Is Dad angry at Dr. Panama?" I asked her.

"No, but I think he's angry Jean doesn't have any patients."

"None?"

"No."

"Not a single one?"

"Nope."

"What's he doing all day?"

"Dunno. But they were talking about it outside, yesterday after supper. Dad was pissed off."

"Dad's crazy."

She turned around and faced me. The sunlight fell across her face and when she closed her eyes for a moment, I saw what was different. She was wearing blue eye shadow.

"People don't get sick as much in the summer," I said. "That's not his fault."

"Dad said people are prejudiced. They're still going to Dr. Bruck in Dover. Even the coloreds."

"Black Americans."

Her blue eyelids were disturbing me. I leaned over Petunia, who was stretched out on her back, and buried my face in the heated skin of her belly. When I moved up to her face and stared into her eyes, she licked my cheek then pulled away from me.

Dad said a dog doesn't want you in its personal space, staring it right in the eye. But it was hard to resist testing, every once and while, whether this was true.

"People are still going to Dr. Bruck?" I said. "When we have the genuine origin of the species right under our roof?"

"Pilgrim, that's not actually funny."

I felt betrayed by her refusal to be amused. "He hasn't had *any* patients?" I asked.

"I told you already. No."

"What else?" I asked, still speaking into Petunia's body.

"I tried to ask a question, but Dad said the subject was closed."

"Why are you wearing eye shadow?"

"Felt like it."

"To bed?"

"Skip it, Pilgrim."

April was right about Dad being angry. As usual, his anger energized him. He took out an ad in the *Dover Weekly*, built a massive sign for the front of the doctor's office, and hung around the stand educating people—more like scaring off customers, remarked Mom. Nothing worked. We just need one patient, Dad said, to get the ball rolling.

That would be me—the one patient—though I never got the ball rolling.

EIGHT

Four, five, or six feet. We would all have different memories of its length, even those of us who never laid eyes on it. But Jean said it was four and a half feet long, and he would be the one to know best.

My father did not believe in killing an animal without good reason and was infuriated by what he saw as the needless destruction of life, but he still had his mind set on Dr. Jean Moss becoming a pillar of the community, so he would keep this opinion to himself.

I found the snake when I went traipsing down the cellar stairs one day with an armful of dirty laundry, which prevented me from seeing it until I hit the bottom step. It was lounging on the cool cement slab in front of the washing machine, its body relaxed and outstretched. I screamed and dropped the laundry and it made an almost imperceptible movement, as though to coil, but perhaps the cold had settled into it too well. I was still screaming as I crabbed my way up the cellar stairs on all fours. I needed to elevate myself. I needed to climb the walls, the furniture. I skipped around on the balls of my feet. By the time April, Jean, and my mother were circling around me, I was on the kitchen table and had stopped screaming but couldn't speak.

Jean looked confused and alarmed.

"Pilgrim saw a huge snake in the cellar," April said, her face paling as she climbed onto a kitchen chair where she squatted. "A goddamn huge one." A shiver convulsed her.

Which was strange, because later that night, alone in our twin beds in the dark, April began speaking as though she was the one who had gone down into the cellar. As though hers were the eyes that had seen the snake.

"That was me," I interrupted. "I was about to put some clothes in the washer."

"What are you talking about?"

"You never even went down into the cellar, April."

"I sure did. The snake was stretched out on the cool cement. It was black and massive. Way bigger than those ones in the trees. Its head—ugh—was drooped over the edge of the cement so I couldn't see its face."

She was describing the snake precisely as I had seen it. But *I* had seen it.

"You're probably just seeing what was in my head," she said to me.

"No, you're seeing what was in *my* head."

"Then Jean touched me," she said. "He was worried about me because I was going into shock."

"You're retarded. That was me."

"You wish."

130

"Liar. Admit it."

"Shut up, Pilgrim."

"No, you shut up."

I knew it had been me, crouching on the kitchen table, my teeth chattering. Mom, who had looked like she would like to get up onto some furniture herself, had glanced from me to April and back to me before demanding, "There's another snake in the cellar? Where's your father?"

We looked outside and saw his truck was gone.

"Where'd he go now?" she said, nearly wailing. "He's always disappearing."

Jean took a step towards me and gripped my shoulders.

"You've had a shock, Pilgrim. Try to breathe."

My eyes were locked on his. I took his attentiveness as evidence he had forgiven me for my childish, rude behaviour over the pea pods and Mendel the Monk. I felt I would do anything to make this young man appreciate me again. I would never speak again, for example, if that was what was required. Conveniently, my teeth began to chatter more fiercely.

"How do you feel about snakes, Jean?" my mother whispered.

I watched him smile crookedly. "Not this kind of fear." He turned to her. They studied each other a moment. Finally he asked her, "Just come to the top of the cellar stairs with me? Would you mind?"

Reluctantly, my mother followed him out of the kitchen. We could hear their footsteps make it partway down the stairs, followed by silence, then their footsteps returning. April was still crouched in the chair behind me.

Mom came quickly back into the kitchen and went and stood by the sink. Jean's eyes were on me again.

"Are you breathing, Pilgrim?"

"Yes, I am."

"Slow and steady?"

I nodded.

Behind me, I could hear April breathing.

"You say the shed?" Jean asked my mother.

"Yes, the first door. On the wall above the wheelbarrows."

Jean went outside. I knew what was on the wall above the wheelbarrows. "What's he going to do?" I asked. "What's Jean going to do, Mom?"

She was pulling some garbage bags out of a drawer and ignoring me. I could tell she had seen the snake.

"I don't understand how a snake that size could get in the cellar," April remarked loudly. "It's massive."

I nodded.

"Your father has some answering to do," Mom was muttering. "He was supposed to have all those holes in the foundation sealed. Where the hell is he, anyway?"

When Jean came back into the house a minute later he was carrying an axe. He took the garbage bags from my mother, then stopped, perhaps stalling. "You're safe. You're all quite safe," he said. "It's a harmless snake. Why don't the three of you go upstairs for a while?"

"He must be old," I said, getting down off the table and beginning to feel guilty over what was about to happen. "That snake? Must be old, he's so big?"

Jean glanced at me and I remembered my decision not to speak to him again, lest I annoy him, but he smiled kindly. "Yes, I suppose he is an old fellow, Pilgrim."

I went upstairs with Mom and April, where we waited in my parents' bedroom without speaking. Occasionally there was the clang of the axe hitting the cement—clear and harsh and able to reach us easily—whereas the blade cutting through snake made no sound that we could hear.

By the time my father's truck pulled in, Jean had long finished chopping the snake up into manageable pieces and shovelling the twitching flesh into garbage bags. The bags were heavy and thumped against the cellar stairs as he brought them up.

"If you had been here, Russell, you could have dealt with it your own way," my mother said, knowing, as I did, how he felt about what had been done to the snake.

My father's only response was to say the nasty smell in the house, not to mention in the cellar, was the result of a defensive spray the snake released when realizing it was threatened. But Dad bit his tongue and did not go on to say that it had been threatened, and then butchered, for no reason other than being a big old snake seeking reprieve from the hot weather. But I knew he was thinking it, and Mom and April did, too. As for Jean, he knew only that he'd accepted a distasteful task in service to a family hysterical about snakes.

After that, we stopped complaining about the heat. I got into the habit of going swimming to cool off, but I went alone, since April had become distant and didn't seem interested in joining me. Each afternoon, after we had done our chores and I was sweaty and dusty from sweeping the barn from one end to the other, and April had gone up to the house without a word, as though she was mad at me about something, I made my way, feeling lonely and sorry for myself, across the marsh behind the barn to a small holding pond. In fall it would be drained and the water used to flood the cranberry bogs, but now it was cool and deep and fresh. Mom didn't like us swimming there because she couldn't see us from the house.

On the far side of the pond was a wooded hill criss-crossed by stone walls built, Dad said he knew for a fact, by the early settlers. "Probably your own ancestors," he'd add. Now it was thick with oaks and hickories and red maple. On occasion, April and I wandered over the hill and down the other side, emerging at the edge of the McNadden farm, though to call it a farm was generous, because all they had was a lot of flower beds, half a dozen chickens and one pig. Here we stopped and sometimes climbed an ancient white pine until we were high enough for a breeze. We passed the time talking and absently watching Mrs. McNadden gardening in her denim skirt, or talking to our father at the edge of her driveway where he'd stopped his truck to have a word with her out his open window, his elbow resting in the sun.

Now, as I approached the pond, waves of heat unleashed by my movement came pulsing out of the weeds. I kicked off my workboots. The water was as cold as I had imagined, and I began to unzip my cut-offs, then stopped, suddenly self-conscious. I glanced around. The pond was ringed by swamp maples and willows standing dead still in the heat. April and I had been skinny-dipping here for years and never met anyone. Even so, I decided against undressing, in case someone did appear out of the blue.

Like Dr. Panama, who was known to go out for a stroll. Especially since he had reduced his office hours until business picked up.

I waded in, and the water inched up my ankles, my calves, my knees, my thighs. As I moved into deeper water, I rose on tiptoes and rolled up my shorts as high as they would go. I felt the cold on my skin, the pressure of the tightened cloth between my legs, the scorching heat on my head and shoulders. I hesitated, not fully committed to getting my clothes wet, and considered the possibility I was being watched. I thought of April slipping away to apply eye shadow, which she'd done again on a few occasions, without telling or inviting me. Finally the sun got too hot, and I splashed out.

As I was putting my boots back on, Petunia appeared at my elbow. She had followed my scent from the barn and now crawled onto my lap and licked my face feverishly. After a while I nudged her off and she flung herself onto the ground and rolled around in the grass, grunting with pleasure. She was a ball of matted fur—not at all like her fashionably trimmed, shampooed relatives who rode in the back of Mrs. Lewis's Mercedes. Occasionally my mother took a pair of scissors to her coat, but often, like now, her fur had grown so long it fell in corded, ropelike spirals.

I walked slowly back to the house. I was as hot as ever. At the bottom of the yard stood my grandparents' old outhouse. Years ago, Dad had given it a quick makeover when we'd had plumbing problems. April and I had been seven. One of us would sit and do her business while the other prepared rosettes from old newspaper. I wondered whether inside the outhouse it would be cooler, hotter, or the same.

Petunia pressed her nose against the back of my calf.

"Hold your horses," I told her. I was bored enough to be curious. I pushed aside an elderberry bush blocking the entrance, releasing a shower of tiny, desiccated petals, and stepped inside. I was prepared for a foul odour, but it only smelled of rotting wood and dampness. I was noticing how the metal bucket of ashes was still there, covered with roaming pill bugs, when the attack began. First a sound like wind rushing in my ears, followed by a dizzying activity all around my face and hair and body. Then something inside my shirt, and I began slapping at myself wildly. I turned and saw the nest—it was massive—lodged there in a top corner like dried-up grey pudding.

I burst out, screaming. Petunia, who'd been sitting on the grass waiting for me, took off into the woods.

At the house I was met by my father, though I was hoping for my mother and a cold washcloth. But he took in my face, red and threatening to swell uncontrollably—which it never did—and made a strategic decision.

It was my first time in Dr. Panama's office. The tires were still scattered across the front yard. I doubted Mrs. McNadden's brother-in-law's kids played with them, as she had claimed, since grass and blue asters were growing up through them.

Inside was no better. Even I could see the place did not look the way it should, though I had only been to Dr. Bruck a few times, once for a broken wrist after jumping from the hayloft. My chief memory of those visits was of the complex odour arising from an empty cocktail glass on his desk.

Dr. Panama greeted us with an astonishment he was quick to mask, then stood aside and welcomed me into the examining room once my father had explained the circumstance of our visit. Dad was distracted by this excellent opportunity to get the ball rolling and was behind me, pushing me along. It was clear he planned on joining us, but fortunately Dr. Panama raised a hand and proposed he take a seat in the empty waiting room.

I scanned the examination room, recognizing those boxes that had come in the mail and that April and I had lugged down to the house. Many were still taped and unopened. Perhaps Dr. Panama hadn't expected to see a human patient after all. Various jars and tubes and metal objects were strewn across a card table and onto plywood shelves built by my father. There were heaps of cotton balls and bandages on the table, too. The air smelled of fresh paint. The colour they had chosen, my father and Dr. Panama, was aquamarine. This was not like the clinic in Dover.

The examining table was the only thing that looked legitimate. I knew on top of it was where I should be, so I waited beside it. The hornets had shocked me, because of the stings themselves and because of the violence of the attack. But now the pain was fading. The two of us were here only because my father had a point to make to the tiny population of Cranfield.

Dr. Panama was looking at my face and arms. "Where are the worst of your stings, April?"

Although I was used to being called April, and normally hardly noticed, I had an urge to correct him. But I was still wary of annoying him, so I just said, "Under my shirt."

I was concerned that any minute my father would barge in from the waiting room. Maybe this occurred to Dr. Panama, too.

"Indeed," he said. "Why don't you climb up there and remove your shirt."

"Huh?"

"We'll determine if you are having a normal reaction to bee stings."

Hornets, I wanted to tell him. "Bra, too?" I asked.

Was he trying to remember something from medical school?

"I've been stung on my mammary glands," I explained.

"Of course. Bra, too." He looked very serious.

I hopped onto the examining table and tore my shirt up over my head. I was embarrassed by my bra. It was one of the original Petal Bursts, and after all these years, it was hard to tell if it was the white one, or the pink. I took it off and hesitated with it in my hands. Dr. Panama stood back a few feet, just staring at my naked upper torso. A dead hornet fell out onto the floor, but we pretended not to see it. We were both a little ruffled by all this. We had not woken that morning and imagined we would be here now, face to face — the table gave me height — myself topless and him taking my clothes from my hands and searching his office for a place to hang them.

"There's a hook on the back of the door," I pointed out.

"Indeed."

Once he hung my clothes — the Petal Burst slipped out of his hands once — he came back and proceeded to count my hornet stings. Eight. Most had been inside my shirt: at the base of my neck, over my shoulders, along the ridge of my clavicle. It could have been the same hornet. The dead hornet.

There was also a sting on the dark bumpy area around one of my teats, which was nearly the same colour as Dr. Panama's hands, which were unsteady.

Not teat, there was a better word.

Nipple.

That made nine. Each of the stings had left a raised red area the size of a dime. I heard someone running down the stairs in the adjoining apartment. A screen door banged and someone started hollering.

"What are your thoughts on this?" he asked.

"I think I'm having a normal reaction to bee stings."

That made him — finally — smile.

"Do you have some ointment or something, to treat them with?" I asked. "My father will expect that."

"April, you would make a brilliant assistant."

I agreed. Dr. Panama may have been twenty-six, but I knew he wasn't really so much older than me. Again, I was on the brink of correcting him, telling him I was Pilgrim, but he was busy going through tubes of stuff on the card table, taking his time to read the labels then picking up another one. He glanced over at me appreciatively. It was cool in the room and peaceful. Especially without a shirt on. A break from the hot weather. I had not yet experienced air conditioning, but when I did, a few years later in Montreal, I would immediately recall that afternoon when I was sixteen and sitting up straight as an arrow on the examining table in Dr. Panama's makeshift office, all of my awareness of the world migrated to my breasts and Dr. Panama's hands.

When my father knocked, we both jumped.

"How's our patient?" my father asked, opening the door a few inches. This was just like something he would do. I should have been prepared. I should not have let Dr. Panama take my clothes.

"*Dad!*" I clutched myself, one hand per mammary gland.

"Oops." He closed the door and from the other side shouted, "Where's the doc?"

"Right here," Dr. Panama called out from the other side of the card table. "We have almost completed the exam."

"*You're embarrassing me!*"

"Sorry." I could hear him chuckling. He was in great spirits now and had completely forgiven Jean for hacking the water snake to bits. "What's the verdict?"

"April has had a normal reaction to bee stings," Dr. Panama called out.

We shared a look.

He found a tube of ointment that satisfied him and came back over to me with it. He applied it meticulously, a modest dab on each of the nine stings, his face implacable.

He was almost finished when he asked, without taking his eyes from his task, "By the way, who is this Dr. Panama?"

I was trying to hold my breath because the sound of my breathing was so loud. "He's you," I said, exhaling with a burst.

He nodded and seemed relieved.

I wished I had 109 hornet stings.

When he was finished he put the cap back on the tube, returned the tube to the mess on the card table, reached for my shirt and bra, and handed them over.

"I'll see you outside," he said, opening the door and looking at me in a new way. I knew it would be impossible for us to return to our pre–Mendel the Monk exhilarating banter, which had given me so much pleasure, but I didn't mind that now. He had clearly forgiven me.

Unfortunately, I had forgotten who I was.

As soon as my father and I got home, we sat down to eat. Mom had made a cold supper since it was too hot to cook: leftover potatoes and macaroni salad. It was the type of meal she liked to both prepare and consume. She tossed the potatoes with mayonnaise and chopped green olives, and sprinkled chives over the macaroni. She sliced cucumbers and bathed them in dillweed and vinegar. I, too, enjoyed these chilled, exotic meals. I liked my mother's hushed pleasure, the raw taste of growing things, the idea that food could relieve you from the heat of a long day.

My father said the meals left him starved.

But he was wound up by the afternoon's events. He was all for putting a notice in the *Dover Weekly*, announcing that Dr. Moss's practice was up and running—his first patient had been seen and cured. It would be within reason, he said, to exaggerate the effects of the hornet stings for the purpose of publicizing Dr. Moss's superb doctoring. Not only had I been discovered with stings from head to toe, but my skin had turned red and corrugated like something left to rust in a ditch.

I nodded, bought over by my father's enthusiasm.

My mother was a little skeptical but wanted to simply enjoy her meal, so she said only that she didn't think it was routine for doctors to put out newspaper articles detailing specific cases.

As for the doctor himself, he missed supper that night. My father had urged him to stay behind to organize his office in preparation for the upcoming flood of patients. Frankly, I think my father had been surprised by the disorder of that office.

But he was so proud of me, I was swept along in his buoyant mood. I had rescued the project. Along with, of course, my father's fast thinking in rushing me to the doc's office.

"She was brave, Marsha. I have brave girls in this family."

I knew he was really only talking about me.

But it was odd, I couldn't get a read on April. It was as though she could have been anybody. Wasn't she paying attention? Couldn't she sense I had something to tell her? I rested my hand on her arm.

"Covered head to toe," my father said again. "You should have seen her. Stings all over the damn place."

I was grinning like a lunatic.

"I don't see one single sting," April said, pulling her arm away. I wasn't sure she had even looked at me.

But it was true. My injuries were fading fast, perhaps due to the ointment Jean had applied to my body with his ten soft fingers. I had a secret now, though I would be hard put to say what it was. I felt excited and frightened by turns, and was increasingly desperate for April's attention.

"I'm sorry you weren't there, Miss Sourpuss," my father said to her. "I'm sorry you missed all the hullabaloo."

"I'm not."

Under the table I pressed the edge of my bare foot against hers. She moved her foot away.

"Mistook her for April." My father was pushing his chair back, laughing. "Kept calling her April," he told my mother.

"He doesn't know them that well," Mom said serenely. "Not like we do." She glanced over at me, and we exchanged an amused look—Dad acting like the all-time expert in telling April and me apart.

"Chicken Palace tomorrow," my father announced. He was banging around in the cupboards.

April and I groaned.

Petunia had followed him across the kitchen. He took a step towards her, pretending to step on her, and she backed away, wagging her tail.

"Come here, girl," I said.

"Except for your mother. She'll be at the stand. Plus, she's faint of heart."

"I'm faint of heart, too," April said.

"Sometimes I think I could be a vegetarian," my mother said to no one.

"Will Dr. Moss be joining us?" I asked.

My father gave me a look over his shoulder. "He has a practice to run, remember?"

"I think I'll have some more of that potato salad, Mom," April said.

My mother was pleased by that. "What are you looking for Russell?"

"Something sweet."

"In the tin, at the end of the counter," my mother said. "I hate the raw smell of their insides. And the way the cats get so nutty."

"What? That's a great smell!" my father shouted.

He was making us all hot again with his energy.

I was late getting to the barn the next morning because I couldn't get April moving in the right direction. She was evasive and hinted at not participating, and I kept telling her she was crazy,

Dad will kill us. I had on an old pair of dungarees I didn't mind getting blood all over, but she was in her white denim cut-offs. I didn't know she had everything planned out already.

I found my father down behind the barn, trying to woo the geese: a male and female and three goslings. The goose's nature is both coy and distrustful, but my father was an expert at winning them over. Besides, animals liked him. A dog visiting with its owner would go right over to my father and sit patiently at his legs, as though hoping for a transfer of ownership.

When I told him April wouldn't be helping, he said, "Tell me something I don't know." He was on his haunches with a hand resting on the back of the gander, who was cackling softly. The female was just inches away from them, shifting her weight from one muddy orange foot to the other. She shat, lowered her head and lunged at me, hissing. I shooed her off with my foot.

I glared at my father. "Huh?"

"Huh?"

"Dad!"

"Were you raised by hillbillies?" He stood and the geese scattered, then kept their distance as they followed us around to the front of the barn.

"No," I told him. "I wasn't. So what about April?"

"She's helping out at the clinic." Suddenly it was "the clinic."

"Helping out? How?"

"Jean will need an assistant now, taking appointments and whatnot. It was a great idea."

"Whose idea?" I asked at a normal volume, though I wanted to shout at him. He was so dense.

He ignored my question. "Mrs. McNadden is going to give us a hand."

"Damn it, Dad, does she have to?"

He laughed and lowered his voice conspiratorially. "Come on. She thinks it's going to be a lark. Let's get some blood flying before she gets here."

"Gross."

I helped my father catch a dozen chickens, which he hung by their feet from a rope running like a clothesline just inside the barn door, where the light was good. I looked away as he went down the line, slitting their throats with a knife, one by one. That was his part. Mine, and normally April's, was to wait for them to die, dunk them in hot water, then throw them in the automatic plucker, a contraption my father had built.

As I waited, the chickens flapped energetically for several minutes, upside down and not looking much like hens with their heads dangling half broken off. I stood back to avoid the blood spraying from their throats. White feathers drifted around us like dandelion thistles and the cats came out of the dark corners or dropped from the rafters, meowing. That's when I heard the geese honking maniacally, and within seconds Mrs. McNadden appeared at the barn door, in coveralls and pearls, her glossy hair tied back with a ribbon. When she saw us she went pale and my father nearly did a little dance. The timing was perfect. I thought he'd kiss her, she was so easy to predict.

He guided her over the threshold, his hand on her elbow. "Welcome to the Chicken Palace, Lois. Time to roll up those sleeves. Watch the floor, bit slippery just now."

She couldn't speak at first, and when she did, she stammered. Normally I would have been entertained by my father's teasing, if only for his sake. Today, however, I felt nauseated, watching the hens gone still and thinking I could already smell their entrails.

"Now that their hearts have stopped—"

"Have...have their hearts stopped?" Mrs. McNadden asked.

"That's what I just said, Lois." My father winked at me. "Pilgrim here is going to show you how to pluck them." As he spoke he went from chicken to chicken, removing their heads with his knife and tossing them to the cats.

"You're not wasting any time." Her eyelids fluttered as she spoke. "Your father is pretty quick at that, isn't he, Pilgrim?"

From out in the run came the sound of the rooster crowing, like he knew what we were doing.

Our family was not well off, but we were not as poor as most of the Negroes. Or those whites who had hit hard times, like the Doucettes, whose father was in a wheelchair and whose mother had gone to visit a cousin several years ago and not come back yet. Mr. Doucette looked like he had once been a powerful man, like a boxer or wrestler. He would watch his four kids board the school bus while he sat in clear view in his wheelchair on their front step, as though by his belligerent expression daring Mr. Philpott to thunder past without stopping. There was an air of dignity about this man, as there was about the four children. Because they were Jehovah's Witnesses, my father had no time for them, but I would have avoided them anyway because they smelled bad. They boarded the bus and sat in the front rows. I wondered if they were relieved when Mr. Philpott shifted into higher gear and their home vanished behind us.

No, we were not like the Doucettes, who still didn't have indoor plumbing. On the other hand, we were not like the McNaddens, who had a new RCA television set that you didn't have to get up and go bang on every five minutes to make the picture stay still, and who had a little green Fiat—a used car but not that used — in which Mrs. McNadden tore around Cranfield. Mr. McNadden worked at the First National Bank in Dover and didn't have much of an interest in the farming life, other than to have a few laying hens and another farmer's cows grazing in his field to keep the woods from coming in and his wife happy.

Mrs. McNadden enthusiastically experimented with bean sprouts, granola, a yogurt starter, and making her own hand soap. Now she was rolling up her sleeves to butcher chickens for their unpolluted meat. My father said she was a "back-to-the-lander," as though it was a reason to forgive her for her silly crazes.

My mother said it was a shame she never had children.

Almost everyone we knew came from Cranfield or nearby, including my parents. But Mrs. McNadden came from Boston. She had met Mr. McNadden when they were both there at college. But whatever she had studied then held no interest for her now, since she was keen to be learning all she could about everything we did over our way.

"I really admire the way you live your lives," she would tell my mother, who was too polite to roll her eyes.

I took two of the dead chickens by their legs, dunked them in the hot water, then tossed them into my father's plucker, a large tub nailed to a motorized spinning platform. The chickens tumbled around like clothes in a washing machine, their bodies knocking against the wooden knobs my father had driven into the sides of the tub, until their feathers were more or less rubbed off.

I was thinking about Jean and April. They would be arriving at his office about now. My mother, full of cheerful encouragement, would have been asked by my father to drive them. This had all happened without my knowledge. And April had kept it from me.

The night before I'd been too giddy to sleep. My legs felt jumpy and I wanted to talk to April, but she had fallen asleep right away, despite the heat. I knew my funny feeling was from being half-naked in front of Jean. When I woke in the morning, I could hear his voice carried up from the kitchen. He was talking to my mother—the two of them were always the first ones up. I had lain in bed, imagining what it would be like to visit the Bahamas with him, to find a cool spot under those coconut trees where the sand was soft and creamy beneath our bare feet.

When I had turned over, April wasn't in her bed.

"May I ask you a question?" Mrs. McNadden said to me.

"Yeah."

"What's the problem with that kitty?"

A tiger cat—not *kitty*—was sitting on the barn floor behind us, swishing her tail.

"She's just waiting for a scrap, Lois," my father said.

"No, I mean her fur has been ripped completely off."

Her fur had not been ripped completely off, though it looked like she'd gotten into some kind of trouble. But I just wanted to think about Jean.

"That's not mange, is it?"

"No," my father said. He was getting impatient. "That's the feral cat probably been around again."

Dad alleged the feral cat was part bobcat because of his behavioural tendencies and short tail. We knew he was in the vicinity when the female cats came mewing around our legs with their flesh torn.

If Jean was topless, his chest would be like a smooth, dark stone.

"Pilgrim!"

"*What?*"

"Just trying to get your attention," my father said. "The two of you are like a couple of nitwits today."

Mrs. McNadden giggled.

"What?"

"Lois asked how your stings are."

I stared at her. It was annoying how she knew about the hornets already. Her nosiness knew no bounds. I shut off the plucker and threw the two chickens on the gutting table. "Dad, is she going to gut them with me?"

I glanced at Mrs. McNadden and caught her shooting my father a knowing, sympathetic smile.

I didn't know which was worse: her presence in the barn or eviscerating chickens. I liked chickens when they were alive, scratching the earth and clucking unremittingly, as though the only way they could think was to think out loud. You threw a hefty, feathery chicken in the plucker and a minute later you took out a lump half that size with baggy reptilian skin. On the other hand, Mrs. McNadden was really getting on my nerves, standing so close to me I could smell her Prell shampoo.

"Watch how the expert does it," my father said, squeezing in between us and smelling of nothing but perspiration.

"Put it on its back. Cut in. Here. Snip. Spin it around." He sliced into the chicken's belly between its legs and shoved his hand in to drag out its guts. It was like the chicken was being turned inside out.

Mrs. McNadden shifted.

"The two of you would be better at this," he said, resting his stinking hands on the table. "Your hands are smaller."

For the next couple of days my father kept me busy. We processed the chickens in small batches, only a few at a time, dragging it out, and he was uncharacteristically picky about getting all the pin feathers off. I suspected he was trying to keep me away from April, so she would be free to help Jean in "the clinic."

Mrs. McNadden did not return to lend a hand, having a number of appointments to keep in Dover.

Yet my father's good mood and optimism that my hornet stings would result in an increase in traffic at Jean's office were short-lived. The only call they got that week was from old Mrs. Henrietta Rosa on Willow Lane, who had a sick cow. Jean and April walked twenty minutes to find the animal in a lethargic but non-life-threatening state, and Jean recommended a salt lick—a remedy, he admitted to us, that had been April's idea.

"A shot in the dark," my father agreed. "Did you charge for the visit?"

"No, Russell, I couldn't. It was a place of some poverty."

Everyone could see my father wasn't pleased.

April was glowing with importance. The veterinary's assistant, I thought scornfully.

A few days after Mrs. McNadden joined us at the Chicken Palace, I set my internal clock a half hour early. The sun was barely risen. While I quietly dressed, Petunia eyed me anxiously from my bed, and I eyed April, who was still asleep. *Okay*, I told Petunia, lifting her onto the floor. She followed me out with her nose pressed to the back of my calf. She was so lightweight she made no more sound than I did.

In the kitchen Jean was alone, as I had hoped, stirring hot

cereal at the stove. It was fascinating the way he could find his way around a kitchen. My father only knew how to open and close the refrigerator. He could feed goats and pigs, chickens and geese. But not himself.

Jean was wearing the same wash-and-wear, wrinkle-free grey pants he'd stepped off the bus in. They had pockets with mother-of-pearl buttons on the backside. Inside one of the pockets there was a pencil and some crumpled notes by the looks of it.

He seemed delighted to see me, as though I had made his day. For a moment, I had the crazy notion he was going to embrace me. He smiled at me and said, "Good morning, April."

There was something about the way he said her name. I froze, my hand on the breadbox.

"Up so early and already dressed?"

I said nothing, not knowing how to respond to this, as April.

"The bee stings?" he asked, pressing me for more. "A-one?"

"Yeah, fine. I forgot about them, actually." I reached for the bread. When I glanced over at him he was nodding at my words, ladling his cereal into a bowl with a puzzled look.

I wanted to touch him. The desire was powerful. As I dropped a slice of bread in the toaster, my back to him, I considered all the ways this might come about. I could turn unexpectedly and bump into him. I could lean out and stretch as he passed behind me with his bowl of hot cereal. I could close my eyes and play blind and walk zombie-like around the kitchen until we collided and I entered, at last, the zesty zone of his body, mushed up against his chest.

Instead, I sat down across from him and began to nibble at my toast with my pinkies out, although eating was making me nauseous.

"All right, then," he said, his meaning utterly unclear. He stared at me like no one ever had before. Suddenly I felt as though I'd just sprinted around the house ten times.

April had also set her internal alarm early. Though not as early as mine, which she must have realized when she opened her eyes and saw my empty bed. That would explain her dazed look as she tottered there in the doorway. By my estimation she'd been conscious no more than thirty seconds. Her sleeping braid was mangled and she was still in her pyjamas. Her mammary glands looked bigger than mine.

We had the same DNA. How could her mammary glands be bigger than mine? Was she doing exercises on the sly? Eating something in particular that assisted in this regard, that she'd read about and not shared with me?

I decided it was simply that they were at liberty inside her pyjama top to do some showing off, which I didn't think was fair.

"Good morning, Jean," she said.

I'd never heard her address him by his first name.

Apparently I was not visible. She strolled across the room to the cupboards, her bare feet going flap, flap, flap.

"April?" Jean asked. He didn't look too good anymore.

My sister nearly pirouetted before meandering in our direction. She was so happy. But she was holding back in some way. She glanced at me.

A cold worry hit me and I put my toast down.

Seconds later my father opened the kitchen door. He had been cutting firewood and was wearing his shorts, and a fine spray of sawdust clung to the black hairs of his legs, his boots, and the tops of his socks. I realized that all this time I'd been listening to the rising and falling whine of the chainsaw without registering it. Though his work boots were not dirty, he stood there at the threshold, stomping and wiping his feet an unnecessarily long time. He was irritated by April and me, poking around the kitchen like a couple of flies that got in through a hole in the screen.

"You two up early," he muttered, finished with his boot-wiping.

We shrugged.

"Where's your mother?"

"The stand, probably," I said.

It was easy to see my father wanted us to get lost. But I wouldn't go until April did.

"Go get some clothes on," he said to April. "This isn't a hotel."

April hesitated.

"Hey!" My father stepped into the room and brought his palm down hard on the kitchen table. My toast shifted on my plate. We felt a quick jolt like electricity through our bodies. April left the room and I shrunk into my chair. Petunia scooted under the table. I was sweating. It was going to be another hot day.

When I looked up Jean was staring at me. He hadn't spoken since realizing I was not April. I was unable to read his look. I felt like I was blind or deaf or in the wrong universe. But I wanted him to stare at me forever. Don't take your eyes off me, I wanted to say. Watch me now as I push away from this table and progress bravely to the sink, ignoring my father's pissy mood. Watch me closely. I am the one who was stung by hornets, not the other, the one who has been alone with you for days in your cool aquamarine office.

"I'm starved," my father said.

I knew April would be into her clothes and back downstairs in a jiffy, vigilant and strange. I leaned against the sink.

"Did you get rid of the nest?" I asked my father.

"What nest? The hornet nest? I'm starved."

"Yeah, that nest." I watched my father, knowing Jean was watching me.

"Why would I do that? They won't hurt you if you leave them alone."

I ran a hand across my bare shoulder and a tiny swelling that might have been the remains of a hornet sting. Or it might have been a mosquito bite or pimple.

"Almost healed," I told them.

"Do you want me to take a look?" Jean asked, turning in his chair to face me.

"Well, I don't want it to scar," I said.

"Come, then."

I pushed away from the sink and went up to him until I was just inches away. Now that I was so close to him, and behaving so shamelessly, I thought my body was going to shatter from nervousness.

He looked at my shoulder.

He looked at me.

"Not charging us for this now, are you?" my father joked.

"No, it won't scar. There is one thing, though."

I waited.

"You're Pilgrim?"

I nodded.

"Positively?"

My father laughed, and I pretended to as well.

"Pardon me. What I meant to ask," Jean said, "was it you who was stung by the bees?"

My father steered me towards the stove. "Yes sir, that one was Pilgrim here. And she is thinking about whipping up her poor old dad a couple of eggs, right?"

"Right," I mumbled, embarrassed by his touch in front of Jean.

"Scrambled." My father took possession of my seat at the table. "Hornets, Jean, not bees. Where's my better half?"

"Dad, you already asked that."

"She's at the stand," Jean said easily, as though the conversation had been this even-keeled all along, but I knew better. "She wanted to be early for the purpose of taking away the tools you left there yesterday. She said customers associate a clean and tidy look with clean and healthy food."

"No rhyme or reason to your mother. Coffee, too, Pilgrim, if you would. Going to be hot as the dickens today."

I gave my father his coffee. This was not his first, or even second, cup. He drank black coffee all day. It was rare for him to have breakfast, so I didn't hurry with the eggs. He would change his mind when he saw them on the plate in front of him.

"So what's the battle plan for today?" he asked Jean. "Bright and early to the office?"

Why did we all love Jean? Did it have to do with him being the origin of the species? Was all our DNA traceable to his? But my father hadn't mentioned DNA or gene pools for months.

"Jean?" my father pressed, surprised by our house guest's silence. "Popping over to the office?"

I sensed Jean gathering his thoughts. He was no longer watching me closely. In fact, I suspected he had decided not to look at me at all.

"I intend on buying a car today, Russell."

My father set his coffee cup down. "What's that?"

"With my own car, I won't have to rely on your kindness."

While Jean and I waited, my father thought this over. "I'll tell you what," he said. "There are several used lots in Dover. They know me. Worked at one, in fact. I'll go with you so you don't get swindled. They'll see you coming a mile away. What type of car are you on the lookout for?"

"I was thinking of a Datsun," Jean said cheerfully.

"A brand new car?"

"Is that a Japanese make?" I asked my father.

Jean looked at me with surprise, despite himself.

"The girls have an intelligence for cars," my father said. "Pilgrim more than the other one."

"I see," Jean murmured.

"Pilgrim's favourite is the Plymouth Road Runner."

"No, it isn't!" I said heatedly. I didn't want my father speaking on my behalf, revealing things about me I'd rather remain hidden. Especially since the Road Runner seemed suddenly contemptible.

My father continued on as though he hadn't heard me. "We nearly got one, but what a bunch of cheap bastards. I know what the mark-up is. I know what I'm talking about."

"The Plymouth Road Runner is *not* my favourite."

"Brand new?" my father asked Jean again.

"That's my hope, Russell. I suspect it will be a custom order."

"Well, Jean my man, that'll set you back a pretty penny."

I was a little worried myself. I turned and looked out the window above the sink. If Jean had wheels, he could get up one morning with the mockingbirds and be gone. Who could blame him? Then I had a thought, and wished I had a suitcase. I could be ready to go, too. I didn't need a suitcase. I could throw a few things in my school bag. I imagined our departure: the dark, early morning, only the songbirds up.

But what about April? For a second, there was a roaring in my ears. Then a screen door flapping.

When I turned my father was gone.

"Where did he go?" I asked Jean.

"Do you think I may have offended him?" he asked me. "I didn't set out to offend him."

I laughed. I couldn't help myself. No one intentionally set out to offend my father.

"Tough," April said. She was standing in the doorway. "Who cares what he feels?"

She was dressed now, and wearing a bracelet of red embroidery thread. She had the face of someone who'd like to chase me off the property. Not my twin's face.

Jean gave April a meaningful look—wariness, regret, sadness. He was also angry, but that was with me as well, which I thought was undeserved.

I dumped my father's eggs into the hot pan.

At supper, April was still wearing her bracelet of red embroidery thread.

Jean hadn't bought his car.

"Did you buy the Datsun today?" I asked him anyway.

April looked up quickly. She didn't know about the Datsun.

"I have to go to Plymouth for it," he explained to me. He placed his knife and fork on the side of his plate, as though sparing any attention to the handling of his food while answering my question would be bad manners. He looked directly at me like he had in his office, and I was furious because I knew everyone could see I was turning red.

"Automatic transmission?" I asked.

"Yes," he answered slowly. It was obvious he hadn't even thought about that.

"What colour?" April asked quickly.

"White with a red interior."

"I've never ridden in a Datsun," I said just as quickly.

"An import," my father put in. "Like the Beetle was. You girls remember the Beetle. A bad buy."

"It sounds pretty," April said. "Will you take me for a drive?"

"Eat your supper," my mother said.

She was speaking to us, but Jean picked up his knife and fork. "I'll take everyone for a drive," he said.

"Promise?"

"What have you got that bracelet on for?" my father asked April. His voice seemed unnecessarily loud when he spoke, as though I had been asleep. "Worried I won't know who you are?" he joked.

"Jean, do you promise me?"

"I have already given you my word, April."

"April."

"What, Daddy?"

She wore the red embroidery thread religiously, removing it only when she showered so the colour wouldn't bleed. I watched her out of the corner of my eye as she slipped it back on. It was as though it carried a spell, transforming her into someone else—a girl more beautiful and vibrant—once it was over her wrist. Feeling slightly guilty, she'd glance over at me, but I was already turning away.

I took solitary walks, wishing there was a way I could soak up some beauty for myself from the bronzed summer landscape, from the liquid song of a wood thrush or morning mist suspended over a bog. I took longer walks, testing to see if I would be missed.

Sometimes as I returned and approached the house, I would see April at the kitchen door, waiting for me. I remembered the time we'd been punished for letting the hens out and our debilitating confusion. Our loneliness. The sudden leak of meaning from our day.

But April was gone when I entered the house, and I had no idea where she was or where to look for her.

NINE

I've been back in Cranfield two weeks when Rodney disappears. I drive past the gas station and Papa Gino's Pizzeria and search for him in the window, but the pizzeria is closed more than it's open. Then one day I notice the "Closed" sign has been replaced by a "For Sale" sign.

Mrs. McNadden has also made herself scarce, even though she was the one who badgered me for weeks to return to Cranfield to sort things out. I haven't seen her since that first day when she met me at the house with the keys, but I know she is home because her Taurus is there when I pass by on my way to the nursing home.

It rains several days straight. The nights become frosty and gradually the sodden leaves are stripped from the trees. Overnight, it seems, the last goldenrod and asters turn brown. Grass begins to lie flat in the fields, and the white-and-pink phlox that held out so long and cheerfully by the kitchen door now rot on the stem. My father's squash and pumpkins become mushy and riddled with black fungus.

I visit my mother every day. We sink together into the sofa, and at first I am put off by her touch, this lightweight, twitching contact with essentially a stranger. But gradually I become accustomed to her softness and faint sweet-and-sour odour. We watch the news on television, with our varying powers of comprehension, as the Dow drops and foreclosures and calls to the National Suicide Prevention Lifeline rise.

One evening I am only half paying attention when I realize we are watching a piece on "the latest casualties" of the mortgage crisis. It occurs to me, as we view cats and dogs locked in rooms, tethered to fences, or waiting at the back door to be let back in, that I might want to flip the channel.

A litter of pit bulls. A crushingly hopeful golden retriever. A tuxedo cat. And then, a small poodle curled up tight on a piece of cardboard in a trashed living room. It lifts its head to face the camera.

My mother stirs. What does she remember?

"I need my work shoes," she says. "I need to get going."

"Don't you worry, Mom," I tell her.

Later, I can't keep these mothers and fathers out of my head —these once-responsible pet owners loading up their SUVs and trucks and deciding what to bring when they disappear: clothes or patio furniture, toys or kitchenware, cats or dogs.

The next morning I stop at Mrs. McNadden's. She opens the door and looks at me suspiciously, then steps out onto her front step and shuts the door behind her, as though my getting inside her house is the last thing on earth she wants. But I'm tired and depressed from seeing my mother in that place and don't care either way. We stand there in the drizzle.

"April?" she asks after a moment.

"No."

This is worrisome.

"I'm Pilgrim."

"Ah-hah. You've come. How was your flight?"

"Mrs. McNadden, don't you—"

"Do you need the key to the house, dear?"

"Mrs. McNadden," I say gently, putting a hand on her arm as though I might prevent this sudden sense of unreality from getting worse. "You already gave me the key. About two weeks ago? You met me at our farmhouse. We talked about Obama, and my mother."

As she remembers, she blushes with embarrassment.

"How is your mother?" she asks after a moment.

I shrug.

"I tried to warn you."

"That's true, Mrs. McNadden, you did."

A smile appears on her face at this news that she was right. She is wearing a clip-on pearl earring in one ear—her left ear. She glances out at the road as a truck passes, and sighs.

"Would you like to come in for a cup of coffee, dear?" When I nod, she leans back on her door to open it. "We could get to work on your father's obit."

"His obit? But he died over a month ago," I say, then immediately regret it.

But Mrs. McNadden has recovered her sense of space and time. "You should do something to mark his passing anyway. It's expected. I advise you skip the *Plymouth Mariner*, too expensive, but we can draft something for you to drop off at the *Dover Weekly* on your next visit to your mother."

"It's expected?"

"A service was what was expected. An obit is the least you could do. Come in, we're getting wet."

Expected by whom?

As soon as I step inside I remember the wet-wood smell and dimness of this house. There is a cavernous passageway to the kitchen, the walls decorated with Marimekko wallpaper of huge fuchsia and gold flowers. Mrs. McNadden drove all the way to Boston for the wallpaper, and my father, April, and I helped Mr. McNadden put it up. It was crowded in here that day, and Mrs. McNadden repeatedly promised to stay out of our way, but didn't. Now, the seams of the wallpaper are lifting off and ragged. It did not brighten the hallway as she had hoped, but I would not have noticed that then.

The kitchen is massive compared to ours and not much has been altered over the last thirty years: the same long wooden table with benches, as though she and Mr. McNadden once expected to raise a pack of offspring, and the same linoleum with its design of brown bricks—an excellent camouflage for dirt. The kitchen does not smell of food, but of bacterial growth that thrives in dampness and cold and human flesh.

"It's a lovely place, isn't it?" she is saying.

"Yes," I say, glancing around, searching for something to single out and praise in this centuries-old farmhouse. "It's a great home."

"Oh, I don't mean this," she exclaims, blushing again. "Sunset Hills."

I am beginning to understand her inability to keep the name of the nursing home straight.

"Your father was lucky to get her in there. They have regular medical care, don't they? Sit down. Would you care for a cup of coffee?" she asks again.

"If you have it."

"Of course I have it. I wouldn't offer it if I didn't. Now get rid of that wet jacket and take a seat."

But it's chilly in the kitchen and I make no move to remove my jacket. I sit at the table, beside a picture window emanating a forceful chill and facing a backyard that was once, I recall, a tidy expanse of flower beds and shrubbery. Now it is one big, wet compost of decaying leaves and tall grass, scattered branches and blown-in litter.

Mrs. McNadden stays close to the counter top, using it for support as she moves about. She is not at all as spry as she was on that first day, when she met me at the farmhouse in her fur coat and white heels.

"Are your hips bothering you?" I ask.

"I'm just a little stiff." She glances across the room and I follow her line of sight to her muskrat coat, heaped into a chair. She turns back and reaches up into a cupboard and pushes things around. A jar of Folgers coffee falls out and hits the counter top.

She slaps at the jar, as though it's hot. "I prefer the taste of Maxwell House," she tells me, once she has the jar open and is scraping into the granules with a fork. "But I find it doesn't mix as well with cold water the way Folgers does — that's so nice on a summer day. Is it true, Pilgrim? They have regular medical care?"

"I don't know how that works. The truth is, I haven't seen any doctors."

I hear a dripping sound and glance around. Water is leaking from the top of the window frame and pooling on the sill. The linoleum floor below is dark and wet-looking. A clip-on pearl earring rests against the baseboard.

"They say it's best to keep warm if you're stiff, Mrs. McNadden. I always find that a little exercise, or dressing in layers—"

"Is that what they say, dear?"

We have our coffee at the long table. She brings over a pad of lined paper and a pencil. Her face has a glossy cast and she's a little breathless now from her efforts.

"It'll be nice for April to see the obit," she says.

"April?" I ask, startled. "How would April see it?"

She slurps her coffee. "Now, Pilgrim, I didn't put any cookies out because I'm not supposed to eat sweets anymore. But did you want some? It's no trouble."

I think how nothing kept her from my father's frozen éclairs, but then I don't really believe there are any cookies in those cupboards anyway.

"No, I had a late breakfast."

"Dr. Bruck said I might be developing diabetes. He told me we would do a blood test, but then he had that awful stroke and retired. I've also been having these tiny memory lapses, nothing serious."

"You should make an appointment with someone else."

She looks at me vacantly.

"Another doctor?" I prompt.

"There isn't one."

"I doubt that's true. Who took over his practice?"

"I went to Dr. Bruck forever, Pilgrim, I can't go to anyone else. I heard his wife has gone crackers."

"About the obituary."

"Righto."

"I don't know if April still reads the *Dover Weekly*," I say carefully.

"No, but they list obits on the great web."

"The *Dover Weekly* does?"

Mrs. McNadden sucks in her breath and gives me an irritated look. "The girl at the IGA, she told me it will go on the great web and everyone on the planet will see it. We had a long conversation. I don't think she finished school but she seems sharp enough."

"All right, then."

We work on the obituary, which is straightforward enough: birth date and location, age at time of death, lifelong resident of Cranfield, Massachusetts, survived by wife, Marsha Carver Bell, and two daughters, Pilgrim Wheeler and April—but here we stall and are forced to back up. We agree to leave out his daughters' surnames, since we don't know if April's has changed.

I wish there was more to say about this man, so sharply opinionated and willful, so often disappointed—no, let's face it, crushed—by the failure of other people to meet his expectations.

We pause, as though Mrs. McNadden and I are sharing similar thoughts.

"Your father was different the last few years," she tells me. "Quite so." For emphasis, she tries to snap her fingers, but produces only a fleshy tap-tap sound. She looks at me and then at her mug.

It occurs to me she is lost without him.

"He was less —" She hesitates.

"Less opinionated?" I say helpfully.

"No, dear. I was going to say less inhibited."

Which is funny, because I never thought of my father as inhibited.

"He regretted his impatience with people. He expressed that to me openly."

"He could certainly be intolerant," I say with a laugh.

"Intolerant. Yes, dear, that's a choice word to describe Russell." She glances at me quickly and sorrowfully.

Apprehensive that a confession may be on its way, I reach for the pad of paper with its brief obituary.

"Are we satisfied with this?" I ask.

"I wish I'd been there when he went," she says.

"Mrs. McNadden, don't think —"

"But I knew something was up when Rodney pulled into my driveway and braked so abruptly. I was having a Lipton Cup-a-Soup. He stood at the door and said I should call the police, who sent the coroner. Rodney and I waited in the barn an awfully long time for that man. He had a phone in his pocket. Imagine."

"I'm sorry you had to go through that."

"Oh, it's no matter to me. The coroner called Tooksbury's and we waited no time at all for them. Mr. Tooksbury suggested I might not want to watch, but I did, out of the corner of my eye — well, someone had to."

"Where was Rodney?"

"He'd taken off." She shrugs. "Tooksbury's had a stretcher contraption they unfolded, reminded me of a beach chair. They rolled Russell out on it."

She dabs at her eyes, and I bend down beneath the table to rescue the lone earring. I place it on the table. She looks at it, covers it with her palm, and draws it off onto her lap without a word.

"I put the death certificate with his things, dear, up at the house."

"Yes, I saw it. Thank you."

"His ashes"—she glances around, including at the ceiling—"are somewhere. I'll get them for you."

"Another day, Mrs. McNadden. I should get to the nursing home."

"Perfect." She looks relieved not to have to start the search.

I promise to drop the obituary off at the newspaper office on my way to Sunny Gardens. Mrs. McNadden makes reference to their medical care again, just before I step into the rain. I get into my car, relieved, not just because I'm out of that house but because I know Mrs. McNadden is back into her muskrat coat.

I don't visit my mother until the afternoon. When I arrive, an unfamiliar woman is hesitating just inside the door, a slender binder tucked beneath her arm.

She gives me what my mother would have called "a nice smile."

Mrs. Godfrey is there, but clearly upset, oblivious to her husband's velvet ribbon resting on his foot. Mr. Milton stands in the middle of the room, his arms folded across his chest in a relaxed, aggressive manner. Allison is at his elbow. I realize Mr. Godfrey is the only resident in sight.

"What's going on?" I ask.

Allison shoots me a look. She is stroking the back of the sofa with her palm. It's clear she would like to convey some information to me. Everyone, with the exception of Mr. Milton, seems embarrassed.

"What's going on? Where's my mother?"

The woman with the binder gives me another nice smile and puts her hand out to me. "Hi there, I'm Sharon Rogers from the Town Office."

"Is this about my mother?" I ask.

"I don't believe," Sharon says, looking with confusion from Allison to Mr. Milton and back to Allison, "I've met her mother?"

"We don't keep track of who you've met here, Sharon," Mr. Milton says.

"No," says Allison.

"Okay," says Sharon, turning to me. "So I just popped over at Mrs. Godfrey's request, you see, to register Mr. Godfrey."

"Not happening," says Mr. Milton. "Not on my watch."

"You have no authority over this," Mrs. Godfrey says.

"So this isn't about my mother?" I ask.

"No, no, no," Allison says, coming to my side.

"I don't want to get in the middle of it," Sharon says to me. "I don't know who has the authority here, honestly, I don't." She turns to Mrs. Godfrey. "I'll speak with the Town Solicitor later today, that's the best I can do."

Mrs. Godfrey puts her hand out. "Give me that form, Sharon."

"Do *not* give her that form," Mr. Milton says. "He can't sign his name."

Sharon looks ambushed. Mr. Milton is not a man many would cross.

"One need not be able to sign one's name," Mrs. Godfrey says. "You ignoramus. He can mark an *X*."

"He does not have the mental competency," Mr. Milton tells her, his body stiffening, "to mark even an *X*." He has not liked being called an ignoramus.

"I know how he wants to vote," she says. "He wants to vote for Barack Obama. I can do it for him."

"Sure as shooting you cannot do it for him," Mr. Milton says. "I won't let you."

"Can he mark an *X*, Mrs. Godfrey?" Sharon asks nicely.

"Of course he can. But that's not even the point," she cries. "Jimmy voted Democrat his whole life! This is the most ridiculous thing I've ever heard."

Allison, who smells deliciously of cigarettes, whispers into my ear, "Twilight zone. Woo-woo, woo-woo."

I'm startled by her proximity. I look at her and see a lot of shimmering green eye shadow.

"Excuse me," I say, and go off down the hall.

I find my mother in her room, trying to open the window, her thin arms pushing against the sash. She's still in her dressing gown and her sleeves have slipped down to expose bruised, speckled wrists.

I take a seat on the edge of her bed, exhausted. It's only three o'clock but the day is already ending. It's still raining, the drops pecking against the window. I can't seem to stay dry, my clothing perpetually damp and pasty against my skin.

"What are you doing, Mom?"

"Oh, you know, just puttering," she answers, breathless. The voices of Mr. Milton and Mrs. Godfrey drift in.

"I think that window is permanently shut, Mom."

"Damn it all to hell." She drops her arms and stands there, humming and watching me intently. "It was lovely," she says after a while.

I sigh. "What was, Mom?"

"The way you two talked to each other in your sleep."

I stare, flabbergasted, at my mother.

Allison appears in the doorway and my mother scoots away from the window.

"What did we say to each other?" I ask my mother.

"How're we all doing here?" Allison says, giving us a big smile.

"What did we say to each other?" I ask again, ignoring Allison.

My mother looks at me blankly.

I turn to Allison. "Why is she still in her dressing gown? In the middle of the afternoon?"

"No one's been able to get near your mother today, Pilgrim. Talk about crabby."

"Has she had her lunch?"

"What she didn't throw on the floor."

"How about a cup of tea, Mom?"

"No. I don't like tea."

"Yes, you do."

"I prefer coffee," my mother says.

"Since when?" I ask.

"Sorry to interrupt," Allison says, winking and letting me know we can only pretend so long that everyone in this room has full mental competency. "Mr. Milton wants to see you in his office, Pilgrim."

"How is it out there now?" I ask.

172

"Sharon's taken off. Mr. Milton is in his office. He wants to see you. Do you need a cigarette? I know I do."

"Tell him I'll be there in a minute."

"Cigarette?"

"No, thank you."

"Just let me know. I got a few with your name on them."

Allison is barely out of earshot when my mother says to me, "I'm not sure who that woman is, but I think she has a crush on you."

"Maybe she's just looking for a friend," I whisper.

"That could be."

"Come out now, let's visit with the Godfreys."

My mother trails obediently behind me to the common room. She sits beside me on the sofa and presses into my side.

I can see that Mrs. Godfrey, sitting with her husband, is still shaken. She won't look at me.

"Perhaps Obama won't need your husband's vote," I offer.

Mrs. Godfrey's eyes flash with gratitude. "You know, I was just telling Jimmy that very thing," she says.

I glance at Mr. Godfrey. I have not heard him speak a single word. Ever. There is not much evidence he comprehended the scene that just took place, or has comprehended anything taking place around him since I arrived. Then she puts a hand over one of his and I see his blue eyes meet hers.

As though they have exchanged some crucial information, she sighs and turns to me. "Please let me apologize for my behaviour, Pilgrim."

"No apology necessary. Honestly."

"That man is just the *worst* kind of man. I could kick myself for losing my temper like that. It doesn't help and it just upsets me. It upsets Jimmy, too."

"Mr. Milton wants to talk to me. Apparently. In his office."

"Well, you better go," she says with defeat, as though teams are forming.

"He can wait."

"Good. Make him wait."

"I dropped by Mrs. McNadden's this morning," I say casually. Mrs. Godfrey nods, but looks uncertain.

"That friend of my mother's? With the fur coat and diabetes?"

"Yes, yes, I remember her. I also knew her years ago."

"You did?"

"Her husband worked at Dover First National. Jimmy was regional manager. That's how I knew them."

"I'm surprised by her situation."

"Why is that?"

"Her lifestyle, you know, it's a bit on the down-and-out."

"Yes, that is a shame."

"What happened?"

"The Republicans happened! Reagan and the Bushes."

"But Mr. McNadden had a good — a regular — job." Not like my father.

"Yes, that's true, but then he died far short of his retirement. Cancer. I'm surmising, even with a plan, drugs were costly. Who knows the details? They may have remortgaged? Investments, if they had them, went poof? She would have her social security, and that's about it. Pilgrim, if you think you recognize this country, you are blind as a bat."

"I guess Mrs. McNadden never worked," I say neutrally.

"Pah!" Mrs. Godfrey gets to her feet. "In those days, we didn't, did we?"

My mother pinches my arm. "Let Russell know I'm ready to go home. I've had enough of this."

"It seems Mrs. McNadden no longer has a family doctor," I tell Mrs. Godfrey.

"It's not possible for everyone in this country to have a family doctor."

"That's absurd."

"No," she says unequivocally. "There aren't enough doctors to go around. That's a fact."

"Everyone deserves to have a family doctor," I say. "They have to fix that."

Mrs. Godfrey halts in front of me, teetering slightly in her agitation. "Fix it how, Pilgrim? There's no money!"

I don't know what to say to this. Mrs. Godfrey goes back to her chair beside her husband, who no doubt shares her opinion —if not overtly, then at his murky core.

"What about Marsha?" she asks me. "I bet she can sign her name. If that's what one must be able to do to vote in this country."

"Huh?"

"Your father hates that," my mother says suddenly, leaning full onto me. "He hates you saying 'huh.' Like a hillbilly."

"You've been feeling a lot better, haven't you, Marsha, since your daughter arrived?" Mrs. Godfrey says pointedly.

Mr. Milton's office is spacious and nearly empty. There is a dented filing cabinet, a desk, two chairs, no paperwork anywhere.

I stand in the doorway and wait to be invited in. Mr. Milton glances at me then back to his desk.

"May I come in?" I ask politely, though I doubt I will be able to embarrass him with good manners.

He nods.

"May I sit?"

He has been reviewing some glossy brochures, which he now shoves in a drawer.

I sit.

"I wanted to get one thing straight with you, Mrs. Bell."

"Mrs. Wheeler."

"Nobody at Sunny Gardens Homecare is voting for an African."

"Does that include Allison?"

"I'm talking about the residents," he says, like I'm dense. "I'm not worried about Allison. Allison Archer has a head on her shoulders."

"Not a fan of Barack Obama?"

"No need to steer the conversation that way. My objective here is to make the situation clear to you."

"I understand," I say. "I have some questions, though, if this is a good time?"

He stares at me. I take this as a yes.

"I wanted to ask about those bruises on my mother's arms."

Mr. Milton turns in his chair and fixes his attention on the filing cabinet beside him for several long seconds. He swivels back to me.

"What are you asking?"

"I'm asking how she might have got those bruises on her arms."

Again he turns to the filing cabinet, but this time he shouts "Allison!" and I jump.

We wait in silence until Allison appears, her blonde hairdo backlit so that I can see through it in places, like it's made of spun sugar.

"She wants to file a complaint," says Mr. Milton, with a nod to me.

Allison looks devastated.

"That's not what I said, Mr. Milton. What I said was that I wondered how my mother's arms became bruised. I wasn't accusing anyone of anything."

"Self-inflicted," Allison says flatly.

"Do you really think so?" I ask in my most reasonable voice. "How would she be doing that exactly?"

"You can file a complaint if you want. Makes no diff to me."

I turn back to Mr. Milton. "Is she being restrained?"

"Absolutely not."

"Is she being given drugs to pacify her?"

He nods several times. "When she first arrived there was some agitation and combative behaviour. It was within our—"

I lean forward. "I don't want her restrained. With drugs, or in any other manner."

"Mrs. Bell, dementia patients are not truly capable of suffering emotional distress."

"You can't really believe that, Mr. Milton."

"I believe the opinion of some of our expert doctors."

He is emitting measurable hostility. Allison begins picking at her cuticles, and Mr. Milton reopens his drawer and returns to one of his brochures. For a cruise, it appears. Blue skies and bikinied women. He is dismissing me.

"Planning a trip?" I ask.

Allison's eyes dart over to the brochure in her boss's hands with, it strikes me, excessive curiosity. He throws the brochure back in the drawer.

"Speaking of doctors," I say. "My other question is whether my mother is receiving any professional medical care."

Allison gasps. "What d'you think she's getting right now, twenty-four seven?"

"You are being very unfair, Mrs. Bell," Mr. Milton says.

"Allison, I meant by an MD. A licensed doctor who has completed medical school."

"Each resident has a physician of their own choosing. Most have the same one—that's a matter of convenience for everyone," Mr. Milton says. "By the name of—" He looks up at Allison. "Kosta?"

"I think it begins with a vowel, Ricky."

"Indian," he says.

"Mmm." Allison shakes her blonde head like something isn't sitting right in her bowels. "Pakistan?"

"Hosta!" Mr. Milton says with triumph.

"Yes, Ricky!" Allison cries, looking as though she'd like to put her hands on him. She turns to me. "Dr. Hosta. He comes out from Plymouth."

"How often is he here?" I ask.

"We have on-call services, but otherwise—monthly-ish."

"When will he be here next?"

"Allison will check the schedule and let you know."

Allison gives me a chilly look. "Consider it done."

I figure I will no longer have access to Allison's cigarettes, but worse, that I've caused her to think me more a troublemaker than potential friend, which may not bode well for my mother.

So I watch her closely when she marches briskly into the common room an hour later to take the residents' vitals.

"Your surname is Archer, is it?" I ask her, trying to sound friendly. I'm sitting with my mother, who is staring at the television.

Allison nods but won't look at me. "So what?"

"Mr. Milton mentioned it. In his office. He said Allison Archer has a head on her shoulders."

She is wrapping the blood pressure cuff around Mr. Godfrey's arm in a no-nonsense manner. But as I expected, this information brings out a small smile.

"Gently," Mrs. Godfrey cautions.

Allison pauses, then surprises me by passing the thermometer over to Mrs. Godfrey, who takes it without comment, leans over her husband, and wiggles it into his mouth.

I wonder if her lenience with Mrs. Godfrey and the thermometer is meant to make me feel shunned—less than two weeks ago I was barely allowed to brush my mother's hair.

"Is Archer your maiden or married name?" I ask.

She gives me a nasty look. "Is this twenty questions?" she says.

When she takes my mother's pulse, blood pressure, and temperature, everyone goes quiet, but as soon as she's finished and has moved on to the woman with the walker, I say, "Just wondering if you're related to a Phil Archer."

She straightens and puts her hands on hips and says, "Seriously?"

The woman with the walker looks nervously over her shoulder.

"Sorry," I say. What am I missing here? I glance at Mrs. Godfrey.

"I *had* a brother—Phil," Allison tells me. She's gathered up her equipment and is moving towards the bedrooms.

"Allison," Mrs. Godfrey says. "With all due respect, how can you be opposed to Obama when he's promised to get our troops out of Iraq?"

"Oh my God. What's your point?" she asks in such a way that I figure she knows exactly what point. "Barack Obama can't do anything for Phil."

"I'm not saying he can, but he's going to get our troops—"

I interrupt. "I knew your brother."

"Yeah, Pilgrim, so what?" She's halfway across the room, but has turned to throw this question at me.

"I had a date with him. We smoked some pot and got high."

They all, including the woman with the walker, who, frankly, is making me the most uneasy right now, are staring at me. Maybe I should have given some thought to sharing that fact before I did.

Allison laughs contemptuously and says, "I doubt that."

"Phil Archer who graduated from Dover Regional High around 1976?"

"Maybe, but Phil wouldn't have done that. That wasn't my brother."

"Bet it was."

"Pilgrim," Mrs. Godfrey says quietly.

"He had long hair and a leather jacket and was one hundred percent against the Vietnam War. He wanted to walk on Washington with my father."

"You're so crazy, you're demented."

I've had a long day with difficult people. I get to my feet and walk over to Allison so I'm close enough to put my hand on her shoulder. She flinches. "If your brother had a blue Pontiac, or access to a blue Pontiac," I say, "then I'm not the one who's crazy, my friend."

She's done with me and can't leave the room fast enough. If I thought she was angry with me in Mr. Milton's office, this is something else altogether.

Mrs. Godfrey begins, "A word of warning—"

"That was a mistake, you don't have to tell me."

"You did surprise me," she says in a neutral tone.

"I can't stand people being stupid."

"No, of course not, no one can. Mr. Milton is a lost cause, talk about stupid, but Allison is a decent soul. You want to stay on her good side."

"Phil Archer was not only a pothead," I say, still revved up. "He was against Nixon, against the war. He was passionate about it. And he enlisted?"

"He was murdered over there, Pilgrim. Blown to bits."

"Shit."

"People change."

"Come on."

"So you believe the person you are right now is identical to that girl who enjoyed some recreational activities with Allison's brother? For one thing, I doubt you were so angry."

Well, she's a good one to talk, but this time I keep my mouth shut.

Indeed, people change. Later that day, after Mrs. Godfrey has gone home for her evening break and as I'm putting on my coat, Allison approaches me—I briefly wonder if she's going to slug me—and without a word hands me a form. Across the top it reads "Commonwealth of Massachusetts." Her manner is shifty and I hope I'm not being served an order banning me from the home. But it's a Consumer Complaint Form, Division of Health Care Quality, Boston.

I take it and shove it in my purse.

Part Three

TEN

Proper lodgings for Jean never materialized, though it is hard to know how committed my father was to this task—a negligence he would certainly come to regret—and so Jean remained living in our house, sleeping in the room under the stairs.

Suddenly, I was an inch taller than April and my hair a shade darker. My mother proposed that this difference in hair colour, although slight, was due to my spending so much time indoors, alone in my bedroom, reading. By contrast, April, whenever she wasn't at the clinic with Jean, couldn't stay still. She moved in and out of the house with an unfamiliar restlessness. Her voice took on a daydreamy, aristocratic quality. She talked back to my father and stepped away if she sensed I was turning in her direction. I rejected all that I had once believed about DNA and God.

Then one day I caught them.

April was still going off with Jean to the clinic every morning, but it was for only one or two hours now, and nobody would admit it was pointless. And while my mother continued to drive them over in the station wagon, Jean seemed to have lost interest in getting a car of his own.

April and I were tending the animals and the smell of manure was strong inside the barn, closed up because of rain. The hot spell had passed, leaving behind a string of wet, blustery days that soaked the parched fields and gardens. April was working the pump, filling the water buckets, and I was lugging them off to the stalls.

I was at the far end of the barn tending to the lambs when I looked up and saw Jean step in. The barn doors were open just a foot or two, the light dim, so he was not able to see me, half crouched and motionless. April was easy to spot, standing just inside the entrance at that creaking pump. Despite our increasing differences, Jean still had trouble telling us apart, and yet somehow, he knew it was her. Was it the clothes she wore, I wondered, a special smile? Or was she wearing that bracelet?

He went directly to her. She kept her hands on the pump but twisted towards him and lifted her chin with a question in her eyes. He placed his index finger against her bottom lip, almost experimentally, as though testing for texture and temperature. She was worrying about me, whether or not I was watching. Yet she let him kiss her. He felt soft, like new leaves. Only then she whispered a warning I could not hear. She said, *Pilgrim's here.*

He glanced around, still not seeing me, turned, and left. I was trapped with the lambs, who were nudging against me, missing their mother, their noses hard and insistent. I didn't want to look my sister in the eye. I wanted her to follow Jean, so I could be alone. We stood, me at one end of the barn, her at the other, listening together to the sounds of hens fussing and flapping, of hay being chewed over and over, of animals knocking their heavy hooves against the wooden floor. Water was beginning to run off the eaves into the muddy paddock out back.

When we were younger, April and I used to hang from the maple tree behind the house, our knees hooked over the lowest branch while we held hands and dangled side by side, fascinated by everything turned upside down. We would remark that this was how the world must have looked when we were being born.

April didn't know whether I had seen Jean kiss her, but if I did not come back out of the stall soon, she would have to assume I had.

I left the lambs and strolled over to her and gave her my empty buckets to refill. I sighed like I was bored out of my mind and felt her search my face for clues.

Once we were finished, I left the barn ahead of her. I was thinking I could remember our apprehension about being delivered into this upside down world, and the relief it was to have each other.

A day later April was summoned by our father to Bishop's Farm Feed over in Hallsburg. It was a half hour's drive each way and my father needed the company to stay awake. It was mid-afternoon and Mom would be working at the stand another couple of hours. The house was so quiet you'd think it was empty, but it wasn't: I was just outside Jean's bedroom, where every minute or two I could hear the creaking of his mattress springs.

After a while I went up the stairs, quietly in my bare feet, and into my bedroom. The clothes April had worn the previous day were on the floor: a white blouse and dungaree cut-offs.

Her red embroidery bracelet lay on her bureau top where she'd forgotten it.

I stripped. Despite the room's stuffy air, goosebumps broke out on my arms and thighs. I was aware of my breasts tightening in that room that seemed suddenly the temperature of an icebox. Although I had clearly seen Jean kiss my sister, I refused to give up on that moment when I was perched on his examining table, without shirt and bra, and he couldn't look away. What had passed between us that afternoon in his office had been irresistible and special. Remembering that, I felt a fine, imperceptible pulse emanating off my body, as though each of my cells had its own heart, beating rapidly and according to its own rhythm.

I picked April's clothes off the floor and put them on. The cut-offs were snug, but this was not something he would notice. Being dressed again was both a relief and a let-down. No socks or sneakers. I released my pigtails and combed my hair. I applied a bit of April's blue eye shadow, my hand shaking as I held the tiny brush, and slipped on her red embroidery bracelet.

Downstairs again, nervous, I pushed his door open with greater force than I'd intended, so that it punched the bedroom wall and shuddered. Startled, Jean looked up from his bed where he lay reading. He was wearing his grey slacks and an undershirt, his arms bare. The bed was made, some clothes folded on a chair, a tidy stack of medical books and a glass of water on his bedside table. A towel hung from a bedpost, which my mother would not have liked. The dampness would spoil the wood. But Jean didn't know that. It struck me that here was a person anxious to give all things their place, and yet he wasn't doing a very good job of it.

I was the essence of discretion. I lifted my finger to my lips, displaying that embroidery thread around my wrist, and gave him April's sympathetic smile. He immediately relaxed, which was alarming. I went and sat on the edge of his bed, my back to him, and felt the old mattress sink beneath me. I wanted to have a thousand conversations with him, but I was afraid that if I spoke, I would give over to being Pilgrim. My nerve began to drain out of me.

I shivered when he placed his hand on my neck and drew his fingers down my arm to my elbow. I didn't know if I was opening a door for them they had not yet fully opened for themselves, or if they had already gone through it by then and it didn't matter what I did. I had to shift because all my cells were buzzing again.

"Come," he said.

I lay down gingerly beside him and the bed creaked just as I'd heard it when I was hovering outside the door. Jean sighed.

I stared at the ceiling and listened to him breathing. I'd no doubt his cells were buzzing, too. His smell was a faint reminder of his first day with us after that long bus ride from Miami. When he moved, I was alive to his body pitching beside me on the bed. His breath grazed me. I felt one of his hands over mine, just above the waistband of April's shorts, and then a moment later his lips moved into my hair and kissed my skull.

I had a yearning to climb on top of him and do something —increasing the surface area of my body in contact with his would be a good start—but I was held back by being April, by the effort it was taking to be only her. When I realized he was waiting, I turned my face away and looked across the room and through the window to a lilac tree outside, the branches lively in a light breeze. My eyes followed the pairs of heart-shaped leaves that grew smaller and smaller the farther they were from the trunk. According to my father, the brain is always searching for a pattern.

"Why won't you look at me?" Jean asked. I turned back, and there he was, just an inch away. I was struck by how his skin glowed and how kind he looked. I felt a madness. A madness for his kindness.

I shut my eyes, worried he'd seen it was me, then felt his hand cup the back of my head. He put his lips on mine. His tongue was a shocker, lush and not all that wet.

I rolled on top of him. Of course, I'd never done anything like this before. My back arched, but I felt slightly irritated—I couldn't really get where I wanted to be. His penis was hard and pleasant and extraordinary beneath me.

He took his mouth away and pushed me onto to my back again. I got limp then and let him take over, excited and curious about his next steps. He reached down and unzipped April's shorts and pushed his hand down there. I raised one knee to the side surreptitiously, the way a dog will lift a scrap of food from the tabletop when your back is turned. I could tell I was gooey where his fingers were.

I was disappointed when he took his hand from April's shorts. He reached for my hand and drew it down, placing it over his crotch. Immediately he began making little growling sounds, his mouth and rapid breath against my ear. I nearly giggled.

But when he spoke he sounded so earnest. "Please," was what he said. He also sounded like he needed to clear his throat of a ton of phlegm.

Tentatively, I began patting, then rubbing him, and was impressed by the result, though unfortunately his pants separated us.

"We should take our clothes off," I whispered.

I knew full well what he had in there and where it was meant to go. I was also dying to see it.

"Please, don't stop, Pilgrim, don't stop."

"I won't," I said reassuringly. "I promise."

A moment passed.

"Pilgrim?"

I carried on with the rubbing, but it was no use.

"Why didn't you correct me?" he asked hoarsely. "When I called you Pilgrim?"

I felt jittery and pressed my body against his.

"Lord help me," he moaned.

"So what?" I said. "You said my name. So what?"

"I didn't mean to."

"But you said it. You said, 'Don't stop, Pilgrim.' I heard you."

His eyes were so close to mine, and he was feeling a lot of things, I could see that. Anger with me, guilt, and something that was pulling him close to me again.

"It was *me* in your office," I said. "It was *me* who was stung by those hornets." I pushed my face against his neck and took a deep breath in.

"I know that now," he said, and he put an arm around me and held me. "But I cannot be with both of you. My world has...I wonder if I might be having a nervous breakdown?"

"No." I pressed my body against his, and though I didn't have a clear idea what he meant, I said, "I don't think you are."

"I cannot be with both of you," he repeated, letting go of me.

He was a warm, lovable human being who was shifting inch by inch away from me on the bed. If only, I thought, he could be a bit braver.

"Pilgrim, you must get out of this room. The family will be home soon."

"Just pretend I'm April?"

We were on our backs now, touching only at the sides, staring no longer at each other but unhappily at the ceiling.

I crossed my arms over my chest. "I refuse to go," I said. "You're being completely undemocratic." This was a phrase my father used when something was not going his way. It had lost its meaning other than as a statement of protest.

"What was that?" Jean asked, amusement creeping into his voice.

I despaired of the speed with which he was gathering his composure. He gave me a little poke in the arm. He thought everything was going to be all right now, like we were just good chums. It made me feel awful. I considered spitting in his face, or biting him.

"What if I tell?" I demanded.

He thought about that. "What will you tell?"

I put my feet on the floor and crossed the room with dignity. I considered informing him that he was going to ruin the bedpost with his damp towel and that, further, I hated his guts, but I didn't want to sound immature. Once out of his bedroom, I bolted through the rest of the house and out the back door, then down to the barn. As soon as I stepped inside, squawking erupted from the chicken coop.

I climbed the ladder to the hayloft. People think a hayloft is a pastoral, romantic place, a pillowy hideaway. But bales of hay are brick-hard and scratchy. They turn the air dusty and asthmatic and make you think of the labour involved with getting them stacked there: of my father tossing them up to us — April, me, and some local boy — from the back of the truck. We may have outnumbered my father three to one, but he hurled them at us. We had to be quick.

I barfed over one of the bales and began to feel better.

I was up there a long time, hours maybe. It was nearing supper-time when my mother began shouting for me. My parents never knew where April and I were unless they could actually see or hear us. Unless we were sitting there across the table from them.

But it wasn't long before I heard April step into the barn, walk a few paces and stop.

"Hey."

Silence.

"I know you're up there. Supper's nearly ready and we haven't done our chores."

I stood. She was already facing in my direction. She didn't have to move her head or anything. We looked at each over a bale of hay and giggled. Maybe it was still possible for things to go back to the way they used to be.

But I just wasn't sure.

She looked puzzled then. "Why are you wearing my clothes?" she asked.

I thought at first I would not be able to survive my humiliation and worked to cultivate an air of indifference around Jean. He had been with us over a month now and it was the rare occasion, these days, when he went to his office. Instead he kept close to us, where I could see and smell him. He lent a hand in the barn, in the gardens, in the kitchen. He would even hang laundry on the line. It was difficult to avoid him, but when our paths crossed, he was cordial and pretended nothing had happened between us in his bedroom.

Or office.

I wished he would go back to the Bahamas—and then, of course, I wished he would never go back to the Bahamas. I would remember his warm arms and legs against mine and a case of the chills would wash over me, while meanwhile he was standing across the room doing the dishes with his back turned and probably not thinking about me once.

The worst of it was that I couldn't share my feelings with April.

One Sunday, Mrs. McNadden appeared at the house, lugging the doctor's-office sign. Someone had tried to burn it, then tossed it onto her brother-in-law's side of the yard. He had not been pleased.

I was in the kitchen with Mom and Dad. It was nearly the end of the summer, but instead of having that feeling of things coming to a close, as I usually did at that time of year, I had a sense of everything being jumbled up and uncertain. I could feel it in my parents, too.

I watched Mrs. McNadden make a show of placing the burnt sign on the kitchen table. She was wearing long pants, which was rare for her. Usually she was outfitted in a Talbots polo tee and skirt. But we all knew what she was hiding: fifteen stitches sewn into her calf by Dr. Bruck after she'd been bitten by Baconer, her pig. She had made the mistake of bringing Baconer indoors to live when he'd first arrived—a velvety pink piglet. But now he was a teenager—inexhaustible, exploratory, and nippy.

My father strode across the kitchen and scoffed at the sign. "That's one piss-poor job of burning a sign," he said.

It was true. The paint had bubbled and turned dark, but the words were still legible, and the wood itself had not ignited at all.

"I'm only the messenger, Russell."

"Kids," my mother suggested.

"Why would you think that, Marsha?" Mrs. McNadden asked.

"If you'd been willing to set an example, like Pilgrim here," my father said to Mrs. McNadden, "this might not have happened."

"I have a connection with Dr. Bruck."

"At least you got the pig out of your house," my mother said soothingly. "And into the pen where it belongs."

"That's ridiculous. A *connection*," my father said. "You know how important this is."

Mrs. McNadden looked like she didn't, though.

"Where's Jean?" my mother asked me.

"Will you tell Dr. Moss about this?" Mrs. McNadden asked.

"Of course not," my mother said quickly.

"Is that wise, Marsha?" Mrs. McNadden wanted to know.

Mom turned to me. She looked exasperated. "Where's your sister?"

"Dunno."

"Find her."

My father took the sign and disappeared outside with it. I never saw it again. Mrs. McNadden followed him, like they had unfinished business.

"They argue like they're married," I said with disgust.

"You don't need to tell me."

The next morning, as I was making Dad's coffee, Mom appeared back at the house. She looked as though her plan had been to sneak upstairs and hide, but on meeting us, she just stood there and blinked a few times. She had left only five minutes earlier. Normally we wouldn't see her again at the house for another seven or eight hours.

"What is it, Marsha?"

"Someone…"

"What?"

"Mom?"

"Someone made a terrible mess of the pumpkins."

"What the hell are you talking about?"

"The butternut and winter squash, too."

"Mom, are you sure?"

"Show me." My father had his arms around my mother, guiding her towards the door. Her legs were stiff. "Are they still there?"

"Yes, Russell. They're just lying there all hacked to pieces."

"I meant the sons of bitches who did it," he said gently.

"I didn't see anyone. I think I'll stay here a while."

"No," my father said. "Customers will be arriving." He glanced at me over the top of her head. "We'll all go take a look. Pilgrim, too."

"And April?" Mom asked.

"She's still in bed," I said softly. I knew the growing distance between April and me bothered Mom.

It was early. The world seemed to have taken pause between the silencing of the night and the waking of the day. There was no breeze, and pockets of cool air held on here and there, stirred only by our hurrying legs. Blades of grass clung wetly to my bare feet, giving me that feeling we'd come outdoors before it was ready for us, though the sun was climbing and blinking yellow behind the trees. At this time of day, on such a day, I was struck by how far away the next night lay and how much time and opportunity we had before us to shape a perfect life, to put things right.

I was still thinking maybe it was only ravens or raccoons.

Mom moved reluctantly as we escorted her down the driveway,

then stood at the edge of the garden while my father and I went in. I remembered gently lifting the pumpkins onto their bottoms earlier in the summer so they would grow round and well proportioned, which they had, though now they were split open, the smashed bits and pieces scattered far and wide, while the large raft-like leaves had been ripped or broken off at the stem and the runners trampled on. It almost looked as though there'd been a dance. A wild, middle-of-the-night dance, while we slept. There was a stench — they were already beginning to rot.

"Who would do such a thing?" Mom said.

"Best not to take it personally," my father said. He was calmer now, picking up the larger chunks and tossing them to the edge of the garden.

My mother, still standing there with her shoulders slumped and her face blank, looked like it was a little too late for that.

"For God's sake," Dad said suddenly. "Don't anyone tell Lois."

Mom nodded.

"Don't tell anyone," I said.

"Won't April notice?" Mom whispered.

"Marsha. Go over and open the stand. I'll get the tractor and wagon, and Pilgrim and me will haul these out in one trip and forget this ever happened."

As far as I knew, neither Jean nor April ever did find out about the smashed pumpkins, or the burned sign. Jean probably didn't even notice the sign had disappeared from the front of his office.

April and I lay on our beds re-reading our *Betty and Veronica* comics. Veronica couldn't fit into her slacks. Neither could Betty.

"I'm bored," April complained.

I turned a page. Betty and Veronica decided to go on a crash diet.

"Aren't you bored, too?"

It was rare for April to be hanging around me. Every day I waited for her to come and confess what was going on with Jean. To tell me about the kiss, or kisses, or promise me there had only been that one in the barn.

"Earth to Pilgrim." But something was going on. She was wound-up and restless.

It was the kind of day that was neither sunny nor rainy, neither hot nor cold. The sky had clouded over and the air was close and bothersome, and April was right, it was boring. A fly was driving me bananas, slamming itself against the window pane over and over again.

I wanted to forgive her, so I told her I was thinking of biking over to Otto's for some penny candy. More than anything, I longed for our life to be normal again. Going to Otto's would be a normal thing for the two of us to do.

"Can I come, too?" she begged. "Pretty please, pretty please, pretty please?"

"It's a free country."

We tossed aside our comics and headed out of the room. "Thank God," she said. "Something to do."

But when we got to the shed, our bikes were gone. They were Raleighs—hers black and mine maroon—that we'd had since we were ten.

We tried to think when we'd used them last—if we'd left them anywhere. We were responsible with our possessions. I watched April suspiciously. I wasn't convinced she was surprised to find our bikes gone. I'd already seen Jean kiss her in the barn. It only fell to reason they would have sought another place and time for that. So they had fetched our bikes and pedalled off. Was that before or after I visited him in his bedroom and we nearly took our clothes off? It made me crazy to think about. Some field, some patch of woods, some grassy area beside a bog that smelled of wintergreen and ferns where he could put his tongue in her mouth and examine her breasts. Who knew? Who cared? Then they forgot to bring the bikes back with them. *My* bike.

"Where did you leave my bike?" I asked her.

"I didn't take your bike."

"You didn't even ask if you could borrow it."

"I didn't take your stupid bike."

"I hate you." But maybe she was telling the truth, I wasn't sure.

"I hate you, too."

We left the shed, and there was the Ambassador.

"We could take it as far as the stand," April proposed. "And walk the rest of the way?"

"Why not."

"You drive."

We both knew that at the stand I would turn onto Assabet Road without stopping. Mom would be too busy to look up from her produce and customers, and if she did, she would assume it was Dad heading off on some errand. Plus, we were sixteen, for Christ's sake. I was old enough to drive a few miles whether I had a licence or not.

A gang of kids was inside Otto's. Otto himself stood in surveillance behind the counter, letting it be known no one was leaving with any unpaid merchandise. April got her bag of candy first and went outside. I had just taken mine when I felt a jolt to my shoulder and nearly dropped the bag. I spun around. April was coming back in across the oily floor towards me.

She punched me.

Behind her, I saw Lottie Barboza enter with her cousin Tina.

I took my bag and circled towards April, avoiding Lottie and Tina.

I hadn't seen Lottie in years. If someone had mentioned her, I would have envisioned the small, serious girl who wore a faux leather jumper and sat between us on the bus until her brother made her stop. That evil Amado, she had called him. I knew Lottie had left school, which somehow seemed in accordance with her present grown-up appearance — she looked too old to be in high school. She was nearly a foot taller than us and her breasts were an impressive size. She could have been married. She was, at the very least, someone's girlfriend.

And she was strong. April's shoulder was throbbing.

"I don't care," April whispered when I reached her side. "She's just a piece of trash."

I flinched, startled April would talk that way. There was laughter from Lottie and Tina, who were now roaming the aisles at the back of the store.

"Are you here to buy anything, Lottie?" Otto was saying in his unfriendly way. "Otherwise I want you out. You, too, Tina." He was coming out from behind the counter to make his point.

April and I left the store. We wanted to get to the Ambassador. I was glad it was there.

"Stop," April said behind me.

She was pointing at two bikes lying on the dirt ground.

"Look, our bikes," she said.

I saw that they were and that they'd clearly been through a lot in recent days. There were new dents, and mud and grass in the spokes. One of the seats had been slashed, as though sliced up like a pie.

"Let's go," I said. "We'll tell Dad. Come on."

But April wasn't ready to leave. When Lottie and Tina emerged a second later, she said, "Did you steal our Raleighs?" Her feet were only inches from the handlebars of her own bike.

I was nervous. *Never mind. Let's go.*

Lottie walked up to April. "We didn't steal nothing," she said. April stood no higher than Lottie's protruding, hard-looking breasts. I thought she might be sticking them out a little to make them look bigger.

"You're a liar," April said back to her.

Lottie sneered at April and reached down for the bike. "That's tough titties for you, sucker." She began to pedal off.

April didn't move. I came up close to her.

"They haven't got no titties," Tina sang out, taking my bike.

"We do so," I said quietly to April, who scowled at me.

We watched the two of them riding off, on our bikes, down Route 17. Suddenly Lottie banged her foot down on the pavement and twisted back, though she didn't look directly at us, and yelled out, "If you need a doctor for that arm, just give us niggers a call, we got our own doc now."

The two of them were laughing so hard they could barely stay on the bikes. Our bikes.

There was an icky sourness in my belly, along with the hammering in my shoulder.

"I'd like to run them over with the car," April said, her cheeks flushed.

I got in behind the wheel and drove us home, where we went immediately inside and upstairs to our bedroom and focused our attention on our bags of penny candy. I was reeling from what had happened at Otto's, and I suspect April was too, though neither of us would speak of it in the few weeks we had left in each other's lives. I was surprised Lottie had stolen our bikes, but not shocked. That she'd hit one of us was different. It had been personal and fierce.

"I'm going on a crash diet after this," I said, rattling my bag.

"Me, too."

It was when we sat down for supper that night that we realized no one had seen Jean since breakfast.

At first, we were bewildered.

"Did he happen to say where he was going today?" April asked no one in particular.

It dawned on me that this was why she'd been hanging around me all day—Jean had vanished and she didn't know where he'd gone.

My mother looked at my father, who shrugged.

"Go see," April said to me.

"Go see? What?"

"If his things are still in his bedroom. His clothes and books."

"Of course they are," my mother said. "Why wouldn't they be?"

"I'm not going in Dr. Moss's room," I told April. "You go, if it's so important to you."

"You're closer," April whispered urgently. "I'd have to come out around the table."

"That's the stupidest thing ever."

Please?

No.

"End of discussion," my father said. He glanced darkly at April. "He's not the type to disappear after all I've done. Without a goodbye."

"That's not what worries me, Russell," my mother said.

I understood what my mother was saying, but I doubted April did. She thought he'd left her. Under the table I nudged a foot against hers. She was holding back tears and her face burned. I felt a little bad for refusing to check Jean's room, but I had promised myself I would never go back in that room as long as I lived.

Suddenly April stood and stormed out of the kitchen, but only seconds later came back and sat down at the table with us.

"Are his things there, sweet pea?" my mother asked.

April nodded and bit her lip.

"I'm worried about this, Russell. The world is so topsy-turvy. You know yourself—"

My father cut her off. "I'm not jumping to conclusions." But I think he felt uneasy.

After supper, April asked me to stay with her in the kitchen while she waited for Jean. She was doing a bad job of hiding her feelings for him. I think her behaviour was an eye-opener for my parents, who were also waiting anxiously for his return, but elsewhere in the house.

I hoped nothing evil had happened—a concern I couldn't share with April. I thought about Lottie's comment that afternoon and about the white parents in Boston hurling garbage at the black kids trapped in those school buses.

Soon, April and I would be returning to school ourselves. I imagined heading off each morning with our textbooks, leaving Jean behind at the house and getting on the bus. I was pretty sure Mr. Philpott would not approve of our guest.

As the minutes passed, I wondered if there was someone we should call. Jean's family? The police?

"He'd never just take off, would he?" April asked desperately, as though that was the only explanation.

But, as we learned, Jean had not taken off. He had walked to the post office directly after breakfast and boarded the bus to Plymouth, where he purchased his white Datsun coupe with red interior. Its engine was quieter than the station wagon's. The first sign of his return was Tansy and Bandit barking in the driveway. April and I were still waiting in the kitchen, and we both jumped to our feet. Relief was like something solid that slid down my throat to my stomach.

April flew out of the house and flounced around the car with the dogs like she had no sense at all. Our parents were right behind us.

"It's beautiful. It's beautiful. Oh, it's beautiful, Jean."

Jean stood there, beaming. The sun was setting and lighting up the interior. He had driven with all the windows down and I could not resist putting my hand inside to touch the warm red vinyl.

"Set you back a pretty penny?" my father asked.

Jean shrugged self-consciously.

"Well, I warned you."

"It's quite a snazzy car," my mother remarked with the voice of someone who is desperate to forgive.

But my parents were mostly watching April.

April tossed and turned all that night. Petunia and I watched her, a couple of times, slip her feet over the edge of her bed and pause there, then change her mind and lie back down. She must have realized that in the quiet of the night every floorboard in the house would creak, and that our parents would be alert to such sounds.

The summer was winding down, the nocturnal creatures exhausted. A few birds were still singing, but the songs were fragmented and dispirited.

I rolled over and looked in April's direction. She was a colourless bundle.

What do you love about me?

The morning after Jean purchased the Datsun, my father informed us we could no longer drive the Ambassador, even around the property, since we didn't have our licences, though that had never been a condition before. We were also, he added, as though it was an afterthought, not allowed to travel anywhere in the Datsun. April was furious. She became obsessed with the Datsun, with the idea of Jean taking her for a drive in it.

"It's not fair," she complained angrily. "I don't see why we can't take a spin in Jean's car. It's okay with him. Isn't it, Pilgrim?"

But I offered nothing.

We were in the kitchen canning tomatoes. Mom, April, and me. Normally I loved this time of year. The three of us, the industry of it, each day those familiar smells—pickled beets, dilly beans, rhubarb chutney, peaches. I was at the sink, slipping the skins off the blanched tomatoes under cold water. The room was humid from the boiling pots, and April and I had pulled our hair back in elastics, while Mom had covered her head with a red kerchief. The blanched tomatoes gave off a fruity odour, like wild grapes. Oddly, this always drew a couple of barn cats up to the house, and they would sit patiently on the other side of the screen door and meow, which incensed Petunia, who tap-danced around the kitchen, growling.

"Drop it," Mom told April. She was to my left, taking the soft tomatoes from me and pressing them into jars, her hands awash in the pink juice. "Your father's not going to change his mind."

"What's the matter with the Datsun?" April demanded. "Why are you and Dad being so mental about that car?" She stood on my other side, at the stove, where she was tasked with gently removing the bobbing tomatoes from a pot of simmering water once their skins had split.

"What time is it?" my mother asked. She did not have an internal clock. "We're supposed to help the McNaddens get that pig of theirs in the truck. They're finally getting him slaughtered, and I want to get lunch over and done with first."

After Baconer bit Mrs. McNadden, he had been banished to the pen built for him in the backyard. The McNaddens did not think he slept. He rooted in the ground with his filthy snout until all plant life inside the pen was annihilated and even roots belonging to trees outside the pen were damaged—evidenced by their paled, curled leaves. In the centre he dug a mud bath into which only half his body fit, usually the rear portion. He repeatedly knocked over his water bucket.

When my mother saw the pen she said it was too small and the site too damp. Someone should have told them, she'd said, looking at my father.

Now Mrs. McNadden was desperate to have him trucked off for slaughtering. But as with so many things, they required my parents' help. You need to know what you're doing if you're moving a pig, my mother had admitted. Especially one as spoiled as that Baconer.

"Eleven thirty," I told her.

"I hate it here," April said, jabbing at the tomatoes with a slotted spoon.

"April, don't let those go too long," Mom said crossly. "Are they ready? They look ready from here. Sixty seconds is plenty."

April lifted the spoon out of the pot and watched the hot water dripping off it.

"April! Can you please pay attention to what you're doing," my mother said.

"I hate it here," April repeated quietly. "Just one ride—"

"Honest to Pete." Mom paused and placed her palms on the counter. "Sometimes I wish your father had never heard about that government program. I wish he'd never found Dr. Moss."

"Oh, boy," April whispered. She glanced at Mom and her eyes flashed. As she did, she leaned up against the stove.

"Careful, April. That's scalding hot. Pilgrim, go help her."

I went over and pushed April away from the stove. "Watch out," I said. "Just give me the spoon. I'll do it."

"You don't like Jean?" April asked Mom, ignoring me. "Because he's a Negro?"

"Of course I like him, and what a thing to suggest," Mom said. "He's a nice young man. Helpful, polite. But the program isn't working, and I'm sure there are better job opportunities for him elsewhere. Maybe at home."

"You're a liar," April said to my mother.

"In the Bahamas," I added.

"We *know* where," April said to me.

"A liar? April, I think you better go up to your room and calm down. You're more a hindrance than a help today."

"You don't want him to go so he'll have better opportunities. You just want him to go. You're a liar."

Mom stood back from the counter and straightened her back. In front of her were several rows of bottled tomatoes. They were wiped clean and shining. I thought they were a splendid sight. "Damn it," she said. "Now I can't remember if I got the air bubbles out before putting the lids on. That's all I need. A jar exploding."

"They'll be fine," I told her.

"It's just a car ride," April muttered. She was overheated.

"Is it really?" my mother asked, taking a few steps towards April and bumping into me. "I've had just about enough of Dr. Moss and this fanciful thinking of yours."

"So what!" April shouted, brandishing that spoon. "You'd have to let me ride in his car if we got married!"

"What was that?" Mom said.

My father opened the door and stepped inside, all in one quick movement. You could tell by his face he'd been listening.

Lunch was nowhere near ready.

He looked at us, then over his shoulder. "Where's Jean?" he asked.

"How should I know," my mother said.

"Perhaps he's admiring his car," I said. I thought the comment might be taken as a joke. My father glared at me, but it was one of those rare days when time begins to click by so unevenly—so strangely—that the wicked and absurd can be spoken aloud and forgiven. He looked questioningly at my mother.

"Upstairs now, girls," she ordered. "And splash some cold water on your face, April. You'll feel better."

"I don't want to feel better," she cried. "I hate your guts."

She was glancing around with a crazed expression. I moved towards her, to tug her away from the stove, but I was too late. She flung the spoon back into the pot and I felt the pain instantly. She grabbed her wrist.

"Out!" my father roared.

"Russell." We all froze. "Pardon me." It was Jean. His face was on the other side of the screen door, which he had not yet opened. He had simply walked up like someone just come in off the road. I hadn't gazed directly at him in days, but it was easier this way, with his face behind the grey mesh. I liked his eyes, his voice. I liked the way he smelled. Occasionally, like now, I would remember—though I tried not to—his tongue and fingers inside me. The cat waiting on the doorstep beside him meowed hopefully.

We didn't have our lunch that day, or our supper, but I can't remember anyone complaining of hunger.

My mother ushered April and me out of the kitchen. As the three of us went up the stairs, we heard the screen door open and my father say to Jean, "I need to have a word with you."

Upstairs, my mother sat on April's bed, and April and I sat opposite her on mine, side by side, a few vibrating inches apart. We were straining to hear what was being discussed down in the kitchen. April was holding her wrist and rocking back and forth, so I reached out and rubbed the back of her head. I felt Petunia squeeze herself between the two of us. She stuck her front paws out over the edge of the bed and looked elatedly across at Mom. It was a treat for her to have nearly the whole gang together like this in the bedroom.

"April?" Mom said. "Has Jean—has he touched you?"

She sounded nervous. Like me, she was still reeling from April's comment about marrying Jean.

"I won't listen to this," April said. She put her hands over her ears.

"Sweet pea, he's much, much older than you."

"Ten years," I confirmed, nodding.

"What do you know, Pilgrim? Has he touched her? Do you understand what I'm saying?" Then she had a wild thought. "He hasn't touched *you*, has he?"

"Don't be preposterous," I said.

"This is no time for the holier-than-thou, Pilgrim."

April was listening closely behind her hands.

"His body has not come in contact with ours," I said. "He has not seen either of us naked, or asked either of us to remove our clothes, or—"

"Pilgrim! Hush. My God, what's gotten into you?"

Petunia jumped onto the floor.

"Yeah, what *is* the matter with you?" April asked, dropping her hands from her ears.

"We just want to go for a ride in his car, Mom, plain and simple."

"Weirdo," April said to me, but she was softening now, even admiring me.

"Brand new cars have such a nice smell," I added and April smiled.

Mom was scrutinizing us. I concentrated on being innocent and clamped down on a tiny convulsion in my throat. Mom looked tired as sin.

"Buying that car was a rash decision. Jean surprised me. I don't know how he plans on getting it back to the Bahamas." She looked back and forth between us. "This is all just about the car?"

We nodded. Our breathing clicked in sync.

"Cross your hearts and hope to die?"

We drew crosses in tandem over our chests with a finger. If our father saw us doing that, he'd want to strangle all three of us.

The house was dead quiet.

"What a morning," Mom said eventually. "I suppose Lois is up there pacing around, waiting for us. It would be a treat for me if her own husband could handle these things."

Then she drew herself up. April and I were now wedged together on the bed, rubbing our wrists and embracing the belief we had been wronged and misunderstood. I hadn't been this physically close to her in a while, and I found she smelled differently.

"Do you want me to have a look at that burn?" she asked April.

"No."

"Fine. Just don't expect to get inside that car," she warned, standing in the doorway. "Pilgrim, I'm going to put some of the bottles in the pot now, before I go. I'll set the timer. Can I depend on you to take them out? We won't be long."

Tomato juice was all over her pant legs. She was not the type to wear an apron.

"Did you hear me, Pilgrim?"

I looked up at her.

"Keep your ears tuned for the timer? Pilgrim?"

"Yes!"

She left our room and called down, tentatively, from the top of the stairs, "Russell?"

"What are you doing?" he shouted back up, as though he had been standing there at the bottom listening. "We promised Lois we'd load that friggin' pig an hour ago."

"Coming," she said, then to herself, though we could hear her plainly, "Damn that Lois."

She went down the stairs, and we heard a brief exchange of softly spoken words between our parents. The kitchen screen door opened, then closed with a bang. One of the dogs whined and the truck started up. I imagined Dad might ram the Datsun, but that would be illogical. Jean needed something to drive away in after he'd packed his suitcase.

April's arms were around me. "It's not about his age," she hissed into my body. "It's about him being colored."

"Black American." I rubbed the back of her head again. "I know. I don't think they want you to marry a Black American."

"Do you think Dad heard that?" she whispered.

I was certain he had, but I didn't want to worry her.

My father was worked up and had been for weeks, what with his doctoring scheme being such a failure and then his irritation with the Datsun. He'd probably been born angry, and I figured you really had to feel sorry for someone born angry, like it was a genetic disorder.

We rested there, slumped against each other in the silence, and were growing dozy when we heard footsteps on the stairs again. We sat bolt upright. Suddenly, our hearts were beating madly. Where had he been? He came up slowly but powerfully and I imagined his thighs flexing beneath his pant legs as he took each step. As far as I knew, he'd never been in our bedroom before, but I had a sudden vision of him sneaking in when we were all outside and seeing our clothes on the floor, our barrettes and elastics on the mantle, the beds unmade and the sheets and pillows covered with Petunia's fur.

He stood in the doorway, his kind, syrupy eyes flicking back and forth between the two of us.

"You're not allowed in this room," I said.

He ignored me and came to the exact spot on April's bed where my mother had sat. "Let me just sit for a moment," he said miserably. "And talk to you."

"Of course, Jean," April said. She shifted an inch away from me.

I figured he wanted me to take off so he could be alone with April, but I didn't budge.

"I'll be leaving in the morning. Russell has a map for me. It's very detailed. It will be an adventure, driving to Miami."

It was so obvious he was trying to be brave that I felt a little sorry for him.

"Dad said that?" April demanded. She flapped her wrist and blew on the burn. "That you have to leave?"

"I agreed it was time. Also, I lied to him. I said he could trust me not to do anything improper."

"Lying isn't the worst sin there is," she said.

"He suggested you had a schoolgirl crush on me."

"I don't care what he calls it," she said.

He hesitated. "I told him if that was so, I never noticed. I said I could not even tell you two apart."

"You can't," I said.

His eyes jerked nervously in my direction. Then quickly away.

"Your mother looked terrible when she came downstairs."

"We didn't tell her anything, did we, Pilgrim? Jean, promise you won't leave? I'm old enough," she said meaningfully. "Jean, you *know* I'm old enough."

He smiled at her when she said that and I had a painful sense of trespass.

I heard the timer go off downstairs in the kitchen.

"Maybe he *should* go away?" I suggested, and April looked at me with alarm.

"We should go away," April said to Jean. "You and me."

"I didn't mean you. I meant him," I said, blowing on my own wrist.

"Shut up, Pilgrim."

"You shut up." I felt like pinching her. Protecting her had been a catastrophic mistake.

"Is there a problem with your wrists?" he asked.

He stood and came over to us. He lifted my hand and inspected my perfectly fine wrist, then April's, which was pink and slightly swollen. He never looked at my face, just my wrist.

"What happened?" he asked her, still holding her hand.

"Promise you won't leave? God, I'd die."

He smiled at her again, indulgently, fondly.

"She burned it on a pot," I explained, because I knew she wouldn't.

"Does it hurt?" he asked.

"Not overly," I said.

"They'll be home shortly," he said. He sounded defeated.

I was surprised they had sat this long without touching. All because of me. Otherwise, I supposed, they would have been all over each other.

I had an idea.

"Let's take the Datsun for a spin," I said.

"Very funny, Pilgrim."

"It may be our last chance," I insisted. "Besides, Mom and Dad won't be home for at least two hours."

"They've only gone to the McNaddens'," Jean said. "To load that pig."

"Didn't you hear Mom?" I said to April. "They're going to Dover afterwards, to pick up the Rototiller at the repair shop. We have plenty of time. Remember she said, 'Keep your ears tuned for the timer'? It'll be forever before they're back."

April turned to Jean. "Why not?" They looked like they had known each other for years.

"I don't think it's a good idea, actually," he said. "Also, I already heard the timer."

"I have to take the bottles out of the pot, that's all," I explained, then added hopefully. "A kind of farewell."

"No, *not* farewell—"

"You're coming, too?" he asked me.

"Her?" April blurted out, then gave me a look that wasn't entirely apologetic.

"Of course," I said to him. "I'm looking forward to it."

It took a few minutes to find our sneakers, which we wanted to wear so we wouldn't get the inside of the Datsun dirty with our feet.

In the kitchen the glass jars of tomatoes were rattling away on the stove and the air was steamy. I got the jar remover and lifted them out onto the dish towel that Mom had neatly folded on the counter. The clinking sound was due to some broken glass in the bottom of the pot. One of the jars had exploded. Perhaps my mother had not worked the air bubbles out of them after all.

"Let's pack a picnic," April suggested.

"We don't have time," I said. The remaining jars were hissing on the dish towel and I edged away from them. "Come on. Let's go."

April looked at me and then at the jars.

"I thought we had plenty of time?" Jean was saying, as April took his hand and pulled him towards the door.

As soon as we were outside I had to marvel at the bizarre progress of the day. I remembered being in the barn first thing in the morning, doing chores, like it had been yesterday. And now it was afternoon. About 3:10. Had we been all day canning tomatoes? And then talking to Mom, and then *him*. Petunia was at our heels, but I didn't think she should get in the Datsun. Her toenails might puncture the vinyl.

I had avoided the car since it first arrived, despite its glamour, because Dad might be cross if he caught me admiring it. I had even pretended I wasn't listening when Jean explained to Mom one evening how the Japanese had concocted a harder, more resilient automobile paint. But every time I walked by the Datsun I was awed by its sheen: the white paint swimming like cream, dazzling and pure in the sun, under the clear topcoat.

Now April was running her hand along the Datsun's hood, while Jean was opening the passenger door and flipping the seat forward so I could climb into the back. They both waited.

"I feel sick," I announced, stopping a few feet short of the car. "Huh?"

"We aren't going without you. I won't bend on this," Jean said directly to me, then turned to April. "For propriety's sake. It's a risky idea, anyway. I don't want to leave on a bad note."

"Stop saying that, Jean. You're not leaving."

"What are your symptoms, Pilgrim?" he asked. This might have been a doctor's curiosity and concern, or a layman's savvy distrust.

"I just feel kind of gross all of a sudden. Stomach region."

"You can sit in the front," he said. "April won't mind."

"That won't help," I said. April studied me. She was beginning to have an inkling that I was up to no good.

"You're lying," she said.

"It's not contagious," I said with meaning.

Both April and Jean seemed about to speak, then simultaneously stopped. I had the disturbing thought that he knew our periods came within minutes of each other, and further, that neither of us should be having it right now.

"It came early," I whispered to April. I stared hard at her. My face was hot with the conflicting urge to have a quick look into his eyes, yet not look anywhere near him. He knew so much about me, and had chosen her.

I seemed to be the only one aware of a series of popping sounds and the tinkling of glass coming from inside the house.

I stared at April. *Can't we both love him?*

But the idea that they might now go off alone, just the two them, was impossible for April to resist. I reached down and scooped up Petunia, who pressed back against me and licked my throat.

"What's the big deal?" I asked loudly, walking backwards to the house with Petunia in my arms.

Inside, I got no farther than the kitchen table, where I sat down and clasped Petunia to my chest so she wouldn't cut her feet on the broken glass. I glanced at the red juice and tomato flesh splattered over the walls, counter, even the ceiling, then didn't look again. I waited impatiently for the sound of the car starting. After a while, I tipped back in my chair and peered out the screen door. They were standing by the Datsun. Jean's doctor's bag was open on the hood and he was wrapping a bandage around April's wrist. Her heart was pounding.

I was impatient for them to get going. The broken Rototiller was twenty feet away from the Datsun by the shed door, where it had been for weeks.

April was distracted, but it was only a matter of time before she noticed it, though I wondered if anything could stop her from getting in that car at this point. Jean probably didn't know what a Rototiller was.

I sat the chair back down on all four legs and held tight to Petunia, who was getting squirmy. Finally I heard the Datsun start and drive off. By the sounds of it, Jean was going at a good clip, which concerned me. The time was 3:25. My parents would be back from Mrs. McNadden's any moment. It would be best if they got caught right away, within minutes of the house.

My actions had not been sisterly. To my surprise, I began to feel menstrual cramps.

Petunia pulled back and lifted a paw to the side of my nose. It smelled of soil and grass, of the outdoors, where she wanted to be. But I wanted her with me.

Normally, loading a pig took no time, and my mother would get bored chatting with Mrs. McNadden. April and Jean might have been intercepted before reaching Assabet Road — at which point it might dawn on them I had deceived them — and a ruckus with my father would ensue. I would not be able to see or hear that from the house. On the other hand, the Datsun could have made it free and clear and be off meandering the country roads, moving farther away until they were lost. I sat perfectly still and panicked.

It wasn't until 4:05 that our truck pulled in. At 4:06 my parents were in the kitchen with me. I had forgotten to turn the burner off and it was only then that I became aware of the smell of scorched metal. My mother raced to remove the pot, then grabbed the broom.

"Are you trying to burn the house to the ground?" she cried.

"Where is she?" my father shouted, his boots crunching on the broken glass. He looked wild with worry but also like he might cripple anything in his way.

But once I apologized for the wreckage, explaining I didn't get to the bottles in time because I was outside trying to prevent April from driving off with Jean, I wasn't the one in trouble.

I had assured Jean and April they had two hours. I just hadn't expected them to take so much of it. I had expected them to leave and return, get caught, and Jean would be sent packing—alone. I chastised myself for not thinking things through. For not considering that Baconer might have resisted being trucked off and slaughtered.

I didn't want to think about the possibility that April and Jean might simply not return.

My father went down to the barn to lock up the animals and I helped my mother tidy the kitchen. We put everything—including the broken bottles and dented lids and rings—on the back porch to think about later. Mom would try to salvage what she could. Her red kerchief had fallen off at some point during the day, and her long, dark hair looked flat and dirty. After Dad returned to the house, I went upstairs and I saw the kerchief on my bed. It must have slipped off earlier, and none of us had noticed, not even her. Then Jean had come in and probably sat on it.

I got into bed and tried to read. Mom came upstairs and poked her head in and asked if I was okay. I nodded.

"Oh, there it is," she said, spotting the kerchief. But after she picked it up she hesitated. I could feel her staring at me and I wanted to be alone. I had a lot of things on my mind.

"What?" I asked without looking up.

"Your father," she said. "I'm trying to stay clear of his path. Are you hungry?"

"No." I turned a page.

She began putting some of my clothes away.

"Is ten years really such a big deal?" I said.

"Oh, sweet pea."

The Datsun came down the driveway and pulled up to the house an hour and a half after it had left. I felt the cold fear in my sister's gut when she saw the truck parked there, and her surprise and anger as it dawned on her there hadn't been enough time for our parents to drive to Dover and back after loading the pig.

I couldn't imagine anything at all about Jean's response to seeing the truck, but I suspected it was not fear.

So I was fearful for him.

ELEVEN

The world went from silence to an explosion of voices as soon as April and Jean returned from their car ride and stepped into the kitchen.

Seconds later April was racing up the stairs and slamming our bedroom door behind her. She glanced at me where I sat on my bed, hesitated, then jumped into her own bed and pulled a blanket up over her head, as though she could hide there. I was disgusted by this drama and wanted to point out no one was chasing her. Downstairs my father was shouting, "Didn't we say no to her riding in that car!" My mother's voice was placating. Jean's was louder than hers, perhaps slightly affronted.

"I agree it was a mistake," we heard him say, then a moment later, "Of course. Absolutely. As you wish."

"He's packing his suitcase," April wailed from under the blanket. "Isn't he?"

It had gone quiet down there and I thought he probably was.

"You shouldn't have been gone so long," I said. "Where were you?"

Petunia jumped up onto April's bed and began sniffing at her under the blanket, wagging her tail and trying to find an entry point.

"Oh, no, oh, no. I don't want Jean to leave." April was curled up into a ball. "Dad is going to be furious with me. He is really going to furious with me, Pilgrim."

I had been feeling guilty, but less so now that they were home again and she was putting on this show. "That's stupid," I told her.

The phone started ringing downstairs.

April threw the blanket off and pulled Petunia into her arms. "You're wrong. She'll tell on me, I know it. I bet that's her now. She's such a nasty, prissy busybody. If she tells on me, I'll kill her, I swear I'll kill her."

"Who will tell on you? What did you do?"

Petunia was sniffing the bandage on April's wrist, her body rigid.

My stomach was hurting me — I figured from lack of lunch and supper. Even though the sun was setting earlier these days, it was still bright and warm outside.

The phone rang and rang. Where was my mother? Finally I heard heavy footsteps and my father's voice, "Hello?"

"Shit, shit, shit," April moaned.

Petunia was trying to worm her way out of April's embrace.

I don't know how long my father was on the phone. In fact, I had forgotten about it. I was thinking how I, too, would never see Jean again. But April was as alert as a squirrel. As soon as my father's foot was on the bottom step she was scurrying from her bed and trying to get out of the room. But there he was, just as quick, knowing she would try to escape, despite there being nowhere to escape to. He looked at both of us with fury, making sure he knew who was who. She backed up and got into my bed this time, and we automatically put our arms around each other. She began to hum.

"Just heard from Mrs. McNadden," he said. "On the telephone."

He was so quiet, that was the strangest part. I knew he was pretty angry, yet he was so quiet.

"I'm trying to imagine this. It is funny." He actually smiled. "Imagine Mrs. McNadden out for a walk in the woods, happy as a lark we got that pig out of her life, then coming upon you and that sex maniac on Cory's Lane in the back of his car? Quiet!"

The humming stopped.

They only got as far as Cory's Lane?

My stomach had knots in it all the way up to my throat.

"Who said?" I asked stupidly. Cory's Lane was an old cart track that ran behind Mrs. McNadden's pasture. It was nothing more than two ruts. Could the Datsun have even gotten down there? I thought of the grass that grew along the track's meridian swishing against the underside of the car as they inched their way deeper into the woods for secrecy's sake.

My father was looking at me like I was a moron, while April rammed herself against me. "Didn't you hear what I just said, Pilgrim? My favourite nitwit was out for her evening constitution, thinking her biggest worry is snakes, and she sees that friggin' foreign car. What I don't get is how long it took her pick up the telephone and ring me."

They were beginning to hurt, April's fingers digging into my back and side.

"That's not all of it," he said to me. "Your sister got out of the car, picked up some rocks, and chased her off. Lois was not pleased with that."

"Mrs. McNadden?" I asked, still trying to keep up.

He nodded. "Yes, Pilgrim, and as it was just described to me, your sister was not fully clothed."

"They were only small rocks," April challenged. "Wouldn't hurt a fly." She gave me a quick look and I knew she'd been wearing nothing but her underwear.

"All right. End of discussion. In the car, five minutes. Jean can take his own car."

We were jolted by this. Where were we going? And with Jean?

"And bring the pillow dog," he added, already out of the room.

There were scratching sounds from beneath the bed and Petunia crawled out between our legs.

We had been driving twelve minutes. I wasn't using my internal clock. I was watching the clock on the dashboard, just left of Mom's sunburned shoulder. She was fidgety, looking everywhere: out the side window, straight ahead, hastily at my father, and several times behind her at April and me.

My father was keeping his eye on the road. He hadn't spoken since we'd left the house. I knew it was best not to speak either —or move, for that matter—but Petunia had grown heavy in my lap, so I shifted slightly, tipping her off onto the seat. She let out a grumpy sigh of objection.

"I never heard a pig scream like that before," my mother said, glancing at my father. "Where are we going, Russell?"

Beside me, April twisted around to look out the rear window at Jean following us in his Datsun. She was running her hands up and down herself excessively, as though checking for something. The movement tugged at her bandaged wrist. Suddenly I was aware of Dad watching her in the rearview mirror. His brown eyes appeared to have no depth.

The car slowed.

"That pig was a screamer, girls. I thought I was hearing a jet plane go over. I thought we would never get—"

"Marsha."

We turned off onto a dirt road I had never noticed before. It was a place closed in by old forest—majestic trees and brambles and shifting sunlight. Birds swooped across the road in front of the car, which was moving more slowly now, but even so, I was pretty sure we were travelling at a speed my father would not normally recommend for the Ambassador on this kind of road. We passed several cranberry bogs where the landscape opened up, and for a moment I felt my spirits lift, as though there was still hope this was nothing more than a family excursion, but then the forest closed back in around us. I felt my sister's hand on mine. She took another look behind her for Jean. I had no doubt he was still with us.

"I feel carsick," she said.

I wanted to know what it had been like wearing just her underwear, next to Jean, against his red upholstery and his body. Had he been down to his underwear, too? Or less? A feeling, like when you hit your funny bone, ran through my arms and shoulders and neck.

Then I smiled and had to look out the window to hide it from my father, thinking of April grabbing rocks and pitching them at

Mrs. McNadden. Served her right. She'd probably walked right up to the car and pressed her nose against the window.

"I'm going to puke!" April cried. "Stop the car!"

My father ignored her.

"Dad!"

"Stop the car, Russell," my mother insisted. "Let her get out and be sick."

My father slammed on the breaks. "You have two minutes," he told her.

April leapt out and went and stood in front of the Ambassador where Jean couldn't see her. I closed my eyes and tried to steady my breathing, but seconds later I opened my own door and vomited onto the road. My father shouted at my sister to get back in the car. We set off again.

Petunia was getting restless and whining.

My mother asked, "How much longer, Russell?"

The track widened into an area that was the terminus of two other dirt roads, though both were overgrown and would not provide exit. On one side a field that had been recently hayed rolled up a slight incline and on the other side was a swamp. There was a parched, undernourished look to the vegetation. Willows grew along the edge of the water, but looked so dull and spiritless they seemed at any moment on the verge of falling in. Beneath their patchy shade my father parked the car. Petunia rose on her hind legs and sniffed eagerly at the unfamiliar landscape.

Once out of the car, the four of us were facing Jean. He hadn't closed the door to his Datsun and it stuck out behind him like it was a wing on a big white insect. I noticed Petunia was beginning to wander over towards the swamp. I hoped she didn't locate something revolting to roll around in that would make her stink on the drive home.

"What the heck is going on, Russell?"

We had never heard Jean speak rudely to anyone.

"Mr. Bell," my father corrected. You could tell he didn't want to speak to Jean ever again.

"Okay then, Mr. Bell. What's going on?" Jean said. "I'd like to know precisely why you have brought us here."

"Interesting," my father said, observing his feet. Then he looked at me. He was behaving so strangely. "When Marsha and I say, no getting in Dr. Moss's car, what does that mean?" When I didn't respond, he glanced around. "Anyone?"

I felt my mother tense and I saw her blinking as though dust had just blown up into her eyes. Her jeans were still damp from the tomatoes. My father put a hand on her shoulder and let out a soft whistle. Petunia glanced up and trotted back to us, her tail wagging.

"April," he said, sounding more himself, which was a relief. "Could you put a collar on that dog?"

"Dad?"

"It's in the front seat."

After April returned from the car with the collar, he remarked, "I find it interesting that you forgot the rope."

April was slipping the collar over Petunia's head. "I didn't see any rope," she lied. She wouldn't look at him. But she knew what rope. We had both seen him toss it in the wayback before we left.

My father hesitated, then went and got the rope himself and carried out the rest of his demonstration, he alone knowing where he was headed with it. The rope was so long he was able to tie one end to the car's trailer hitch, loop it through Petunia's collar,

227

and then tie the other end to a small alder. As he worked, he grew increasingly sloppy and erratic, as though his own actions were feeding his agitation.

I was frightened, but I also sympathized with my father. I didn't want April to leave any more than he did. Someone had to take control of the situation.

Petunia's range of movement, the limits of which she had immediately tested and established, was not much—a few inches. She lifted a paw and looked at my father contritely. Her scraggly tail lay motionless in the dirt.

"Moss, you're fired," my father announced. "Your medical practice in Cranfield is terminated. If I ever see you again, I'll shoot you."

Jean laughed.

"Funny? You think that's funny? How interesting."

Each time my father repeated the word "interesting," a chill went down my spine.

Petunia began panting, her pink triangle of a tongue throbbing like a small heart in her open mouth. I told myself she was getting herself all worked up over nothing. Dad just didn't want her wandering away and getting lost.

But then he went back to the car and took something out of the glove compartment. At first I thought it was an oddly shaped cucumber. I felt the position I had silently taken—of being on his side—drain out of me. I had forgotten that the best punishment was separating you from someone you loved.

I clenched down on my jaw until my teeth hurt.

"Dad," April said calmly, as though he hadn't just taken a pistol out of the car. "This isn't about the Datsun." I was struck by her bravery and poise—standing there with her arms loose at her sides, her expression blank, relaxed.

"Hey," Jean said to my father. He was nervous. Except for April, we were all nervous. "You need to cool down."

"You're telling *me* to cool down? April is hardly more than a girl."

"Russell, dear."

"Mr. Bell, this is—"

"Shut up, Jean, or I'll shoot you, I'm this close." He turned back to April and struggled with his expression. "Listen to me. Your mother and I said *no getting in that car.*"

We watched him glance around distractedly, the pistol swinging from his hand, as though he couldn't find his way back to his plan.

Suddenly he took aim at Petunia. "You should have known better," he said to April. "Besides, you don't really love this dog. She won't be missed."

"No, no, no," my mother whispered. She sounded as though she couldn't draw her breath.

"But she's my dog, too." When I spoke I tasted the vomit in my mouth.

"Stay out of it, Pilgrim," my father ordered. He flapped his free arm in front of Mom and me, as though to keep us back, but neither of us had budged.

He was still pointing the gun at Petunia.

April put her hand out. "I'll do it, Dad. I'll shoot her."

"What?"

"Give me the gun. It should be me who does it. Right? This is my fault."

I knew what she was thinking: *let's just get the pistol out of Dad's hands.*

He glanced at me and I nodded, and he smiled weakly, almost as though he were embarrassed by his relief.

"Of course," he said. He held out the pistol and April took it with her bandaged hand, then stepped gingerly back from him. She swivelled to face Petunia.

My thoughts were coming rapidly, probably too rapidly for April. *You don't have to do it. Not now. Run. Throw the gun in the swamp.*

"This is perverse," Jean said angrily. "It's idiotic."

My father's eyes slid over to glare at Jean. "I've already warned you, Moss, not to interfere," he growled, and with that, he began to regain his purpose.

April was having trouble holding the gun properly in her bandaged hand. She refused to look at me and I couldn't tell if she wanted me to take it from her or not.

"Maybe use your other hand," my father coached. He sounded both encouraging and troubled.

"But I'm right-handed, Dad. I can't use my left hand."

I still wasn't sure if this was a charade on her part or not.

"Are you all crazy?" Jean said.

My father paused to give Jean a long, mean look. I almost thought he might tackle him.

"Shut up, Jean," I hissed.

Dad turned back to April and said, "Okay, honey, okay. Then get closer. I'll count you down."

With horror, I watched my sister step towards Petunia and train the gun on her. She moved deliberately, yet as if in a daydream, the way she had been moving all summer. Like she was already thinking of being somewhere else.

Don't do it, I thought. *It's not fair.*

"Let's not go through with this, Dad," April said. "It's not fair to Petunia. You know that."

"Deftly put, April. But if you don't do it, I will." And he took a step towards her.

"No! Stay there, Dad. I'll do it."

"Then hook your index finger over the trigger. Yes, that's right. One, two..."

I had a sudden desire to make a dash for it—to sprint out into that field among the bales of hay or dive into the swamp or run in circles around my family. My attention was drawn to a group of birds fussing loudly in the willows bordering the swamp, and I caught a glimpse of blurry movement in the foliage. It was a relief to look elsewhere, if only for a moment.

"Three."

April fired the pistol three times. The first two times I thought she was aiming for the swamp, but it was hard to tell, because her hand was so shaky. Petunia began bouncing around on stiffened legs, straining on the rope and yapping like a maniac.

I was confused by what she did next—like she was trying to hide the gun in the folds of her clothing. *That's not going to work. Dad can see what you're doing.* Then there was the third shot.

I had expected the shots to be louder. Even so, several cawing crows emerged from the tree tops and into the sky, taking less time to react than April, whose expression was slowly shaping up as puzzlement.

Well, what did you expect? I thought angrily.

Her face had quickly paled and lengthened. She looked unfamiliar, a little like this girl who'd sat in front of us in Biology in tenth grade. The girl had expensive clothes and chalky skin, and rarely smiled or spoke. She'd been unmemorable, but now, out of the blue, I was thinking that kids must have been picking on her—was it that group in the back? And that right now, my sister looked exactly like her.

April, who didn't look like April, had shot herself. I thought it again to be sure: April shot herself. Yet her body did not seem to obey gravity. She was floating upright, while my own legs were as rooted and graceless and unable to move as in any bad dream.

She put a hand to her belly and sunk down to her knees, then positioned herself carefully on her side in the dirt. She struggled to pull her knees up. Her blood, no longer safe inside her body, began to come out darkly near her waist.

Jean and my father were moving on her. I watched Jean crouch and scan her face, then speak her name with detachment, like he was a teacher doing roll call. His fingers scrambled through her clothing and he examined her with a quick, adept manner that prevented us from seeing what he saw. His face was unemotional. He covered her wound with both hands, looked up and locked eyes with mine. He nearly spoke to me.

But he changed his mind and turned to my father, who was kneeling beside him, and said, "Grab my medical bag. Back seat. Now, please."

My father sprang to his feet and got Jean's bag. His face was flushed. Jean withdrew his bloody hands from April's waist and pressed a wad of bandages against her, somewhere in the vicinity of her belly button, and spoke her name again. She might have made the sound of one word, but I wasn't sure, and Jean told her to stay with him as he got an arm beneath her. As he shifted her, I saw the back of her T-shirt was covered in dust.

Somehow he managed to carry her to his car and keep that bandage pressed to her belly without help from any of us. Likely he was in a territorial mood. There were no objections from my father, anyway.

Jean was laying her in the back of the Datsun when he spoke to my father again. "Dover Clinic. I'll ride in the back with her. You'll drive. Hurry!" He was speaking loudly and I had a hunch he was starting to panic.

My father got in the driver's seat and had the car moving before he'd shut his door.

"We'll take the Ambassador," my mother said to me eventually. It sounded like such a dumb thing to say.

It took several minutes to free Petunia, who had spun around so many times she was tangled in the rope and wanted to do a thorough apologetic licking of my hands and face first. I ordered her to get in the car, and she went directly to the Ambassador and hopped up into the back seat. I threw the rope in beside her.

My mother and I got into the station wagon and closed the doors. She reached for the ignition and stopped. We were both looking at the gun where April had dropped it in the dirt. I felt like I'd been running. I was wet between my legs and realized I'd started bleeding a week early.

"That shouldn't be left there," I said.

"Will you fetch that thing?" Mom asked, as though I had not spoken. "We should get home. We should be near the telephone."

It was dusk suddenly. Above the hayfield, fireflies were flashing on and off.

233

TWELVE

April was not detained at the Dover Medical Clinic more than ten minutes before being taken by ambulance to Jordan Hospital in Plymouth where we had been born. She was rushed into surgery.

I didn't visit April in the hospital. My parents wouldn't allow it, as though April shooting herself was symptomatic of something they didn't want me to catch, or a tendency to do myself in they didn't want roused from its dormancy.

But I didn't want to shoot myself any more than I wanted to visit her.

My mother explained she'd had an operation. I pretended to be interested.

"They had to remove her womb," she said, sounding as though everyone's life was now ruined.

Meanwhile, my period was unusually heavy.

"I'm glad we were there when she woke up."

"What did she have to say for herself?" I asked.

"Not much," Dad said moodily. "She was sluggish from whatever they used to put her under."

"She was horribly thirsty. She was begging for water, wasn't she, Russell?"

My father was standing in front of the closed refrigerator as though he could see through its door. He was always scolding April and me for standing with it wide open and letting all the cold escape.

"The nurses said she could have one sip of water," Mom said. "But your sister grabbed the cup and gulped down nearly all of it. They had to struggle to get it out of her hands."

My father looked sideways at me and we both grinned.

"And then she threw up," my mother said, annoyed the two of us would admire April's disobedience. "Those nurses know what they're doing."

But my mother changed her mind about the nurses knowing what they were doing when April slipped out of the hospital ten days later, right under their noses, and disappeared.

A note appeared in our mailbox at the end of the driveway, across the street from the stand, the next morning. It wasn't even in an envelope. They must have driven over in the Datsun in the night. I wondered where he had been all this time. Sleeping in his car in the hospital parking lot in Plymouth? Would that have been a smart idea?

The note said:

Dear Pilgrim, Mom and Dad,
I'm going with Jean. I'm all healed. I'm just fine.
Don't come looking for me.
—April.

"Does that sound like your sister?" my mother asked me. She was grasping at straws.

"It's her handwriting," I pointed out.

My mother went to speak with Dr. Bruck late one afternoon. She didn't tell us she was going, but she couldn't stop herself from telling us when she got home. She said he'd been particularly unhelpful. He was having a cocktail at his mahogany desk when she walked in, and though the sight of it caused her to immediately lose hope, she asked him how in heaven's name those nurses could have let April go.

"She's sixteen, Marsha," Dr. Bruck told her. "She has certain legal rights she didn't have a year ago. She can leave home, for example. She can leave school, for cripes sake."

"But how could they just let her go?"

I imagined Dr. Bruck took a minute then to study my mother. Maybe he had been looking forward to his manhattan since lunch, when he'd had his last one, and now he had to speak and breathe and make eye contact with this woman, all under the pretense that it wasn't sitting there at his elbow, the ice cubes hissing faintly.

Dr. Bruck had never met Jean, but it was likely he'd been hearing about him all summer and was more than a little surprised to see my mother. I imagined he still wasn't over the fact that Russell Bell had orchestrated the setting up of a practice by a Negro doctor over in the Cranfield sticks without conferring with anyone in the medical community first. Even so, he may have felt sympathy for my mother, especially since he must have sometimes wondered if she was a few spoons short of a set.

"I did have the chance to speak with April's attending surgeon," he said. "I was at Jordan Hospital on another matter. I hope you don't mind?"

My mother shook her head numbly. She had no idea what he was asking. Her daughter had shot herself then disappeared.

"I realize I may no longer be April's physician, but I have known her since she was an infant and naturally I was concerned." He put a fingertip on the side of the cocktail glass and withdrew it.

"I can tell you that April has made a promising recovery. It's unfortunate what's happened. What she's lost. But she's healthy and strong. For small girls, those two were always hardy."

He smiled and added, probably because my mother looked as though she needed more, "I remember when Pilgrim came in with that broken wrist. April stood over there against the wall. Mute, pale as that ceiling. Frankly, I was more concerned about her. I tried to get her to wait outside with you, but she wouldn't budge. She's a loyal girl, Mrs. Bell, you don't have anything to worry about."

I thought my father would lose it when my mother repeated this conversation to us, given his disdain for Dr. Bruck, but he just nodded. Perhaps he was mulling it over and wondering, like me, whether that business about being sixteen and having certain legal rights was baloney or not.

My mother brightened at my father's lack of reaction. "What are you going to do, Russell?"

"Nothing," he said. "She'll be back in a couple weeks."

My father expressed no sense of responsibility for the shooting, nor did he consider April's disappearance a kind of reckoning. When I think of the two years that followed, which would be my last in Cranfield, I think of three things—apart from our loss of April. One was Jimmy Carter's appointment of Andrew Young as US Ambassador to the United Nations, the first Black American to this position, which for weeks my father spoke of daily and took as a rattled affirmation of his action in bringing Jean to this country, more or less illegally, despite his later action in firing Jean, more or less at gunpoint.

Another was my father's renewed interest in the cranberry-growing business, which was a cooperative venture not with my mother, but with Mrs. McNadden.

The last was the return of the feral cat.

Later, I heard there were people who thought my father should have been charged for what happened to April, but the police said there was nothing with which they could charge him, not even cruelty to animals. I read this in the *Dover Weekly,* which included a photograph of my father, then I threw the paper in the woodstove.

I avoided looking at myself in the mirror, because it was April's face I saw, not mine. There were days when I could barely speak to people, both at home and at school, because it was April's voice I heard coming out of my mouth, not mine. I didn't know what to say anymore, what words to choose, what thoughts to express. Some mornings I spent an excessive amount of time trying to decide what to wear to school, where everyone knew about the shooting. I got into the habit of waking late in the silent house and missing the bus.

Sometimes, I simply forgot she was gone. At school I glanced up from my desk to see where she was. At home, stirring a glass of milk and Nestlé Quik, I expected her to request one, too. Or, putting my coat on, I waited for her to call out, asking me where I was going.

I was worried sick about her, knowing she was finding people perplexing and unfriendly, and the land not just hot but parched and suffering. Nothing at all like either of us had imagined it. And the food. The food was strange, and I wasn't there to sample it with her, as I had been when we were little. I almost hoped she tossed the food on the floor and upset Jean. As time passed, I felt her homesickness lessen, and I don't know if that was because of me or her. Sometimes I thought she was coming home, but maybe she was only thinking about it.

But I knew something she did not: Jean would not be allowed back in the country, so if she did return, she would have to return alone.

It was Dr. Bruck, of course, who contacted the Immigration and Naturalization Service, which led to our learning that Jean did not have a licence to practise medicine in the Commonwealth of Massachusetts. Or in any US state, for that matter.

"The law takes that quite seriously," said the sweaty immigration officer who drove down from Boston to interview my parents.

"Well, he didn't practise, now, did he?" my father told the officer. "Racism turns out to be the name of the game around here."

The man was sitting at our kitchen table with my parents. Dad was not being friendly and Mom was remote and despondent, which I thought was understandable. When the man spoke his lips stuck together and he tapped his pen on the back of his hand. Someone should have offered him a cold drink, but no one thought of it. I was leaning against the refrigerator. Twice the man glanced at me and back at my mother as though it might be wise to excuse me from the ensuing conversation. He had a pack of Winstons in his breast pocket that he never touched.

The officer brought out a photograph to confirm we were talking about the same Jean Moss. My father examined it a full minute before handing it to me. The officer inhaled sharply at this but said nothing.

It was a high school graduation photo. Jean wore a jacket with a crest and striped tie and looked shockingly young—skinny, boyish, and oddly not all that dark. He'd been someone else before we knew him. Now he was someone else again. Despite everything, I wished I could keep the photo.

"So? Is it him?" the officer asked.

"What if I said no?" my father challenged.

"It's him," I said. "Where is this?"

"That one's taken at the London prep school he attended. Name escapes me. The Brits have been very helpful."

When I offered the photo to my mother, she grimaced as though she couldn't stomach the sight. "Surely any blame lies with the program," she suggested.

"What program?" the officer asked.

"The joint state and federal program that brought him here."

"This is news to me."

"It doesn't matter now," my father cut in. "They lost their chance. Let them drive to Dover to see that quack Dr. Bruck."

"Has it occurred to you, Mr. Bell, that Mr. Moss did not have any patients because he was not a licensed doctor?"

My father cocked his head at me. Please, I thought, don't say it.

"He had one patient, my daughter here. He did a real cracker-jack job, too."

The man turned to me as though maybe I was the key to this case after all. "You weren't feeling well?"

"I'm fine now."

He stared at me without speaking for several seconds. I wondered if he was trying to decide if he should continue with this particular line of inquiry, or let it pass.

"Hornet stings," my father said.

"That was the nature of the complaint?" the officer asked. "Hornet stings?"

I nodded.

"Did he examine you?" he continued, his tone warm and phony.

"No."

He put his pen down. "You mentioned a government program, Mrs. Bell. I'd like to get back to that. This is something we'll need to look into. Sounds like we might have a problem with screening."

"No," my father said. "That doesn't have anything to do with you."

"I'll be the judge of that, Mr. Bell."

My mother had perked up. "Russell?"

"Yes, Marsha."

"Tell the man the name of the program." When my father did not respond, she turned to me with a wild look. "Pilgrim, do you know?"

I shook my head.

"Russell!" We were all staring at my mother, including the immigration officer.

My father looked fed up.

"There was no goddamn program, was there?" my mother said.

"No, Marsha, there was no goddamn program," my father said in a whiny voice that was meant to imitate my mother but did not imitate her at all.

"Shit, Dad."

"Was this some kind of an experiment of yours, Russell?"

"Experiment?" the officer repeated. "Jean Moss broke US law."

"And now April is gone. I've just about had it, Russell, with your antics." My mother turned to address the officer. She looked like she was going to fall apart any moment and it was awful, watching her.

"Do you know where she is?" she asked him.

"What does it matter if he had a licence?" my father said. He was staring at me, as though there was still time for me to become his accomplice in this. "He was a doctor in another country, right? I don't get all the hysteria."

"Mr. Bell, the University of the West Indies is not one of your offshore medical schools that trains our kids to practise here at home. It's one of their own schools. Students are meant to practise in their own region. Do you see the distinction?"

"I repeat—"

"Can you just tell me where she is?" my mother said to the officer. "I just want to know she's okay."

"I'm sorry, Mrs. Bell, runaways aren't our concern, to be blunt," the officer said. "However, if you think of anything later and want to get hold of me"—he placed a business card in front of my mother—"you can give me a ring."

"She'll be back," my father assured us.

"Shut up, Russell."

"Dad, you don't know that."

"Let me share a little something with you," my father said, and how I wished the immigration officer did not have to hear this. "When our neighbour caught them, he was cowering in the back seat of that pansy car. With his face in his hands. April will be back. Mark my words."

It's doubtful the officer knew what my father was referring to, but it was at this point that he put his paper and pen, and the graduation photo of Jean, back in his briefcase, along with a bunch of forms he must have decided were not going to be necessary after all.

"There's one thing I can offer you," he said just before leaving, looking at my mother and me by turns, and ignoring my father. "If this Moss character knows what's good for him, he'll have returned to the mumbo-jumbo country from whence he came." The officer stood by the door. He was jiggling his shoulders, perhaps unconsciously, to loosen the damp fabric that had become bunched under his armpits.

"The Bahamas," my mother said, as though it were no closer than the moon.

"Right. And I daresay he better stay there. If he knows what's good for him," the officer repeated.

After he left, letting himself out since no one got up, the three of us sat there, avoiding each other's eyes.

"Runaway," my mother said softly. "God in heaven."

It's true, none of us had used the term "runaway." A runaway was a hard case who had to get out of a hard case situation. Runaways were in the news. They lived on the streets, they met the wrong types, they were never seen again.

As I was leaving the room, my father mumbled something about instinct being the voice of DNA. "If you run, you run," he said scornfully.

He had not mentioned DNA for so long, I was surprised.

I had started up the stairs when I heard my mother saying, "I want that weapon out of this house." Until that moment, I had not thought about the pistol, and I stopped to listen. "Do you understand me, Russell?"

"You've made your point."

"And I don't want to hear the word 'racism' in this house ever again. Racist? Face it. If we hadn't overreacted, she wouldn't be a runaway."

"She wanted to marry him, Marsha. Is that what you wanted?"

"That was nothing more than a bit of dramatics, Russell. It didn't mean anything. We could have handled it. We could have waited it out until she got over him."

"I didn't see it that way."

"Suggesting she shoot that poor dog? It's appalling what you did, Russell. And I stood by and let you. I'll never forgive myself."

"I didn't suggest it. She did. That ludicrous excuse for a dog—"

"And everyone from here to Plymouth knows about it."

"—should be dead."

I figured he must have glanced around the kitchen then, searching for Petunia, because my mother said hotly, "Don't you dare do anything to Petunia. Don't you dare."

I continued up the stairs to my room—my very own room now—where I flopped down on April's bed and stared at the poster of Rod Stewart tacked to the ceiling.

I figured my father's secret wish had been to shoot Jean. Shooting Petunia—whom my sister loved, too—was the next best thing. And within the law.

Jean can take his own car, he'd said. *And bring the pillow dog.*

But it was risky. You lead a bunch of jumpy, overwrought people to a clearing and take out a gun, and someone is bound to get hurt.

Dad and Mrs. McNadden could often be seen inspecting the abandoned cranberry bog behind our house, both in rubber boots, their heads swivelling every which way with indefatigable enthusiasm and scheming. Once I was shovelling manure from the chicken coop and saw the two of them crossing the bog under a sky filled with shiny sunlight and fast-moving black clouds. It was October by then. Dad was carrying a bucket of sand that he was spreading over the plants with a gloved hand. Another time I saw him, alone, going at the brush and tall weeds with a scythe.

My father alleged it had once been a fully operating cranberry bog. He remembered it from when he was a boy—in the fall the Portuguese pickers moving over it on their knees, working their scoops, and along the banks the wooden boxes piled high and orderly. Now the bog was filled in with cattails, goldenrod and Joe-pie weed, but the cranberry plants were still there—my father would be happy to show them to anyone who doubted. His first order of business was to control drainage, and God only knew how he was going to do that, my mother remarked. My father responded by saying Lois had volunteered to make some calls.

But Mrs. McNadden's brother-in-law was still waiting for his rent and Jean's medical supplies had been costly. Mom was furious when she learned Dad had taken out a small loan against the farm in order to equip the doctor's office, with the expectation the loan would be paid back by patient fees.

Without ready cash for irrigation equipment or machine harvesters, my father and Mrs. McNadden undertook to dry-harvest. It was an inspired decision. It would meet a growing demand by the nature folks for fresh berries, and was the traditional picking method besides. The wooden cranberry scoops and rakes were cheap — in fact, Dad predicted they could be picked up for next to nothing in antique stores and flea markets. It was a win-win.

"He's delusional," my mother told me. "He still has to irrigate. He knows so little about plants. He's out there trampling all over them."

Mrs. McNadden joined my father on other projects as well. She got over her fear of butchering chickens and took my place dunking them in hot water and tossing them in the plucker. The first time my father requested my assistance after April was gone, I flat out refused. My father turned away from me, as though it only stood to reason that he continue to be disappointed in his family, and drove off in his truck to find Mrs. McNadden.

Mom began pestering the immigration officer. This went on for a while, until he became unavailable to take further calls. Yet she did learn a few things he'd not been inclined to share the day he visited. Such as that while Jean had spent much of his childhood in the Bahamas, after the age of twelve he attended London private schools. He returned to the Caribbean, where he was accepted at medical school in Jamaica. His mother, deceased, had been white. He'd had one sibling, an older sister who passed away young, and he was in possession of a house and property on a small island. Information on his father was thin, but Immigration assumed he had been—or was—black, and that his parents had not had, as they put it, a matrimonial relationship.

"Your father feels betrayed," my mother tried to explain one morning as she drove me to school. I'd missed the bus again and she and Dad were cracking down on my absenteeism.

I thought she meant because of April. "That's why he won't try to find her?"

"No," Mom said. "Betrayed by Jean. Your father thought he was giving a poor Bahamian boy the chance to change his life."

"But then he bought the Datsun?"

"Exactly," Mom said.

"Dad assumed Jean was dirt poor because of his colour?"

She nodded.

"When he found out he wasn't dirt poor, he didn't like him anymore?"

"Perhaps not as much," Mom admitted.

"That's sort of like being prejudiced, isn't it?" I said.

"I think they got off to a bad start with the snake."

Mom and I never mentioned the other matter, though, the one that was there in the car as we drove, next to the table while we ate, over our beds as we slept, which was that April and Jean might be married. In fact, within a few weeks of April's disappearance, we didn't speak of her in relation to Jean at all, as though the two had never crossed paths. Mom might have said to me, "Can you put this blanket on April's bed?" or "Are these boots yours or April's?"

But neither of us ever said, "I wonder if they're married now."

I was often first awake in the morning and would come down-stairs to find my mother asleep on the sofa, Petunia pressed against her side. After the stand closed that fall, Mom became aimless, wandering from room to room, where she paused brief-ly, or from chair to chair, where she sat briefly. Her normal fall activities—spreading the fields with manure, planting spring bulbs, bottling jams and jellies, pencilling notes in her planting journal, and thumbing through seed catalogues—were forsaken.

It was late in the fall when the feral cat reappeared. We first noticed him making a dash at dusk from one of the sheds, where he took up lounging during the day. He was quick-moving and hugged the earth with his solid rectangular body as he disappeared into the woods. My mother loathed him. He chased the barn toms away and wouldn't let you approach him, even if you did have a saucer of milk or pat of butter.

"He's bad news, Russell. He can't be tamed. I don't see why you won't trap him."

My father refused. He said he didn't have good enough reason.

"Trap him, Russell," my mother begged. "He scares Petunia."

My father was never rude to my mother. He did not say, "Will you shut up." But he looked as though he would have liked to. In fact, he looked as though he would have liked to go upstairs and pack some things and get in his truck.

"Give me a break," he said. "She's a dog. She can't remember anything beyond a minute in time."

After he left, my mother began whispering. I didn't know if she was speaking to me or to herself. Then she was right up close beside me.

"What?" I asked, backing away from her.

"He's out to get Petunia."

"Dad?"

She shook her head.

"Mom, what are you talking about?"

"That cat."

"Huh?"

"He terrorizes Petunia. I've seen him. He stalks her."

I had gradually begun to ignore Petunia. I was aggravated by her silent, needy looks and developed an aversion to the smell of her breath and body. I did not welcome her into my bedroom anymore, and eventually she kept out of my way as much as I did hers.

"Where's the dog now?" I asked my mother.

"In the closet."

"She can take care of herself," I said, not believing this for a minute.

"If you say so. She doesn't go out anymore, so that's good news."

"It is," I said, without feeling. My mother put her hand on my back. A gesture of gratitude. I waited for her to withdraw it.

It was true that Petunia, curled up in a ball in a closet or turning in circles as she snapped at imaginary flies, never left the house, and I didn't know how she and my mother worked around this and the calls of nature, but the feral cat got her anyway.

THIRTEEN

After April ran away with Jean, I took up smoking—which so baffled my father he could barely reproach me—and applied for scholarships at a dozen or so colleges and universities. The applications were still in my room, but had been shoved under April's bed and forgotten. Montreal seemed exotic, intriguing. I pictured devout Roman Catholics moving among gloomy gothic buildings blanketed in snow.

Identical twins are indistinguishable from a distance. Never in my life had a person, other than April and my mother, called out to me, confident it was me they saw and whose attention they sought. But this was what I experienced at McGill, first with classmates, later with Ethan. These people were not making a fifty-fifty guess. Suddenly I was aware of myself as never before, as though I had drifted out from beneath a shadow or haze.

From the start, I was early for classes and study groups. It was a way to control things in a place where everything was unfamiliar, where I was terrified by being alone. I struggled to choose a major. Engineering, biology, chemistry, philosophy, literature: I was curious about them all, but none excessively. Identifying a major would describe me. Make me unique.

At the end of my first semester I went home for Christmas, but it was a journey I would repeat only a few times.

Mom and Dad picked me up in Dover—the bus no longer made stops in Cranfield—and the three of us went to Dairy Queen for supper. Dining out was something our family had rarely done, and I could see they were making an effort to mark my visit. My father commented that if a cherry dipped cone was still my favourite, I shouldn't hesitate to get one for dessert, which I did, even though it made my throat scratchy. Cherry dipped had been April's favourite. I told them about Montreal, the dorm, my courses, and they listened without asking a single question. It was almost as though they found my words incomprehensible, which surprised me, since my father had always been so inquisitive about the world and it had been his idea that I pursue education in Canada.

He explained he was doing a lot of reading on alternative methods of cranberry harvesting. Mom said he was up against serious competition, and my father said he wasn't doing it to make the big bucks, it was experimental farming. My mother took a bite out of a french fry and gave me a look, but her protest was weak. I had missed her in Montreal that fall, which struck me as a normal thing for a daughter to experience, and I was looking forward to spending time with her.

I was tired from the travel and went to bed early. The bedroom I once shared with April had not been touched in my absence, and as I drifted off, I decided to only come into the room to sleep and dress. Otherwise I risked being swamped by memories of her.

Before going downstairs the next morning, I stopped at the door to my parents' room and looked inside. The bed was unmade, the sheets and pillows and woolen blankets in a tumble, evidence that two people had slept there and that my mother had stopped camping out on the sofa in the living room.

On the kitchen table there was a note from Mom saying she and Dad were doing errands, including a run to Bishop's Farm Feed. I could not remember them both going off on an errand of that sort together, ever. It was gloomy and rainy out, so I wandered around the house with Bandit at my heels until my parents returned, but almost as soon as Dad had taken his coat off, he put it on again and went back outside.

"I waited to have lunch," I told my mother, who was putting away a bag of groceries. I was tracing my finger along the grains of wood on the kitchen table, just as I'd done a thousand times.

"Oh, sweet pea, we ate," my mother said apologetically. "Your father was starved. We stopped at that place in Hallsburg."

"Where did he just go now?"

"He has to repair the electric fence."

"Then why did he drive off in the truck?"

"Pilgrim, I don't have the answers to everything."

I was hungry, but when I opened the refrigerator I couldn't think what I might like to eat. Mom came up beside me to slide a tub of margarine into the fridge and said, "I'll be out of your way in a jiff." After she left the kitchen I heard her going down into the cellar.

Later that day the rain stopped and I went out for a walk. Everything was either brown or yellow, and the trees bare except for the oaks, whose stiff, papery leaves would hang on through the winter. But the sun was out, gleaming on the wet surface of things, and the air smelled earthy and sweet. Bandit and Tansy came along, one ahead of me, one behind, as though to keep me where I needed to be. I considered checking to see if in fact the charge was out of the electric fence by touching it lightly with a finger, but then thought, why bother? I headed back to the house.

It struck me that my parents were managing better now —better than before I left. I wondered if having a single daughter around the place was a sad reminder that there had once been a pair. That it was too hard to have only half of what had once been one.

When I returned to Montreal I was ambushed by a longing for April, despite having been successful at not thinking about her in Cranfield. It was a heartsickness I couldn't shake. I despaired of the snow and biting cold, which had not turned out to be in any way exotic or intriguing.

Then spring arrived, creeping up on the city, whose air became soft and blue-hued. On my way to chemistry lab one day I stopped to linger over the sight of crocuses emerging through the thinning campus snow.

I was thirty minutes early and alone in the lab when a young man burst in.

"I'm sorry I'm late," he said, then looked around, puzzled.

"You're not late, you're early."

"Doubtful."

"The lab doesn't start until three."

"You're positive about that? Dr. Aramack's Chem 297?"

I nodded and turned my back on him and opened a book.

After a while he spoke to me again, but in a more conciliatory tone: "I thought it started at two thirty. My mistake."

Goosebumps rose on the back of my neck. There was something about the way he spoke. I turned slowly around and stared at him.

"I'm the new teaching assistant," he explained.

"What happened to Monique?"

"She broke her leg. Skiing over the weekend. What a winter. So much snow."

Monique was his girlfriend, I later pieced together.

"Well, the snow is melting now," I said neutrally.

He frowned. I gave him an encouraging look, and he barely hesitated before launching into the importance of understanding the action of sublimation as it related to the chemistry of weather: the transition of snow directly into damp water vapour when heated by the spring sun.

He articulated each word so precisely he almost sounded wooden. I didn't know what to make of him. The other students were coming in and getting settled.

"I'm sorry if that was pedantic of me," he remarked, sounding bewildered, then walked to the front of the lab to introduce himself to the class.

His name was Ethan Wheeler, a graduate student in chemical engineering.

I decided I would get the highest mark in the lab.

Over the term I learned as much as I could about him. He'd grown up in Stockholm. His father was an American businessman and his mother was British, a translator. He'd attended American

255

expat schools—the reason, I decided, for his careful, proper pronunciation of the English language.

But this was the only thing about him that reminded me of Jean.

Ethan was confident, rigorous, predictable, and openly affectionate—even in the lab, in front of the other students, even before he and Monique split up, a fact he clumsily shared one day. If I asked an astute question or had the textbook answer, or sometimes, made a mildly successful joke, he might throw an arm around my shoulders and squeeze me against his side. It seemed he'd find any excuse to praise me, but he was jovial about it, buddy-buddy. Each time I would steal a whiff of him: airy and subtle, a hint of laundry soap.

Eventually I became aware of two students, Mary and Adelaide, watching me, often when Ethan was hovering near my desk, but sometimes when I was alone. People had always stared at April and me because we were twins. I was used to it. But now when I walked into a room and someone looked at me, I grew anxious. Was there something wrong with me? With the way I dressed, or walked, or spoke?

Mary and Adelaide were lab partners, confident and cool, the type I never expected to speak to me. Their experiments generally resulted in disaster and muffled laughter. Ethan, unimpressed, mostly ignored them, and I was shocked by how easy it was for them to sail through class with such little care. It wasn't just that they were wasting money, they were wasting time.

As the weeks passed I grew more and more uncomfortable under their scrutiny, until one day Mary arrived early, just a few minutes after I had. When she came through the door and looked at me, I could see she knew I'd be there alone, though

I never asked how. She immediately launched into a string of banal comments, including how dead boring the course was and I nodded, though I felt I was betraying Ethan and the truth was, I genuinely liked chemistry. Eventually she dug out her lab book.

She said she was failing and asked if I would mind explaining a few things.

When I saw the cover of her lab book I realized I'd had her name wrong: it was Merry. Merry Whittaker. I wondered if her parents had given her this name, or if she'd given it to herself.

I told her sure, I didn't mind.

For several weeks Merry arrived early and we reviewed the previous week's lab. Soon we began meeting at a coffeehouse. I was giving her the answers, but I didn't care. Once I explained a concept, she got it. She was quick, but seemed to have a lot going on in her life. She waited tables and lived in an apartment full of students, all of which kept her busy, up late, and in high spirits.

She was short, like me, but softer, a little plump. She had wavy blonde hair and wore a stud in her nostril and smelled of garlic, patchouli oil, and hash. She seemed to have a string of boyfriends. We became friends, which astonished me.

"Adelaide?" Merry said dismissively when I asked. "I went to high school with her. I don't really know her."

The two had grown up in Westmount, an affluent anglophone suburb of Montreal. Like me, Merry didn't see much of her parents, though I never knew why, especially since they were no distance away. But it was something we liked about each other, that we shared a quiet, unexplained estrangement from our families.

"There's something about you," Merry said one day as we were having coffee. "You're brainy and conscientious, but different.

Peculiar. Oh, I mean in a good way! Everyone else is so boring. You're not insulted, are you?"

But I wasn't insulted. Her words came as a surprise and filled me with wonder. They were like a gift.

Ethan didn't make an appearance at our last lab, and I told myself he'd never acted as though I was anything more than the student with the highest marks. Monique came instead, still on crutches but keen to apologize for breaking her leg in three places. She wished us the best of luck. I waited in vain for her to mention Ethan—her gratitude, and our good fortune, that he'd been available to take over from her. His whereabouts. Anything.

The next day I moved out of the dorm and into Merry's apartment. It was on the second floor of a triplex, with a wrought-iron external staircase that wound up to an ornate balcony and the entrance to the apartment. Though it was crowded, Merry saw to it that I had my own room, which was small and faced onto the back courtyard. She also got me a job waitressing at the restaurant where she worked.

My first day, Merry introduced me to Matt, the dishwasher. I suspected she had once dated him but she never confirmed this. He had shaggy blonde hair and a sloppy, dishevelled appearance, but he hosed down the kitchen floor at the end of the night in an aggressive, dramatic manner that attracted me to him. We slid into a relationship easily, without fanfare, with barely any courtship. He was undemanding, perhaps because I never knew what he was thinking. I didn't tell my parents about him.

I telephoned home every week. My mother commented on the lack of rain, a tornado that had touched down in Worcester County without warning and killed five, an accident in front of the stand when a truck hit a parked car—bad for business, with the customers overreacting and asking what if there'd been a child in the car. I rarely spoke to my father.

Midway through August, Mom asked whether I planned on coming home for a visit that summer.

"Can't," I said. "Classes are starting up again soon."

It was a relief for me she hadn't mentioned this until it was too late. I think it was a relief for her, too. That evening a few friends came by, including Matt. We smoked hash and listened to Fleetwood Mac. Merry was on the floor beside me, and across from us, one of our roommates, Lily, lay with her head in Matt's lap. Her eyes were closed and she was singing along to the music, barely coherently.

Merry leaned over and asked if I cared.

I shook my head.

"Pilgrim, you're too generous."

"What did you say?" Lily asked, opening her eyes. "She's what?"

"A woman of integrity," Merry told her.

"I think Pilgrim's shy," someone else offered. "Shy and sweet."

"Shy, but I don't know about sweet," Merry said.

I had that feeling again — of surprise and wonder — that people could have any impressions of me at all.

"Sit up, Lily," Matt groaned. "I think my legs are gone to sleep."

I woke the next morning to the sound of church bells ringing. Beside me, Matt was breathing rhythmically, and I stared at his bare shoulder, thinking I didn't want him to stay over anymore. I slipped out of bed and went to sit in a chair on the other side of the room to wait for him to wake.

I'd left my window open a few inches because of the previous day's heat and humidity, but overnight it had rained and the air had turned fresh and glossy in the morning light.

I was suddenly exhilarated with the idea of Matt leaving and of being alone in my room. It was a feeling like bliss, like something physically pleasing. As though a lid was opening on the top of my head in the middle of winter and letting the sun beat down into my core. I wanted only myself for company.

The fall semester began and I chose a Communication major and Business minor, while Merry continued to struggle with building up any enthusiasm for her coursework. In November, she stopped going to classes and announced she was moving to Japan to train at a Zen monastery. She bought a huge backpack and filled it with clothing, trail mix, and condoms. I accompanied her to the airport. I didn't ask about the absence of her parents.

"I may never see you again, Pilgrim," she said solemnly. "I may never return to Canada."

We hugged each other goodbye, then I watched her, dwarfed by that backpack, disappear through Customs.

I hung around through Christmas, alone in the apartment, my remaining roommates dispersed for the holidays. There were several blizzards in a row and instead of plowing to bare pavement, the city trucks bladed the snow to a level pack. I loved the look of our street, with its rows of metal staircases, now hung with icicles, twisting down from the second-floor balconies. For the first time, Montreal seemed exotic, the way I had imagined it back in Cranfield. I bundled up and took long, fast hikes through the city, and then one day I entered the nearly empty McGill library and began researching identical twins.

From the time that April and I were toddlers, my father had wanted us to believe we were extraordinary, so the first thing I looked up was the birth rate of identical twins and was not overly surprised to learn it was about one in 250 births. Ours was not the only fertilized egg in the history of humankind to mysteriously split within the first two weeks of conception, forming a pair of siblings with an identical arrangement of amino acids—siblings who may have once imagined God was a little man who crawled inside their mother's belly to build them piece by matching piece.

I read about twins as alike as if they had been factory-manu-factured, whose sense of being was not of one person, but of two, and I felt a cold chill of recognition. I read about twins who pushed and punched each other in the womb, whose separate identities were developing before they were even out of the gate, and I was dizzy with relief they had not been us.

A week after Christmas break, I was leaving the library late in the day when a voice called out my name—something that still startled me.

Ethan came bounding up the steps. He said he'd been in Aberdeen, on work term. He embraced me and the side of my face sunk into his thick parka.

"I think dinner is in order here," he declared, speaking in that slightly formal, stilted way of his. "You're not busy, are you?"

I laughed and shook my head where it still rested against his shoulder because he hadn't yet let go of me.

"I've been looking all over campus for you," he said. "Did you know that?"

"I had a hunch," I told him.

"There's something different about you," he said, awkwardly trying out his new Scottish brogue.

Unlike Merry, Ethan pressed me for information about my home and family. It is possible he would have accepted anything about me, yet I told him I'd been an only child and my parents were dead. Linked to them meant linked to a runaway twin sister who'd shot herself, and whenever I considered exposing her, I felt the encroachment of our DNA on my growing sense of self. I feared stepping back into that haze where my identity was a shared identity—where, in Ethan's eyes, I might not be as special as he seemed to think I was. I believed myself best revealed through secrecy.

I stopped reading about twins. I was busy, seeing Ethan almost daily, and I had a lot of coursework.

Despite my new life and new identity and the passage of time, a part of me was always aware of April. Occasionally I would wonder where she lived, if she worked, if Jean was still in her life. Was she even alive? I was certain I would know if she wasn't.

I would imagine what we might have shared if we had not lost each other, and I would remember details about her, like the smell of her breath and dry, summery hair, or those cold nights when I climbed in bed with her and she'd wrap herself around me without waking.

FOURTEEN

During my three weeks back in Cranfield, I've been allowed to talk to Katie only twice. When I call she is—Ethan claims—taking the dog for a walk, already in bed, or at a friend's house. It appears he has decided to shield her from me. Or punish me. He is finding it difficult to forgive me for lying all those years, and I am finding it difficult to care that he can't.

Then, in early November, I wake one morning before dawn and hear Katie's voice so clearly inside my head, she could be in the room with me. I don't move, but wait beneath the quilt for the grey room to take shape and offer me a three-dimensional, familiar living room. The furniture, fireplace, and jars of dried flowers slowly emerge. I glance at the silent wall clock. Behind its dimpled glass the pendulum hangs eerily still, as though mocking my understanding of place and time.

I flip the musty quilt off and put my feet on the floor and sit up.

At nine o'clock, I telephone a lawyer recommended by Mrs. Godfrey and make an appointment for later that morning.

Dan Boucher is young and jumpy, with a close haircut and expensive suit.

Right away we hit a snag. My father named his daughters executors of his will, and various petitions and forms will require both signatures.

"He named your mother, originally," Dan says, playing with an elastic band. "But he asked me to change it, after she went into care. How difficult will it be to chase down your twin sister? Do you need our assistance on that?"

I don't like the way he puts it, like my family's history is everyone's business.

"Your father had an outstanding invoice with us," he adds. "Whoops." The elastic band launches out of his hands, nearly clipping my shoulder on its way across the office.

"Just give me the documents," I tell him. "And the invoice."

I head to the nursing home after the lawyer's appointment, but instead of going in right away, I sit in the car and take out my cell. The sky is cloudless and the sunlight is angling through the leafless trees, as bright as it will ever be at this time of year.

"Fred started obedience school last night," Ethan tells me right away.

"How's Katie? She doing her homework?"

"Of course she is."

"Obedience school?" I ask, because I know he's waiting for me to ask this.

"Yeah, Fred bit someone, the Cunninghams had guests. They were very nice about it, but that was the agreement. Obedience school. It's not a bad idea. He's been picking up some bad habits."

"What were you doing at the Cunninghams'?"

"They invited us for dinner."

"Us?"

"Katie and me. Katie was over playing with Ella," he adds. I'm not sure if there is an implication of wifely neglect or not.

Marie Cunningham, the quintessential Country Walk Estates wife and mother. In my mind's eye I try to get a fix on the neighbourhood and surrounding landscape. I see huge homes, spruce woods, tree lichen like Christmas tinsel, wet snow falling half the year.

One day I walked into the Cunninghams' to collect Katie and discovered a girl in a black dress and white apron vacuuming their living room. A white paper crown on her head.

I appreciate our heated floors, heat lamps in the bathrooms, argon gas windows. Never a winter's night when Katie has to wear her clothes to bed to stay warm. But I'd had an uncomfortable, tumbling feeling, standing there at the Cunninghams' and exchanging an embarrassed look with the cleaning girl, as though I'd briefly lost my footing.

"You brought the dog with you to the Cunninghams'?" I ask Ethan.

"I walked over."

Katie had been campaigning for a dog since before we left

Calgary. I would find newspaper articles photocopied and taped to things around the house: "People with Dogs Live Longer, Study Shows" on the bathroom mirror; "Pets Good for the Soul" on the microwave.

I said no. No dog. Absolutely not.

"Come on, Mom, please?" Katie begged. "Didn't you have a dog when you were a little girl?"

"No. My parents didn't allow pets."

The last was "Man's Best Friend Reduces Risk of Heart Attack" propped against the crystal salt and pepper shakers on the dinner table one evening. As I reached for my napkin I was aware of Ethan and Katie's stillness across from me. When I saw the article I wanted to crumble it brutally with my hands. Stamp on it. Roll over it on the floor with my flailing, protesting body. My lasagna — with porcini mushrooms and pancetta — was separating, the top layer slipping off and crashing into my salad. It was disappointing to see. I looked at Katie and Ethan.

"Okay," I told them. "I give up."

Katie ran around the house for ten minutes screeching with joy.

The animal shelter people said Fred was a year old. Half border collie, half Labrador retriever. He had a shaggy black coat, one erect ear and one floppy, and a white stripe between glassy, worried eyes.

One evening, as Katie practised her dance routine in the dining room, banging into furniture and ignoring her homework, I spotted Fred coming into the kitchen.

"Not a good time," I said, waving an arm at him. "Out you go."

He froze, briefly seized by an interest in something on the floor, and backed out of the kitchen.

"Mommy," Katie said, coming in a minute later.

"Write it on the calendar," I said. "So we won't forget."

"You don't even know what I'm going to say."

"Your recital dates?"

"You hurt Fred's feelings. Why can't he come in the kitchen?"

"I'm making dinner and the last thing I need is a dog under-foot. Have you finished your homework, Katie?"

"Blizzard warning in effect. No school tomorrow."

I looked out the window. Indeed, it was starting. Big, doughy flakes that were quick to accumulate. Once I had the sauce made and poured over the chicken and everything put in the oven, I wandered into the family room. I watched the snow collecting around the purple crocuses in our backyard, leaving them the only colour in the world.

In the morning I was up before anyone else, listening to the radio. High winds and blowing snow. Schools, banks—everything closed. But I had no interest in returning to bed. I took a mug of coffee to the family room and sat in the loveseat by the window, and there were the crocuses, exposed by the winds, ripped and finished for the year.

"What gives with that look on your face, Mommy?" Katie was standing in the doorway.

"Come here, honey. What look?"

"Like this." Katie pursed her lips and drew all the skin in around her eyes.

I looked at her and laughed, marvelling at how effortlessly she was becoming a unique person. "Really? I look like that?"

Katie nodded and snuggled in against my side. She was wearing baggy pyjamas with clouds and sheep.

"Look at the crocuses, Katie, they're like something landed from another planet."

"You look sad, Mommy. Are you crying?"

"Of course not." I pressed my hands into my eyes. "Just tired."

"That's your excuse?" Then, repentant: "No school?"

"No school."

"I was right."

"You were right, honey."

I heard the clatter of someone racing through the house, released from his kennel, and there was Fred, tearing into the room. I raised my foot to block him from leaping onto the loveseat with us and spilling coffee everywhere, and felt the impact shudder through his small frame.

Ethan appeared in the doorway, already dressed for work and gazing at us fondly.

Katie slipped off the loveseat onto the floor to begin anew Fred's lessons. "Paw, Fred, give me your paw." He swallowed several times and his good ear bristled alertly, but his attention span wasn't enormous. He glanced at me, then suddenly attacked his tail and chewed at it vigorously.

I looked over at Ethan. "You're going out in this?" I asked.

"All-wheel. I'll be fine."

"Coffee's made."

"Perfect." He looked handsome in that offhand way of his, nicely dressed and all squeaky clean, as though scrubbed down to some elemental goodness.

"Fred! Give me your paw."

Fred rolled over onto his back, exposing his belly and trying his best. "No!" Katie scolded. "I said *paw*. Not *roll over*."

"He's a dog, Katie," I reminded her. I thought what my father might have said and added, "He can't remember anything beyond a minute in time."

———

I light a cigarette and tell Ethan, "I've booked a flight home. Day after tomorrow."

"That's good news. I was afraid I was going to have come down and get you."

"Not sure what my next steps are here, anyway," I say vaguely.

"When you get back, we'll talk. I keep telling you I can help. How's your mother?"

"Just about to go in and see her," I say, staring at the home. "Every day is different. Some days"—I pause to take a drag on the cigarette—"she's all sweetness, while other days she shouts bloody murder if I just touch her."

"Are you smoking?"

"Right now?"

"Yeah, right now."

"Why?"

"That way you paused. Reminds me of talking with the guys out on the rigs."

"Sound sexy?"

"So you *are* smoking? Christ almighty, it's like I don't know you at all."

I press the button on the automatic window, which still lowers at a snail's pace, and wave the smoke out. I'm not sure what the policy is on smoking in rentals.

"I meant to ask, how's the mood there?" Ethan says, deciding to ignore my smoking for now. "In terms of the economy?"

"Bizarre. Awful. People just packing up and driving away, disappearing."

"Remember Murray and his new wife?" he asks, a little excited.

"Gone. She had a mother in Ohio, lost everything. They went down to try to sell the house. We made the right choice, coming here." He laughs. "They're still pumping out the oil here."

"Good thing," I say without enthusiasm.

"I guess the Americans are all worked up about Obama, one way or another?"

"They are. Put Katie on the phone."

He hesitates. "She's still sleeping."

"Why are you doing this?"

"She gets upset after she talks to you." He lowers his voice. "She misses you."

"So let me talk to her, Ethan."

"Listen, I'll let her know you're coming home. You'll see her then. I'm glad you're coming home, Pilgrim."

When I get back to the farmhouse that evening, I go into the living room and lift out the shoebox tucked under the card table.

Inside are a few photos, my parents' marriage licence, letters, and several Christmas cards from me with my return address on the envelopes—so this was how Mrs. McNadden found me.

Laid on top, as though it was the last item my father, or Mrs. McNadden, looked at, is a piece of schoolwork with the poem "Trees" copied out in a young, blocky hand. Below the poem is a brief summary: "In his poem Alfred Joyce Kilmer compares Trees to the beauty of the natural world especially the female form which is noted by his use of the words; BREAST, BOSOM and HAIR." In the top corner it reads, "Russell Bell, Grade Ten, Essay No. 5, Miss Freeley."

He received a C–. The grade is underlined twice and circled. Miss Freeley wrote, "Russell Bell, you can do better."

I smile. My father: once a relatively obedient, albeit lazy, boy. This was not the father I knew, yet somehow I recognize him, as though this boy had been secreted away inside my father all the while.

I sit back on my heels and glance around the room.

Suddenly I wish I could see him, talk to him, sit in the same room with him, even if only for one last time. We would talk about the gardens needing rain, that fall is early this year, how one of the Muscovies has abandoned her nest after laying twenty eggs. He'd whistle through his teeth and shake his head at this record number.

But the gardens are grown over with weeds. The ducks are gone.

I blow on my hands and rummage through the shoebox. Finally I find it—a postcard so faded I'm not sure what it was meant to depict: maybe a parrot, or maybe a huge frog, in thick vegetation of a monochromatic grey-green. The note on the back reads:

> Dear Russell and Marsha,
>
> April has recovered quite nicely and is reclaiming both her strength and love of life. As you can see from this postcard, I also come from a land of exquisite beauty. We look forward to a visit from you very soon.
>
> Warmest regards,
> Jean

No mention of me. Should I be surprised?

In the margins of the postcard someone has scrawled a phone number and an address for a place called Pineyard Island in the Bahamas. I guess Mrs. McNadden's sleuthing had its limitations, which, after my recent visit to her, is not surprising.

I hunt down my cell phone and dial the number.

April answers after the first ring.

"Hey," I say. "It's me."

Frost shimmers over the fields the next morning as I drive to Sunny Gardens Homecare. I pass the sagging vegetable stand, the closed Shell station, the Congregational church where my parents were joined in matrimony.

A part of me is hoping to avoid Mrs. Godfrey, but once I'm at the home I find myself waiting for her, sunk into the sofa with my mother, watching the news.

I soon realize—how could I have forgotten?—it's November 4. The Obama-McCain election.

I start to worry that Mrs. Godfrey is late, but when she finally marches in, I learn she's been at the Dover Democratic office, where enthusiasm and optimism are running high. She heads off down the corridor, flinging her coat over the back of a chair as she exits the room, and returns within minutes, wheeling Mr. Godfrey, who, like his wife, is wearing his Obama-Biden button.

When I tell her I'm driving to Boston today, she stops moving and says, "You're not going now? Of all days?"

"I have an early flight in the morning."

"I see." She checks me over, noticing, probably, that I'm less casually dressed than usual. "You're on your way."

"Could I ask a favour of you, Mrs. Godfrey?"

"It's going to be an historic day, you know." She waves a hand. "Of course. Of course, you have to go. What do you need?"

"Could I call you every once in a while?" I ask quietly, looking over my shoulder. "As a way to keep tabs on my mother?"

"Absolutely," she says. "I'll give you my number. Call me anytime. You know that." She moves past me to stand in front of the television. She listens briefly before changing the channel.

I stay until mid-afternoon, pulled in by Mrs. Godfrey's excitement. Allison, along with various residents, including the woman with the walker, joins us to lean into the television and stare at clip after clip of Americans lined up at inner city voting stations, and listen to commentators jittery with excitement. In Taos, New Mexico, a bride stops off to vote on her way to church — one of her bridesmaids stands to the side, smiling patiently but as though time is of concern — while Hillary and Bill Clinton arrive to cast their ballots at a New York school gym, both of them sleek and casual in black outfits.

"The First Lady," the woman with the walker says. "That's the First Lady."

"Obama's leading, though I'm hardly surprised," Mrs. Godfrey announces more than once, and I am reminded of her generation's stunning capacity for hope. "I like what Hillary is doing with her hair," she adds — then, perhaps to needle: "It suits her, don't you think, Allison?"

But Allison is being uncharacteristically taciturn. "Ricky isn't going to be happy," she admits to us.

The woman with the walker takes a hankie out of her sleeve and wipes her nose, then nervously tucks it into her shirt collar.

My mother is dozing off and on, not paying close attention to the events of the day, though she seems peaceful and content. We sit close together, side by side, our heads against the back of the sofa. Occasionally she flattens an invisible wrinkle on the arm of my sweater.

"You used to do the cutest thing," she says, rotating her head towards me, "when you were little."

"Me?"

"You'd look in the mirror and say your sister's name. You'd have a conversation with the mirror."

"Do you know *my* name?" I ask quietly, so no one else can hear us.

"Pilgrim."

"Mom, you know my name."

"Of course I know your name," she says dreamily. "I named you, didn't I?"

I lean closer and kiss her.

She smiles and closes her eyes. "You're good girls."

I stare at her. Several seconds pass. "Didn't Dad name us?"

One eye opens and takes me in. "Why would you think that?"

"I just assumed."

"My, my." She strokes my arm. "That's a mother's job."

I glance at Mrs. Godfrey, but she is consumed by the election. I don't think I can take her telling me one more time that my mother is really quite functional.

A screech travels out from the dining room. "Give that back!" a voice cries. "That's mine!"

Just before leaving, I bend down to give my mother another kiss, but the spell has been broken. Startled, she draws her hands up to her chest.

"Your mother is not fussy about being touched," Allison remarks. "Some are. Some aren't."

"The aged and infirm are not a separate species, Allison."

"So you've said, Mrs. Godfrey."

Part Four

FIFTEEN

Barack Obama is elected the forty-fourth president of the United States, and the next day, instead of returning home to Ethan and Katie as promised, I reverse direction to follow the southern route my twin chose thirty-three years ago. The small prop plane, which has been flying alarmingly close to the watery surface of the earth since leaving Nassau, gets even closer as we are tossed in the air above a trail of islands. The land is sandy and supports a single species of conifer—telephone-pole-straight trees with branches restricted to rounded crowns.

The forest parts and down we go onto a field. The two other passengers and I crawl out of the small plane onto Pineyard Island and straighten.

Then I see her, and for just a moment, the world turns upside down: it is my own body coming across the dusty ground to greet me. A slight squint, a sideways glance, and of course the lazy way we walk—part swagger, part shuffle—that frustrated our father.

Then the moment is gone. As she draws closer, I see her hair is long, a mix of dirty blonde and grey blowing across her face—frankly, a mess. She's wearing a pink skirt and puffy-sleeved peasant blouse with an embroidered neckline, and she's barefoot. She has that youthful, carefree quality I often envy in other women.

I wonder what she is thinking about me: my hair bobbed, brown with subtle highlights. My khakis, blazer, scarf, flats—all deliberately chosen for their neutral, earthy tones.

We grab each other's hands the way we used to after being apart—an instinct to connect through touch. But we hug awkwardly, suddenly remembering we are more strangers than sisters, and spring apart. That night I tell myself I should have known, right then and there, to turn around and get back on that toy plane.

We laugh nervously.

"You look...the same," I say, though of course she doesn't, not really.

"You, too," she says, using a huskier version of my voice.

We steal timid glances at each other and our talk is broken and meandering as we make our way to a large shed that serves as the terminal, where I collect my suitcase. Five minutes later, we exit out the other side of the building and cross the parking lot to her car, a Mazda Protegé they've had a while by the looks of it. I tell myself her car has no bearing on anything.

April unlocks the Mazda and we get in and I immediately roll down the window to release the heat and a cloying whiff of incense. As she backs out, a collection of bangles clatter down her tanned arms, and she informs me Jean left the clinic early today and is preparing a special Bahamian meal to welcome me. I am surprised by what a simple matter it is to know exactly how she feels about this.

"It will be something traditional, with fish and rice and peas," she adds, and I can tell she is both proud to be sharing this with me and worried that I might take something from her life. I didn't realize until now that I might be capable of that—of taking something from her. Things are shifting in ways I did not expect.

The air is dry and pleasantly hot. I welcome it after New England's damp autumn and the chilly farmhouse. I remember when Dr. Panama—not yet known to us as Jean—arrived, how my life sprung alive as we drove back to the farm, Tansy and Bandit shifting around in the back of the Ambassador and my father, an enemy of small talk, humming "Molly Malone." I remember the back of Jean's head, how April and I had stared at it.

On that day I popped open like a jack-in-the-box. Like I had never before felt curiosity or anticipation or attention to anything new.

I feel this again now.

April turns off onto a street lined with stucco bungalows painted in faded pastels. The houses range from the run-down, with missing doors and windows and no attention to landscaping, to the more affluent, with neat-as-a-pin gardens and bright white patio furniture beneath porch awnings. Most of the lawns are dry as straw.

"Welcome to the Bahamian suburbs," April jokes, pulling into a driveway. She bites her lip.

Like others, April and Jean's front yard is decorated with cement statues of dragons and alligators and empty urns, but overall it looks neglected and parched. The house is powder blue and fronted with a deep porch shielded by arched lattice work. It is small and dark and looks deserted.

But inside we are met by an earthy coolness and cooking smells that are sweet and tangy.

"We're home," April sings out, both of us wanting to get this over with.

And then he is there. So much shorter than I remember. And now with white, woolly hair and a paler, more spotted complexion. He is wearing a sleeveless tee and loose drawstring pants—gone are the polyester slacks—and like April he is barefoot. He brazenly takes my face in his hands and scrutinizes me. I had forgotten how different he was from other people.

"Ah," he says. "A decidedly simpler matter to tell you two apart now."

"She styles her hair differently," April points out, as though this is our essential difference. "Here." She takes my bag from me.

He's still holding me by the sides of my head. He's come so close to me so fast.

"You're embarrassing her, Jean."

"Am I?" he asks me.

But I find I am unable to speak.

"Come in, Pilgrim," she says, wanting to rescue me.

Finally he lets me go. April leads, and Jean follows me, his hands now firmly on my shoulders, as though to make sure I do not get lost in their tiny house. We go through a cluttered kitchen, where they stop to point out things, from a painting of islands and tall ships—a Bahamian antique—to their new coffee maker, then through a clattering curtain of plastic beads to the dining room, where they launch into their ordeal in getting the table and chair set, ordered from Miami, through Nassau Customs.

"By the end of it, I wish we hadn't bothered," April says, and Jeans claps his hands in protest, then ushers us out of the dining room and down a narrow hall.

April stops at a bedroom door and says shyly, "Here you are. This is a nice room, even if it is small." She sounds apologetic, almost ashamed.

"If you're lucky, you hear the parrots in the morning," Jean says.

He takes my bag from April and places it just inside the door. The two of them have to press up against the wall to let me pass into the room.

I cross to the window, which faces the backyard and a wall of vegetation so dense and tangled it looks impenetrable.

"Don't be silly. It's perfect," I tell her.

When I turn back, the two of them are watching me. They exchange an amused look.

"What is it?" I ask, smiling.

"You seem very, you know, urban."

"Slick," Jean says.

"No, Jean, that's not what I meant," April says. "Sophisticated."

"In what way?"

"Your hairstyle, your clothes." April shrugs. "Just everything."

I don't know what to say. It's difficult to know if she means this as anything more than a harmless observation, or if it carries some judgment.

"But the green parrot is rare now," Jean informs me. "Occasionally, a small flock."

"She does not care about the parrots, Jean, honey."

"He has a distinctive voice. High-pitched. Your daddy saw a pair."

"Excuse me?"

"Jesus, Jean, forget the parrots." April turns to me. "Mom and Dad visited," she says awkwardly. "Once."

She knows exactly how I feel about this. "I'm so surprised to hear that," I say anyway.

"We'll finish getting dinner ready, Jean and I." She motions him out. She is annoyed with him for not being able to keep his mouth shut about our parents. "Unpack, Pilgrim. Take your time. The bathroom is next to our bedroom. We've only the one."

"Thanks."

"We'll talk about it later. Okay, Pilgrim?"

"Thanks."

I am not going to unpack—this information changes everything—so I sit on the edge of the bed. I set my wait time at five minutes. I'm sweating now, the heat having finally gotten to me.

I hear sounds of the table being set, the rattle of that wacky beaded curtain, and most of their conversation.

"I told you not to say anything about that, Jean."

"How could I not? Tell me! Cut out my tongue, woman, if you must."

"Stop talking that way."

I hear a soft thumping noise.

"Don't provoke me, Jean. I'm serious."

The fish, I'm told, is mutton snapper. Jean caught it himself. "At our beach house, on Little Dove Cay," he explains at dinner. He looks at April. "We should take her there?"

"Sure," she says without commitment, giving me a quick glance.

"When were Mom and Dad here?" I ask, seeking a mild, conversational tone.

Jean and April look at each other, trying—or pretending—to recall.

"It was a long time ago," she says.

"Maybe 1980? Maybe 1981?" Jean suggests.

"They only came once?"

"They didn't like it," April says. "I mean, they were interested in the plants, because they were so different, especially Dad. But Mom complained a lot. How many times did she say the soil was too sandy?"

"Many times," Jean says.

"It drove me nuts."

I can't stand how factual they are being about this. Surely there had been tension with my parents? Roaring, angry words? Pleas to return home? Apologies and recriminations?

We finish dinner. Jean clears the table and disappears. I didn't want the first day to be like this, but I can't stop myself.

"They only came one time?" I ask. "You never saw them again?"

"Don't be upset with me, Pilgrim, please. I couldn't go back there. It would have been too hard to see our bedroom and all our things without you there."

"Tell me about it."

"Plus I didn't want to ask Jean to go. He was just setting up the clinic. I was afraid to travel alone."

"Jean? Jean might have a little trouble entering the United States."

"Why do you say that?"

"He was never licensed to practise. Surely you knew."

April shrugs. I can't tell if she never knew or doesn't care. Her face has a droopy, tired look it didn't have when she met me at the airport.

"Well, I'm sure that doesn't matter now," she says.

"Really?"

"Really, Pilgrim. It was so long ago."

I imagine my father spotting the parrots out the bedroom window. I imagine they arrived as swooping, flashy creatures crying out in jarring voices. He probably kept it to himself—not sharing the sight of these beautiful birds with my mother, who was lying in bed, staring at the ceiling and grimly considering the sandy soil.

I wonder if my parents spoke of me when they visited.

"Mom wasn't the same," April says. "She was vacant and distant. I knew they'd never come again. If it weren't for Jean, I doubt we would have stayed in touch."

"I've no idea what I'm doing here," I whisper.

She reaches across the table with her hand. The hand looks like mine. I imagine stabbing it with a fork.

"Let's start over," she says.

"Okay."

"Okay, good."

"But."

"What?"

"Mrs. McNadden claimed she didn't know where you were. When she first called, she told me you'd disappeared off the face of the earth. Her words."

"You've been talking to crazy Mrs. McNadden? That woman has a convenient way of forgetting things. I wouldn't waste my time on her, Pilgrim. Not my favourite person, as you can appreciate."

I remember standing on Mrs. McNadden's doorstep the rainy afternoon when she forgot who I was. That I had already arrived in Cranfield.

"After Dad died," April says, "she called me night and day. The gall."

"Wait—you knew Dad died? Before I called you?"

"Pilgrim, listen, I didn't want to get into that with you on the phone. It seemed too much for us to tackle right off."

"I can't believe what I'm hearing."

"She called and called. Each time, she forgot she'd already called me. I would have unplugged the phone, but Jean can get called out for an emergency. So I made him talk to her. She never liked him."

"So you know about Mom?" I ask, incredulous.

"The nursing home? I could tell she was declining over the years, when I spoke to her. The conversations were challenging."

"The place she's in—it's, well, grim."

"Dad didn't have much choice, did he?"

"It's depressing."

"Are you accusing me of something?"

"You knew."

"I've never been there. And we are not in a position to help. Doctors here don't earn what they do in the States, or I suppose Canada."

"What's your point?"

"Just that our resources may not be what you imagine."

I observe her trying to make excuses like she's a stranger.

"It's easy to see," she continues, "just looking at you, that you don't have to worry about paying the bills."

"Have you thought of visiting Mom? We could go back together."

"That's a nice idea, Pilgrim," she says. "Let me think about it."

We sit there in silence. Three minutes. I suspect Jean has either slipped out of the house or is standing in the kitchen as still as a mouse, listening to our every word.

"Would it be too much trouble if I made a call?" I ask coolly, glancing across the room at a black phone sitting on the window ledge.

April nods, pushes back her chair, and leaves me alone in the room.

Ethan is so furious he can barely speak to me. "We'll talk later," he decides, though he can't stop himself from telling me they were at the airport nearly two hours. "Katie and I waited for the very last person to get off that plane," he says. "Those imbeciles won't tell you anything. Even when the passenger is your own bloody wife."

I hang up, relieved how little explaining I had to do, and glance around the small, chaotic room. A narrow bookcase by the doorway is jam-packed, books lying on top of each other at all angles. Some of them, I notice, are about twins.

I feel guilty over Ethan and Katie, and saddened by how badly it's going with April, but mostly I'm exhausted. I return to the little guest bedroom and stare blankly at the forest backdrop. It's nearly dark outside now—night is coming on quickly.

April always got away with things. She had that knack. And the knack of keeping matters to herself. We were once so similar, and now I can only see the differences. I feel lost in a way I haven't in years.

She was the sister who ran away, annihilating our twinship. And yet, once I was gone—for what choice did I have?—she snuck back in. Three, maybe four, years later. And my parents forgave her.

In the night I wake suddenly, my thoughts on Mrs. McNadden. Perhaps I should have been paying better attention to her, visited her more than once, and recognized that she knew more about April and Jean than she had shared—or remembered.

When I wake the next day it's nearly noon. Someone is moving around in the kitchen. I shower and get dressed, and when I come out Jean offers to make me a breakfast, he says, "fit for a queen."

"Just coffee," I tell him, having decided not to get cozy with him. I am upset with both of them, and he is hard to read. Last night, before and during dinner, his gestures towards me seemed at times too intimate, as when his hands guided me through the house. But this may just be his way—boyish, innocent, probably meaningless.

"A coffee and cigarette?" he asks.

"What?"

"Like your sister?" He shakes his head with disapproval. "That's her breakfast."

"April smokes? Really?"

"Mostly in the morning. You?"

"Lately, yes."

"Go ahead. The window is open."

"I'll go outside."

"Absolutely not. I insist. Sit."

So I take the chair nearest the window. I lean back and try to direct my smoke out-of-doors. He brings me coffee and sits down opposite me and stares.

"Smoking is a stress reducer," he remarks, then asks, "Do I look changed to you?"

I laugh. "It's been a long time. Yes, you have changed." What strikes me most about him is that he seems smaller, although no less powerful. Wiry, agile. The muscles at his neck are ropey and every inch of his arms smooth and taut. Though I can't really know this, I suspect his stomach would be firm and unyielding. Then I think, what kind of a thought is that?

"Would you recognize me?" he asks.

"I don't know, Jean. Probably. Yes. Where did April go?"

"I would recognize you."

"Of course you would recognize me," I say, smiling despite the awkwardness. "I look a lot like your wife."

"No, no. I would recognize *you*. By the way, Pilgrim, how nice to see you finally smile."

Not quite the uncertain, polite young man anymore. That's one way in which he's less recognizable.

I hear the front door open.

Jean is shaking his head. "We aren't married," he says softly.

"Excuse me?"

Then April is in the doorway. "You're home early for lunch," she says to Jean, tossing a newspaper on the table. On the cover is a photo of Barack Obama with his wife and daughters on election night celebrating before a vast crowd. The headline reads, "Obama Wins Historic US Election."

"And Dad just missed it," April says to me. "He would have been—"

"—over the moon."

"Are you two serious?" Jean demands. "Have you lost your twin minds?"

He sounds annoyed, almost hostile. It troubles me how abruptly his mood has changed.

"There were campaign posters for Obama in the Nassau airport," I say, thinking to move the conversation off my father.

"Are you serious?" Jean asks again. "That's rubbish that Russell would have been over the moon."

"I'm not surprised," April tells me, ignoring him. "I saw one here, too. Like his election is their election. Like he has been elected leader of the world."

"People are ignorant," Jean says. "I don't understand what they expect. What rewards do they think this Obama will bring them? Is there a magic pill?" He turns to me and asks in an overly earnest manner, as though he is speaking to a child, "Did you bring a magic pill with you from America, Pilgrim?"

"Don't be so negative," April says, then looks at me. "He's handsome—Obama—isn't he?"

I shrug.

"They will be crushed when there is no change," Jean says. "Day following day following day."

"Okay, Mr. Sunshine. Finish your lunch. You have patients waiting for you."

I am surprised by the intensity of his bitterness. After he's gone, April and I exchange a look.

"Wow, his mood can turn on a dime," I say.

"No kidding. Welcome to my world."

"Magic pill?"

"He's a bit cynical about Obama," she says, drawing her lips down in a caricature of woe. "You might have noticed?"

We look at each other. When we laugh, the world flips and just like that, in a single moment, April exists as she used to: radiantly and absolutely familiar to me—more than any human being has ever been or ever will be.

She says, "I still love you, you know."

"I missed you."

"It's been hard to feel a purpose."

"I know."

"I'm sorry I ran off like that."

"We never got to say goodbye."

"I know. Then all these years."

"If you cry, I'll cry."

"And I'm sorry I made it up to them without telling you."

"How could you tell me?" I say, forgiving her entirely. "I was gone. I was too stubborn to look for you."

After that, it's as though our decades of separation were no more than a handful of months.

Each morning, April and I emerge from our bedrooms at the same time and pass through the beaded curtain into the small kitchen, where we make coffee to take outside to drink on the porch behind the latticework. Then we have a cigarette, lighting them in unison, as though we have rehearsed it. The watery sunlight criss-crosses the porch floor and warms our bare legs in bands.

Eventually, Jean pops out of the house, ready for work, for which he dresses casually in slacks and T-shirt, and we all mutter our goodbyes. April and I watch him drive off in the Mazda. Or he'll walk, if April and I need the car that day.

The days are hot but the nights cool, and I sleep wonderfully, rarely waking for nine or ten hours. I realize I was exhausted from being cold, from facing my mother in that urine-sodden place, and from the ghostly dilapidation of the farm. I start to tell April about all of that, but she becomes too sad and asks me to stop.

I accompany April on her errands and help her cook, clean the house, and occasionally make a half-hearted stab at gardening.

I avoid Jean. Each night, he and April withdraw to their bedroom and close the door. When I hear them — that throaty, broken language that means only one thing — I put the pillow over my head.

By the end of November, Obama and his daughters are deliberating over their choice of hypoallergenic dog. The US continues to shed jobs. I call Mrs. Godfrey a few times, but there is no answer at the number she gave me. I assume she is at the nursing home, which is a comforting thought.

I am allowed to talk to Katie now. In fact, she is the one who typically answers the phone. It is Ethan whose voice I begin to miss. My guess is that he can't trust his temper. When I tried to explain where I was and why — in the Bahamas, visiting a relative — he said nothing. He doesn't want me to know what he's thinking, and I don't.

I ask Katie if she's done her homework, taken the dog for a walk, keeping her room tidy.

"Tell Daddy I'll be home before Christmas."

"Yes, Mom," she says quietly. "Okay, Mom."

Neither April nor I refer to the length of my visit, and I fall in love with the heat, the smell of sand cooked all day by the sun, the severe shadows at dusk, the amplified sounds of night. April and I discover, but are not surprised by, what we have in common as adults: we prefer vodka to gin; we're hopeless at baking; we despise yoga; we have a weak left ankle; our teeth still ache when we're hungry; in our mid-thirties we briefly struggled with weight for the first time, gaining ten pounds and a sudden, embarrassing sentimentality—a tendency to well up at a sad news story or sappy commercial.

Even our jobs—or what were our jobs—followed a parallel track, though it's possible this was more by happenstance than design. For years, April ran Jean's medical clinic.

"I retired," she says, "so I could stay home and enjoy my hobbies, like gardening."

At first I think she's joking. I don't want to point this out to her, but their yard looks like the surface of Mars.

I describe my job with the Calgary Community Health Centre, which I left when Ethan's company offered him a position in St. John's, Newfoundland.

"I was sorry to leave it," I confess as we prepare lunch one day. "But his promotion was impossible for us to turn down."

"They don't know about me, do they?" she asks, slipping a knife into a papaya. "Ethan and Katie?"

"No," I say, worried, but she smiles, neither surprised nor hurt, and reaches out to lightly rub my back.

I watch her gather plates and cutlery, and it's as though I'm observing someone doing an impression of my own movements, in my own kitchen, thousands of miles away.

Although we are so alike, there are differences. April's face is narrower than mine, and she's slightly shorter, but she was always smaller. Her long hair is lighter, bleached by the sun, and looks dry as bone. I suspect she goes days without brushing it. She wears a large, floppy hat whenever she steps outdoors, but I had to buy sunblock since there was none in the house, which would account for her face being browner and more weathered than mine. In some ways, she reminds me of our mother.

Jean departs for the satellite clinics on the out islands and is gone several days. April and I grill fish outdoors and drink our vodka tonics.

April makes a point of talking about Jean while he's absent, and I wonder if she is protecting him in some way, as though she wants to ensure we not forget him. She seems to hold him—and his practice—in high regard, although as far as I can tell his days are spent treating earaches, cuts, rashes, and "tummy viruses," as he refers to them, and I think I hear a touch of boredom in his voice.

One afternoon, perhaps sensing my failure to be awed by Jean, April launches into the story of a young girl suffering from acute tetanus. We are driving home and she pulls the car over to the side of the road to finish an ice cream dripping down her hand.

"Out on one of those tiny islands," she says, pausing to lick the cone. "The poor little girl couldn't open her mouth to say one word. Horrific pain. There were delays in evacuating her by plane, but Jean refused to leave the island until she did."

A regular superhero, I think, reaching over to wipe a splat of ice cream off her arm.

"She nearly died, Pilgrim."

The inside of the car is quickly growing hot. Jean is due back that afternoon, and I find I am looking forward to being around his peculiar vigour and straightforwardness again, but at the same time I am reluctant to share April with him.

"What's that? Is that someone's house?" I point to a small shed. Some dirty blankets and a mattress have been brought outside to air, yet the building has no windows.

"The Haitian Embassy," she says, shooting me a quick smile.

"Seriously?"

"No. Of course not. That's what Jean calls it. It's where the Haitians who collect the garbage stay."

"So 'Haitian Embassy' is a joke?"

"Yeah."

"Huh."

"What?" Finished with her ice cream, she lights a cigarette.

"Just seems, you know, a little politically incorrect for Jean."

"Pilgrim, really."

"Well?"

"It's a joke."

"Right."

"I'd know if it's just a joke or not. You didn't marry Jean. I did."

We are both a little shocked by her words.

"Except you're not married," I say after a moment.

She smokes her cigarette in silence. I wish she would start

the car. The harbour appears more crowded than usual, with its hodgepodge of sailboats, motor yachts, and those fishing boats that sit so low in the water they look as though the merest wave would sink them. Each day seems hotter than the previous, despite the approach of winter. There is a baking dryness inside my nostrils, and in the ditch not far from the car broken bottles and cans glitter brilliantly, hurting my eyes. I shift in my seat and feel the dampness on my back.

"When did he tell you that?" she asks eventually.

"Day two. Right off the bat. It was a very odd conversation."

"The thing about Jean—"

"Don't lecture me, April."

"Listen to me. The thing about Jean, he's easily misinterpreted."

"By whom?"

She sighs. "By women, of course. I've seen it. They think he's up to something and really, he's just like, I don't know—"

"A cat with a mouse?"

"No! Of course not. It's just how he is. He's just being who he is."

If you say so, I think.

On the other side of the harbour is a teal-blue marina decked out in plastic candy canes and snowflakes. A sleigh, reindeer, and the word "NOEL" have been strapped to its roof. The place is busy, with people getting in and out of dinghies, hovering around the bait shop, or just strolling up and down the public docks.

"What's the date?" I ask.

"December first, maybe the second."

"Shit. Christmas." I feel a little panicky.

"Christmas isn't a big deal with us," April says.

I've noticed a growing habit in her of pointing out any difference between us.

"You must miss Katie," she says.

It's like holding a heavy block of wood under water, this trying not to think about my daughter. I know that I have the stubbornness to do it, but April's question weakens, and then irritates, me.

"You haven't asked what happened to Petunia," I say. "Or did they tell you on one of their visits?"

"I think we've established there was only one visit. No, they didn't say. What happened to her?"

"It's not important."

"It seems important to you."

"Start the car, April. I'm roasting. Why don't you have air conditioning? You should get air conditioning in your next car."

"Noted."

"Mom asked me about the dog. In that place she's in. More than once."

"So are we going to talk about this now?"

"After you ran away, Mom worried about Petunia excessively. Like she transferred her feelings for you to that dog."

"I'm confused. Would you have preferred I had shot Petunia?"

"I would have preferred you shot nobody."

"I hardly ever think about that day—"

"That's convenient."

"May I continue?"

"Go on."

"Don't you remember? Dad was off his friggin' rocker that day—if not that entire summer. I never truly considered shooting Petunia—how could I? Besides, even if I did, Dad was still going to make Jean leave. Shooting myself was immature. Reckless. But it was the only solution I had in the moment. I was sixteen."

"Okay. I get it. Start the car. I'm roasting."

"Would you have shot Petunia?"

"Possibly. I don't know."

"Well, that's one big difference between us."

When we pull up to the house, Jean is standing on the lawn, a medical bag and small suitcase at his feet, talking to a slender man with skin as black and shiny as a crow's.

"Look who I found," Jean calls, gesturing at us to hurry over.

The man watches us with joy as we approach. A scar in the centre of his bottom lip widens his smile like the opening of a fan. If not for his obvious delight I would wonder if it pained him to smile. He glances at me. There is a flicker of surprise, but he turns back to April immediately. His green pants and dress shirt are worn and damp-looking. One of the sleeves is rolled past his elbow and the other flaps, unbuttoned, as he holds out a photograph he has been displaying to Jean. Excitedly, he shows the photo to April, then, with some hesitation, to me. He points to the girl and the large doll she's gripping. I recognize it immediately: an American Girl doll. Katie has three of them.

April scolds, "Patrice, we haven't seen you in such a long time. We thought you forgot about us."

"No, no, don't worry that," he tells her. Satisfied that we've all had a good look at the photo, he slips it into his breast pocket and pats it several times. He touches his abdomen and says to Jean, "I have some medicine, Doctor?"

"Still plagued with gas?" Jean asks.

"Yes, yes, plenty plagued with gas." His smile has not let up.

Next to Patrice, Jean is small and hardly dark at all. In fact, he and April, with her deep tan, seem closer in complexion than Jean and Patrice.

Jean kneels and rummages through his medical bag, then rises with a large bottle of Tums. He shakes a handful onto Patrice's palm.

"So we'll see you in the morning?" April asks. "Promise?"

"That right. In the morning, me working."

"All right, Patrice," April warns. "I'll be expecting you."

But Patrice has already turned away. A rip in one of his pant legs travels up his calf to the back of his knee. He looks once more at April and flashes her his jagged smile.

Inside, April immediately asks Jean, "Where was he?"

"Walking down the road. I had to do some convincing"—Jean rubs his fingers together—"to get the taxi driver to pick him up. He was anxious that we see the photo of his daughter," he adds.

"Have you met his daughter?" I ask.

April ignores my question and says to Jean, "Of course he wanted us to see it."

"Why?" I ask.

"That doll was from us," April says with pride. "Last Christmas."

Jean positions himself behind April, puts his hands around her waist and lifts her a few inches off the floor. "She wants an iPod this year," he informs her, his face tilted into her hair.

April smiles. "Well, that's too much. Would you mind putting me down? And how would we get it in time?" She turns to me, shaking her head, and explains, "It takes weeks to get things here, but Patrice, he thinks we can make anything happen."

Jean puts her down and comes up behind me, places his hands around my waist, and lifts me. My back brushes against his chest and belly. "What are you doing?" I ask sharply.

"Jean, come on," April says.

After he puts me down, he attempts to pick April up again. She and I look at each other, realizing in the same moment he is comparing our weights.

"He better come back in the morning," April says, pushing Jean away. "Like he promised."

"He'll be back," Jean assures her. "He was intrigued by Pilgrim's presence."

Not until it's obvious Jean has given up his investigation and won't lift me again do I feel that unmistakable shimmer of desire. I glance at him and catch him watching me. "He didn't know April had a twin," Jean tells me, stepping my way but not touching me. Even so, I grow warm. "He'll be back just to see you again. Keep an eye on you."

"Why?"

"Haitians think twins have special powers, but can be dangerous. My guess is he's gone to find his buddies to tell them about you—about what he's just seen."

"Where are they?" I ask. "His buddies?"

"Probably the woods."

"Not the Haitian Embassy?" I say.

"Don't be ridiculous," Jean says, frowning. "If they're lucky, someone's boat shed."

"He'll be okay," April says quickly. "The weather is fine."

Jean rolls his eyes. "She mommies Patrice," he tells me.

April smiles fondly. "He was only ten when he first showed up here, Pilgrim, looking for work. He'd come across from Haiti with some older boys."

"You do what you do, when the chips are down," Jean says. "Isn't that so, Pilgrim?"

"I was worried the big boys weren't being nice to him," April continued. "He had some bruises, but Jean examined him and made sure he was okay."

Jean winks at me. "His mommy," he teases, and I laugh.

"He barely knew his own mother," April snaps.

And just like that, my days of peace and equilibrium begin to unravel. Another week passes and I feel Christmas drawing closer, but each day I put off making a decision about when to go home. The intervals between my phone calls to Katie increase.

Each day, Patrice arrives early, without announcement —sometimes, I suspect, before dawn. He weeds and clears away brush, waters the barren gardens in which April has set new annuals, and tidies and washes the conch shells that border the lawn and pathway to the house. April becomes increasingly concerned with finding things for him to do.

Now she and I rarely emerge from our bedrooms at the same time. If I'm up first, I go out onto the latticed porch and see Patrice's soda can and sack of food and clothing placed at the edge of the driveway. But he's not easy to spot, camouflaged as he is by the flickering shade. When he finally steps out from the shadows, he waves enthusiastically, but waits for April before approaching the house.

April frets about Patrice's stomach and asks him several times a day how he's feeling. She wonders if he needs more serious attention than a handful of Tums, but Jean assures her Patrice has simply got a touch of nervous tension.

"You don't help, April," Jean points out good-naturedly, "by reminding him of it every hour."

I silently agree. He's a grown man, not a child, but I'm smart enough not to say this.

When she's not worrying about his health, she worries about giving his daughter an iPod for Christmas, although time is running out for her to order it in from Miami. Patrice mentions it almost every morning shortly after arriving, assuming they have been discussing it in his absence, which they have. Their indecision baffles and gradually annoys me.

"Just buy the damn thing," I say at dinner one night. "What are you waiting for?"

"We must control his expectations," Jean explains. He is sitting beside me. When I turn to look at him, he winks at me. I wish he wouldn't do that.

April is nodding. Her face is flushed—from the heat, and because it was early afternoon when we had our first vodka tonic. Patrice failed to show up today, and April stayed inside the house, aimless and out of sorts. Then Jean, who only works to noon on Fridays, came home in a wound-up holiday mood that is grating on us both.

"It's expensive," Jean adds.

"But it will break his heart," April protests. "And his daughter's."

"Just buy the damn thing," I say again.

"I'm sure he has an ulcer, Jean," April says. "Can't you order some tests?"

"He doesn't have an ulcer," Jean tells her firmly.

"How do you know?"

He stares at her. "Stop worrying about him."

"I'm curious who his daughter thinks these gifts are from," I say. "Santa?"

"From us, of course," April says, though she doesn't sound entirely certain. "By the way, Pilgrim, I've been meaning to ask you about that ring."

Jean places his arm along the back of my chair and leans towards me. "Do you worry about your daughter the same way she worries about Patrice?"

"Pilgrim and I are not the same person," April snaps.

"Really," I add.

"Can you get me another drink, Jean?" she asks. "Pilgrim wants one, too."

As soon as he's gone, April puts her hand out. "Can I see that ring?"

My twin and I react to alcohol the same way: we grow quiet, and sometimes a little mean. Reluctantly, I pass her the ring. When Jean crashes back through the beaded curtain with our drinks and asks if we can read each other's mind, we don't even look at him.

I light a cigarette, though the window is not open and I have no intention of getting up and opening it.

"I used to think you two knew what the other one was thinking," Jean says, giving me my drink, which is so full some of it spills onto the table. "Back in the days of Cranfield."

"Shut up, Jean, honey."

"Well, I knew where you were hiding," I tell her. "When we played hide and sneak."

"Hide and *seek*," April says, trying the ring on different fingers. "Huh?"

"Hide and seek. You said hide and sneak."

I look at Jean. "Did I?"

April lights a cigarette. "What are you asking him for? He won't take sides."

Jean winks at me again. This time I'm sure April sees it.

"That's bullshit anyway, Pilgrim."

"Like hell it is," I say. "I always knew. You knew, too. Admit it."

"Do you honestly think we're the same?" April asks Jean. Then she gives me a tight smile. "You're right, I knew where you were hiding. I was actually better at it than you."

I don't think this is true, but I let it go.

"I didn't say you were the same," Jean tells April. He's tiptoeing around her now, which surprises me. He puts his hand over his heart, an apologetic gesture meant for her, but it draws my eyes right to his body.

April and I smoke our cigarettes in silence while Jean drums his fingers on the tabletop. April glances at him with irritation. I realize her expression is a carbon copy of one I sometimes give Ethan. I didn't realize it was so unattractive.

"Petunia also knew," I say after a while. They both look at me. "Where we were hiding," I explain. "She could sniff us out."

"Please," April cries. "You're not bringing up that dog again, are you?"

"Poor little mutt," Jean says.

"She wasn't a mutt," I say. "She was a purebred miniature apricot poodle."

April finishes her drink and tells me, "I knew, as soon as you stepped off that plane, I wasn't up to the look on your face." She stands. "I'm going to bed."

"You'll regret saying that in the morning," I say.

"Yeah, even if I do, you'll never know."

I light another cigarette and smoke it, looking straight ahead at April's empty chair. Eventually, I pick the ring back up where she left it on the table. I sense Jean's eyes glued to me.

I put out my cigarette and rise, wobbly.

I have taken only one step before Jean jumps up and catches me with his body, embracing me awkwardly.

"Bad idea," I tell him.

"It was you," he says into my neck, like he hasn't the guts to face me. Like this is his main purpose in burrowing his head beside mine, so he doesn't have to look me in the eye.

"Okay, fella," I say lightly. "We've both had a lot to drink." But I'm afraid. His strong smell disarms me, and any inclination to resist him feels distant and buried.

"It was you," he mumbles into me. "First you, then her. But after we came here, I knew I made a mistake. I had taken the wrong girl."

"We're not interchangeable."

He shakes me. "Remember when you came into my bedroom in Cranfield? Pilgrim, do you remember?"

"You're talking about something from a long time ago," I say. But I find that I am not really surprised by all this. I expected it. Gradually, almost hoping he won't notice, I let myself slump against him. I need to know what he feels like.

"I think about that, Pilgrim. Often."

"I don't believe you," I protest, yet I don't move. "You're just saying that because you're drunk."

"What should we do?" he asks.

From the hallway comes the sound of the bathroom door opening and April going into their bedroom. I disentangle myself from him with care, as though an explosive is lodged between us.

"I should go home," I say.

"Where?"

"Canada." For the first time, I'm scared I might not get back in time for Christmas.

Jean steps away and lifts his hands in defeat. "As you wish."

He's gone. When I turn into my room I half expect him to be hiding there, but he has obviously made it to his own room. I get into bed and wonder if he will have forgotten our conversation by morning. I put my head on the pillow. The room spins.

SIXTEEN

I wake the next morning to wheezing sounds coming from Jean and April's overgrown backyard. For a moment I am home and Katie is still a baby and Ethan has stepped on one of her squeaky toys. By the time I am fully awake, the cries are gone and instead I hear distant footsteps followed by a door slamming. Then the house is quiet and vacant. I sit up with a jolt. Where is Jean? Only vaguely do I recall the plan I made before falling asleep, to make it home in time for Christmas. Frantic, I dress. Shaking. Hurried. Nauseous. I rush through the empty house and out the front door and onto the porch.

My head is clouded and my thinking evolves slowly. Patrice has returned and, as usual, is tending a number of small fires that give off a spicy, woodsy odour. April is kneeling not far from me, her face hidden by her wide-brimmed hat and her hands cradling another wilting annual meant for this sun-baked flower garden.

Those plants need shade, some organic matter, and a lot more moisture, and April knows that.

Jean?

He's in the Mazda, behind the wheel. I'm not sure if he's coming or going. April lifts her face and stares at me, telling me nothing, which is no surprise. I glance back to the car and Jean is no longer inside. He is outside, moving towards me.

"Where are you off to?" I ask, hoping to sound casual, but not a good judge of my success.

"An emergency at the clinic," he says. "Would you like to come along and watch me in action?"

"Yeah, okay." I lurch down over the steps towards the car.

"Like that?" he asks me softly, throwing the words to me over the roof of the car.

"Yes."

As the car backs out, I cannot look at April, to whom I have said nothing, but I glance at Patrice, who is standing at the edge of the property and wearing his alarm shyly.

"You look worked up," Jean tells me once the house is behind us. I believe he is telling me this not because he needs to know why, but as a warning. But I'm not sure.

"In what way?" I ask.

"Your hair is uncombed."

"Oh, well."

"Your shirt. Inside out?"

"Shit." I rest my elbow on the open window and hold my forehead in my hand.

"Okay?" he asks.

"I'm just realizing I'm hungover."

He nods without speaking. He rummages in the compartment between our seats, comes up with a stick of Juicy Fruit gum, and hands it to me with something that reminds me of impatience.

"Where are we going?"

"I told you. The clinic."

"Oh."

"Where did you think we were going?"

"I wasn't really sure."

"Maybe you needed a bit more sleep."

Now I'm worried. I hold the stick of gum in my lap. I want to ask him if he remembers his declaration last night but am afraid to. He's not the same man now. He's sober.

"I think I heard those parrots this morning," I tell him as we pass the harbour and its various second-rate tourism operations. "Like a child's squeaky toy?"

"That sounds about right," he says, but he's not as impressed as I'd hoped, and he turns into the same shopping area I have visited a number of times with April. I hadn't noticed the Pineyard Island Medical Clinic before, nor had April pointed it out to me, even though she worked here for years. With the exception of a single taxi, the lot is empty.

He parks and gets out and I follow him, embarrassed now by my inside-out shirt and puffy skin and stale breath. As he unlocks the clinic, the back door of the taxi opens and a woman emerges. I watch her lean back in, lift out a child, and hurry over to us. She's tanned, well groomed.

"You must be Dr. Moss," she says, all business-like, to Jean. She has pretty eyes and a big, toothy mouth and diamond stud earrings. "We spoke by phone earlier." American. Midwestern perhaps. The child lifts a feverish face from her mother's chest and blinks at us. "Thank you for coming out on a Saturday, Doctor. She's been running a fever for close to a week. We've been sailing."

"Not a problem," Jean tells her. He smiles at her intensely for several seconds and she seems slightly caught off, as though a piece of her confidence has been loosened. She looks at me for the first time.

I try to think of something to say.

"My wife," Jean explains. "We are just on our way to our beach house on Little Dove Cay for the weekend." He pushes open the door and nods to her. "After you," he says.

"Thank you kindly." She steps inside with her child. "Little Dove Cay? We just spent two nights there. Such a quaint island."

Then he nods to me, and I follow her in.

I don't know what I expected. Not aquamarine walls exactly, or medical supplies dumped out on a card table; nonetheless, I am surprised to find a bona fide medical establishment: the quiet hum of electronics, the sharp coolness of round-the-clock air conditioning, the smell of air fresheners and disinfectants. A waiting room. A table with magazines and toys. Red-and-green Christmas garlands.

Aroused by the change in environment, the child whimpers and begins to squirm.

"She's prone to ear infections," the woman apologizes. She rearranges the child in her arms. "I'm sure that's all it is. We didn't have a thermometer on the boat, which frankly surprised me because they are supposed to come fully equipped, but I think her fever has been a bit high. It's okay, Becky. She claimed to see a rabbit last night. She really has not been herself."

"If you'll just follow me this way," Jean says to her. "And we'll have a look." He heads down the hallway, flipping on lights as he goes.

I can't inquire after the location of the washroom, now that I am supposed to be his wife, so I hang back, figuring it's nearby, which it is. Inside, I take off my shirt and put it back on properly, then wet a wad of paper towels. I sit on the closed toilet seat and shut my eyes, the towels pressed to my face. I count to ten. Years ago, when Katie was in full tantrum, I'd slip into the nearest closet and count to ten. Or I'd step outside, even in winter.

After a while I stand and examine myself in the mirror. I run my fingers through my knotted hair, which has lightened from the sun and from the grey that is starting to come through. My face, on the other hand, looks darker—I keep forgetting to apply sunblock. I rub my teeth with a finger and bit of hand soap, then gargle ferociously with handfuls of water. Finally, I unwrap the stick of gum and pop it into my mouth. It's delicious and energizes me. I go back out and creep down the hall. The door to the examining room is open.

"What about her chest," I hear him asking. "Much coughing?"

"She *was* coughing. But less now. I have to say she just seems so darn listless."

When I reach the doorway he is leaning over the child with his stethoscope slipped up under her T-shirt. His look is concentrated and stern. "Take a few big breaths for me, Becky," he coaches. The little girl is sitting on the edge of the examining table, white-faced and breathing audibly.

She inhales and her chest heaves up once.

"Good girl," he says. He takes his otoscope and bends to look in one of her ears.

"Ah-hah! You were right," he says. "She's got a whopper ear infection." He checks the other ear. "Both ears. Would you like to see, Mommy?"

"Well, I guess so. Why not?"

He steps aside to allow the woman, who seems hesitant, to stoop and view her daughter's ear. I note that he and the woman are not that far apart from each other.

"Do you see that?" he asks quietly. "Bright red? Glowing like hot embers?"

"Yes," the woman says politely. When she straightens I can see she is wondering about the point of this. "She has an ear infection. I rather thought so. She's prone to them."

"And pneumonia."

"Oh no, oh dear. Don't tell me."

"I'm ninety-nine percent certain she has pneumonia. After the chest X-ray, we'll know for sure."

"We have to go for an X-ray?" the woman nearly wails. "Honestly, can't you just treat her? Where would we have to go for that? My husband is waiting for us at the marina."

Jean takes a moment to smile again at the woman, though it seems to only be confusing her. He steps to the door and beckons us to follow him. "I'll warm up the X-ray generator. It'll take five minutes at most to get it cracking."

"You have an X-ray machine here?" she asks. "Actually?"

The question seems to bother Jean — briefly. "This clinic also serves the out islands," he explains. "You may be surprised to learn we are centrally located in the world that exists here."

The woman pretends to appreciate the meaning of this remark, then gathers up her lethargic child and looks at me with relief and gratitude. "Thank God. I'll tell you one thing, you people really are a life-saver."

I nod, chewing my gum and still feeling my way into this role. "He does his best," I say, trying to sound casual.

"My God," she admonishes. "I'd say he does better than that!"

I make a face at her behind her back as she leaves the room.

Down the hall is a larger, cooler room housing several machines meant to take the measure of, I assume, various bodily disturbances.

Even I can see that the child is quite sick and having respiratory issues. I leave them to it and go sit in the empty waiting room.

When they come out a while later, the woman has a bottle of liquid antibiotics in one hand. She repositions the child in her arms and thanks Jean repeatedly. She glances down at me where I'm collapsed into one of the chairs. Her expression implies I do not fully appreciate the value of this man.

If only she knew.

"I wonder if you could call me a taxi?" she says to me.

Before I can even begin to think about how I want to respond to that, Jean sprints over to the phone on the receptionist's desk.

The three of us wait awkwardly. The woman moves the girl from hip to hip. "She's getting so heavy," she tells Jean.

"I'm not surprised. You've had to hold her for a long time."

"I'll tell you one thing, it will be my husband's turn when we get back to that boat. This trip has actually been a tiny bit of a nightmare," she confides, looking to me for sympathy.

I nod. I reach for a tissue and spit my gum into it. The woman looks away. Then her taxi arrives and after thanking Jean twice more, she is gone.

I stare at the floor.

He sits down in the chair beside me. After a while he says, "You're getting a nice tan."

I frown.

"You weren't particularly friendly," he says.

"You were flirting with that woman."

"I was not flirting with her," he says with surprise.

"Take me back to the house."

"I was not flirting with a patient," he says, growing more heated.

"She wasn't the patient. The child was. She was a stupid American."

He makes a throaty noise of frustration.

"You were flirting with a stupid American woman."

He stands and storms off down the hallway.

"Hey, I want to go back to the house," I yell after him.

I'm starting to get goosebumps from the air conditioning. I'm also thirsty.

I find him in his office, sitting at his desk, writing away at something.

"So are you going to just sit there?" I demand, glaring at him and wishing I could stop myself. "And scribble out your notes and pretend you don't remember what you said to me last night?"

He lifts his head and gives me that slow smile of appreciation and surprise that I remember so well from his life with us in Cranfield, and which even now I long to earn.

"Have a seat, Pilgrim." He gestures towards a black couch with

316

pancake-thin cushions and metal arms. I wonder if he takes the occasional afternoon nap here.

I flop down dramatically and he comes and settles beside me. Both of us are wearing shorts and he sits so that the skin of his leg presses against mine. He leans close and runs his hand along my thighs, up the inside of my shorts, not roughly but forcefully, and my breath catches. I immediately think of that day in his bogus doctor's office when I was sixteen and just stung by hornets.

"Now," he says. "Pilgrim. Are you and I on the same page?"

We contemplate each other, our faces just inches apart, and I see a playfulness in his eyes that makes me smile. But more than that, I see the brazen honesty and kindness that set him apart the first day I met him—the moment he stepped down off the Greyhound bus from Miami.

It's dusk when he returns to the clinic. I'm waiting for him in his office, sitting on his black couch, unable to make a decision. He has been pleading with me all afternoon to run away with him to his beach house on Little Dove Cay.

The plan was that he would retrieve my purse and luggage, because the one thing I do know is that I cannot face April, but he steps into the office empty-handed and mumbles something about not being able to get inside the house. He makes it sound as though this is of little consequence.

"But I need my wallet and passport to get home."

"Home? Where?"

"Canada," I say, astonished but amused by his inability to remember this.

"Is that what you have decided, Pilgrim, to leave? When Little Dove Cay is paradise?"

"Shit, I don't know what to do." I drag my hands through my dirty, tangled hair. "Let me call home. And don't ask me where that is."

He looks disappointed, but tips his head towards the phone on the desk and says, "I'll wait for you in reception."

I dial the number, my hand shaking. I should know what to say.

Panicking, I hang up, pause, then dial again. This time I force myself to wait for the ring.

It rings, and I'm thinking neither Ethan nor Katie wants to talk to me. That they just don't know how important it is for them to pick up. I keep the phone pressed to my ear, letting it ring, refusing to believe the house is empty, certain that eventually someone will give in and decide to talk to me.

Jean appears in the doorway.

We stare at each other. Isn't it wrong to consider this? I want to ask him. Monumentally wrong? But he looks like it isn't. What about April? Is she in his thoughts at all? But he looks like she isn't.

The ringing phone is still at my ear.

He turns and walks away.

Agitated, I shift from foot to foot and turn around and back again. Movement across the room catches my eye and I gasp.

What's she doing here?

My heart races. It only takes a second to realize I've seen my own reflection in the mirrored door to a cabinet above a sink. Yet, for a split second, in this darkening room, I thought I'd seen April.

The message manager finally kicks in.

When I enter reception a minute later, Jean is standing on the desk, adjusting one of the Christmas garlands tacked to the ceiling.

"I'm coming with you," I say. "To Little Dove Cay."

"Ah, fantastic news," he says and leaps off the desk. An end of garland drops from the ceiling and dangles behind him. He takes my hand and leads me to the door. I remember him comparing April's weight to mine a week ago.

"We have a full moon and clear sky," he says. "We'll go straight away."

I nod, not sure I fully comprehend what this means. We drive a long time in the car, at least half an hour, and I start to doze with my head against the window. I wonder if I am coming down with something after spending most of the afternoon underdressed in that air-conditioned office. Or maybe I caught something from that sick girl, Becky. I make a wish that she will be as good as new soon. Then I forget about her.

Later, we are in a whaler in the night, crossing water as clear and sheer as glass. I am sitting with my back to the bow, facing Jean, who looks past me, his hand on the tiller.

I stare at the twinkling yellow lights marking Pineyard Island as we move farther and farther away from it. I don't know where we are going or how long it will take.

The air is gauzy and warm. The ocean is no more than a few metres deep throughout our journey. Under the full moon, it's almost like day. I can't see the surface of the water—instead my eye falls directly to the seabed, where clumps of brown seaweed sway on the sandy bottom. Without a visible water surface, it feels as though we are suspended in the air.

After a while Jean reduces the speed and the sound of the engine dulls. The land comes on us suddenly, alarmingly close on either side as we pass through a narrow opening. Up ahead loom tall structures with single pale lights at their summits. As we draw closer, they pitch almost imperceptibly on the water and produce a gentle hum, as though they are alive and breathing. Yachts. Towels and bits of clothing left to hang from deck rails glow brightly. I am thinking surely I am sick, or in need of sleep, if boats have become living creatures, just as Jean cuts the motor altogether and in the silence we slide along the water surface until he warns, "Hold on, Pilgrim," and the boat abruptly shudders. I turn and see the bow is knocking up against a dock. At the end of the dock sits a whitewashed cottage.

I wake early the next morning, alone in the narrow bunk bed where Jean and I slept the night. But there is no sign of him now. It's noisy, not just from the raucous trilling of birds, which I grew accustomed to on Pineyard Island, but from people calling out across the water, the rise and fall of outboard motors, the rattle and clanking of sailboat rigging, the sounds of machinery: drills and saws and whatnot. Tentatively, I sit up on the edge of the bunk. I look down between the floorboards to see water moving below.

The beach house is a single room with built-in bunks along one side and a kitchenette, with a small sink and two-burner stovetop, along the other. Windows ring the cottage, the shutters propped open by short sticks so that I have to twist down to see out. I glimpse the dock and a strip of blue water and mangroves growing along the shore on either side. The place smells salty and rank.

I discover the toilet in a closet-sized outhouse a few feet from a back door and separated from the cottage by a short path bordered by hibiscus. When I step back inside moments later, Jean is standing in the hot, watery light. His face collapses into relief when he sees me.

He immediately comes over and runs his hands all over me as though I might be cold, which does in fact give me goosebumps.

"I was afraid you'd left," he says.

We spend the afternoon in the bunk, the heat like a third body on top of us. I don't ask where he went that morning.

"Do you think the people here will think I'm April?" I ask him.

"Don't wander around without me," he says gently.

But the next morning he is already gone again when I wake.

I go outdoors, but stay close, lingering between the cottage and outhouse, the hot sand between my toes and the sun beating on my skin. I am protected by the cottage and vegetation, but have a partial view onto the busy harbour, as small and cozy as a pocket. We are located in a row of cottages. Each has a dock with small boats tied on and stained gutting tables. Yet I have not seen a single soul except at a distance on a moored yacht or whaler zipping past. Most seem to be vacationers, people like Becky and her family, on boats with names like *Our Destiny*, *Epilogue*, *Mañana Maybe*, *Instead*.

There is no landline here. And my cell phone is back on Pineyard Island and Jean doesn't carry one. We are cut off. I think of April, Ethan, Katie. My mother in that home. My father abruptly dead on the floor of the barn.

I go back inside the cottage to wait for Jean, who doesn't return until noon, bringing fruit and bread, fish he boasts he caught himself at dawn, and enough coffee for me to drink all afternoon in an effort to combat the sluggishness the heat brings on. We have only the clothes we were wearing when we left Pineyard Island, but it's so humid that mine are already turning sour and I wear the minimum, either just my T-shirt or just my shorts. Jean wears his drawstring pants loose, low on his hips. He has a small, round belly like a cushion, not as firm as I had imagined. He puts a shirt on only when he's going out.

When I mention how hot it is, he apologizes for the weather, saying it is unseasonably warm, more like May than December. At this time of year the place belongs to the Americans and Canadians and a handful of Europeans escaping winter on their sailboats. He prefers the summer, when the tourists are gone and the Bahamians who own these cottages come out for the ocean breezes.

"What ocean breezes?" I say.

We climb back into the bunk together. Later, as dusk falls and it grows marginally cooler, he begins asking me questions about the farm in Cranfield. He reminisces about the tall, leafy trees, the strange bog behind the house, the rows of corn with their ears of milky-white kernels like babies' teeth.

It's gone, I try to tell him.

"I dream about Cranfield," he says, which astonishes me.

He quizzes me about the vegetables we grew, the animals in the barn. He wants to know about the Dover Clinic and Jordan Hospital—are they still there? I shrug. I report that Dr. Bruck has retired. I don't mention that his wife has gone crackers.

"Perhaps we should go back for a visit," he says.

"You're kidding, right?"

322

On the third afternoon, Jean returns wearing new clothes. He presents me with a batik skirt, purple flip-flops, and a gaudy green T-shirt decorated with shimmering fish.

"Time for us to make a move," he announces.

"Why?" I say. I am in my shorts and bra. I cross the room and lift his shirt and press myself against him. "Where?"

"Somewhere more private," he whispers, kissing my ear.

"Tomorrow. I promise." The skin over his belly feels heated through and through, like a stone baking in the sun. "Cross my heart."

Jean shakes his head. The expression he gives me is uncompromising.

I look at the clothes he's chosen. They are so not-me.

"It's too hot to wear all those clothes," I protest.

"Come now, Pilgrim. It's not like you to be meek."

He seems different. "Where will we go?" I ask.

"To the beach house."

"I thought this was the beach house."

"No, this is the dock house. The beach house is on the other side of the island, the ocean side."

"Oh."

"You'll find it cooler there."

"How far?"

"Ten-minute walk. We don't even leave the property."

"In that case I don't need to change."

He laughs. "Yes, you do. We cross the Queen's Highway. And the woods are maggoty with Haitians."

"Really? A highway?"

"Of course. However—" He puts his hands over my damp bra and cups my breasts. "Better to cover these properly."

I nod. He's probably right.

"And it will do you good to bathe in the sea, at the very least. Do you see my point?"

"I don't have a bathing suit."

He grins, as though waiting for this very objection, and takes from his back pocket two colourful strips of cloth and dangles them in front of me.

"A bikini? I'm too old for that, Jean."

He makes a throaty noise of disbelief that I suppose is meant to flatter me.

Does April wear a bikini? It has not escaped me that there is no evidence of April here. No clothes, no toiletries, no books, no knick-knacks. Nor can I smell her anywhere.

"I think we should dispose of your other clothes straight away," he tells me, scrunching up his nose comically and putting the bikini into my hands. I examine it with dread. It has blue-and-yellow sailboats and a fringe on the bottom front and across the top.

"I guess it could serve as underwear," I say.

"Good girl," he says, kissing me again before moving off to collect his own things in a small canvas bag.

We set off. I feel foolish, like a flower child, in my kooky skirt and the pink hibiscus Jean tucks behind my ear as we leave the cottage. The bikini bottom riding up my ass.

We follow a path through dense, knotted woods bordered with greying conch shells, like those in front of the house on Pineyard

Island that Patrice idiotically washed each morning. They separate the white sand of the path from the dark litter of leaves that cover the forest floor and look as though they would take a long time to decay. There are a number of intersections with other paths, and before long I know I would have trouble finding my way back. At one point we cross a wide track of hard-packed earth, barely space enough for one vehicle. The Queen's Highway.

"Where does it go?" I ask.

"The other side of the island."

"Are there paved roads?"

"No."

"Cars?"

"No. Most people use golf carts."

He seems reticent and distant suddenly, as though I've done something to offend him. Or he's changed his mind about me. I wonder again where he's been the last few mornings.

I ask, "What about your work? Don't you have appointments to keep on Pineyard Island?"

"I left a note in the office," he tells me.

"Can you do that?" I say to his back. "Just take off like that?"

"There's a nurse. I explained I was coming here."

This certainly strikes me as lacking in responsibility.

"There's a clinic on Little Dove Cay," Jean adds. He looks over his shoulder and catches me tugging at the stupid bikini bottom. "Where did you think I was each morning?"

"I see." Now I'm peeved he didn't tell me this before. "You're working at a clinic on this island?"

"Precisely."

"Just mornings?"

"Just some mornings. Soon it will be the holidays."

Christmas. I stop. "I want to go back," I tell him.

He turns and stares at me. "Where?"

"Where we were. The dock house."

"Why?"

"Everything has changed, even you."

"No, no." He walks back to me, but I can see that he is worried, too. He takes my hand. "Just follow me," he says. "We can return to the dock house for sleeping, if you prefer." He holds me and presses his face into my hair, breathing deeply. We stay this way until I lose my balance and we stumble together in the soft sand.

But we don't return. In fact, I never see the dock house again.

After a while the path rises onto open ground where a dozen short, arthritic-looking trees stand. Dark green fruit litters the ground. Jean tells me it's the orange orchard.

The beach house takes me by surprise. It's wooden and unpainted, yet grand, with a second-story balcony built over the porch, both of which extend on three sides of the house and sport decorative railings and balustrades. It will take me a few days to realize the crude jigsaw pattern cut into the balustrades is meant to resemble pineapples. The balcony is accessed via the upstairs bedrooms, but we will never venture out there, since Jean feels the balcony floor is too rotted to be safe.

I follow him up flared concrete front steps to the porch, which is deep and shadowy beneath the balcony and looks out through the trunks of evenly spaced coconut trees to the sea. In the farthest distance a row of whitecaps falls repeatedly over a reef.

"I thought a beach house was a place to change into your swimsuit," I joke.

"This is where I grew up," he says abruptly, going through double front doors lodged open with rocks. "With my mother and my sister."

I look up. The colour of the porch ceiling is sky blue, though the paint is peeling in fat, tongue-like curls. Flakes of paint are scattered across the porch floor and several grime-streaked chaise lounges.

While there had been no sign of April in the dock house, the beach house is saturated with her. I smell her the instant I trail inside after Jean, and for a moment I panic that she might be just around the corner—that, perversely, Jean has been keeping me at the dock house and my twin here. I am surprised by the strength of my fear. Then, without asking, Jean informs me that while April never liked either place, she preferred the beach house. Though now, he says with considerable self-pity, she won't come to the island at all.

"Don't talk about her to me," I say. "I don't want to even hear her name, Jean."

"As you wish," he says, shrugging.

But my twin is here, invisible. Clothes belonging to her, I will find, are hanging in the bedroom closet on the second floor. Various broad-rimmed sunhats hang from hooks in hallways, behind doors, in bedrooms, even in the dining room, the most formal of all the rooms, which is closed off and stuffy. Her brand of hand cream awaits me on her dresser top, a rusty razor in the shower stall, her sluggish electric toothbrush—which I brazenly appropriate—beside the marble bathroom sink.

Everything is from yesteryear: chipped and stained and losing colour, yet solid, holding up in a manner that conveys it was once the best money could buy.

"Who built this house?" I ask.

"My mother."

"Is there a phone?"

He laughs and shakes his head, then passes through a set of swinging doors into the kitchen, leaving me alone in the hallway.

The wooden floor is gritty with sand under my new flip-flops. I gaze out through the open doors at the coconut grove where the grey trunks slope upwards in unison in a kind of botanical choreography, creating bands of shade on the white sand. Their tangerine-orange and green fronds are so bright and jubilantly coloured, I think of a bird, or fire on a planet with more oxygen than Earth. The sea is clear and turquoise. Farther out it turns abruptly blue. On the horizon, soft lavender clouds lie fluffy and fragile, a pale sky above them.

I hear water running and the clattering of pots and pans.

Jean comes back through the swinging doors. When I turn, he is staring at me. "We will have a new life now," he says encouragingly.

Early each morning, dozens of chartered fishing boats roar out to sea in front of the house, navigating through the reef in single file. Eight hours later, they return at the same enthusiastic speed. Otherwise, time passes unmarked.

We make lavish, manic plans for our future, argue over little things, then fall asleep clamped to each other. One night he rouses me, his hands on my body, and not a word passes between us. This quickly becomes a habit—and often I am awake before he is.

I tell him everything about Katie, down to the last detail. I confess my fear she will turn on me. I decide the only thing to do is bring her to Little Dove Cay to live with us. There's a small school in town, Jean admits vaguely, mixed grades.

But I will have to be strategic. Ethan will fight for full custody. I used to listen to him at night, walking back and forth along the upstairs hallway, doing business on the phone with people sitting at desks in distant time zones.

"He takes no prisoners, Jean. You know what I mean?"

I pester him daily about finding a telephone in order to put these plans in motion.

Each morning I accompany Jean on his way to the clinic only as far as the Queen's Highway, at which point he kisses me and I promise to go straight back to the beach house, where I spend most of my time waiting for him.

He returns mid-afternoon, bearing fruit or gorgeously iridescent fish.

He doesn't want me to go exploring on my own — though he has little time to go exploring with me — but neither do I relish finding myself lost in the dark, hot woods in my bikini, so I wander around the property, generally within view of the house. The ocean side turns out to be only marginally cooler and the heat makes me lethargic. I visit the orange orchard, dragging my feet, and suck on the green oranges whose tough rinds I tear open with my teeth. Like ripping apart a baseball. The hot juice runs down my body, leaving a sticky film on my skin and bikini.

I stop combing my hair or bothering with a hat. The shower head falls off the first time I try to use it.

Behind the house is a dilapidated chicken coop on stilts, the run fallen away. Jean says his mother was proud of her hens. Such morsels of information I solemnly receive and tuck away.

"Hey, chickie, chickie, chickie," I call out each time I pass the coop.

Eventually I begin poking around the house. The bedroom we share is the only upstairs room that is fully furnished. The others are half-emptied, with wrought-iron beds and wooden chairs but bare, smudged walls and boxes stacked in corners. It's as though someone set out to gut the house, then changed their mind. Was that April?

There's a tall, stately secretary desk in the living room. Beneath the desk I find a hen's nest, empty and ancient, but neatly shaped. At one time handy, I suppose, if anyone wanted a poached egg for their breakfast. A 1940s sofa, with tufted orange upholstery and rock-hard throw pillows, extends nearly the length of one wall.

At first I wonder if I'll discover objects put away in unexpected places like I did in Cranfield, but everything in the desk is more or less as one would suppose: a bundle of coloured pencils held together with a dry rubber band that breaks the moment I touch it; a sewing kit; a pack of playing cards; a tin box of buttons, seashells, and chunks of coral; a notebook with elegantly handwritten recipes.

A few photos are loose among these objects, as though hastily thrown in, and most are of a white girl. In one, she is a toddler, sitting on the porch in the sun in her underwear; in another, she is older and wearing her school uniform and sagging knee socks. "Nassau Photo Studio" is stamped on the back. There is also one of her with a younger boy, whom I recognize instantly as Jean. They sit at a table, bent over work of some sort.

Most of the photos are black-and-white and remote, the way photographs were then, as though you are looking down the wrong end of a telescope, but two are in colour. One is a Polaroid of a woman posed in front of the chicken coop behind the house. Her skirt reaches just past her knees, and her blonde hair is fallen forward over one of her shoulders in a single braid. She is heavyset and has a smile that exposes large, white, even teeth. It is easy to see Jean in her face, particularly around the mouth.

The other is Jean's graduation photo — the same the immigration officer brought us over thirty years ago. I feel a stab of sadness for our lost time, the desolation that comes to everything. I flip the photo over and on the back it reads, "My son, Jean Moss, March 1968."

So this was Jean's family, the mother and sister the immigration officer eventually revealed to my own mother, after her constant telephoning. There is no evidence of a father, black or white, in any of the photos.

"Where is your father?" I finally ask him. "Is he alive?"

He doesn't answer me right away. It is twilight and we are walking along the beach, holding hands. He is swinging my arm and thinking.

"No idea, I'm afraid, who he was," he says finally. "Or if he's living."

"Did you ever meet him?"

"I wouldn't know, would I, Pilgrim, if I didn't know who he was?"

"Maybe he lived here on Little Dove Cay?"

"Not a chance. This was a white island then."

"You were the exception?"

331

He turns us back towards the house, hidden at this distance by the coconut trees.

"My mother took us to another island once, much larger," Jean says. "I was so young I can't tell you where it was. There were black people, more than I'd ever seen. My mother held my sister—she had started crying—in one hand and me in the other, and marched us through that town, up and down the streets. We stopped at a house with a narrow front but very long out the back—called shotgun houses. Two boys were sitting on the steps, staring at us. My mother told me they were my brothers and that their name was Moss."

"What did you say?"

"I just wanted to go home."

"You don't know where that was?"

"No."

Some days, Jean doesn't go to the clinic at all and stays close to the house. It seems to be a last-minute decision, especially if it's a nice day and on seeing the coconut grove and the dazzling turquoise water he can't drag himself away. I wonder aloud about vomiting children, gaping cuts, unexpected burns and breaks. He says it's not that busy and there's a government nurse. I think, slightly annoyed, well, that's news to me.

On such days, he goes fishing or keeps himself busy with small jobs that usually involve sand, which must be swept from the house daily—though it will only be back the next day and has long ago scoured away the floor's polish. Or he rakes the coconut grove from end to end, but it too will be disturbed overnight by wind and various creatures. He's particularly vexed by the nocturnal hermit crabs, which leave behind a network of zigzagging tracks that look as though a fleet of drunken cyclists passed through in the night, so he traps them in small pits baited with birdseed.

And then there is the transporting of white sand from the beach to scatter over the woods paths. He carries the sand in a small bucket and in his shorts pockets.

"Why do you bother?" I ask.

"It gives them a clean and tidy look," he says.

One day I find an old pamphlet on the history of Little Dove Cay, published in 1980 by the local heritage society. I take it out to the porch and sit in one of the chaise lounges, under the blue ceiling. Chips of paint float down from above and cling to my hot skin.

I read about pockets of islands settled at the time of the Revolutionary War by American colonists loyal to the British Crown. I learn that Little Dove Cay was settled by Loyalists fleeing New England.

After a while, I see Jean striding up from the beach with a bucket of sand and his sand-filled pockets dragging down the sides of his shorts.

I call over to him, "What did you mean when you said this was a white island when you were a boy?"

He keeps walking a few paces before abruptly turning in my direction. When he reaches me, he stops and sets his bucket of sand down and squints up through the balustrades with the pineapple cutouts.

"It was a settlement of native whites only," he says. "Black Bahamians were excluded."

"Your mother was a native white?"

He nods. His face is shiny with heat.

"Her ancestors were from New England?"

He nods again. His look is peculiar, unreadable, and it silences me. He picks up his bucket and I stare after him as he walks away with that heaviness in his pockets from the sand, and an ache comes over me. I think about the young man he was when he came to us in Cranfield: a fearless boy who had never doctored yet was eager and willing to begin. Ready to do what politeness required of him: listen to my father's schemes and opinions, my dumb chatter, April's sneaky silence. Hack up a water snake, treat benign hornet bites, witness a young girl shoot herself.

He was mysterious, with his accent and wash-and-wear clothes and gentlemanly ways, but in truth it was his powerful sense of self that captured us. We were not used to people who were so gravely, yet unquestionably, certain of themselves. It led to us abandoning each other. But he could not belong to every one of us. And not every one of us could belong to him.

Had he never come to us, duped by my father's promise that all manifestations of DNA were welcome in Cranfield, and never met my sister and me, what man would Jean be now? Despite everything, he liked us, he liked the farm—even now he talks about Cranfield.

But I worry we eroded something in him. That we plucked him off a life track where everything had a place and decisiveness ruled—because sometimes, watching him, I question his conviction, that drunken night on Pineyard Island, when he declared he'd taken the wrong girl.

334

SEVENTEEN

There is a side entrance to the beach house through the kitch-en. It's a Dutch door with upper and lower panels that open independently of each other. A nocturnal tree frog sleeps all day on the outside of the upper panel, its gooey appendages holding it fast to the wood even as we go in and out.

I'm unaware it's Christmas Day until sometime in the afternoon I ask Jean why he didn't go to work. When he tells me, I turn and walk away. I never sent Katie a present. My plan was to send her a plane ticket, but I haven't even managed to telephone her.

Two days later I wake and, clear as a bell, hear Katie speaking to Fred. One sentence, matter-of-fact but imperious. "Go find your new toy, Fred."

My stomach is growling from hunger. I slip into my bikini and go downstairs and rummage through the cupboards in the kitchen, using a footstool to get to the higher reaches, and find a bottle of green olives. There is peanut butter in the refrigerator and bread that requires some plucking away of mouldy bits. I set the ragged bread on the counter and cover one slice with peanut butter and the other with chopped olives. The morning sunlight comes in the window and the food glistens and lifts as though it has been placed under an invisible magnifying glass, or as though I have Superman vision. I've never noticed that pimento strips are covered with the tiniest of black specks.

It's 9:38 in the morning.

I crawl out through the bottom panel of the Dutch door, not wanting to disturb the tree frog. I find Jean in the coconut grove, standing over one of his hermit crab traps, tying the prisoners together in pairs by their legs before dropping them in his bucket. Later he'll fling them out over the water where they'll sink and drown.

"You and me, we're going to town," I say firmly. "I need to phone Katie. Today."

He looks up at me and smiles. I hand him half a peanut butter and olive sandwich.

"Also, we're running out of food," I go on. "We need groceries. We've got almost nothing left."

"Nothing? Not a crumb?"

"We have some things, canned salmon and pasta. But I'm sick of those, and of your oranges and fish. I want some cookies, a candy bar or something. I want to hear Katie's voice on the phone and I want to tell Ethan he has to buy her a ticket. Let's go. Now."

"Will your husband agree?" he asks innocently, making it sound as though he is the only sane one here.

"We're going to town," I repeat, my voice rising. "It'll be an excursion."

"An excursion is a brilliant idea."

"To town, Jean. To find a phone. Get food. Maybe some new clothes." I pull at my bikini with its grimy nautical scenes.

He gives me a kiss. "I'm sorry."

"Okay."

We fetch our hats and sunglasses to protect us from the sun, which Jean remarks will be useful, as it's scorching where we're going. He searches under the kitchen sink and finds a couple of army surplus canteens. As he fills them both with water, he suggests I wear a long-sleeved shirt as well.

I'm suspicious and feel like I'm negotiating with a child. "We're going to town, right?" I ask.

It's nearly noon when we trudge off past the hen house and orange orchard.

When we get to the Queen's Highway, beyond which I have not been since leaving the dock house weeks ago, Jean turns left and I follow. Instinctively, I sense this is not the direction to town, but I am wary of challenging him. At least we are moving, I tell myself, reuniting with the passage of time.

"I'm so happy to be doing something," I say. "I was starting to think the earth had stopped rotating on its axis."

Jean laughs and glances back at me appreciatively.

"I'm happy we're doing something together," I continue, watching his back and purposeful strides. Despite his white hair and rangy limbs, in many ways he is still the restless young doctor roaming around the farmhouse, inquiring after my mother's zucchini squash or some other matter of importance to her, too naive and good-natured to know how these questions irritated my father.

Gradually the parched trees give way to flowery spikes, like giant asparagus, and a twisting orange vine that blankets other plants and that Jean informs me is called lovevine. Other than that, he keeps his thoughts to himself.

The Queen's Highway narrows. Under the shimmering heat, I feel a touch of vertigo. I know by now we are definitely not going to town. The land seems to roll and tilt like milk in a saucer, and I am grateful Jean recommended the hat and sunglasses. Then the highway dips, out of view of the sea, which unaccountably makes me nervous. The temperature is oppressive. Fallen leaves crack like china plates underfoot.

When the highway crests again, a breeze hits my sweating face, and we are facing dozens of above-ground caskets set among sand and sea grass. Jean passes through a white wooden arch and I follow, though there is no fence or other barrier to mark the cemetery's perimeter.

"Jean," I mumble. "Wait."

The stone caskets are laid out randomly, without rows or any discernible planning, and I stay close to him, not wanting to step anywhere he has not. When he stops, I stop just behind him. I want to keep moving, to stir the air, but I don't want to touch him. It's too hot.

He points to a grave marker near our feet.

In Loving Memory of Emma Sybil Johnson
Beloved Daughter
Born February 15, 1946
Died September 7, 1955
SHE WAS AFFECTIONATE AND LOVED BY ALL

The heat is like a furnace, a drug, but "Emma Sybil Johnson" rings a bell. Her name is on a baby's mug, in a songbook, on the back of a child's rocking chair in one of the half-empty bedrooms.

"You were asking about my family," he says.

What an effort to think. "Your sister, Jean?"

"Half-sister. We did not share a father. But perhaps you already know this, since you've been rifling through those old photos."

He nods at a larger casket within inches of the other, though its marker is smaller and the inscription simpler:

Lillian Cole Johnson, 1923-1973
JESUS CALLED HER

His mother. I am still reluctant to touch him.

I imagine him bringing April here decades ago. I imagine her learning all this about Jean — that he was not really the whole, perfect young man we'd thought. That he was broken, that he had a sister and a mother — a family — already dead when he came to us. All the time he was in Cranfield, he was carrying that around and never told us.

But there's something else, something ominous and difficult to put into words. I sense I'm being punished, or that April once felt punished, right here in this very place. Suddenly it is 1975 and I am April, only sixteen and homesick, being led across this hot land and taking the blame for having a father that drove Jean out.

"How did your sister die?" I ask, feeling shaky.

"A coconut."

"Sorry, what did you say?" Something is wrong with me.

"Her skull was split by a falling coconut. Mother rang the dinner bell, then sent me out. Emma was flat on her face in the coconut grove. It was a bright day. But very windy."

"How old was she…" I say, staring at the grave marker and struggling to do the math.

"Nine. She died instantly. Head injuries are a more common cause of death than people realize. If she had lived, she may have had lifelong disabilities."

"How sad. Terrible."

"It was a freak occurrence," Jean assures me.

"I'm so sorry," I say.

"Mother fell apart."

I wonder if this was when the hens moved into the house.

"Jean."

When he looks at me his eyes linger. "You should start drinking your water, Pilgrim."

"It tastes like plastic, from that yucky canteen."

"For God's sake, just drink it," he says. But as we exit under the white wooden arch, he says apologetically, "It will help you."

I wish we could go back to the beach house and upstairs into bed, where we would hold each other for the rest of the day, but at the Queen's Highway he takes my hand and leads me in the opposite direction. It's as though he is drawing me deeper and deeper into something I won't get out of easily.

"Don't you find this heat crippling?" I ask, but he doesn't seem to hear me.

Does this island go on forever? Maybe it's not really an island?

"I don't want to get lost," I say to his sweat-splattered back.

"No one is getting lost."

"I don't want to be so far away that we won't be found." I am finding it difficult to speak. My ankle is beginning to cause me pain and my legs feel funny, as though a rare disease is creeping up my body.

The Queen's Highway ends at a crumbling stone lighthouse where we disturb lizards, and even with my dulling mind, I can see this is someone's camp. A piece of carpet, a flattened paper cup and the sole of a shoe sit near an extinguished fire that emits a cloying, fruity smell. Bits of torn cloth cling to bushes, and flies hover over a pile of fishbones. Haitians, probably.

"Pilgrim. Look at me."

Or is this where he comes when he's not with me? That would be absurd. Again the landscape begins to tilt and shimmer.

I try to focus on him.

He puts a hand on my cheek. "You're on fire," he tells me.

"Why?" My voice sounds loud.

"Sunstroke."

"Are you cross with me?"

"You're confused. It's my fault. This walk was too much for you."

This time he puts me in the lead, his hands on my shoulders as he steers me down through the bush to a small beach that comes upon us suddenly. He sits me at the water's edge and forces me to drink the water left in my canteen, then his, one small sip after another. He scoops up the warm, syrupy ocean water in his cupped hands and dribbles it down my back and neck.

Although my head has begun to throb, I gradually feel better. I prefer the island at my back like this, and being close to the water, where it seems safer. After I while we stumble out for a brief swim, his arm secured around my waist.

Later, we lie together in the sand until the sun is low in the sky.

"Better now?" he asks.

"Recovered. Thanks, Doc."

"Your eyes are not so glassy. That's a good sign."

My mind drifts as he talks about fishing—triggerfish, hog-fish, mutton snapper, yellowtail—and I enjoy this meaningless chatter, so uncharacteristic of him. The sand gives way beneath my body, surrendering to my elbows, buttocks, heels, the back of my head.

I may have fallen asleep for a moment when I realize he is reminiscing about Cranfield again.

"I think you're fixated on that place," I murmur.

"You don't know what it meant to me," he says. "I took the invitation as an honour."

"Of course, Jean. I know. I'm sorry."

I guess he never knew his practice in Cranfield was illegal—a sham. I hope he never knows.

"Although it was another story when Russell took his pistol out of the glove compartment."

I sit up. My head is pounding. Snowy white seabirds are flying left to right, low over the surf precisely where it crumbles on the sand, where earlier I sat while Jean revived me. The sun is going to set any minute.

"Jean, I don't want to talk about that."

"There's something I've always wanted to know," he says. "Something I'd like to ask you."

I sigh. "What?"

"Did you know the pistol was there, in the glove compartment, Pilgrim?"

"Of course not! Is that what you think? Is that what *she* said?"

Yet. I encouraged their car ride. I lied about the Rototiller. I did nothing while the bottles of tomatoes exploded over the stovetop and my father plummeted into rage.

"I have to go away for a while," he says.

"You're mad at me. You're punishing me."

"No. But my clinics are scheduled to start on the out islands tomorrow. I'll be gone two days at the most."

"Why didn't you tell me before now?"

"I didn't think of it."

"I'll be alone?"

"Stay around the house, don't go anywhere."

"How long?"

"I just told you. Two days. I have your word you'll stay around the house?"

"Can't we find a phone first?"

"As soon as I'm back."

"You have to go?"

"It's my job, Pilgrim. Believe me, I'd rather stay here on Little Dove Cay with you."

That night we sleep soundly in each other's arms, not waking once. The next morning I walk him to the Queen's Highway. He heads off to catch a ferry to Pineyard Island, and from there a float plane to begin his rounds. I promise to stay around the house and he promises to return safely.

Two days pass. Then three, then four, but there is no sign of Jean.

The monstrous fishing boats roar out each morning like an alarm clock, then back, eight hours later, snaking in through the reef. The tree frog stays glued to the kitchen door. I am wakeful and nervous at night. The noise of barking dogs lifts and falls, sounding at times as though the dogs are on the other side of the island, then as though they are just out there in the coconut grove. Insects rattle on through the hours like they're on amphetamines, and when the sun rises and the Bahamian mockingbird starts up, it's a relief to get out of bed.

I eat the last can of salmon, then make a meal of macaroni tossed with some dubious ketchup. I finish the peanut butter, the olives, but look askance at the powdered mashed potatoes and hearts of palm. Beyond that, there is little other than some brown sugar, margarine, an old bottle of Pepto-Bismol.

Where the hell is he?

I scour the house for money and come up with some coins. Not only is my purse still on Pineyard Island — with April — but it appears Jean took his wallet with him. He should have considered leaving money for me, I think testily, given the chance he'd be delayed.

I set off for town with the loose change. At least enough to make a collect call. When I get to the Queen's Highway, I turn right.

Three different golf carts pass, but the occupants — stout blonde men and women dressed in long pants and shirts — ignore me, though I am right there, pressed up against the dense foliage and smiling at them eagerly.

One of my flip-flops gives out and I toss both into the dusty woods, causing a bird or other hidden creature to respond with a noise like someone smashing two stones together.

Abruptly, the Queen's Highway exits the woods, enters a settlement, and becomes pavement, which means Jean was lying when he said there are no paved roads on the island. I am surprised and relieved, but feel betrayed by Jean, to find civilization so close at hand. Pastel houses with gingerbread trim along the eaves and porch railings dazzle in the sunlight, their darker shutters closed. The yards are tidy and neatly clipped.

There is a small church at a crossroads with a letterboard that reads: "Keep Thy Tongue From Evil." I smell something familiar and sweet—like strawberry Jell-O being made—as I pass a house with a picket fence engulfed by bougainvillea.

I keep walking, descending towards the harbour where I notice, despite a general busyness, that every sailboat, fishing boat, and motor yacht is tied up to the docks. I wander through the town barefoot and sweaty, trying to make eye contact, but no one will look at me.

I just need a phone, I want to explain, I just need to hear my daughter's voice. A gust of wind careens down the narrow street, spraying me with sand. I am infuriated with Jean for putting me in this position.

The Little Dove Cay Souvenir Gift Shop is being closed as I pass. Beyond it is a grocery store, which turns out to be air-conditioned, peaceful, and cool. I go up and down the single aisle and look longingly at chocolate bars and bottles of Coke in a refrigerated display case. I figure I have enough money for a Mars bar. The woman behind the counter is putting her cash drawer in order, so I put some of the coins in a neat pile on the counter and wait for her to look at me. Finally, I give up and walk out of the store, leaving the money.

Outside again, I glance at people and devour the Mars bar but am afraid to use my voice to ask for directions to a pay phone. I feel like I'm in kindergarten without April and can't whisper to her for help, for comfort. After half an hour, I turn back. As I trail along the higher ground through the gingerbread houses, the wind picks up. It whistles down the wires overhead, incongruously bringing to mind a howling snowy landscape.

By the time I'm at the beach house, the coconut trees are bent nearly to the ground and their fronds are opening and closing like fans as they slash the air.

I yank at the heavy front doors to close them and at once it becomes dark inside the hallway until lightning flashes and, for a moment, the house is awash in light. I can hear the wind and rain entering through the open windows upstairs and am thinking about going up to close them, when the thunder sounds. I shrink back against the wall and feel the house moving. I spring away. Everything becomes excessively loud: furniture being flung down the length of the veranda. Sand, rocks, branches hitting the house.

I panic, imagining Jean in a tiny plane, light as paper. Or perhaps the storm caught him as he dashed between islands to save another girl with tetanus in some boat now smashed, overturned, dragged out to sea? I realize I have no real idea where he went. All I have is his promise he would be safe and return in two days.

When the wind lets up, I hear the rain and feel the temperature drop. Even my feet are touched by this cooler air. I don't go upstairs, though it's likely the rain is soaking the floors, and instead I turn into the living room and make a dash for the 1940s orange sofa. I huddle at one end. A glass of water Jean left on the coffee table tinkles with each blast of thunder. Rain falls sideways against the house for a long while, then turns to hail, bouncing into the room like marbles. Eventually the lightning appears out over the water, its thunder muted, and by dusk the storm is gone.

I tiptoe onto the veranda. The chaise lounges have disappeared. Branches are scattered everywhere and the sand is dark and soaked like quicksand. The shining vegetation is motionless. There are no sounds of birds. Puddles formed in Jean's white sand paths look like blue milk.

I return to the sofa, and although the storm has passed, I am awake all night as the nocturnal noises of the out-of-doors re-establish themselves with vigour, and Jean fails, minute after minute after minute, to return. I imagine Haitians, having abandoned the drenched woods where they had been camping or the collapsed boat sheds where they had been squatting, on the hunt now for new lodgings.

Shortly after dawn I hear voices, then the padding of bare feet on the floorboards. Someone has come into the house through the kitchen door. It could be anyone. It could be Jean.

It's my sister.

"Are you alone?" I grumble, rubbing my jaw. I haven't risen off the sofa. I haven't even raised my head.

"Patrice is with me."

"I hope you didn't disturb that tree frog on the kitchen door."

"Didn't see any tree frog."

"Why are you here?"

"They saw you in town yesterday." She circles around and perches on the coffee table and her face moves into the light. She looks concerned and angry. She's wearing one of her billowy dresses smelling of incense. "Penny, from the grocery store, she telephoned me."

"No. They did not see me. I could have been a ghost."

"They kept looking at you, knowing you weren't me, thinking you were me, and so on."

I sit up on an elbow. "I'm telling you, April, no one was looking at me. Not one person. Not once."

"I'm telling you, Pilgrim," she says, her voice rising, "they were looking at you, all right."

I flop back down on the sofa, yet keep my eye on her as she checks the room to see how I might have changed things.

"Where is he?" I demand.

"No idea."

"You're lying."

"As far as I know, the out islands."

"Is he okay?"

"Of course he's okay," she says scornfully.

"I was worried about him in the storm."

"Were you. Well, he's working."

"Is that the truth?"

"He's my husband, I should know."

"Except you're not married."

She pounces on me and digs her fingernails into my wrist. She says something, but I don't know what, it sounds like a snarl. Her face is pious, twisted, hot. If she kills me, no one will hear me cry or know. Patrice will probably dig the hole in the ground.

"We don't need someone to tell us we can be together," she hisses. "We don't care about all that bullshit."

"Really? 'Cause he wants to come back to Cranfield with me."

"No he doesn't!" Her fingernails release me only to clamp down farther up my arm. Later it will look like a badly done allergy test.

"He dreams about Cranfield," I say.

"Cranfield is nothing."

"He wakes me in the night with his hands all over my body. So *haw-haw*."

"Let me guess? Around two, three o'clock?"

"Go to hell."

"That was a habit we got into in Cranfield, Pilgrim. You can appreciate we had to be careful. The middle of the night was the safest time. It was *our* time."

"Nice try," I tell her. "What's with the outfit, by the way? Little old for a hippie, aren't you?"

"At least I don't look like a bum. Have you seen yourself? Honest to God, you stink."

"*Me?*"

"All my life" — she's so enraged she has to stop and take a breath, her face inches from mine — "I shared things with you. Everything. But not him. That's why we ran away. We could never feel safe around you."

"I don't care what you come up with to hurt me."

"You cast a fucking shadow. Wherever I was, whatever I was thinking."

"You don't think it was the same for me?"

"He was the only thing I wouldn't share. The *only* thing."

"Where is he?"

"None of your business."

"Where is he?"

"He had to leave, that's the God's truth. He had to get away from you. He can't stand you. You were smothering him, kept asking him questions, kept touching him, you wouldn't leave him alone. You have to control everything."

"You're a liar."

"You smothered him. You smothered me, all the time. You did. You probably smother your daughter and husband, too. They probably hate you."

She's a monster.

"You're the monster," she says, her voice hoarse now from yelling. "Sure, right, perfect, go on, start crying. Perfect."

I wipe my nose. I hate her. Did he really say I smother him?

"Crybaby."

She disappears and goes into the kitchen. It sounds like she's unpacking. Better be groceries.

She reappears and demands, "Why are you rubbing your jaw like that?"

"My teeth hurt."

"Great. You're starving. You know there's no food in that kitchen. What were you planning on doing if I didn't show up? Huh?"

I ignore her and she stomps out.

After a while, Patrice tiptoes in and places two grilled cheese sandwiches and a glass of chocolate milk on the coffee table, then tiptoes out. I almost ask him if his daughter got an iPod for Christmas, just for the hell of it.

I gobble down the food, then hurry upstairs and crawl into the bed I shared with Jean. I've not slept in any other room and I'll be damned if I'm going to start now. Plus I'm dead tired.

But I can't sleep. As the afternoon passes, I listen to the footsteps below, April and Patrice conferring, doors opening and closing. Sounds like she's doing a thorough wash-up in the kitchen.

Late in the day, I go to the window and see the ocean is still torn-up and murky. Above it, strips of grey clouds criss-cross the sky. Below, Patrice is dragging away the broken branches and fallen coconuts littering the grove.

In the night I sense someone getting into bed with me, but I'm finally too deeply asleep to be roused.

Near morning, I dream I'm trying to find my way back to the farm. I meet some children lounging in half-broken beach chairs who tell me I've gone the wrong way. *Go back to the road and turn right,* they say, laughing merrily—not mocking me, just happy like children are meant to be. *It's that house right there,* they say. When I go in the house, it's a shambles. Dozens of plastic toilets and potties are lined up along one side of the kitchen, each holding a few inches of urine. The counters are as tall as trees, with recipes and notes tacked neatly to the outside of the cupboard doors. A woman in a ruffled apron stands with her back to me.

I say, *Mom, there you are. How did we get separated?* But when she turns, she doesn't recognize me.

I open my eyes and look into those of my sister's. She—not Jean—has slept the night in the bed with me.

"What a sad dream." I put a hand over my eyes.

I can smell and feel her breath on me. "Cranfield?" she asks. I nod.

"I try to think of it as just a place," she says, "that's gone." She's watching me. "You're so angry," she whispers, like she's amazed.

"So are you."

"But I'm talking about you."

"Why is it okay for you to be angry, but not me?"

"I didn't say it was okay for me."

"Talking to you is like talking to myself. Like being caught in one of those awful mental loops."

"Pilgrim," she says softly. "Do you realize how filthy you are?"

"Yeah, well, we had this slovenly thing happening."

"You do, actually, stink. I say that nicely."

I don't dispute this, and she gets out of bed and disappears into the bathroom. I hear a drawer opening and closing, water splashing into that chipped marble sink. When she returns she's wearing the blue housecoat that's been hanging on the back of the door and which I never touched, as though I knew she would eventually arrive and put it on. I watch her set a basin of water, along with a towel, soap and nail clippers, on the bed beside me.

"Jean likes to get all primordial out here," she says matter-of-factly.

She sits on the edge of the bed and lifts one of my hands and begins washing it, thoroughly, one finger at a time.

"I couldn't find towels," I say. My hand looks lifeless and unfamiliar. "Where were they?"

"Everything is put away," she says, by way of explanation. I don't know what this means. "Pilgrim, your nails are a mess."

"I looked for towels. But then the shower head fell off, so it didn't matter."

She pauses, my hand in hers. "This is my old mood ring, isn't it?"

"I think so. I found it in the refrigerator in Cranfield."

"I knew it was mine."

"You can have it back," I say. "It's yours, after all."

She waves a hand dismissively, then picks up the nail clippers and begins trimming my nails. She works slowly and with care, squinting a little in the morning light.

I feel myself growing sleepy.

"The shower head is easy to fix," she says after a while. "Jean should have done that for you."

"April?"

"Yeah?"

"When we were little—I mean before we could talk—I used to try to see the air between us. Did you do that, too?"

She shakes her head. "I don't think so."

"I realized later I was trying to see something that can't be seen with the human eye. Oxygen, carbon dioxide, nitrogen—we can't see air."

"Wow," she says. "Have you seen your feet?"

"I'm lacking footwear," I point out.

"You should shower, okay? I'll fix the shower head for you."

"I would stare at you, puzzled that I couldn't see it. The air between us."

She circles around to the opposite side of the bed with the basin of water and toiletries, sits, and picks up my other hand.

"You'll take a shower?" she prods. "I brought shampoo and conditioner, by the way. I knew you'd need it. There's nothing here."

"Okay, I'll shower."

"You know, after Jean arrived—"

"In Cranfield?"

"Yes, yes." She pauses. "The moment he arrived, and moved into the room under the stairs, all I wanted to do was touch him." She looks at me. "But we didn't know how to be with a man."

I remember.

"Right?" she says. "I thought he would be like you. The way you and I were. Easy to understand. Easy to love. Words not necessary. But with special—exciting—touching."

"He was unprepared for Dad."

April's smile is lopsided, like a shrug.

"What I can't wrap my head around," I say, "is Dad coming down here and being civil to him. It boggles my mind to think he forgave Jean."

"He wasn't civil. He was rude. He didn't forgive him. He didn't like him." She pauses and contemplates me. I am overly aware of my hand in her stilled hands. Then she picks up the soap again. "They asked about you, Mom and Dad, if I'd heard anything. They said they couldn't reach you. I think Canada just seemed too vast and unmanageable to them."

"They did? Why didn't you tell me this before?"

"I guess I should have."

Birds are singing again, and I listen with my eyes closed, marvelling at the strength of their voices after yesterday's vicious storm, until—suddenly alert—I open my eyes and look at her.

"Don't cry," I say. "Please don't cry, April."

"It was awful," she tells me. "I wanted to die."

"Hey." I reach out. "Come here."

She crawls onto the bed and lies beside me. We hold each other.

"You lived in this house first?" I ask quietly.

She nods.

"How long?"

"Months. No one would acknowledge me. A black man with a white woman? That didn't go over too well here, either. I missed you so much. Mom and Dad, Petunia, even Dad's geese. Even that nasty horse."

"Happy."

She laughs at the name. "I know you don't believe me, but I just wanted to die."

"I believe you."

I knew this. Of course I knew this.

"We haven't done that in years," she says sadly. "Wake up together like that."

"In the middle of the night?"

"I had to be quiet," she says. "I used to sneak out of our bedroom and creep down the stairs. He'd be waiting for me, in his bed. Everyone was in the house and none of you knew."

"True. Wow. I didn't know."

"He was so tender."

I wipe her hair off her face and rub her head, then stroke her arm. Her forearm resembles mine — coppery hairs, the wrist joint knobby and narrow — which is unremarkable, except that no one in the world looks as similar to us as we do to each other.

"Pilgrim."

There's something else.

"When I said that all I wanted to do was touch him, the moment he arrived? I was lying. It didn't happen like that."

I'm not sure I want to hear this.

"At first, I was just trying to keep you and Jean apart. I was jealous. You trailed after him like a puppy, and to be honest, I thought he was a pompous jerk. So I started wearing make-up and pretended to care about him, only because you did. I needed to keep —"

Stop.

"— pace with you. Remember how attentive he was to you, when you saw the snake in the cellar? Then you were stung by the hornets, and I knew something had happened. I only wanted to drive a wedge between you two. By being you."

Almost-me, I think. *Not me.*

"But then everything changed," she says.

"What do you mean?"

"I grew fond of him."

When I wake again it's noon. I'm alone in the room and my suitcase is waiting for me beside the bed. I consider how it got here: Patrice lugging it from Pineyard Island to Little Dove Cay, then up the stairs, ever so quiet, while I napped. Beside it sits my purse, with money and passport.

In the bathroom I find the containers of shampoo and conditioner. After my shower, I brush out my hair, which turns glossy now that the salt and sand and dirt are out of it. It has grown considerably since last October, and I'm thinking I might keep it long like this. Maybe just a trim when I get home.

I dress in my own clothes: long pants, flowered blouse, pale blue sweater. I feel fantastic in them.

The day is cloudless but cooler. Perhaps what Jean would call proper Bahamian winter weather. April and I take a stroll through the coconut grove where the sand now has a yolky yellow sheen. We leave our footprints everywhere.

"Where is he?" I ask again. "Is he back on Pineyard Island?"

"No."

"Where did he go?"

"Not certain. There are a couple of settlements on the out islands he likes. Not my cup of tea."

I'm pretty sure this is not the truth and that she knows exactly where he is. But that means he's safe. I guess he had to choose one of us to rush to before the storm.

I change tack. "His mother must have been an unusual woman."

"She was an outsider. After Jean was born, her husband—the father of her daughter—left her. It's a close-knit religious community. I can't stand the place. I don't know why Jean is so attached to it."

"I suppose it's his home. He can't let it go."

"Anyway, the husband abandoned her, never spoke to her again. He still lives here. He owns the Souvenir Gift Shop in town."

She arranges ferry passage for us back to Pineyard Island, but I insist I need to make a call first. We pack, and April, Patrice, and I walk to town. April leads me out onto a pier around the back of Penny's grocery to a pay phone located where only someone in a boat could see it.

While I listen to the ringing—four, five, six rings—and imagine Fred in the empty house, barking, I stare across at a small beach bordered by dark, leggy mangroves. A Haitian is shovelling seaweed onto the bow of a rowboat dragged up on the sand. An elderly white man sits slumped at the stern, gazing out across the water.

I'm startled when Ethan picks up. I'm also relieved it's him and not Katie.

"We've had an unbelievable amount of snow this year," he says. "I just came in from clearing the driveway and steps."

We haven't spoken for weeks and this is what he tells me. He sounds tired. It hits me he has no faith anymore that I'm coming home.

"I'm coming home."

He hesitates, but when he speaks again he sounds stronger. "Where are you?"

"Didn't you get my message?"

"You left a message, oh right, something about moving to a different island. Which I could barely hear, like you were whispering. Why would you be whispering? What's the matter with you? Is this some kind of joke? Does Pilgrim Wheeler still exist?"

"The phone situation is tricky. I've been trying to call. There was a hurricane."

"Really?"

"I'm coming home."

"Certain?"

"Promise."

"What makes you think you're welcome?"

"What about Katie?" I ask, suddenly nervous.

I remember my plan to bring my daughter down here to live the remainder of her childhood with Jean and me in that ramshackle beach house. A plan as poorly considered as any of my father's.

"Funny you should ask," Ethan is saying. "The other night she had this idea you'd been killed in a car accident and nobody told us." Abruptly, he drops the sarcasm. "I don't know how to handle these things."

The elderly man puts his hands on his knees and pushes himself up off the rowboat. He turns stiffly and speaks to the Haitian, who nods and takes his elbow.

———

We take the ferry—a souped-up fishing boat—back to Pineyard Island. April and I huddle near the front, avoiding the exhaust fumes, while Patrice stands at the stern, bracing himself with a hand on the boat's canopy.

Jean isn't at the house, though I would have been surprised if he were. Patrice slips away without my noticing. I phone the airlines and book an afternoon flight to Nassau, then on to Boston. I also phone Mrs. Godfrey, but again there is no answer. April signs the various legal documents drawn up by Dan Boucher without reading a single word.

I take a last look at the little bedroom backing onto a wall of plant life and the remote chance of parrots.

Together we sit inside the small terminal building with four other passengers, waiting for the pilot to fetch us. April is antsy. She goes over and asks for two Cokes from an old woman selling hotdogs and conch fritters out of a space that might have once been a closet.

She comes back and hands me the Coke.

"Your starter's about to go," I tell her. "On the Mazda?"

"I know that, Pilgrim."

I sip my Coke, which is warm and definitely not Coke. "Is this ice tea?"

"Might be. That woman is blind. I mean literally."

"Well, you should get it fixed, April. You don't want to break down somewhere."

"You were always better with cars," she says, a tremor in her voice.

The pilot comes in and announces the plane is ready to board. He doesn't look old enough to have finished high school. The other passengers gather around him and he begins checking their boarding passes against a print-out in his hands.

Together, my sister and I get to our feet. I recognize the pressure of her hand on my back as she gives me a small, guiding push. But when I take a step, she grabs my sleeve.

I stop and look at her. "Please don't cry," I whisper, and she nods.

The four other passengers have wandered, unescorted, out onto the tarmac. The pilot glances at his print-out, then in my direction. "Pilgrim Wheeler?" he asks a touch impatiently, his soft, young face serious and unsmiling.

"That's you," April says and lets go of my sleeve and, for the second time, gives me a slight push.

I show the pilot my boarding pass, then follow him and the other passengers across the tarmac. Once in the plane, he directs me to the co-pilot's seat, as though I'm someone he'll need to keep his eye on now. He straps me in—a little excessively, it seems—making it difficult for me to twist around and wave to my sister, if indeed she is standing outside waiting to see me fly off.

The plane taxis to the end of the runway where it turns, the engines rising and falling in pitch, then heads back, gaining a rocky speed. Both the sound and heat pin me as though amplified by the casing of blue sky above. As we pass the terminal shed, I strain against the straps, searching, and there she is, nearly to the Mazda and almost gone. At the last second I see her stop as Jean emerges from behind a stand of palmetto.

We both knew he had to be somewhere close by.

EIGHTEEN

I land in Boston and rent another Honda Civic. Patchy snow and silence have fallen over the fields and woods and houses. Last year's corn still stands in places, its lanceolate leaves flicking in a blustery wind, and late-season cabbages, still awaiting harvest, nestle like rows of human heads in the fields.

It's late afternoon when I arrive at Sunny Gardens Homecare. When I first step in, the common room looks empty and is poorly lit, the only illumination coming from the television. *Deal or No Deal* is on and though the volume is low, I recognize the voice of Howie Mandel coaching contestants. A cardboard Santa with full troop of reindeers is still taped to the wall, and a nearly desiccated poinsettia sits on the coffee table, as though the plan is to let it fully die before chucking it out.

There are sounds indicative of mealtime and, closer, something knocking. That's when I see her, trapped in a wheelchair pulled up tight to the wall. Her hands are folded on her lap, while her toes thump against the wall in a feeble, absent-minded protest. The odour of reheated food grows stronger as I cross the room.

"Mom?"

I switch on a nearby table lamp and, once I figure out how to unlock the chair, roll her away from the wall. When I see the crust of food on her collar, I know I haven't made a mistake in coming here.

She blinks a few times but doesn't look at me. Her lips are chapped and cracking.

"I think you're a little drugged there, Mom, what do you say?"

She doesn't say anything.

I hear a muffled sound from another part of the building. A groan? A creaking floorboard? Then, the ding of a microwave timer. I feel crazy with the need to get my mother out of here before Mr. Milton appears, although as the minutes pass, I begin to doubt my arrival has been noticed.

I push the chair over to the television, which seems to revive her slightly. "Did you find the dog?" she asks.

"Yes," I whisper.

"Her name is like a flower?"

"Yes. She's safe."

"What a billy I am. I'm just being so billy."

"I think you mean silly."

She stares at me.

"You're not silly, Mom, but just don't try to stand."

I hurry down the corridor. On the outside of her door is a piece of paper with a new warning: "OCCUPANT TRYING TO RUN AWAY." I search her closet and under her bed, but there is no suitcase. I'm not thinking. My father delivered her here; they unpacked her things and gave the suitcase back to him.

She was never going anywhere after this. But I do find a large envelope stuffed with papers; hopefully it includes an ID of some kind. I shake her pillow violently from its pillow case. I grab the photos — of the house, the farm, the birthday party — off the wall, a few shirts and slacks, pairs of underwear. I stuff everything into the pillow case.

When I return she is still slumped in the wheelchair but seems mildly interested in the television. Still no one else. I wonder what happened to Mr. Godfrey.

"Do you have a coat, Mom? A coat? Marsha? Shit."

She blinks, as though someone has just yelled at her. She rubs her elbows and says, "Is that a nice way to talk?" She sounds a bit like Allison. I don't want her to sound like Allison.

A few coats and jackets are hung on a coat stand by the door. I choose a green jacket and carry it back over to her.

"Where's Mr. Godfrey?" I ask.

"He went to sleep."

"Did he? Let's get you into this. Mom, please listen to me."

"He went for a walk."

I manoeuvre one arm, and then the other, into the jacket.

"He had his cookies." She is swallowing with effort. "He went back to bed —"

"Hey now." I press my cheek against the top of her head, which feels hot and smells sweet and musty, yet faintly of April. I realize that in an olfactory sense, I have no memory of my father.

"Are you thirsty?"

She has no idea, but I fill a paper cup with water from the bathroom. It takes her a while to drink it. The microwave timer dings again.

Finally, I help her to her feet and guide her to the door. She stops to pick up a plastic chrysanthemum that will sit on her lap all the way to Boston.

As I back the car out, she leans forward and puts her hands on the dash and asks angrily, "What is that place?"

"Right there?" I ask, pointing at the home.

"Yes, that building there. What is it?"

"Nothing. It's no place."

I notice Milton's Motors for the first time as we leave Dover, perhaps because of the way it stands out, glowing yellow behind its glass walls. Inside, a few salespeople sit at desks, their heads down among the sleek showroom cars, not a single customer in sight. Despite the hope that Obama's election has brought to many, I sense a swollen, prickly danger.

I drive until my pulse has levelled out, then pull off the freeway at a rest stop. I still have the complaint form Allison gave me in October, which has a contact number to the Department of Public Health's Patient Complaint Unit. It claims to be a twenty-four-hour-a-day, seven-days-a-week phone line, but a voice prompts me to leave a message. I tell them the administrator at Sunny Gardens Homecare in Dover is an ignoramus by the name of Ricky Milton and the facility should be investigated for negligence and abuse. I don't leave my name and I don't feel overly hopeful. My mother stares out the window into the darkness.

● ● ●

Initially both my father and I went after Petunia. She hadn't made it far. She was heading down the driveway towards the vegetable stand, but when I called her name she stopped, saw me, and quickly slunk off into the milkweed and meadowsweet, doing her damnedest now to avoid all other living creatures. The feral cat had gotten into the house by busting through the screen door, then tackled her in front of the refrigerator and broken her back. Petunia was dragging one of her hind legs, and there was something creepy about the way she couldn't hold up her head. The way it nosed along the ground.

I stood bawling in the driveway, my love and affection for that dog rushing back from some hidden place inside me. I was thinking how in the end we hadn't been the family Mrs. Lewis imagined we would be when she brought us Petunia. I remembered her as a silky puppy, her eagerness and loyalty, how it took her several months to realize she had the DNA to jump expertly onto my bed like a big, fluffy flea. I remembered the smell of her paws — of dirt and worms and new shoots. The winters when she slept against my back, keeping us both warm, and the popping, sipping sound of her little snores, her breathing never rhythmic, as though her dreams were too important, too vivid, to allow her a restful sleep.

Now, she was wild-eyed and frantic to escape us, the dense vegetation snagging and tearing at her matted dreadlocks. I couldn't bear to watch her, or be reminded of her eyes following me as they had every day since April left, hoping I would look her way, waiting for me to touch her. I didn't understand who I was anymore.

Mom was in the house, shouting hysterically. We could hear her all the way out there. My father glanced at my teary, snotty face as he went past and ordered me back to the house.

"Go check on your mother, Pilgrim."

Instead, I detoured into a thicket of raspberries that smelled tangy and comforting. Their prickly stems tore at my ankles and shins.

It was a year since April had disappeared, but it wasn't until that very moment that I knew for certain she was never coming back.

My father came out of the milkweed gripping Petunia tightly to his chest, and I watched him head in the direction of the house. But he passed the house and went on down to the barn, and after several minutes I heard his pistol firing. So that's where he'd been keeping it.

My mother abruptly stopped shouting, and as everything fell silent, I stepped out of the raspberries and gazed stupidly at the rows of tomatoes on the other side of the road. They were ripe but badly staked, so that those on the lower branches were rotting on the ground.

I was thinking, what a waste. Why haven't they been picked? Why hasn't Mom organized a day of canning? Nothing seemed right. An icky, terrifying feeling came over me that everything —the house, barn, animals, gardens, stand, Assabet Road—were dissolving. That soon there would be no meaning to this place.

That fall I was a recluse in my bedroom. Mom suggested I needed something to do with my hands, so she bought me several skeins of yarn, and I took up knitting. I found cigarettes on my own. I began applying to colleges.

In New York City, David Berkowitz was apprehended after a spree of shooting people in their parked cars, and my mother feared I'd encounter the same incomprehensible dangers in Montreal. Even so, I applied and was accepted and, though frightened for different reasons, left home the next year for McGill.

• • •

To the best of my knowledge, the only time my mother has travelled by air was when she and my father visited April in the early eighties.

On the flight from Boston to Halifax, she sits quietly in her window seat, but there is a new energy about her, a sparkling. As the other passengers board the plane, she watches them with an intensity that would be rude if it weren't for the sweetness in her eyes and the sudden flash of her smile each time she succeeds in making eye contact. She observes, fascinated, as I reach across to lower her tray and place her boxed lunch before her. I open my own lunch. She watches me for a moment, then opens hers. She peers inside, takes out the cookie and looks back to me. I take out my cookie and bite into it. Cautiously, still watching me, she bites into hers.

When I notice the red crescents on my wrists where April gripped me with her nails, I tug at my sleeves to hide them.

I'm worried about our two-hour layover in Halifax and how we will spend the time. After passing through Customs, we go up the escalator to the second level, but my mother enjoys it so much we go back down the other side in order to ride it up again. We do this several times until a Customs official begins heading our way.

We scour the terminal. We do not rest. My mother takes a sharp, prolonged interest in one woman getting a shoulder massage and another a manicure. We examine nearly everything in the gift shop, from magazines to chips to T-shirts to neck pillows. We are in there so long, I feel compelled to buy a stuffed toy lobster I would have difficulty separating from her anyway.

When our second flight is called we join the line and I explain to her we are getting back on the plane. She nods and, in her eagerness, steps on the heels of a woman in front of us. When I try to pull her back she presses even more insistently against the woman's backside.

The woman turns around, I assume, to give us an exasperated look or a piece of her mind. My mother is standing only inches from her.

".You could have done pre-boarding," the woman says, looking over my mother's head at me. She speaks matter-of-factly, almost forlornly. "I used to do it with my father. And once upon a time, my children. Naturally they were always on their worst behaviour in an airport."

My mother reaches out and touches a gold button on the woman's sweater.

"This is my first time travelling with her," I say, removing my mother's fingers from the woman's sweater. "I didn't think of it."

"It's hard to think of everything." Behind her, the line has begun to move.

"They were probably just excited," I tell her.

"Pardon?"

"Your children."

"Shoo," my mother tells her.

We board the plane and everything is repeated. We settle into our seats and fasten our belts. My mother stares at the passengers coming slowly up the aisle, then out the window, then back again at the passengers. In front of us, a teenage boy is struggling to stuff his carry-on into the overhead. My mother sighs sympathetically.

After we are airborne, an infant across the aisle begins crying. Its young mother covers it with a blanket and tries to interest it in one of her breasts. But the infant is having none of it. I watch the man in the adjacent seat. The reserved way he glances once or twice at the mother has me thinking they're strangers, until he plucks the baby out of the woman's arms and presses its little head to his lips. But the infant's cries only intensify, and I smile when the man quickly hands the baby back to the woman.

My thoughts return to April's confession — that she first regarded Jean as a pompous jerk — and I realize how surprised I am by this, when all these years I thought we'd seen the same things in him in the same moments. But I'm more surprised by my relief, and a sense of liberation. Even back then she wasn't, after all, what I had most wanted her to be: *me*.

Meanwhile, the monitors are demonstrating how to inflate the life vest stored in a pouch in the seat beneath us.

My mother makes a faint sound.

"Mom, what is it?"

She looks distressed. I put an arm around her.

"You know how the sound of crying babies always makes me blue."

I know, of course, no such thing.

It's fog throughout our descent until the last few minutes. The runway becomes visible just before we touch down, first with one set of wheels and then, a long painful second later, with the other set.

The plane taxis—it seems forever, as though we've landed miles from the terminal—until coming to a shuddering halt. Passengers spring up around us. My mother's nose is an inch from the window. I've no idea what she's feeling. Apprehension, curiosity, hope? She touches the glass with the toy lobster. Could she have imagined thirty years ago, or yesterday, that such a place as Country Walk Estates—this far-flung, exclusive settlement set among stunted spruce and peaty bogs—would be her future?

"We'll let everyone else get off first, Mom. Okay? We'll take our own goddamn sweet time."

They don't know she's with me. When we reach the top of the escalator, I see them both. We are the last passengers to emerge, my mother pressed up close to me, and Ethan looks both puzzled and irritated. His eyes glance off me and I am stunned. My husband doesn't recognize me.

"There she is! There she is!" Katie tells him, springing up and down.

His eyes sweep back and this time he sees me. He starts towards the bottom of the escalator. There is something familiar in his movements—is it eagerness? I wonder if he will pull me to him in that brusque, jolting way of his and wrap his arms around me.

I imagine us in a couple of hours, standing next to our bed.

He looks exhausted—probably from many things, including my long absence, but because I know him so well, I also suspect meetings that ran late in the day, as evidenced by the suit he is still wearing and the loosened Ralph Lauren silk tie. The tie was a gift from me, though it's likely only a coincidence he's worn it today. Despite his exhaustion, he soldiers on—this is my husband, at the top of his game. I watch him with fascination and longing as he lets Katie approach the escalator ahead of him.

I'm so happy to see her I almost feel sick.

My God, what did he let her do to her hair? It's streaked with blue.

My mother is behind me, pushing, because all of a sudden she has no time for escalators and wants to get to the bottom without delay. Neither Katie nor Ethan is making the connection. They aren't expecting her. Or the story she will bring.

I step off the escalator, her hand in mine.

"There you are, Mommy," Katie says, still hopping around. "Fred's in the car. He can't wait to see you."

Handsome Obama goes grey in patches and no one will work with him in Washington. I see him on television, each time thinner than the last, and imagine the stooped form his tall body will take in later years.

As far as I can tell, my mother is pleased with Country Walk Estates, pleased with her outings with Fred and me in the Pathfinder to collect Katie, the groceries and dry-cleaning. She and Fred share a passion for walks in the country, and although we've tried to explain to her she can't leave the house without another person, Fred follows her around so tenaciously the two of them have managed to slip out more than once unnoticed.

The farm is on the market. Ethan is handling that. Most of the time, I think of Cranfield as just a place that's gone.

But there is the odd morning when I wake, still drowsy, inside the hum of my modern home, to find a view of the farm has crept up on me. I'm not sure whether this is a true memory or part dream. I don't know if it's dawn or dusk—an ambiguous light hits the wings of birds lifting over the bog, and at first the scene lacks temperature, smell, and taste.

I'm standing in the kitchen, behind the screen door, peering out. All at once the rust of the screen fills my nose and mouth, and agitation seizes me. My eyes are fixed on April, who is walking—that slow and idle way we do—away from the house, out towards Assabet Road.

The moment she stops and looks back to make sure I'm there is the moment I know she will. I can see every detail of her face. She's so pale she's nearly white. A fledgling, sexless—we haven't yet met Jean. Her face is like a stamp on my inner world, as though I'm looking in a mirror.

ACKNOWLEDGEMENTS

Many thanks to everyone at Goose Lane Editions — most especially, as always, to my editor, Bethany Gibson; to Lisa Moore and all the Burning Rock members; to my agent, Anne McDermid; to copy editor Peter Norman; and to the Canada Council for the Arts for financial support during part of the writing of this novel.

A number of books on twins provided context, insight, and inspiration. Particular acknowledgements are due to the following: *Twin Stories,* by Susan Kohl; *Raising Twins,* by Eileen M. Pearlman and Jill Alison Ganon; *One and the Same,* by Abigail Pogrebin; *Indivisible by Two,* by Nancy L. Segal; *The Silent Twins,* by Marjorie Wallace; and *Twins: And What They Tell Us about Who We Are,* by Lawrence Wright. I am also grateful for *Out-Island Doctor,* Evans W. Cottman's lively memoir of his experiences in the Bahamas.

Photo: Vatcher Photographic

LIBBY CREELMAN's collection of short stories, *Walking in Paradise*, was shortlisted for the first annual Winterset Award for excellence in Newfoundland and Labrador writing. *The Darren Effect*, her first novel, was published by Goose Lane Editions in 2008. Her stories have also been published in literary magazines across the country and in *Best Canadian Stories* and *The Journey Prize Anthology*. Creelman lives in St. John's, Newfoundland.